CW01662762

Spartan Quest

Salvation

Anthea Laurelton

Book 1 in the Spartan Quest duology

Published by: Anthea Laurelton

First Published – 2022
This edition published 2022 by Anthea Laurelton
Sydney, New South Wales, Australia
www.anthealaurelton.com

The National Library of Australia Cataloguing-in-Publication

Creator: Laurelton, Anthea, author

Title: Spartan Quest – Salvation / Anthea Laurelton

ISBN: 9780987640727 (paperback)

Subjects: Romance fiction.

Historical fiction.

Cover art by Sheridan Kent
Printed and bound in Australia by Ingram Spark

A catalogue record for this book is available from the National Library of Australia

AUTHOR NOTE

Dear Reader,

The Ancient Spartans did not record their own history. Researchers look to the likes of Herodotus, Plutarch and Xenophon—to name a few—who wrote about the Spartans, sometimes without having even lived in Sparta itself.

While this is a fictional love story, I have endeavored to portray as closely as possible, the societal norms the Spartans adhered to and the way their society functioned. Even for myself, writing this book has proven to be a fascinating journey of discovery.

The city of Apollysis sprang from my imagination and was placed at the far north-western end of the Peloponnese. Likewise, the Hidden Shrine of Apollo is created for the purposes of the story as an important pilgrimage site for the Apollysians. There are references to real historical sites such as Delphi, Olympia and the temple of Apollo at Amyklai.

For readability, clothing and weapons are referred to by their English names except for the xiphos and kopis. The Spartans used both types of swords in battle, and since they are very different to each other, I elected to keep their Greek names.

A large slice of creative license was taken which affects one of the characters. Readers familiar with Greek myths and legends will spot it late in the book.

Happy Reading!

Anthea Laurelton

Born and raised in Sydney, Australia, Anthea Laurelton fell in love with Greek mythology at the age of thirteen. Her love of the Spartans began after reading *Roger Lancelyn Green's* THE TALE OF TROY at around the same time. Leaving behind a career in IT to write love stories set in Ancient Sparta, and pander to an extremely spoilt German Shepherd, she can be found power walking with Zali, spending time practising yoga, going on long car trips, writing and too many other interests to list here.

One day she plans to breathe life into her contemporary story ideas.

ACKNOWLEDGEMENTS

My sincere gratitude to an amazing group of women writers who encouraged and believed in me.

Catherine Evans and Sheridan Kent for their critiques in the early days when I was stumbling through the story, not really knowing the direction I wanted it to go. Vanda Vadas for her words of wisdom as my writing journey unfolded.

Donna Munro and Susannah Kade for offering up their time to both beta and proof-read.

A big thank you to Donna for her expert advice and assistance when I decided to dip my toes into the waters of self-publishing.

Special thanks to Sheridan for noticing I kept losing Diokles's helmet from one scene to the next, and A L Maze, who, besides proof-reading, lifted my game by wielding that dreaded green pen which is deadlier than any Spartan sword!

You ladies rock.

CHAPTER ONE

North of Sparta, around 450 B.C.

Failure was not an option.

Jaw clenched, Diokles stared at the ridge of hills in the distance until his eyes burned. Shrouded by low-lying clouds, they drew his gaze like the enchanted voices of the Sirens drew hapless sailors to their doom. He and his peers would march over those hills this very night.

By dawn the next morning his goal would be in sight.

An angry whinny brought his attention back to the organized commotion behind him. Hoplites settled on places to rest for the remainder of the day, while helot servants prepared the pre-battle meal. The aroma of roasting meat mingled with fragrant wood smoke. He breathed the scent in deeply watching the smoke curl upwards into the azure blue of the sky.

His mouth watered. The fight was yet to be waged, but he could taste it. Excitement thrummed in his veins, every cell of his hard disciplined body already celebrating success.

Overwhelmed by an urge to set out immediately, he crushed it down through sheer will. To act with rashness was to invite defeat. One failure already blighted his life. Its memory still possessed the power to flood his body with raging heat.

"The portents were good."

Dousing his anger, Diokles turned to acknowledge his friend and second-in-command standing beside him. From the day they met in the agoge, the training ground for all worthy Spartan boys, they remained firm friends. Acastus had saved him from near death, or worse, being maimed for life. He trusted him like no other.

"Thanks to the gods they were. Even the priest pronounced them auspicious."

No Spartan would prepare for war without invoking the aid of the gods through a sacrifice. A bull had been offered; the meat not burnt for the gods, would be shared amongst all. With the priest's words ringing in his ears, Diokles had ordered the men rest at this site prior to the final march.

"Zeus will grant us victory," he spared Acastus a glance. "As well as the knowledge to take Apollysis with the swiftness of the north wind. I will not spill the blood of our men needlessly."

This was his first command since leaving the agoge. The responsibility of conquering the city of Apollysis was more than just another battle to him. More than privilege in knowing he would command so many of Sparta's finest hoplites.

It was personal.

"I know you will lead us to victory," Acastus assured him. "I pray, too, that Zeus grants you the answers to the questions which have plagued you."

His friend's gaze was fixed on his forearm. Diokles flexed his left arm where a jagged scar served as a continual reminder of what he'd once risked and lost.

He clasped Acastus by the shoulder. "It is behind us. Besides, there will be opportunity aplenty to add other scars."

He looked away, turning his focus inwards, recalling the moment he had stood before the Gerousia—the ruling council of Sparta which he hoped to one day join if he lived long enough—being given the tidings of an unseen threat brewing within the city beyond Olympia.

Surprise had been his first response. The citizens of Apollysis were peaceful. Yet the half-dead man found in the great marketplace pleaded to be brought before the council. What he had to say, he insisted, would save Sparta.

No doubt, Diokles thought cynically, the man hoped to save himself, too.

Hard on the heels of that initial surprise, satisfaction had followed at being informed he would be leading a force of his peers to Apollysis. He was now a Spartiate—a full citizen. Pride lifted his chin. He had served his time in the agoge. Fought in battles where he repeatedly proved his courage, leadership, and prowess.

The memory of those battles curled his lips into a grim smile. The outcome had never been good for the opposing force. Every enemy hoplite had not just been an opponent to engage and win against, but a representation of those who needed to pay.

Of those who had slipped from his grasp.

Then the priestess of Athena descended from the temple which overlooked the city, to foretell bloodshed if the spy's warning went unheeded. Fixing him with a look he would never forget, she delivered a message for him alone. A Spartan lived in Apollysis, one who fled years before, taking the treasure of his household with him.

Standing in the still warm, late afternoon sun, Diokles felt his blood turn to fire then ice. Pushing the bitter memories into the deepest recesses of his heart, he willed the muscles in his neck to relax. They were stretched tight enough to make him light-headed.

If this Spartan was who he suspected, then he knew what the treasure referred to. No gold or jewels were as valuable. This 'treasure' rightly belonged to him.

The betrayal by those closest to him continued to sting like an open wound pierced by a thousand spear thrusts. Diokles clenched one fist so hard the veins stood out along his entire arm. What a pity he had not been born fifty years earlier. He would rather have faced the might of Xerxes army and died in glory beside his king, than endure this agony of body and soul. An agony which still smothered his spirit after ten long years.

All because of one woman.

A girl at the time but grown to womanhood by now. The girl he had not stopped searching for. The girl he ached to see again. To hold in his arms as man to woman, not just the boy and girl they once were when they pledged themselves.

Was she even alive?

Wedded?

A combustible mix of desperation and jealousy seared him.

Then his heart lurched in his chest. If she was with this Spartan, how could he protect her once his men overran the city?

Diokles raked stiff fingers through his hair as he pushed self-doubt and fear aside. Both emotions were insignificant gnats to a Spartan warrior.

It was time for action.

He broke from his brooding to give instruction to Acastus.

"Make sure all the men know that the temple of Apollo is to be taken only by me." He dropped his voice so only Acastus heard. "The spy gave me knowledge privately which will help my search."

He lifted an eyebrow when Acastus made no move to leave.

"You are sure this spy is trustworthy?"

"Perhaps not." Diokles narrowed his eyes. "The proof will come once we are in Apollysis. This high priestess is the only one who can wear the coronet he told the council about. The description he gave of her will make recognizing her easy. I will take her to this hidden shrine to reveal what the threat to Sparta is."

"They are fools to plot against us." Acastus paused. "What of the words the priestess spoke to you?"

"After I learn what the threat is and inform the council, I will search for this man. If it is who I suspect, his daughter will be with him." He breathed deeply to calm the exhilaration coursing through his body. "Prepare to march at nightfall."

"I wager the men are even now ready and eager to leave, Diokles."

A half-smile curved his lips. "Yes, they would be."

Watching Acastus stride away to carry out his orders, he knew his peers were ready. Eager to fight. Eager to prove themselves.

They were Spartans.

Bred for battle.

Bred too, for love, although it would be a weakness to admit this.

He thought of the estate owned by his family for generations. Duty-bound to continue its ownership, the law required him to take a wife. Having reached the age of thirty he would be ridiculed if he did not.

By Zeus! He would not allow himself to be made fun of.

Yet, if he took a wife, it would dishonor his pledge, carving his heart in two which still beat for the girl lost to him.

Every instinct insisted the man in Apollysis was Aeschylus.

Father of his betrothed.

Betrayer.

A thrill of anticipation traversed his spine at the thought of seeing her again. Whatever the man's faults—and there were many—he would not have left his daughter.

Waiting until the men found what shade they could to eat their meal, Diokles resumed his contemplation of the distant ridge without really seeing it. Instead, his inner vision presented an image of an empty house, empty as his heart, which sat beyond the boundary of his estate. Her pleading cries echoed in his ears. Cries which begged him not to desert her while her father dragged her away. His own father—older and stronger—holding him in a death grip while his younger self shouted curses against both men.

Bile rose in his throat. He had failed her.

No Spartan failed.

Ever.

This was his chance to fulfil a pact he made that day to reverse the failure.

Knowing no-one would follow or disturb him he walked until he was out of sight of the camp.

He had no wife or mother who could have spoken the parting words every Spartan woman sent her husband or son into battle with. Sorrow filled the deep wound where the memory of his mother lived. Healing it would begin when Apollysis was taken.

It fell to him to speak those words. He would not go into battle without them. Would not go seeking his betrothed without vowing to return home.

And somehow return her with him.

With the sun beating down on him Diokles threw his head back to swear to the heavens.

"With my shield or on it."

CHAPTER TWO

The bronze cup was cold between her trembling hands. Icy cold from the crystal-clear water within. Water so cold it could have only come from the depths of Hades.

The faces of the men circling her always wore the same expression—expectant, eager, exultant. For the thousandth time, she prayed to the gods to recognize those faces.

One of the men spoke but she heard no words. Another pointed to the cup. She lifted it slowly, solemnly, saluting these men. Pressing it to her lips, she drank deeply.

Fire burned her body first. Then came the fingers of ice tearing through her mind, freezing her memories, her very sense of self. Her screams were high-pitched, piteous, agonizing.

Struggling to escape the grey mists sent by Hypnos, god of sleep, she woke—

Moaning and thrashing against the last of the dream which haunted many of her nights, Calliope hurled herself upright off the sleeping pallet, her momentum stopped by a hand gripping her shoulder.

"No!"

Her sleep-befuddled mind registered the panicked shout echoing off the walls. She grabbed the restraining hand, pushing with enough force to surprise even herself.

She must escape before those nameless men made her drink from the bronze cup again.

"Calliope, it's me. I heard you cry out."

The familiar voice penetrated her panic. Calliope shook her head to clear the last vestiges of the dream that never failed to leave her in a cold sweat. Blinking her eyes against the light coming through the small window, she breathed deeply to bring her racing heart under control.

Still feeling that her mind somehow remained disconnected from her body, she cast a bleary-eyed gaze around the small room. In one corner huddled her fellow priestess, Lysandra. The wary look on the woman's face prompted Calliope to give her an apologetic smile.

She reached into the calm center of her being to quell her shaking limbs. The deep, private place in her spirit where she heard the voice of Apollo.

Lately, she struggled to hear it.

Unease stroked her spine like a cold finger. She knew the reason for the struggle.

Calliope buried her head in her hands. Her nightmare visited her sleep more often. A nightmare which became progressively worse ever since a nameless foreboding took hold of her mind. With each recurrence it took longer to calm herself.

The sound of skin rubbing against skin broke into her turbulent thoughts. A pang of remorse shot through her. Lysandra rubbed her hand, wincing as she did. Calliope sighed. She never deliberately harmed anyone—physically or otherwise—although her own heart continued to weep every day from as far back as she could remember.

"I am sorry, Lysandra. Did I hurt you very much?"

"No. The pain is almost gone. I didn't realize how strong you are."

The knowing smile curling Lysandra's mouth drew her brows together. If she did not know her so well, she could almost believe the woman, who had become her confidante from the time they entered the service of Apollo, was weighing up the small incident and considering how best to use it.

Calliope gave herself a mental shake. It must be the after-effects of the dream that made her so sensitive.

Her physical strength she took for granted. Some indiscernible force drove her to maintain her strength. Every day in the privacy of her room she completed the almost martial-like moves which came effortlessly to her. During that time she released a tiny measure of frustration at not knowing her past.

Memories of her childhood and coming to Apollysis remained shrouded behind an impenetrable grey mist. The clammy film of old fear cloaked her skin. If she strained her memory, she could recall entering the temple, throwing her whole heart and soul into becoming a priestess. She belonged here now, the other priestesses becoming the family she could not remember.

Then the kindly Aeschylus adopted the frightened and confused young girl she had been. She loved him as a true daughter would yet questions about her past were met with non-committal replies.

Discontentment had settled like a heavy weight in her soul. Even the prayers and sacrifices she offered to Apollo remained unanswered.

What great wrong had she done to be punished like this?

Still, she wanted to repay Aeschylus's love for her. Becoming a priestess, then high priestess at his urging, was the first step in the repayment. She pushed aside misgivings as to why her new father would suggest she leave his house so soon after taking her in. Grateful for his protection, she did not want to hurt him or give him reason to abandon her.

Her dedicated service to Apollo, the decision to take a vow of virginity, won her the exalted rank of high priestess, thereby gaining the privilege to wear the famed sapphire coronet to see through the eyes of the god. But it was not for this reason alone she wanted to keep her maidenhead. Calliope had harbored a secret—that wearing the coronet would restore her memory.

Beads of sweat broke out on her brow.

She had worn the coronet once, barely surviving the inconsolable anguish which had wracked her entire being. She could never remember what she saw.

No power on earth or Olympus would induce her to wear it again.

Calliope wrapped her arms around her chest, much like she wrapped the cloak of her vow around herself. It kept her safe from whatever subliminal heartbreak lurked in her very bones, safe from the normal drives of her body, safe from—

"Today is the start of the week-long festival," she groaned, slapping the palm of one hand against her forehead before pushing herself to her feet.

Lysandra straightened and moved to the doorway. "Lykos is asking where you are."

Calliope gritted her teeth at the mention of the high priest. Caring nothing for her vow, the weak selfish fool blighted her life. She had given up counting the number of attempts he'd made to persuade her into his bed. She loathed him. Loathed him for presenting her with an impossible choice. To stay and endure his presence or leave the city she loved and thought of as home.

If she left, there was nowhere for her to go.

Damn him! Only her sense of self-preservation stood between Lykos and her priestess knife embedded in his heart.

"Lykos can wait," she fumed. "He has become insufferable lately. He thinks he is the lord of all he surveys. It will do him good to learn patience."

"You must not speak like that about the high priest," Lysandra gasped. "The consequences could be great."

"I am not afraid of how Lykos would try to punish me. You may tell him what I said since I am more than ready to say those words myself."

"I would never betray you! You are my friend."

Pausing in her task of choosing the ceremonial robes she would wear Calliope sent a probing look at Lysandra. Her friend's assertion she would never betray her, while vehemently delivered, somehow did not ring true. Despite the earnest expression on Lysandra's face, a discordant note thrummed in the air between them. She looked hard into the woman's brown eyes and caught a glimmer of some carefully concealed emotion in their depths. Apprehension crawled over her skin.

The old nightmare must have shaken her up more than she realized. A slight shrug of one shoulder buried the uneasy feeling. She began to fold a single piece of pale blue cloth to drape into a tunic which she would wear this first day of the festival.

"Go and tell Lykos I will be there shortly."

Calliope received the supplicant's offerings. Quietly, she uttered the familiar prayer for their wishes to be granted. She never tired of helping the citizens of Apollysis.

Unlike the man standing before the altar.

The proprietary, almost predatory, glint in Lykos's close-set black eyes curdled her stomach. It never changed. Year after year during the festival of thanksgiving and fertility, the high priest redoubled his efforts to seduce her. Instead of being free to enjoy herself, she was compelled to play a cat-and-mouse game to avoid him.

Resentment seethed like the roiling waves of the Ionian Sea when Poseidon shook the earth beneath its depths. One hand moved to her waist where her knife was secured.

No. Not now. The time will come when he feels the sharp point of a blade ending his life.

A whoosh of air parted her lips. Had she just received a portent from Apollo himself?

Possibilities sizzled through her.

Calliope did her best to ignore the high priest. As part of the ceremony she was obliged to hand him the gifts brought to Apollo. The lingering slide of his hands over hers nauseated her so much, she struggled to resist the impulse to snatch her hands away, and run to cleanse them.

Instead, she speared him with a warning glance.

"High priestess, the next supplicant is waiting."

Lykos stood close enough for her to smell the overpowering scent of narcissus he used on these occasions. Nose wrinkling, she drew back, not missing the angry tightening of his thin-lipped mouth. Her ear buzzed in protest as though he had spoken directly into it. Raising her chin at his audacity, she composed herself, turning gracefully to receive the next offering.

It was her father.

Her heart filled as they shared a smile. His presence ensured Lykos would not attempt to get her alone. Aeschylus was a prominent citizen who wielded considerable power without abusing it. She loved him so much, although an inexplicable distance remained between them. It saddened her because she could not bridge it.

Calliope reached for the basket he carried, wrapping her hands over his. “May Apollo shower you with blessings, father, and grant you many favors.”

“Thank you, my daughter,” his voice choked. “May he likewise smile kindly on you.”

The tears which sprang into her father’s light brown eyes, astonished her. “What is it? Share your grief so I can pray to the god to take it away.”

When Aeschylus simply shook his head, Calliope squeezed his hands. She wanted to reassure him, take away whatever troubled him.

She needed his reassurance just as desperately.

For a while now she had been unable to shake a growing uneasiness that some great tragedy brewed, ready to strike Apollysis. The hairs on her arms rose until her skin prickled. If only she could run far away from this nameless threat and not look back, but she did not want to leave the temple and her people. They were her family, the bedrock on which she had rebuilt her life.

Calliope swallowed, willing her tense throat muscles to relax. “Can you not tell me?”

Her father gave her a shaky smile.

“It is a burden only I can carry,” he sighed. “Be assured I am here for you and will always protect you.”

She drew back. It seemed an odd thing to say but gave her certainty that if she decided to leave, Aeschylus would come with her.

Relieving him of the basket, she gave him an extra blessing before turning thoughtfully to the altar.

“Did you have a vision, Calliope?” Lykos asked with an intimate whisper as he loomed over her. “It must have been something of great importance to engross you so deeply.”

“No,” she muttered through clenched teeth. “My thoughts are my own, Lykos. I do not divulge them to anyone.”

Certainly not to him. If he knew of the creative ways she imagined getting him out of her life, he would not be so complacent. She glanced at her nails, grown and hennaed for the festival, and wondered what it would be like to drag them across his cheeks.

"Were you perhaps thinking of the fertility rites which are yet to come," he leered. "You never attend those with me even though I have asked you many times."

"Do I need to remind you I have taken an oath of purity," she hissed in an undertone. "I serve only my god. I am wedded to his service and nothing more. Now is not the time to discuss this."

"With you it is never the time. But that will change."

Her eyes widened. Accustomed to Lykos's petulance when he did not get his own way, these subtle threats were another matter. Calliope worried over his remark while she smoothly continued with her duties.

Just like the sense of impending doom grew within her, so too did concern about Lykos's recent behavior. A chill shuddered through her body. He involved himself in the political life of the city in ways a high priest should not. He swaggered through the temple, giving orders, threatening anyone who stood up to him.

Was Lykos's thirst for power another reason her old nightmare had grown worse? Calliope drew a shaky breath. The threat to Apollysis drew closer—she could feel it in the marrow of her bones. No precognition she experienced prior to this time could compare.

Fighting another powerful urge to grab Aeschylus and flee, she restrained herself until the last supplicant presented their offering. She would slip away before anyone could stop her. Later, she would return to pray to Apollo to spare the city dedicated to him; the city which had given her shelter, purpose and meaning.

She would not run. She would stand and confront this yet-to-be revealed threat even if it meant losing her life.

Calliope angrily wiped a solitary tear from the corner of one eye. She was strong enough to hold tears back. Strong enough to face whatever fate threw at her.

Even dying held no terror.

CHAPTER THREE

"Death has come upon the city!"

For the second morning in a row Calliope was shocked into wakefulness. Heart beating a deafening tattoo in her ears, she struggled to orient herself. Pushing her long hair off her face, she tried to recall if she had relived her nightmare.

Again, the warning reverberated through the room. This time she heard the words clearly. The urgency in the voice shouting them caused her to spring to her feet, eyes widening in concern.

Surely the nebulous fears she harbored were not about to be proven real.

No time to marvel at the speed with which she draped her tunic. Snatching up the brooches she had readied the night before, she secured them at the shoulders, then gathered in the loose folds around her waist with a belt.

Throwing a light woollen shawl over her shoulders, Calliope ran in the direction of the cry as swiftly as if Kerberos, the hound of the Underworld, sped after her with all three heads snapping hungrily at her heels.

Between the outer columns of the temple, she found Lysandra, eyes bulging in terror. One quaking finger pointed toward the hills that ringed Apollysis. Calliope whirled to see what horror threatened.

She clutched a hand to her throat. Helmeted figures covered almost every hill.

The frantic thudding of her heart drowned out the words coming from Lysandra's lips. She leaned in closer to hear the priestess croak one word.

"Spartans."

A strange buzzing filled Calliope's ears. Her vision wavered. Struggling to breathe, she exhorted herself to not give in to panic. Eyes staring fixedly into the distance, she could just make out some of the emblems wrought upon each shield.

Lysandra was right.

Apollysis was a peaceful city so why were the Spartans attacking?

Calliope leaned back against the cool stone column, its solid strength keeping her legs upright. *Spartans!* The whole region of Achaea, perhaps all of Hellas, trembled before them. She knew of their fearsome reputation in battle; had overheard Apollysian hoplites saying they would rather fight the Minotaur than a Spartan.

A dazzle of light caught the corner of her eye. She looked toward the east where the first rays of the sun shimmered over the horizon. Pushing away from the column she lifted her hands, turning the palms toward the rising sun.

Calliope closed her eyes, welcoming the warmth seeping into her cold body. She was high priestess of Apollo. If the Spartans were bent on destroying Apollysis, Apollo would reveal to her how to thwart their plans.

Shouts and screams added to the cacophony of noise filling the temple. Below her she could see people already milling about, others beginning to run in all directions. She needed to go to them, calm their panic, organize their escape.

Before she could act on the inclination someone called her name.

Calliope glanced over her shoulder, eyes narrowing. Lykos was running toward her. The look of fear on his weak-chinned face confirmed the belief she always held of him. A coward.

"It is time to leave the temple," he ordered, grabbing her roughly by the arm.

Wrenching herself out of his hold, she rubbed a hand vigorously over the skin where the impression of his fingers still lingered.

"Leave?" she snapped. "Fly to safety if you must, Lykos, since you are so determined to save your miserable skin. I will stay to save as many as I can."

"Do not be a fool," he shouted, attempting to grab her arm again. "You must come with me."

She moved out of his reach, planting her feet against the stone floor. "I go nowhere until I am sure everyone in this temple is safe."

Lykos's face flushed, his nostrils flaring. "Your recklessness will be your downfall, high priestess."

"Your cowardice will be yours, *high priest*." Giving him a cold smile, she crossed her arms over her body.

His cry of outrage she dismissed with a disdainful wave of her hand. It was past time she dropped the outward respect she had schooled herself to show over the years.

"Yes, Lykos, I called you coward. I may face death today, but if I do, it will be in full knowledge I have told you the truth of what I think of you. I am not the frightened girl who first entered this temple. The novice who pandered to your every command. I—"

"Silence!"

Chest heaving from the outpouring of long-held anger, Calliope curled her lips in a grimly satisfied smile.

"The day will come when you will regret those words." He wagged a warning finger in her face. "It is easy to insult me now with the Spartan threat hanging over us, although be assured I will not forget what you said."

"If this invasion means I can speak the truth, then it is worth whatever danger your threats pose to me," she hissed. "Do not think I am unaware of what you wanted, Lykos. I held my tongue because I owe it to Aeschylus."

She sensed he wanted to say something else, but he only sent her a glance of pure loathing before running into the temple.

It took her several deep breaths before she calmed the euphoria bursting inside her. Later there would be time to reflect on her victory. Now she must consider possible escape routes. Thinking hard, she knew only one that would guarantee those escaping would not be seen by the invaders.

Turning to the silent woman at her side, she started. A look of shock, mixed with smugness, crossed Lysandra's face before the priestess swept her eyelashes down.

Why is she veiling herself from me?

"Find as many of the other priestesses as you can," Calliope urged her. "Then meet me at the entrance to the underground tunnel."

Lysandra made no move to comply.

Calliope grabbed her shoulders, giving her a gentle but urgent shake. "Lysandra, go! Please, there is no time to lose!"

"You were foolish to speak to Lykos in such a fashion." Lysandra cocked her head to one side. "What can you do on your own? Take on the Spartan army single-handed?"

Calliope threw her hands in the air.

"I have more to worry about than Lykos's disapproval. I will stay here and pray to the sun god to save our city." She pressed a trembling hand on one solid pillar. "This is the only home I have known, Lysandra. Serving as priestess is the only reason I have for existing. I cannot abandon Apollysis and its people as I was abandoned."

"You must not do this, Calliope."

She gaped at the woman whom she always considered a close friend. A stranger stared back at her. "Why are you of all people trying to stop me? Who will save us against Spartans if not the gods? Now go, go quickly! I will come and seal the secret entrance after you."

She pushed Lysandra into a run, watching until she disappeared. Only then did Calliope turn back to look at the hills ringing the city; to the army massed on their peaks.

That army was your past, is your present, will be your future.

The words gusted through her like a mighty wind blowing down from the snow-capped heights of Olympus.

Never would she allow those words to be true and there was no time to divine their meaning.

The distant figures were moving.

It was time.

Diokles studied the city spread out before him resembling a sacrificial offering. He welcomed the pounding of his heart, beating its own battle rhythm, pumping blood through his veins. His muscles contracted, biceps bulging, from the effort of holding the pair of black stallions that pulled his chariot.

A smile curved his mouth at their restlessness.

Soon, he would give them their heads and they would fly like the wind. Soon, he would be in the city of Apollysis. Soon, it would be groaning under the weight of Spartan warriors.

And if he did not find the answers he needed, it would be left a ravaged shell.

"The men are ready, Diokles. All the preparations are complete."

He acknowledged Acastus with a curt nod. "And the order is clear, no harm is to come to any priestesses they find."

"Yes," Acastus replied.

"And no leniency is to be extended to anyone who stands in their way?"

"The orders were given as we agreed." Acastus paused, then lowered his voice. "Diokles, what if the spy lied about the threat? What if the priestess's words were misunderstood and your betrothed is not here?"

Pain ripped through him, its clawed talons sinking into his heart.

"If the spy lied, he would be better off dying before we return." He would make sure of the man's death. "I trust in the message of Athena's priestess to me. Every instinct tells me she is within those walls below us."

He pulled back on the reins as the horses tossed their heads, hooves churning. He understood their impatience, for it was his own. He too, could not wait any longer.

Diokles leaned in so only Acastus could hear him. The one man who alone knew both the reasons why taking Apollysis was imperative to him. "I have waited a long time for this moment," he said harshly. "In one fell swoop we take the city. I take the high priestess to her shrine where she will reveal the threat to Sparta. Then, I will find this man and if his daughter is not with him, he will meet and pay Charon the same day."

Acastus gripped his forearm. "May the gods grant you the victory you deserve."

With his friend beside him victory would be certain. Diokles wheeled the chariot to face the hoplites under his command. He snatched up his spear, the fighting weapon made lethal in Spartan hands, and roared in a mighty voice. "Apollysis will be taken today. Your orders have been given. You are Spartans. You do not fail."

Every man shouted in agreement, lifting their spears high in salute. He allowed himself a moment of pride at the sight of his fellow warriors, fierce and tried in battle. The rising sun cast a golden glow on their burnished, bronze shields.

But its warmth on his skin was not enough to melt the cold darkness swirling in his heart. He could still hear his mother's dying words, feel the grief that tore at his heart. The revelations of loss and betrayal which fueled his vehement need to exact justice from the one man still alive who had wronged him.

His blood boiled recalling the suffering his father had caused. Bitterness clouded the memories of his mother. Bitterness for not telling him what she knew sooner.

Wrenching his attention back to the present, Diokles gave the signal to move, his focus now directed at the city below. A battle was about to be waged and won. Questions waited to be asked, and inside the walls of Apollysis were the answers.

He would get those answers or die trying.

No-one would stop him.

No-one.

CHAPTER FOUR

Frantic to find any stragglers, Calliope sped along the pteroma—the passageway between the outer columns and the walls of the main part of the temple. She found two terrified girls crouching in the cella—the inner sanctum where the statue of Apollo stood. Grabbing their outstretched hands she pulled them after her.

The city horns continued to sound the warning: invaders approaching. Hampered by the girl's fear, she stumbled down the stone steps leading to the secret entrance to the tunnels beneath the city.

Only two people knew how to open the entrance—herself and Lykos. Pulse thumping in her throat like a sacrificial drumbeat, she registered the race of her heart, fast enough to beat the immortal horse, Arion, in a race.

Seeing Lysandra waiting amongst the other priestesses, some sobbing, some clutching each other as though believing they would ward off looming disaster, Calliope expelled her own sob of relief on joining them.

"Come this way." She hurried toward the steps leading further below the temple.

One glance showed they followed without question. Except for Lysandra.

Calliope ran back to her. Reaching for Lysandra's hand, she pulled in the direction of the subterranean entrance. Meeting resistance, she slipped, feet scrambling wildly to find her balance. Pressing a hand to her middle when she regained it, she muttered a prayer of thanks. An injury would be untenable given the situation she was in.

"What is the matter?" She threw the priestess a concerned look. "We must hurry so I can seal the entrance behind you before anyone finds me."

"Then you must come with us, Calliope, or are you hungry for more glory?" Lysandra accused in a vexed voice. "Why should you stay here to be sacrificed?"

Calliope's mouth opened and closed; precious time lost in trying to find words.

"What glory?" She stared at Lysandra, blood turning cold. A strange light glittered in the other woman's eye. A mix of envy and malice, prompting Calliope to take a step back. "I do not stay for glory but to pray for the salvation of our city and all our people. If you want to stay with me to pray, then stay, else I implore you, flee to safety."

Witnessing the sly half-smile spreading across Lysandra's face, a shudder raced through Calliope.

"I will go if you insist," Lysandra said, her brow arching. "Lykos will not be pleased you chose to remain behind, but then, he always showed you special favors."

"Lykos is a fool and so are you if you do not escape immediately."

Why did Lysandra choose such a time to indulge in petty jealousies? Well, she would not give her the satisfaction of discussing them in front of the other priestesses, who appeared to have forgotten their terror and were listening avidly.

"Enough of this foolishness. Now, come."

The others did not hesitate, clinging to her tunic in the belief she would lead them to salvation. Calliope dragged them in her wake until she reached a familiar section of wall. Fingertips traced the solid rock, locating the barely visible seam. Using her body weight, she pushed against it. The concealed door opened into a chamber bringing gasps of surprised relief from her companions.

"This tunnel will see you safely beyond the city and out of sight of where the Spartans have massed," she told them. "Do not stop, do not turn back, no matter what you may see or hear."

Chill underground air bit into her skin. Her sense of urgency grew while she ushered them into the narrow tunnel.

Am I rushing them into the realm of Hades?

The temptation to follow them almost overwhelmed her. Calliope reached deep into the well of courage she possessed. She knew her duty—unlike some. Flaming torches already illuminated the underground passage, which meant only one thing. Lykos, along with the other priests were already gone, guaranteeing their own safety first.

She bit back a sound of disgust.

Lysandra was the last to enter the tunnel. Calliope reached out to touch her friend's arm lightly in farewell. "May Apollo light your way out of the city." They held each other's gaze for possibly the last time. Again, Calliope wondered at the calculating expression wreathing Lysandra's face.

"May Apollo help you find your way to us," she replied, then turned and left.

With a heavy heart, she waited, needing to satisfy herself all the priestesses were out of sight. Stepping out of the tunnel she closed the door after her, ensuring no trace of the opening remained.

Whatever Lysandra truly wished her, it did not reflect in her words. Calliope wracked her mind, struggling to comprehend what past sin she may have committed to make Lysandra so cold toward her.

And, why now?

The friendship they shared over the years had become a beacon of light in her lonely life. Yet today her supposed friend had stabbed a barb into her heart without qualms. Right when Calliope needed her support the most.

The blaring horns pulled her out of her melancholy.

No-one must find me here.

Gathering the length of her tunic in one hand, she fled. Free of the enveloping fabric, her legs carried her swiftly upwards toward the cella.

She let go of all thoughts except one—to pray for as long as she could.

Arms outstretched in invocation, Calliope knelt before the statue of Apollo, praying for the safety of the priestesses, imploring his aid for the defenders of the city dedicated to him. Shrieks of pain and terror drew closer, growing in number with each heartbeat.

Calliope prayed, too, that Aeschylus had been able to escape before the city was overrun. A lump formed in her throat. A caring, compassionate man like him did not deserve to die.

Her arms shook from the effort of holding them upright, droplets of sweat running down her forehead to pool in her eyes. She blinked, lessening the stinging saltiness. Shifting to ease the pain in her knees, she stiffened her limbs, willing herself to stay in a prayerful stance on the hard stone floor.

The clang of clashing weapons grew louder—the invaders were inside the temple. Soon enough the slap of feet pounded on the stone floor. Calliope closed her eyes. She would not give death the satisfaction of acknowledging its presence. If she were to die, she would do so kneeling strong and brave before the god she served.

No spear pierced her as expected. Instead, something far worse than death arrived. Her arms were seized by two hoplites, pulling her from her place of refuge. She fought to find her feet, stumbling as they dragged her away.

Struggling against their hold, she kicked at their legs.

"Dare to touch a priestess of Apollo and you will pay with your life," Calliope yelled. Never did she feel such strength, fueled by a combustible mix of terror and rage. But her slim body was no match for the brawn of two hulking, battle-hardened warriors.

Laughing at her futile efforts to free herself, one of them sneered, "Our commander is the beloved of Zeus. We have nothing to fear from your god, priestess."

The taunt galled her, the insult to Apollo grating over frayed nerves.

"Curse you for a Spartan dog!"

Without thinking she sank her teeth into his forearm.

An angry roar filled her ears before she found herself flung to the ground. Landing on her hip, Calliope flinched. Winded, hip throbbing from the impact, she dragged air into her lungs far too quickly. Her chest tightened, the frantic thump of her heart echoing painfully in her ears. Fearing it would crack her ribs she strove for calm even breaths.

Not taking her eyes off the two men, she scuttled backwards out of their reach. The tunic snagged under her foot, falling off one shoulder.

Their angry expressions turned to leers.

Calliope stilled.

Tremors wracked her body. She tried to think, clenching her hands when her mind refused to work. Backing up against the altar, she placed both hands on it, praying they would respect the sanctuary she sought.

Praying for salvation to arrive.

The thickset man on her left swaggered closer. Eyes wide and staring, Calliope swore a silent oath the brutes would not take her without a fight.

Waiting until he was almost on top of her, she thrust a hand beneath the shawl still clinging to her other shoulder, groping for the ceremonial knife she always carried.

To find nothing except her belt. The rasping of her breath hurt her chest.

The hoplite leaned down.

Her fingers curled into talons, ready to scratch his eyes out.

An angry shout reverberated through the room. Calliope's wild-eyed gaze sought out the new menace.

Her attackers leapt away as if burnt by an invisible fire.

Caught up in giving thanks for her reprieve, she failed to see they were suddenly standing to attention and seized her chance.

A surge of power flooded her, demanding she flee for her life. Bracing herself, she leapt forward like a runner in a foot race, seeing nothing except the doorway leading to freedom. Heart beating wildly in exhilaration, she ran, taking two paces, only to thud into an armored chest.

Air whooshed out of her lungs. Instinct driving her, she jumped sideways. Only to lose her shawl, miss her footing and collapse in an ignominious heap on her bottom. Pushing her hair out of her eyes with an unsteady hand, she collected her scattered wits, her vision coming to rest on the pair of feet in front of her.

Her exultation that a god had appeared to save her was short-lived.

These feet were human, planted apart in an unmistakeable attitude of command. Leather sandals cradled grazed, tough-looking skin; the lower legs sheaved by bronze greaves reflecting the red of the cloak hanging to the calves.

Calliope looked up. And up. Her gaze travelled past muscled thighs left bare by the short tunic, past the burnished cuirass which had halted her bid for freedom, her bulging eyes moving past his chest to look upon his face.

A choked gasp escaped her throat.

It was like looking into the face of something not quite human.

The helmet, with its transverse crest denoting his high rank, covered the Spartan's face. All she could see were his mouth and eyes. A mouth compressed in a hard line; unfathomable eyes boring into her. Held in thrall by his unyielding, obsidian gaze, Calliope could only stare back until her eyes began to water. The aura of threat and power enveloped him like a second skin—so palpable it required all her self-restraint not to reach out to touch it.

"We discovered this woman praying to Apollo. She must be a priestess of the temple."

She didn't need to hear the respectful tone to know this was their leader, the beloved of Zeus, who continued to keenly assess her. Seeing him glance at her bare shoulder, her cheeks flamed. She grasped the fibula and pulled it up with a determined jerk. If possible, his lips thinned into an even tighter line.

Some of her terror had subsided, bringing awareness of the disadvantageous position she found herself in. Sitting at his feet gave him power over her—this man would value courage.

Thrusting her chin out, Calliope stood, holding her head high. After confronting Lykos earlier, she'd discovered a long-buried vein of defiance.

"Are you not going to run your kopis through me?" she taunted, wishing her voice sounded stronger. The wicked, curved sword the Spartan carried looked lethal enough to cut through anything.

"I do not hurt women," he growled. He looked around the cella. "Where are the others?"

An unfamiliar emotion skittered along her nerves. The harsh words did not disguise the richness of his deep voice, smooth like the nectar drunk by the gods. Calliope remonstrated with herself for even noticing. Whatever the temptation, she must not forget he embodied a threat to her and her home.

She pulled her shoulders back, the small movement lending her confidence.

"There are no others," she countered, looking directly into his eyes. "I came here alone."

Well, it was partly true, even if the cold look he favored her with, clearly declared he did not believe her.

"Let us not play games," he warned. "Do not dare to hope I will believe you are alone. Where are the priests? The other priestesses? Tell me or it will go hard for you."

His questions rained down like arrows from the bow of Apollo. Her mouth turned down at the corners.

"You just told me you do not hurt women. So, everything that is said about Spartans is true." Disdain dripped from her voice. "None of you would think twice about raising your hand against a woman. You are all the same, high-born or not."

He raised a brow. "As you seem to not value your life there is always a first time."

Calliope's lip trembled. The top of her head barely came up to the impressive width of his chest, reminding her how easily he could snap her neck should he choose to. She shifted her feet, unnerved by the way he scrutinized her features. Did he find something displeasing about her appearance, given the time he took to examine her face?

Every muscle in her neck began to protest from tilting her head back to lock gazes with him.

He walked around her, appraising her in the same way he would assess a horse he coveted. Heat flooded her cheeks, an angry hiss whistling through her teeth. Refusing to be intimidated she hoped her eyes hurled daggers.

Calliope blinked.

She would have sworn she spied a hungry, almost yearning, look in his eyes. Even as her brows drew together, the look disappeared, replaced by the considering stare directed at her now.

"You are the high priestess of Apollo. Denial is useless. You were described to me." He paused to let the words sink in. "Tell me, do you have the gift of '*the sight*'?"

A swarm of angry hornets buzzed in her head.

She must lie.

She needed to lie.

Calliope opened her mouth to reply but her dry throat would not form words. Willing moisture into her parched mouth she managed to croak, "I have never divined anything."

He took one step toward her. "Then you better start now." His voice held more menace than the roar of the Nemean Lion. "Consider this your tribute for protecting your friends. I know some escaped. Perhaps you helped them."

"I have never divined. Never!"

If she let herself, she could recall the knife-like pain which had skewered her heart and soul. Could hear the cry of anguish as she called out a name before the icy fingers scored her mind again. By whatever intervention of the gods, this memory remained with her while all else was lost.

Her knees buckled.

She would not allow herself to collapse at this man's feet again. Catching hold of his upper arms to brace herself, the muscles beneath her gripping fingers were like hard rocks warmed by the sun. She felt the start of his body, followed by an unfamiliar spasm in her belly which shocked her.

Calliope snatched her hands away, surprised when he gripped them to steady her.

"It is a coveted honor to be an oracle of the gods," he pronounced before releasing her hands. "Unless there is someone else to take your place you will divine two things for me."

"I will not betray anyone," she flung at him. Even as the words left her mouth, she knew he had tricked her into revealing she was alone. "Damn you, Spartan," she cried. "The wrath of Apollo will fall upon you. You cannot come here, raze my home to the ground and not expect punishment."

Allowing herself a moment to savor the fire blazing out of his eyes, she vowed to thwart him at every turn.

"Spare me your threats. I have no fear of retribution from any god whatever you may believe."

Her breath hissed. The audacity of his words, the certainty in which they were uttered, were calculated to inflame.

Calliope tossed her head and stared him down.

"You dare speak for the gods of Olympus? You, a mortal? Beware they do not strike you dead for your arrogance."

The wretched man smiled at her. The curve of his lips caught her off guard, her stomach free-falling. Perhaps some malady was about to overcome her.

"They will not strike me down however much you may wish it. Your threats and insults tire me. Your assistance is required. It will be given."

She gritted her teeth. "What do you want from me, Spartan?"

Instantly she regretted the rash words.

Female hostages were often taken as slaves to their conqueror's whims. Calliope crossed her arms, hoping somehow to shield herself against his intent. She doubted he would respect her rank.

"Do not worry you are safe for the moment." A knowing smile played around his mouth. "Of course, your safety will depend on your willingness to assist me."

"How safe?" she demanded hoarsely over the lump in her throat. "What is this assistance you expect of me? How long can I expect to live after I help you?"

A muscle worked in his jaw. Good. He was angry. Angry people made mistakes.

Calliope suppressed a bitter laugh.

You fool. Do you truly believe this is a man who would make mistakes?

"I have already told you I do not hurt women. But I warn you, do not try any feminine wiles on me. You will only fail."

Calliope wondered about the dissonant tone he delivered the assertion in. Whatever caused it, might prove a chink in his armor.

She was in danger, yet something about him pulled at her; drew her in. It was more than just his commanding air and magnificent physique. Had she seen him somewhere before? Delphi perhaps, where she had once visited? Her brows drew together in a confused line.

"You will have my co-operation," she acquiesced with a shrug. "But it will depend on what you expect me to do. Death would be preferable in some instances."

Her choices were limited. He could simply carry her off, yet he gave her the illusion she possessed a choice. Wariness bubbled in Calliope, clearing her mind to make some plan.

She would feign going along with his plans using every wile she possessed, even the long-suppressed feminine ones. Anything that would provide her the means of escape from whatever purpose he wanted to use her for.

Calliope waited.

His dark gaze swept around the temple, returning to study her in a way which made every fine hair on the back of her neck rise.

"I will not allow you to die," he stated bluntly. "You appear to love your city, to value your life. If that is so, you will journey with me to the shrine of the Hidden Apollo. You will wear the legendary coronet we in Sparta have learned of, the Sapphire of the Sun God. If I am pleased with what you tell me, your city will be spared, and you will be free to return home."

Waves of darkness crashed through Calliope, flooding her trembling legs, shaking them with such force, she sank to her knees, not caring if he thought she was begging.

"Nooo!"

Stretching her arms out, she gazed up, imploring him through tear-filled eyes. "I cannot wear it," she choked. "Please do not make me wear the coronet."

"A woman's tears will not help you. Do not seek to appeal to my better nature. That part of me was lost long ago."

Calliope burned to tell him she did not believe he possessed a single spark of goodness in him.

"Then take pity on me and sacrifice me on the altar of Apollo, for I cannot do what you ask." Hanging her head to hide her flaming cheeks, Calliope found herself considering the unthinkable. "I will go as your hostage to your house, but I will not divine for you."

"You are the high priestess. Despite what I said before, I know only you are allowed to wear Apollo's coronet," he insisted with implacable determination. "Why are you afraid of it?"

A tiny spark of hope lit a fire inside her. If he was prepared to listen she would tell him the truth. Wiping her eyes dry she sat back on her heels.

"I wore it once," she admitted, noting his compressed lips as he saw through her previous lie. "The high priest never allowed me to return to the shrine after then."

He did not need to know the reason why she had been barred from there. The icy-cold fingers of her dream threatened at the edge of her mind. Calliope lifted her head, utterly resolved to stand her ground.

"I will not wear it again."

CHAPTER FIVE

Staring down his patrician nose at the woman collapsed at his feet, Diokles clenched his teeth to ward off the pain twisting his heart. The ache in his jaw proof he was losing the battle.

But he would not allow the priestess's tears to soften him, even though it strained his sense of honor to witness her distress. He had come too far, invested a lifetime believing the gods would not fail him, to stop now.

From the moment he laid eyes on her hope and pain mingled in a swirling eddy. Memories swamped his mind—of secret meetings, of stolen kisses, of promises exchanged.

Promises unfulfilled because of two men.

The muscles in his neck bunched.

Her eyes alone almost undid his hard-won restraint. They were not the deep soft brown of his missing betrothed, but liquid amber, drawing every cell, every nerve, every beat of his heart into their hypnotic depths. Her thick mane of hair shone with coppery hues rather than golden ones.

His hand lifted.

Was it her?

An imperceptible shake of his head brought him to his senses and banished the impulse to grab a handful of those lustrous strands to ensure the color was real. The priestess appeared to be the right age; her features reminiscent of Callisto's who had been coming into womanhood when she had disappeared from Sparta.

His vision clouded; the urge to lash out strong. What kind of love did he bear Callisto if he could not recognize her regardless of how much time had passed?

Fierce resolve hardened him. Rage blinded a man. He could not afford to be anything but a clear-headed leader. The lives of his peers depended upon it. His own success depended on it too.

Turning his attention back to the priestess, doubt ate at him. She showed no signs she recognized him. In fact, she stared at him with a mixture of wariness and intense dislike. He would never admit how much he admired her courage; her refusal to be cowed. He smiled inwardly. Her defiance was so like his beloved's who had always stood toe-to-toe with him whenever they argued.

With an abrupt gesture he dismissed the two hoplites standing nearby as though carved from stone. They removed themselves from his presence immediately. Like himself, they were the product of rigorous training. A matchless training guaranteeing discipline and loyalty, which did not forgo punishment if orders were disobeyed. Those two would be dealt with. Had he not arrived when he did, he suspected they would have given in to their baser urges.

And, if by some marvel conjured by the gods, this priestess somehow proved to be the woman he sought, their deaths would be swift.

He wanted to prise the truth from her here and now. His hand clenched around the handle of the kopis. He must cultivate patience—a quality he was not renowned for. During his training he had shown supreme skill as a master strategist. All he needed to do was use those same skills to find that truth.

No stranger to feminine beauty, the fierce tug of desire nevertheless stunned him. The long straight hair framed an oval face, her slim form sculpted by the gods, the smooth skin glowing honey-gold. He looked into her eyes again—luminous jewels pulling him into their depths, as dangerous as the depths of the Ionian Sea.

His body stirred, hardening with a speed foreign to him. A grunt of disgust vibrated in his throat at this weakness, this lack of control over his physical urges.

Why did this priestess have such power over him?

Only one woman had ever been able to arouse him the same way. Brows snapping together, he stared at her again.

No. It could not be possible.

"What is your name and where do you come from?"

Her eyes opened wide to shoot daggers at him.

"What difference would it make to you to know my name? I am a priestess of Apollo. That is all you need to know."

"Telling me your name, where you came from, and anything you may know about your city preparing for a war, could mean the difference between wearing the coronet or not."

Her audible gasp, coupled with a hopeful expression, curled his mouth in a satisfied smile. If she chose to be honest with him, he would have his answers sooner than planned. A shorter occupation promised less bloodshed.

"My name is Lysandra," she declared, rising to her feet. "I have lived in the temple for as long as I can remember."

Diokles drew in a swift breath. Beneath her words he detected a subtle jarring in her low tones. She was lying. The way she could not meet his eyes told him all he needed to know.

"You claim to be a native of Apollysis."

"Yes. My memories are of this city; therefore, I have lived all my life here."

Every instinct went on alert at her odd choice of words. Diokles considered her beautiful, deceptive face. She gave off the impression of great calm, but her eyes gave her away. The skin was pinched, the amber depths clouded. They appeared determined to hide the truth.

"You are different to the city's inhabitants. You are taller and your coloring is different. Even the way you talk is different."

"What do you mean?"

The guarded tone revealed he was close to breaking the armor of her composure. "I mean you are lying." His next move came to him in a blinding flash of insight. Looking beyond her toward the main door he called out in a loud voice, "Lysandra."

"She cannot be here! She has—"

The moment she clapped a hand over her mouth triumph flooded him. "You have lied to me a second time and sealed your fate. You will accompany me to the shrine as my hostage."

Loathing blazed in her eyes. She flew at him, his superb reflexes no match for the fists viciously pummelling every part of his body she could reach.

"Damn you, Spartan! May the gods curse you for all eternity! May—"

"Stop this foolishness," he growled, catching her fists in a vice-like grip and forcing her arms behind her back. She slammed against him, her wild struggles testing his control. One arm bent awkwardly, her wince drawing a muttered curse from him. Diokles eased his hold, alert for any attempt she might make to break away.

A subtle movement warned him to twist away from the knee being driven up toward his vitals. The blow landed on his thigh with bruising force. Surprised by the power behind it, by the wildness suffusing her face, he conceded she would not listen to reason.

This left him one course of action or risk being permanently maimed by the Fury in his arms. He released her wrists, wrapped his arms around her before she could flee, and pulled her hard against his body.

Time stopped.

He sensed her sudden stiffness, the subtle withdrawal into herself. Despite her bent head, he spied a blush turning her cheeks red like clouds caught in the rays of the setting sun. Against his cuirass her chest rose and fell with a speed that matched his own thundering pulse.

Hooking a finger under her chin he brought her head up. She might channel a Fury although in no way did she resemble one. His gaze feasted on the perfection of her lips. Slightly parted they emphasized the shape—just like the bow of Eros. The temptation to taste their sweetness beat at him, daring him to slake his thirst.

With infinite slowness he came closer, until barely a finger-width separated their mouths.

The hitch in her breathing sounded in his ears.

Cold reason flooded his mind.

One moment of oblivion would not cure years of hunger.

"Do not try to distract me with your charms," he bit out. He was being unreasonable, but it was his only defence against the enchantment gripping him. "All you will achieve by tempting me is to delay reaching the shrine. Which means your city stays under my command unless you give me the knowledge I have come to discover."

"I hate you," she whispered. "You call me a liar; tell me I am a hostage and now blame me for your own failings."

She pushed against him. He let her go, confident she could not outrun him or the cordon of his peers ringing the temple.

He rubbed the back of his neck. "Give me a good reason why I should spare you this task?"

"If you prefer to see me lose my mind, make me wear the coronet. If you want me dead, take me to the shrine. If you have any compassion, set me free."

Her words sank into his conscience until it fought against itself like two evenly matched phalanxes—one berating him for causing her fear; the other reminding him of the reasons why he was there.

The spoils of victory went to the latter.

"I cannot afford compassion. Nor do I believe you will die."

Standing about bandying words was not the Spartan way. Grabbing her wrist, he turned to leave.

"Please! My shawl."

Not trusting her motives, Diokles did not relinquish his hold. He bent to retrieve the discarded piece of clothing, then, ignoring her startled glance, threw it over her shoulders.

Swift strides propelled him out of the cella. They needed to leave without delay. Given the amount of time already wasted he hardened his heart against her demands he not walk so fast.

There was too much at stake to give in to any weakness.

Stepping out into blazing sunshine Calliope beheld a scene so alien she reeled back against a column. Gripping the warm stone, she dug her fingers into it with enough force to bend the nails.

The large square in front of the temple teemed with enemy hoplites. Not one inhabitant of the city could be seen no matter where her desperate gaze turned.

Her heart sank.

Where were her people? Had they been able to flee? Even worse, were they all dead? How could she find out?

A tug brought her attention back to her captor. In the light she could see his eyes were a deep, deep brown. Eyes which bored into her soul. Tossing her head back, she followed him down the steps, dragging her feet in the hope he would find her too much trouble to take with him. Beads of sweat dotted her forehead when he ignored her efforts.

Knowing she possessed the same chance of breaking free as cracking the stone columns with her bare hands, Calliope dug her heels in for one last determined attempt to make him see reason.

"Wait! Please."

Although he held her wrist without hurting her, the hold remained unrelenting like the narrow-eyed look he speared her with. "What now?"

Calliope swallowed at the sharp tone. If she pushed him too far, how long would he hold himself under the restraint he showed? If she didn't plead her cause, how could she find the courage to wear the coronet which terrified her more than he did.

She prayed desperately to find the words to change his mind.

"Why did you not bring a priestess from Sparta? Why come to Apollysis?" Stopping to draw breath for another assault, her heart sank. A muscle worked in his jaw, and in that moment, she knew she would not sway him.

He pointed a warning finger at her. "No-one questions me. You have brought this on yourself since you will not tell me where I may find another to take your place."

Calliope took in the determined set of his features. She wanted to rage at him that he was wrong. She swayed, nausea churning her stomach.

There was no time to dissuade him again before he released her from his stare to cast a sweeping glance around the square.

"Wear the coronet or your city burns."

Her shoulders sagged under the adamant authority the ultimatum was delivered in. Bending her head to allow her long hair to cover her face, she wept quiet tears—for her home and for herself. His strong fingers tightened against her wrist. If he discerned her tears it was not enough to stop him urging her forward. Surrounded by the enemy, Calliope choked back a sob, following in the direction he pulled her.

He had left her with no choice. In this bleak moment all thoughts of escape crumbled into dust.

Escape?

A glimmer of hope brightened the dark cloud shadowing her spirit. The journey to the shrine would last several days. Surely an opportunity to slip away would present itself.

The tears stopped.

Yes. She who had endured so much in her life would summon the courage to endure this trial and emerge the victor.

The back of her neck prickled. Raising her head, she met leers and suspicious looks from the gathered hoplites. Calliope drew the shawl more tightly around herself. Head held high she fixed her gaze on the Spartan's broad back. Trudging after him across the square her eyes bored holes between his shoulder blades. One day he would pay for the humiliation he heaped on her.

The square was not large but it took an eternity to cross.

Reaching a chariot, Calliope released the breath she had been holding. She forgot her discomfort, admiring the two black stallions harnessed to it, their glossy hides shimmering in the sun.

An elusive wisp of memory tantalized and slid out of her mind before she could capture it.

She scrunched her face, fisting her hand when she failed to recall what the memory showed.

Something about horses. A something arising from the depths of a time she possessed no memory of.

"A rope."

Rope? What did he mean?

Slack-jawed, Calliope stared disbelievingly when a rope materialized, long enough to bind her with. She jumped when it touched her skin.

"Do you expect me to run behind the chariot like a slave?" she asked incredulously.

His burning look was hot enough to melt bronze.

"I do not trust you. This is my guarantee you will not try to flee."

She ground her teeth. How dare he treat her no better than a slave? How dare he consider her no better than some prized horse he won in battle for himself.

Calliope muttered insults under her breath. He would probably treat the horse better than he treated her.

“So, my unwillingness is to be exhausted by making me run after your chariot?”

The Spartan’s answer was to hook his arms around her shoulders and knees, lifting her with the effort it would take him to lift a leaf. The warmth of his arms scorched her skin through the thin tunic. Her heart skipped a beat. No man had ever possessed the power to discompose her like he did.

In one smooth movement she found herself dumped into the chariot. He stepped up behind her, the floor dipped, forcing Calliope to shuffle her feet to keep upright. Toying with the urge to stomp on his sandalled foot, she submitted to the indignity of having her wrists tied to the side railing of the basket.

He stood too close for her peace of mind, evoking shudders whenever his hands brushed her skin. The heat radiating off his body stoked an answering warmth within hers. Awareness ran like a swift current from the top of her head to pool between her legs.

Calliope gasped.

He was the enemy. An enemy she had no right to be aware of in such a manner. She must remain true to her vow. Hunching her shoulders she avoided touching him as best she could.

He left to speak with one of his officers enabling her to breathe more freely. Her curious gaze noticed the ease with which they spoke to each other. Calliope half-closed her eyes to study them both, straining to hear what they were saying. It proved impossible over the noise of restless horses and men moving about. Exhaling a resigned sigh, she turned her attention to her bound hands. Cautiously flexing her fingers, she found enough give in the length of the rope to grip the railing easily.

Her eyebrows rose at this unexpected consideration for her comfort. A cynical grimace twisted her mouth. Of course he wanted her to be comfortable. He could not afford to have her toppling out of the chariot, perhaps breaking her neck. At least not until he had used her for his purpose.

A purpose which fomented fear within her.

The Spartan returned in time to stop her giving into it. Brushing past, he took the reins in his large capable hands. Another wave of feeling crashed through her. She gulped, striving to ignore the fluttering in her chest.

Catching his brief glance, she averted her gaze, pulse pounding to a heavy beat. By all the gods, she would not let him see her fear or the way his presence affected her.

The slap of reins over the horse's rumps was her signal to grab the rail. The stallions leapt into a gallop, forcing Calliope to widen her stance so she did not crash into him. It would be bad enough hurting herself against the bronze armor he wore without worrying about touching any exposed part of his body. With a twist of her lips she saw men scatter out of their path and a small group of mounted hoplites fall in behind them.

Heart weighed down by grief, Calliope spared one last look at her home as the city walls shrank out of sight.

Would she ever see it again?

CHAPTER SIX

The punishing pace was relentless.

Calliope opened her mouth to demand to be taken back, face twisting when only a hoarse croak emerged. He would not hear her over the pounding hooves and the jangling harness anyway.

Clamping her grit-coated lips together she sought distraction in her surroundings. The familiar landscape lifted her spirits. They would reach a small river soon, and if they did not stop, it would be worth risking life and limb to throw herself over the rail, bound hands and all, rather than slowly die of thirst.

No sooner than the thought occurred the pace dropped to a walk. Leaning forward, Calliope spotted the silver ribbon of water. Her groan of relief accompanied their halting on the pebbled bank.

Without a word, he brushed past her, jumped out, and led the horses into the shallows. Incensed by his lack of concern, Calliope fumed until she swore she could feel steam coming out of every pore. All around her men dismounted, some already watering their mounts.

Hot, tired, desperate to remove the grit clinging to her lips, Calliope's frayed nerves snapped.

"Am I to be offered a drink? A dead priestess is of no use to you."

A reproving sideways glance was her reply. She bit down on her lip to stop more rash words tumbling out. It was not sensible to provoke him yet she could not restrain the impulse. She looked away and wondered how she would survive the next few days.

Loud splashes drew her attention back to the river. The Spartan crouched in the shallows, washing the inside of his helmet. Narrow-eyed, she watched him fill it from the fast-flowing current.

Calliope forgot her thirst the closer he came. Her gaze swept over the face of a man born to command—strong, rugged—the bold features making him entirely too pleasing to her eyes. The strong nose dominating his face, the full, sensual lips, the dark brows, curved like eagle's wings. Her breath stopped halfway in her chest, every cell humming in primal awareness.

He stepped up beside her and held the helmet up to her mouth. "Drink."

Dragging her gaze away, Calliope guzzled the cool, life-giving water too fast and doubled over coughing.

"Slowly."

The impatience in his voice earned him a lethal glare. "I know how to drink," she wheezed. Sipping more calmly, it annoyed her to admit he was right.

Pulling away when she had drunk enough, her consciousness of his forceful presence grew unbearably. Not just of his scent—a mix of leather and something earthy she could not describe—he exuded an indefinable air of strength and assurance. Calliope shifted her feet and risked a glance at his face. Her worldview narrowed to his eyes. In them lurked the hungry, yearning look she had spied earlier. His concentrated study of her face left her shaken to the point she took a step away from him.

The spell broke.

She could breathe again.

Through half-closed eyes, she watched him finish the rest of the water, the muscles of his throat strong, like the rest of him. A cursory wipe with his cloak and the helmet was back on his head, hiding all expression on his face. She would guard her emotions just as fiercely.

A shouted order to mount was her signal to grip the rail. Reaching the other side of the river he set the same punishing pace. The rumbling of her stomach reminded her she had not broken her fast.

Glowering at him, she hoped she managed to stay on her feet until they stopped for the night.

The abrupt drop in speed roused Calliope out of a bone-tired stupor. Her dazed mind registered they were leaving the road, moving in the direction of a thick stand of trees some distance away.

She loosened her death grip, weariness weighing down every limb. Her fingers ached; her legs ached from standing in one spot; the skin on her palms burned from bracing herself whenever the chariot lurched over uneven ground.

"We will rest the night here."

Given he had not spoken a word to her most of the day, Calliope started at the sound of his voice.

"Is this how you treat all captives?" she rasped, arching her stiff back. "Never have I travelled in such a fashion—hungry, thirsty and dirty. Now it appears I am to sleep on hard ground, too."

One black eyebrow arched mockingly. "It will make you stronger."

"Stronger! I am a high priestess who journeyed with all the attendant honor due to me."

She broke off. Fear rose like a many-headed Hydra. It always came back to the coronet. No matter what part of her fear she conquered another tendril grew to take its place.

"Your life in the temple has softened you," he declared, striding to where the escort waited.

Despite her distress, Calliope could not help observing how the others deferred to him, their attentiveness while he spoke. It galled her to admit he was a respected and revered leader.

But when the mounted hoplites wheeled their horses around to ride away, her chest tightened, the breath coming in shallow gasps.

It would just be the two of them.

Alone.

Alone with a man, at night, for the first time in her life. He might try to pressure her in the same way Lykos had. What could she do about it? Yet, the Spartan seemed different to the priest as day did from night.

It did not mean she could trust him. She must keep herself vigilant all night in case—

An idea struck with the speed of a lightning bolt.

It could be her opportunity to slip away.

He was striding back to her looking tireless. How long would that last? Even he needed to sleep. And she knew enough of the secret practices to direct her will to stay awake.

"Have you sent your men away because I am to spend the night bound in your chariot? Are they not to witness how you treat me?" Weighed down by weariness she did not care that her words brought a scowl to his face.

"Do you want to sleep tied in the chariot?" he retorted, pausing in the act of untying her. "You are in no danger from me."

Calliope made a choking sound deep in her throat.

"Safe with you? I think not. I don't want to sleep in your chariot, I want to return home!"

Her loud protest startled roosting birds to take flight, squawking in alarm.

"Impossible."

She cast a baleful look at his bent head. He untied the rope, helping her to the ground, but not letting go. The touch of his hand sparked a tingling in her fingers. A light film of sweat clung to his skin, the earthy scent of him raw, its potent maleness teasing her.

Again, the unfamiliar warmth spread from her scalp like hot lava, pooling to a stop between her legs.

She clenched her thighs, furious her mind chose to replay the giggling whispers of priestesses, those unshackled by the oath she had taken, of what a man and woman did together.

Sudden understanding tilted her world on its axis.

No! She could not possibly be attracted to this man who had stolen her from everything she knew.

Sidling away on unsteady legs, she demanded, "Release me."

His mocking laughter grated over her ears. Glancing at his kopis, her fingers itched to grab the weapon and drive it through him.

"Release you so you can escape." Tugging his helmet off he quirked an eyebrow. "You remain bound until we reach the shrine."

Calliope ground her teeth, hating him for the humiliation she would endure.

"I need to relieve myself," she mumbled, eyes downcast, wishing the ground would open beneath her.

"I will escort you."

Her mouth dropped open. "You will not! I need privacy."

Studying the conflicting emotions crossing his handsome face, hope grew she could persuade him to change his mind.

"I promise not to run away." A promise easily kept tonight. Her rumbling stomach curtailed the initial thought to escape. She needed to eat. And needed a weapon. Somehow, she would secure both.

"You would be unwise to try," he declared. "Wild boar and wolves hunt at night."

"I would rather face the creatures of the night than stay here with you." Night was dangerous but he represented a greater danger to her peace of mind. "A quick death is preferable to a painful one or to losing my sanity."

"I do not believe you are afraid. If this is another lie to avoid wearing the coronet it will do you no good."

She met his distrustful look with all the aplomb she could muster. "I have already told you I do not know why the coronet is a danger to me."

A muscle twitched in his cheek. He remained silent for so long her nerves stretched to breaking point.

"I will untie you, but if you disappear from the grove—"

Despite the curtailed threat sweet relief flooded her. Rubbing her freed wrists, she quickly sought out the nearest dense cluster of bushes. Her captor followed hard on her heels. Muttering under her breath, Calliope crouched, doing her best to appear invisible. Once finished, she stood, nose thrust in the air, lips flattened in a tight line of disapproval.

Holding on to the shreds of her dignity, she followed him back to the center of the grove. If only she had her knife, he would be wearing it between his shoulder blades.

Losing her temper would solve nothing. Relaxing the tension in her shoulders, Calliope strolled within the ring of trees, breathing in the late afternoon scents. A soft cry of delight escaped on finding a small pool fed by a shallow stream.

A whinny brought her attention to where the Spartan was unhitching his horses. He must possess great wealth to keep such magnificent stallions. They tossed their heads, evoking a smile as she admired their gleaming hides. His lips moved in what she imagined to be a soothing voice, his touch masterfully settling them.

An image burst before her eyes with overwhelming clarity. A younger version of herself sat astride a horse, laughing, delight crowning her face. It faded swiftly, leaving behind cold tendrils icing through her brain. Calliope rubbed her arms. She had never ridden in Apollysis. Did the fleeting memory come from the childhood she could not remember?

If so, why did it come now? The hoplites of her city rode and often escorted her during festivals. Yet, seeing this man handling his stallions had thrust her into an unknown place. A hidden place buried in the deepest recesses of her mind.

The hair on her arms rose on end.

Coming back to the present, she saw him marching to where she stood, a purposeful look fixed on his face. Calliope thrust her chin forward, readying herself for the next battle.

"Do not stand there like a temple statue," he ordered. "Gather wood for a fire."

She planted her hands on her hips. "You dare. I am a high priestess, or have you forgotten, *Spartan*?" The emphasis on the word was meant to insult. Her courage high, she found perverse satisfaction in the displeasure hardening his face. "I do not gather wood, nor do I cook, nor am I a statue!"

"It will prove a long tiresome journey if you keep arguing with me."

The reluctant half-smile transformed his face. Calliope felt she was being granted a glimpse into the real man buried beneath the armor. Humph! Why did she even care?

Yet, she focused on his mouth, still curved in wry humor.

What would his mouth feel like if she touched it?

If it touched her lips.

He may be mocking her but her blood heated to boiling point. She threw caution to the four winds.

"You kidnapped me. Now you want me to build a fire and cook for you. I will do nothing of the sort. It is not my failure we have no servant. Go after your men. Bring them back to gather the wood."

"The men have their duties. We do not need a servant. It is just you and I."

Calliope dropped her hands to her sides trying to ignore the frisson of excitement stealing through her. Tried to ignore the wicked voice in her head whispering he intrigued her.

Knowing he would not relent she cursed under her breath. Stomping off in search of wood she made sure every step conveyed her disapproval. If he insisted she wear the coronet, she would lull him into a false sense of security by agreeing with his every demand.

Then, she could plan her escape.

Diokles watched the priestess stalk away, rebuke in every line of her supple body.

By all the gods, he would go mad if she continued to defy him. He did not like having his authority questioned. The foolish few who had challenged him learned very quickly it was not their wisest choice. On some occasions it had turned out to be their last.

When he lifted her into the chariot earlier, he had looked into her face and been transported to a time better left forgotten. *Where did this woman come from*? Her lies this morning aroused certainty she hid much more than where her friends had fled to.

So many of her mannerisms reminded him of his betrothed. It did little to assuage the guilt of how his body tightened in her presence. His reaction betrayed the woman he sought. The woman who still held his heart despite her absence from his life.

He kept a vigilant eye on the priestess while she collected the firewood. The longer he watched the deeper his forehead creased. Despite her protests about not stooping to menial tasks, the way she meticulously selected the correct kindling, intrigued him. An odd skill for someone who insisted she spent her entire life in a temple.

She was returning with her arms full. Diokles invoked Hermes—the god whose cunning outwitted both mortals and immortals alike—to help him discover the truth of her past.

"You deceived me again," he stated, relishing the burst of color spreading over her face.

"What do you mean?"

"You told me you had never gathered wood. Just like you told me you had never spoken a word in prophecy, then lied about your name." He spared a pointed glance at the branches she clutched against herself like a shield. "Yet you have brought me kindling dry enough to start a fire. How did you know which to choose?"

"I cannot explain. I—"

Her gaze skittered away but not quickly enough for him to see the bewilderment clouding her eyes.

Quashing the insistence of his conscience to be gentle with her, he pressed further. "What else are you hiding? Truth will help you better than lies."

"Truth!" she yelped. "There can be no truth between us. If you want me to be truthful, then yes, I will try to escape. Yes, I will run you through with your own xiphos if I can. Is that truthful enough? And do not stare at me as though I have grown horns!"

Diokles rocked back on his heels

He did not see horns. Instead, his eyes were drawn to her lips. Her soft, eminently kissable lips. "You presume too much. You may not have horns but you are as troublesome as any Harpy."

Her eyes almost popped out of her head.

"A Harpy! It is you who presume too far!"

He crossed his arms over his chest. "You have carried on like one ever since we left Apollysis."

She shot him a look full of indignation. "Here is your wood."

He stepped back to avoid the pile of branches thrown at his feet. Diokles watched her march to the pool and drop to her knees beside it. He would jump into it later to douse the fire burning in his loins. He could not possibly be attracted to a woman whose name he did not know, but grudgingly, he admired her spirit. She was afraid—of him, the coronet, or something else hidden from his knowledge—yet she continued to be the defiant, haughty priestess.

Her courage stirred something in his heart. Starting tonight he would dig deeper to find out more.

Calliope splashed cool water over her face, a tiny smile playing around her mouth. She could feel every particle of dust being washed away.

Removing her sandals, she swung her hot feet into the water, relishing the relief it brought. The last pinpricks of light pierced the horizon, although warmth still hung in the air. Closing her eyes, she breathed in the sweet scent of myrtle carried to her on a light evening breeze. Her shoulders relaxed bringing relief to the tense muscles there.

The day had taken its toll. The invasion, the war of words with her captor, left her drained. She allowed herself the indulgence of a drawn-out yawn and rubbed her eyes. As dusk beckoned, she meditated, going deep into the calm center of her being, feeling the limitless energy of the earth rise up to replenish her own.

For some time she sat in blissful oblivion until the notion of escape once more nudged the edge of her mind.

Cupping her hands, she scooped water into them, drinking deeply to cleanse her gritty throat. Shaking them dry she gazed into the distance and considered her options.

Escaping alone by night, unarmed, would be dangerous. She drew her knees up and rested her chin on them. Perhaps if she kept to the road there was a good chance to see an animal before it saw her. Then again, what if there was no tree tall enough she could climb? What if the predator proved swifter than her?

Calliope sighed. Her frightened self insisted facing the night creatures would be better than wearing the coronet. Her practical self argued she needed sustenance to restore her strength and to wait for a more opportune moment.

Her stomach growled long and loud. Bowing to more practical concerns Calliope decided she could wait. She would not get far without eating something.

She caught the scent of wood smoke. Getting to her feet, she looked round, surprised to see a blazing fire built from the kindling she had gathered earlier. Keeping a wary eye on the man tending it, she walked over to join him, unsure of her reception.

Drawing closer she saw he was skinning a rabbit. “Where—?”

His withering look stopped her.

“We need to eat.”

Too hungry to let his terse replies bother her, Calliope wondered if all Spartans spoke with the same economy of words.

She studied him beneath her lashes. His hair shone black in the firelight, tamed into a braid which fell down his back. He had removed his cuirass, giving her an enthralling view of the muscled torso honed to perfection; the fitted tunic outlining every ridge of his abdomen.

A fine tremor shook her hands.

Whereas his were steady while he prepared the food. Those capable hands looked strong enough to defeat any enemy.

How would they feel on a woman's body?

She froze. What possessed her to wonder how this man's hands would feel on her body?

Worried her shaking legs might collapse Calliope hurriedly sat beside the fire. Folding them to one side she arranged her white tunic to cover their bareness. She had chosen white to drive home to Lykos her virginal state. Now, she stared resignedly at the patches of dirt splashed around the hem. She expected it would get even dirtier and there was nothing she could do about it.

Quivers of sensation raced across her nerves. She was alone with a man who, equally fascinated and angered, her. Scowling, needing to hide how much his presence rattled her, she went on the offensive.

"I am not used to eating in a man's presence, nor am I hungry enough to share food with you." Her stomach gave its loudest rumble yet. She met his pointed look with gritted teeth and battled a furious urge to hit him.

"Is that all you are worried about? Eating with a man? I will not compel you to eat but you need strength for the journey."

Her disapproval evaporated like the moisture in her mouth.

"So long as I am fit to wear the coronet otherwise you would not care if I starved."

His dark eyes bored into her. "I need answers. You claim you may die or succumb to insanity if you wear it. Is the coronet cursed?"

She dug her fingers against her temples. "I do not know. How can it be cursed?" Why did the wretched man not understand? "The priests maintain the coronet is protected by Apollo himself. Anyone who tries to wear it without proper ceremony, or steal it, dies. As high priestess my duty is to speak for the god, yet I cannot bring myself to do so."

Calliope stopped, surprised he had drawn out this admission. Her sense of self-preservation had obviously deserted her if she almost revealed her deepest, darkest secret. The one she did not possess answers for. Dropping her face into her hands she pushed back the bile rising in her throat.

Eventually she looked up, once more the calm unflappable priestess she had schooled herself to be.

Caught in the thrall of his relentless scrutiny Calliope struggled to find something to dislike about him. The scar across his brow had to be the legacy of some battle. It should detract from his looks, instead it strengthened his features. His eyes, dark as the night creeping across the sky, reflected the flickering flames. The strong lips, full and decidedly masculine, pinched in a taut line.

Dizziness assaulted her. She reminded herself she sought to dislike this man not assess him as a potential mate.

She linked her shaking fingers studying them as though her life depended on it. "Is something the matter?" she challenged.

"You ask too many questions." He turned his attention back to the simple meal.

Calliope stiffened, stung by the unwarranted admonishment. If he thought one question too many she would not say another word.

The aroma of roasting rabbit tickled her nostrils. Her mouth watered watching him prod the flesh to test if it was cooked. At long last he removed it from the fire, using a shorter xiphos than she had seen Apollysian hoplites carry. The sharp, dual-edged sword sliced through the rabbit with unnerving ease.

She gave him credit for ingenuity. He used the wooden underside of his shield as a table, placing slices of meat on borage leaves arranged over it. Hunger overrode patience and manners.

Calliope snatched a portion without waiting to be asked. He could smirk at her all he wanted but no amount of knowing looks could dissuade her from savouring every sustaining mouthful. Licking her fingers, she longed to ask what herbs he had used to flavor the meat with. One look at his impassive face convinced her not to bother.

Warm darkness enveloped them. The soft calls of nocturnal birds provided a gentle melody in tune with the crackling fire.

Hunger sated, Calliope wrapped herself in the shawl and lay down. Shifting about until she found a comfortable position, she closed her eyes. The sound of more wood being thrown on the fire lulled her, the spurt of heat warming her tired body.

Faint rustlings told her he, too, prepared to bed down for the night. But not before he tied her ankles with a knot she was certain she had no hope of undoing. Mouth twisting, she watched him wrap and tie the end of the rope around his waist.

She wriggled as far away from him as the rope length allowed. He need not worry about her running away tonight. Eyelids drooping, she promised herself tomorrow night would be another matter.

CHAPTER SEVEN

Like a wolf scenting prey, Lykos scented the air, nostrils flaring. Somewhere Calliope slumbered in the company of a man he needed to stop.

At any cost.

Was the man touching her the same way he hungered to?

He bared his teeth as every muscle clenched in outrage. If his nemesis had broken through Calliope's self-imposed barriers he would kill him. Then show her the consequences of letting another man touch her.

First though, he needed to deal with the squabbling in his own small encampment, safely situated far enough from Apollysis, but close enough so his reinforcements could reach him. Reinforcements not enclosed by city walls.

"You are a fool, Aeschylus," he yelled, spittle flying in all directions. "If Diokles has her, you know where he will take her. Are you certain it was him?"

Lykos studied the lean figure circling the fire. Aeschylus had changed little from the man who arrived unexpectedly in Apollysis all those years ago. Despite the problems he lived with, the dark hair barely showed any grey, he stood tall with no stoop to his shoulders, his strength remained undiminished.

Lykos curled his lip. Only the permanently haunted look in the older man's eyes betrayed the tortured soul within.

"I am certain," Aeschylus answered. "I recognized the scar on his left arm."

Lykos growled. For too long he had plotted to get Calliope into his bed. This meant keeping his desire a secret from his benefactor. Without Aeschylus's generous support he would not be high priest.

It mattered little. Once Calliope was in his power her adoptive father's usefulness ceased. He would be quietly eliminated leaving Calliope to inherit all of Aeschylus's wealth. No-one would suspect Lykos, the great high priest of Apollo.

Naturally, the fortune would become his when he married her.

But the time was not yet.

"We must reach the shrine before them," Lykos muttered to himself. What options did he have? If he sent Aeschylus after them now, perhaps he would challenge Diokles and one of them would be conveniently killed.

No. They both must die by his hand alone. "I will send a small party of hoplites to recapture Calliope. Your world will collapse if she wears the coronet."

Seeing Aeschylus blanch curved his mouth into a feral grin, until he sobered with the realization that even possessing the means to limit the damage, it would affect him too.

"Have you lost your reason?" Aeschylus gaped at him and waved a hand around the camp. "Where are these men you intend to send? There is one priestess with us yet you speak of hoplites?"

Lysandra's melodic voice flowed over their argument. "Our high priest will have secured our safety."

Lykos looked down to where she sat, lips pouting in invitation. The flames flickered against her light brown hair, turning the strands red. In his mind her features morphed into Calliope's. His insides twisted and burned, lust turning him hard. What he would not give to take her now, concealed behind a tree, their cries smothered, heightening his excitement.

"Our priestess is correct." He stared beyond the ring of trees shielding them, expectancy tightening his gut. "Soon we shall be joined by armed men from Apollysis. I have assembled a small force if it ever came to this day. Do you see how my foresight has been rewarded? We will rescue Calliope and kill Diokles in one swift sally."

Then he could finally take what he had waited for so many years to take. His breath quickened. Triumph lanced all the way into his black soul.

His exhilaration was short-lived, shattered by Aeschylus's disparaging laugh.

"Oh Lykos, you truly do not understand Spartans," he gasped. "If you believe your men can defeat even a small company of Spartans you fail to understand who you are dealing with. There is a germ of truth in the belief that one Spartan hoplite is worth twelve others."

"I do not care," Lykos roared. What did he care of a stupid belief? The day approached when they would all bow to his commands. "I will have the high priestess back. I will kill the man who stole her."

Her innocence was his to take.

When he was crowned the first king of Apollysis.

A secret ambition he revealed to no-one no matter how trusted or sycophantic. The power and prestige of being high priest no longer satisfied his hunger for the greatness he believed he deserved. He rubbed his palms together at the thought of dissolving the city's governing council and ruling in his own right.

Calliope's vow of purity meant nothing. She would be his consort; bound to him, whenever he wanted her. Together they would be a force to be reckoned with.

Provided she did not resist.

He would realize all his plans using the small army he continued to build in secret, gradually increasing their number with men bought to carry out his revenge.

Lykos summoned as sincere a smile as his cunning, ambitious heart allowed.

"Come Aeschylus, let us not cross words," he deliberately softened his tone. "It pains me to disagree with you."

Beneath his feet the ground trembled. Barely discernible at first, he paused to listen. Yes. The sound of drumming hooves grew closer. "Our men approach. We will sacrifice to the gods in thanksgiving and nourish ourselves for the journey ahead."

Hubris expanded his chest as he watched the hoplites ride in. Men loyal to him alone. He could count on them to be his eyes and ears; protect his back. No-one in Apollysis knew they were in his pay nor that they followed only his orders.

The first task for three of their number would be to retrieve Calliope before she reached the shrine.

His insides quivered. Soon she would be back in his power.

The dancing flames of the fire lulled Aeschylus into a trance. The conversation with Lykos replayed in his head. Drawing the cloak about him he pondered over the priest's words and the almost crazed anger consuming the man.

He shifted uneasily as he recalled the glint in Lykos's eyes when Calliope had first entered the temple to train as a priestess. Witnessing the priest's over-attentiveness to the girl who had somewhat healed the wound in his heart, he began to spend his days in the temple. He always visited at different times, ostensibly to pray, using the opportunity this provided to keep an eye on her.

Lykos's behavior tonight justified his move to buy spies within the cohort the priest thought loyal. Aeschylus paid them handsomely, and with families to feed, men were easily bought.

A soft noise snapped him out of his reverie.

Peering beneath half-closed lids he spotted someone inching toward him. Recognizing the hoplite Aeschylus released the breath he held. This man had proved many times he was worthy of his trust.

Waiting till he reached him, Aeschylus leaned in, keeping his voice low. "What are Lykos's plans?"

The man first cast a glance around the camp. Nobody paid them any attention.

"He insists we travel to the shrine in all haste," he murmured close to Aeschylus's head. "He has already sent scouts to find the Spartans who left with the high priestess. My lord, he is a man possessed. Any cautionary word is swept aside."

"I worry about Calliope," Aeschylus muttered, turning his head to look at his co-conspirator. "You have done well. When she is restored to me and we can return to Apollysis, I will personally ensure you are amply compensated. I swear this by Zeus himself."

"Thank you, my lord," the man inclined his head. "Apart from a small few, every other man here has sworn allegiance to the high priestess and yourself. Lykos has been plotting something these past years. I do not know what, but I do know he is dangerous."

"Then he is more of a threat than even I believed." Aeschylus frowned. *What was Lykos up to*? Somehow, he must find out, so he could thwart him to keep Apollysis safe. "I am indebted to you for this news."

The hoplite nodded and slipped away, leaving Aeschylus frowning into the flames. Vowing to keep his adopted daughter from suffering any more than she already had, he determined to keep a watchful eye on Lykos. Suffering was an emotion he understood intimately. After all he had already lost two daughters.

His heart contracted. He could not endure to lose a precious child a third time.

Following the faint trail into the woods Lykos spied the soft billow of a tunic behind a tree. With the stealth of a predator about to pounce on its prey he stole toward it. His body stirred when the woman standing behind the trunk came into view.

Calliope!

"Ah, my sweet," he stepped into her welcoming arms, eyes closed, grinding his hardness against her. Her panting taunted him, fired his blood. "You are so good to me. Let me show you how grateful I am."

Tongue thrusting into her mouth, he worked one hand under her tunic to fondle a breast, kneading its fullness. The whimpers of need deep in her throat inflamed him, her frantic rubbing against his body igniting passion until his mind went blank.

He felt her drag her tunic up. Growling deep in his throat, he cupped her mound, lights erupting in his head at how wet she was. His free hand pushed aside his tunic to release his throbbing erection.

Calliope's image filled his mind. Mentally undressing her he buried his aching length into the woman before him.

Behind tightly closed eyes, he savored the friction as he repeatedly thrust into her welcoming heat. *How would Calliope look when he possessed her? Her body arched like Eros's bow. Head thrust back; the satiny skin of her neck exposed to his delectation. The long red hair draped over his swollen member.*

His climax neared. Muscles tensing in anticipation, he thrust faster.

Hands clamped over her buttocks, he howled his release the exact moment she screamed in ecstasy, her hot passage clenching around him. He pumped hard, imagining his seed filling Calliope.

Breathing heavily, Lykos withdrew and stepped away.

And baulked at the sight of the woman who had just serviced his need.

Lysandra?

Always Lysandra.

Despite the bitter aftertaste in his mouth, she remained a useful tool in his arsenal. Important now; later discarded like all the rest once her worth to him ended.

"Why do you always turn away from me?" she hissed, dropping her tunic to cover her nakedness.

He shook his head at her flushed, angry face. "My sweet priestess," he crooned. "I value your generosity in sharing your body but that is all."

She surprised him with a smug smile.

"Would you show the same *generosity* to the high priestess if she allowed you into her bed?"

Lykos blinked, then stared until she bit her lip, her gaze dropping to the ground. "Have a care, Lysandra," he warned.

Smiling, he closed the space between them. Dipping his head to nip her neck, her renewed moans of pleasure rekindled desire. But not enough to entice him a second time. "You will do something for me," he murmured into her ear, pushing the top of her tunic out of the way. Licking his lips, he brushed his fingertips over her breasts, flicking the erect nipples.

"Anything, Lykos."

Her soft breathy voice did not fool him. Ambitious and cold like himself she complemented him.

"After we reach the shrine, you will conceal yourself inside the cave," he instructed, lips brushing against her breast. Taking the peaked nipple into his mouth he bit none too gently. "If Calliope attempts to wear the coronet you will stop her however you can."

Lysandra tore herself away. He smirked—she was so predictable.

"Always Calliope," she spat. "You are mad with lust because you cannot have her."

"Tell me what you desire my sweet, ambitious Lysandra." Greedily he eyed her bare breasts. He knew what she wanted. Perhaps he might condescend to grant one of her requests. "Is it the coveted position of high priestess you lost to Calliope? Or something else?"

Amused by the myriad expressions crossing her face, Lykos waited. He read her mind with the same ease he read the portents in the entrails of a sacrifice. Lysandra could never hide anything from him.

Her face settled into a sweetly false smile reminiscent of a poisonous snake.

"You read my heart so easily, Lykos," her voice mellowed to liquid honey. "You know I should have become high priestess, but Aeschylus intervened." Her hips swayed with every step she took. Reaching him, she laid a hand possessively over his heart. "I will stop Calliope wearing the coronet provided you elevate me to high priestess." Sliding her hand down his body she stroked him to seal their pact.

Such an easy wish to grant given his plans for Calliope. Thinking of his future consort made it easy to grab Lysandra and kiss her senseless. "I shall grant your desire. Return to your rest. There is one small thing left to do here before I re-join you."

She thrust her breasts forward, coyness in every line of her face. "Can I help," she purred.

"No, it is something I need to do alone. Go now."

He ogled her shapely rear while she sauntered back to the camp, drawing her tunic up to cover herself. No remorse tainted his thoughts over taking what she so freely offered. She used him like he used her.

Delving between the folds of his cloak Lykos retrieved the hidden pouch secreted there. The prayer he chanted under his breath called on Hypnos to cast a deep slumber over Lysandra and the others. No-one must come upon him and witness what he was about to do.

He cleared a small patch of ground so only bare earth remained. Silver beams of moonlight helped him find stones to make a ring large enough to light a fire. Heaping leaves and small twigs inside the circle he struck two stones together until the kindling caught alight.

Fingers digging into the pouch to retrieve the carefully selected herbs, he threw them into the flames, pinching his nose against the acrid smell.

Sitting back on his heels Lykos admired his handiwork. Oblivious to the thunderbolts streaking across the sky, his face contorted, summoning the vengeful fury that raged unceasingly in his spirit. Fists clenched, he spread his arms out and gazed fixedly into the darkness around him.

"Hear me, Hades, dark lord of death. I call on you to cast this curse on Diokles. If he learns the truth of what he seeks strike him down to your realm."

The smoke began to weave and twist in grotesque shapes over the ground.

Euphoria filled him.

It was done.

CHAPTER EIGHT

The pungent smell of smoke woke her.

Calliope sat up and groaned in sympathy with her protesting muscles. Arching her back, she stretched her arms to their fullest in a vain attempt to loosen the knots in her shoulders. Hands rubbing the grittiness out of her eyes, she yawned, feeling like she had not slept at all.

Surprised to find herself untied she stifled another yawn. Maybe a wash in the pool would help clear the tiredness away.

A hacking sound caught her attention. She glanced over to where the Spartan was placing a piece of speared flesh over the fire. He looked so rested and refreshed she wanted to punch him. Running her fingers through her dusty hair, Calliope wondered why the gods did not smite him for what he had done to her.

Stiff all over from lying on hard ground she eased painstakingly to her feet.

"Stay where you are."

"I will not," her voice croaked from her dry mouth. "I need to drink and……wash." Not for anything would she admit she needed to attend to other bodily needs in case he insisted on accompanying her again.

Kopis in hand he rose to tower over her. "I am coming, too."

His tone brooked no argument.

She did not care.

"Must you keep humiliating me." The thought of him hovering behind some bush each time she relieved herself was intolerable. "I promised last night I would not try to escape."

"I do not trust your promises." His hard eyes clashed with hers. "I will bind and carry you if I must."

Calliope drew in a swift breath.

Not against his threat but in defence against the warm rush of blood at the thought of being held against all that maleness. In the morning light she grudgingly admired his muscled limbs, defined in a way she had never seen on a man.

She had heard it said Spartans trained their men hard. The proof stood before her.

Chin held high Calliope stalked past him. He followed close behind and it felt like a subliminal cord bound them together. Every cell in her body hummed in familiarity.

Familiarity?

The shock of the previous day must be playing tricks with her mind. She had only met the man yesterday.

Or had she?

Was he buried in some part of her mind that remembered her life before Apollysis?

She missed a step.

The Spartan sprang forward grabbing her arm to stop her falling in a graceless heap at his feet. Sizzling heat sparked and spread outwards from where his fingers rested.

Her gaze flew to meet his.

To be instantly held captive by dark depthless eyes. Losing herself in them, for what seemed like eternity, she began to sway toward him.

Then remembered who he was and what he had done.

Calliope shrugged out of his hold. "Thank you," she muttered, trying to forget the moment. Those eyes had almost penetrated the grey veil shrouding her mind.

Skin tingling, she walked between the thick bushes growing to one side of the pool.

To her relief he kept his distance. *At least he possesses some honor*.

After a short wash, she marched back ahead of him, hoping her erect posture convinced him she cared nothing for his presence. Only to stop mid-stride on seeing their escort had returned.

"Where do your men go when they are not with us? Are you not afraid of attacks in their absence?"

His answer was to stride past her without a word. Unused to being ignored by anyone, Calliope sniffed, then nonchalantly strolled closer to where they huddled in a group. Knowing where they went and what they did could help her plan the best time to escape.

Pretending to admire a spray of heliotrope, she held her breath, inching closer until she could just discern their words.

"We kept watch through the night. No-one followed, but—"

A stick snapped beneath her feet. A blunt reminder of Spartan efficiency came when they turned as one to glare at her. Nowhere was suspicion more pronounced than on the commander's face. Cheeks burning, she beat a hasty retreat.

Flopping down beside the fire she crossed her arms. The aroma of roasted boar flesh wrinkled her nose. Her captor walked over to join her. She glanced away when he dropped to his knees to check the meat.

"The orders I give are not meant for your ears. Nor would you profit by hearing them."

Calliope looked down her nose and favored him with her haughtiest glare. "I am not interested in what you discuss with your men."

"Then why listen?"

Caught out, she pressed her lips together. Let him think what he liked. She just wanted something to eat.

The Spartans gathered around the fire, like her, keen to fill their bellies. Uncertain whether she would be able to eat such a heavy meal without gagging she sat out on her own. Normally starting her day eating fresh bread, fruit and honey, she was amazed to find the flesh palatable, seasoned with the same herbs he used the previous night.

Beneath her lashes she studied the man who promised to make her life a misery. He had cut equal portions for all, handing a portion to her himself. Observing the easy camaraderie of the group, the sound of his laughter jolted her. Tension eased from her shoulders. If he could laugh there must exist a spark of humanity deep within him. A spark, which if she appealed to, would convince him to return her home.

Before long they broke camp. After giving the horses a drink, the Spartan hitched them to the chariot. While he was occupied, Calliope considered another attempt to run, but with a supreme effort tamped down the urge. It was futile. She would not even reach the road despite half their escort having already left. Giving a resigned groan, she climbed into the chariot and submitted her hands to be bound.

A bird darted across their path as they left. She envied its freedom. How long would it be until she reclaimed hers?

The sun beat down without mercy.

Despite their early start beads of sweat formed on her face. Droplets trickled down her neck to pool between her breasts. Strands of hair stuck to the damp skin of her cleavage.

The itch grew unbearable. Resentment simmered because she could do nothing about it. Why had she not thought to braid her hair like him? She threw baleful looks at the man beside her uncaring whether he noticed.

He was a brute forcing her to suffer this way.

Brute or not, she could not keep her gaze away from the bulging muscles of his arms, rippling beneath the bronzed skin. Sweat dotted his neck and biceps. Her inner vision teased her with images of her tongue licking the moisture away, savoring each flick which carried the flavor of his skin.

Calliope became aware of her tongue moistening her dry lips and burned from the hot wave of confusion enfolding her. If she did not guard her heart, she would end up like the pitiable hostages she saw brought to Apollysis. The ones who fell in love with their captors.

She stiffened. All her life she remained immune to human desire.

What enabled this man to evoke such feelings in her?

Her gaze skittered from him to the straight stretch of road ahead. The black stallions pulled at their bits, prompting her to tighten her grip. The Spartan lengthened the reins and they leapt eagerly into a gallop. Wind whistling in her ears, she caught the half-smile curling his mouth. He was reveling in the speed; she longed go slower. If they continued at this pace they would reach the shrine sooner than she wanted.

A single solitary tear escaped. How would she survive wearing the coronet again?

Then her world changed.

A fleeting glimmer caught the edges of her vision. Her head whipped round to look behind them.

Flinching as her neck cricked, Calliope stared fixedly through the shimmering haze on the horizon. Did she really spy something glinting through the swirling dust?

As if by a gift of the gods the shapes of three riders materialized.

Her pulse quickened. Willing the unknown horsemen to ride faster she uttered a prayer for their horses to be granted wings. They closed on them, one painful stride after another.

Quickly. Quickly.

A darting glance proved no-one else had seen them. Yet. Heart pounding in anticipation, she waited until they were near enough for her to see the bronze cloaks and the sun emblem on their shields. Elation flooded her.

Hoplites of Apollysis. Her rescue was at hand!

A cry of joy escaped before she could stop it.

The Spartan threw a swift glance over his shoulder, lips curling in a menacing snarl. Ferocity blazed from his eyes lending him a savagery worthy of Ares, the god of war.

Calliope gulped. *How much restraint has he shown me if he is this fierce*? Cursing herself for having uttered a sound, she held on with a death grip as he brought the horses to a sliding halt.

"Keep going," he roared to the remaining men. "Make sure there are no ambushes ahead."

"You think you can defeat three mounted hoplites by yourself?' Voice shrill, she shook her head at his arrogance. "My freedom is close and your death closer still."

His eyes bored into hers.

"Watch and learn, little one."

A fierce smile wreathed the visible part of his face. Her breath hitched in her throat. Still reeling from this display of over-confidence, she stared in disbelief as he unsheathed his kopis, hauling the shield up from where it hung.

"After today I will not need to learn from you at all," she hissed.

But he was already gone.

Mouth agape, Calliope watched him lope *toward* the riders bearing down on him, weapons held at the ready. Reluctant admiration filled her when he stopped in the middle of the road, feet planted apart, a mountain of a man ready to let no-one pass. Her heart knocked painfully against her ribs.

He looked magnificent.

The pursuers were very close. Before she could shout a warning her ears rang with a great battle cry.

She must help them. They had no idea of the calibre of man who waited to fight them. Her fingers clawed at the rope binding her, only succeeding in painfully chafing her wrists. Her frantic efforts increased as the riders came to a halt amid a flurry of hooves.

The Spartan took a flying leap between the wheeling horses. One man was knocked to the ground by the heavy shield. Another fell backwards over his horse's rump to avoid the kopis slashing at his throat.

Stunned at what she witnessed, Calliope remained rooted to where she stood, her attempt to untie herself forgotten amid this display of raw, masculine strength.

"Come with me."

She yelped. Engrossed by the fight she had not noticed the third man had rushed over to release her.

"No!" Her panicked shout rang over him. "Go help the others!"

"They are two, he is one, priestess Calliope."

"Leave me! Numbers will not matter to him. Leave—"

A horrible gurgling scream reached them. Her would-be rescuer froze, fear written over his face.

"Go, quickly," she sobbed.

But the scene which met her eyes told her it was too late.

Her stomach turned over, bile rising to burn her throat. How she wished she had not looked.

One man lay dead bleeding from a slash to his throat. The second was almost beaten to his knees. He collapsed under the relentless blows being rained down by both kopis and shield alike.

Morbid fascination held her gaze. The Spartan fought with unwavering energy, never missing a step, never failing to defend a blow. She now witnessed the proof of his earlier words. Calliope clenched her hands and resigned herself to the inevitable outcome

The man who freed her attacked from the rear. She uttered a cry when he was swatted aside with the heavy shield like a mere insect. Calliope called out; her warning drowned out by the clang of weapons striking against each other. Neither man came close to matching the Spartan's sustained skill. He struck unceasingly at his attackers.

In the next heartbeat both men lay dead on the ground.

Calliope bent her head and covered her face. Tears flowed unchecked over her palms. She sniffed, rubbing them roughly away. She had been so close to freedom.

Not wanting to draw attention to herself, she bit down hard on her knuckles, holding back curses she ached to throw at him, seething when he began to drag the bodies behind the dense clusters of tamarisk bushes lining the road. Desolation hollowed her heart. They would be left there without a coin placed in their mouths to pay Charon to ferry their souls across the Styx.

Her head reared back like an angry snake ready to strike. Right now she hated her captor; enough to kill him with her bare hands.

Leaping out of the chariot, she stalked toward the man she blamed for the torment she endured. He had taken her away from her home and refused to recognize her distress. Killed her fellow Apollysians.

Now he would pay.

A clang of metal against rock, followed by a sharp pain in her foot, stopped Calliope short. She looked down. A xiphos lay glinting at her feet. Devoid of blood stains it bore grim testimony of how futile their attack had been.

Her fingers tingled as she lifted burning eyes to where he moved among the bushes. The weapon was a gift from Apollo, granting her a chance to teach this arrogant man a lesson. The chance to avenge the deaths of the men sent to save her.

He would be back soon. He would find her ready to continue the fight.

Wrapping both hands around the hilt, she drew the xiphos up, weighing it. Heavy, but not too heavy, and longer than the Spartan's which would give her the advantage of reach. She marvelled at how comfortable and familiar the weapon felt in her hands. Slashing it through the air, she swung it left, then right.

White hot rage erupted in her chest. Hands curled tighter around the grip while she waited for him to appear.

Her lips curled into a feral smile.

She was invincible.

Now she would show him she was not the pampered priestess he thought.

CHAPTER NINE

Sweat poured from beneath the helmet. Diokles swore as it rolled into his eyes.

Ripping the offending helmet off he dropped it on the ground and wiped a hand over his face. Fingertips brushed the vein throbbing in his temple.

His chest tightened.

He had seen three pursuers coming to snatch something which was his. The sight of them brought forth every bitter, futile, savage emotion that lived within his soul.

His father, alongside two others, had restrained him while Callisto's father dragged her away.

Hands trembling from the adrenaline still elevating his heartbeat, he sucked in long, deep breaths to dissipate it. Killing these men did not relieve the aching loss inside his heart.

He spat out a savage oath. He had lost concentration. Betrayed the discipline he took utmost pride in.

It would not happen again.

On an explosion of breath he dragged the last body behind the tamarisk bushes.

Their weapons still lay on the road. He could bury them, although that required digging, meaning another intolerable delay. Warm air brushed over his hot skin. He frowned up at the cloudless blue sky. Shelter from the midday sun needed to be found sooner than he liked. Thanks to the rescue attempt, he would not cover the distance he'd planned to. The enemy hoplites had fought bravely but why had all three not attacked at once? About to wipe his face again, his raised hand instead fell uneasily to his side.

While he engaged his first two opponents what had the third been doing? Fighting a growing sense of unease, Diokles reran the fight through his mind, certain he had seen the priestess descend to the ground.

His heart lurched in his chest.

Had one of them untied her? Would he still find her waiting?

Long strides carried him quickly back to discover the answer as soon as he emerged onto the road.

He stopped, senses on high alert. Two xiphoi lay on the ground. A movement to the right turned his head in that direction.

His blood chilled.

She waited, holding the third, her unwavering gaze full of deadly intent.

Heeding his danger sense Diokles unsheathed his kopis. His pulse accelerated to energize his body, ready it for battle. Narrow-eyed, he watched her march closer. Every measured step signalled her determination to fight him.

Keeping her in his sights he kicked the remaining xiphoi into thick undergrowth. In a real battle he would use every weapon available, but confident in his superior skill, they were unnecessary for this fight.

She was almost close enough to strike. Trapped in eyes glowing the color of dark honey, for a heartbeat caution gave way to something more elemental. She clutched a xiphos that should never have reason to be in her hands. Those soft, feminine hands should be stroking his skin, their silken touch soothing away the sorrow in his heart. They should be wrapped around—

A sharp tug of desire pulled at his groin.

Diokles hissed out an angry breath. He had allowed himself to be distracted a second time. Distraction meant certain death.

"I do not fight women," he declared, circling her, determined to discover why she affected him the way she did.

"You are very arrogant, Spartan." Mockery laced her voice. "Do you not fear the gods will come to my aid? That with Apollo's help I can defeat you."

He smiled like a cat toying with a mouse.

"You will not win and you place too much faith in one god. The god I pray to is stronger than yours. Now, give me the xiphos." He closed the distance between them.

She retreated a pace, raising the weapon to line the tip up with his throat. "Let us see who is stronger."

Diokles's jaw dropped. She was serious. Her feet shifted into an attacking stance, her fierce gaze assessing him. He had seen men do stupid things on the battlefield but this bordered on insanity.

"Are you mad?" he thundered, shaking his head incredulously. "If you are searching for a weakness in me you will find none. Are you so weary of living that you wish to die?"

"I do not want to die. I want to kill you so I can return home!' Her voice rose, strong and resolute. "Come, Spartan commander, let us fight. Unless you are afraid to fight a woman? If I win, I win my freedom. If I lose, then—"

Diokles growled, uncaring when she shrank away. A rising tide of dark rage ripped at his control. She could not have hurled a greater insult.

"You dare call me coward? Then fight me, high priestess, who is afraid of divining the truth from the god she professes faith in. Pit your courage against my skill. But you will not die by my hand, or yours, until you give me the answers I seek."

He raised his kopis and readied for battle.

Surprised when she did not rush in wildly, he studied her intently. It was like watching a skilled tactician planning their next move. Anger at her insult receded to be replaced by a half-smile quirking his lips.

Her refusal to bow to him, her tenacity in wanting to fight for her freedom, filled him with admiration and an elusive emotion which fled before he could name it. She circled, no, stalked him, her almost-too-perfect face fixated on him. He had trained too many men not to notice how she tracked his every move, searching for an opening, waiting for him to let his guard down.

She would be disappointed.

His impatience to leave was tempered by the lure to see how she would handle herself in a real fight. It might reveal things about her; things she was unwilling to reveal herself. He could give her the fight she wanted without hurting her.

She sprang forward, slashing the weapon at his neck.

Diokles blocked the strike. The power behind the blow knocked him off balance. Recovering quickly, he surveyed her with fresh interest. A rapid reversal of direction and she came in lower, trying to slash his abdomen. He had no time to anticipate the strike, but still blocked her easily.

Pay attention to her every move or she will kill us both.

He allowed one part of his mind to detach and assess her. She fought with scant regard for her own safety. Her eyes blazed; her hands were steady on the grip; the strokes familiar to him. He had learnt those same strokes during his training.

The realization hit with the intensity of a thunderbolt.

In two strides he reached her. “Enough,” he ordered.

A fast, lunging thrust left him little time to block her next blow. With a man’s strength behind it he would be dead. She struck repeatedly with a skill which betrayed her, forcing him to parry every attack. Lingering questions about her identity vanished like wisps of cloud on a summer breeze.

Only a trained Spartan woman could fight as she did.

Exchanging more blows he tempered the force of his strikes. The clang of iron blades coming together resounded in his ears.

It had to be his Callisto.

But why did she not recognize him? And why was she hiding as a priestess?

A vice squeezed his heart.

He fell to his knees clutching his chest. Taenarum, the cave where souls first entered the Underworld, swam in front of his fading vision.

Then a fiery pain exploded in his head followed by a voice whispering he deluded himself. She was a priestess not a Spartan.

The vice eased. He could breathe again.

Blinking in the bright sunshine, a whinny distracted him, then air swirled toward him.

Instinct twisted his body away. The sharp edge of her xiphos cut across his arm. He roared in furious disbelief as warm blood seeped over his skin. Diokles sprung to his feet, relentless purpose filling his mind. All he saw was an opponent to defeat.

Two skilful thrusts and the weapon flew out of her hands. She lunged for it; he reacted faster. A powerful kick sent it flying into the distance to fall somewhere out of sight and out of reach.

Glaring at the priestess, he seized a corner of his cloak and pressed down hard over the wound. “You would have regretted a greater injury to me. It is a long trek back to Apollysis.”

Amazed she wasn’t snarling at him he studied her expressive features. She appeared dazed, as though she could not believe what had happened. He could not believe it either. Death had beckoned. His eyebrows met above the ridge of his nose.

Why had she not killed him when he collapsed. She possessed the skill.

Concerned she might be in shock, he wanted to ask whether she felt faint until he looked into her eyes. The fire blazing in their amazing depths was no doubt meant to reduce him to a pile of sacrificial ashes.

“Huh! I would have driven your chariot back to Apollysis.”

Diokles threw his head back and roared with laughter. “After this fight I have no doubt of that.” He sheathed his kopis. “But you would not have gone far. My stallions would have killed you. No-one except myself can handle them.”

“I would have managed, Spartan.”

Her use of the word, *Spartan,* the way she looked down her nose when she said it, snapped his restraint. Leaning in he wrapped his uninjured arm around her waist to haul her against him.

“What are you doing?” she gasped, struggling to free herself.

He had no idea. No comprehension of the madness which had possessed him to fight her. “Your insults weary me, *priestess*.” He bit the title out like an epithet. “I need no reminder of who I am. Taunt me and you will learn we are not noted for our even tempers.”

“Yes, I can see that, *Spartan*,” she hurled back, still wriggling against his hold. “You were too busy dragging me from the temple to observe the respect due a priestess. You did not even have the courtesy to tell me your name."

Her outrage drew a strangled laugh.

"I do not introduce myself to my enemies. Especially those who lie. When I ask questions, they are answered truthfully. The consequences are not healthy otherwise."

The color in her cheeks ebbed, then returned to cast a rosy glow over the golden tones of her skin.

Desire ran like wildfire through him. His body stirred in the same way as when he first saw her in the temple.

The heat, the road, the landscape, faded away. His world narrowed to her parted lips. They looked so soft. He wanted to feel their softness; feel them move against his own. Wanted to taste them, to kiss the dust covering them away.

Wanted to be certain this woman was not the Callisto he sought.

Amber eyes blazed into his. Capturing her chin, he wondered whether she would bite him, or spit and snarl like an angry cat. Holding back a smile, he brought his head closer, unaware she trembled in his iron grip. Her hot breath feathered across his mouth, promising the taste of ambrosia in her kiss.

He felt her swift intake of breath. Heard her soft voice whisper, "No."

The plea brought him to his senses. He let her go, seized her wrist, and pulled her toward the waiting horses.

"No." She dug her heels in and struck his injured arm repeatedly. "Let me go. Take me home, take…."

Curbing the instinctive urge to lash out, Diokles grabbed the hand pummelling him. "You will hurt yourself," he warned when she started to kick the greaves covering his shins.

"I do not care," she hissed, now aiming for his knees.

The last of his patience evaporated. "So be it. I am not to blame."

The sight of her startled face drew an impudent grin. This time he would allow himself to give in to the driving need to taste her lips.

Dipping his head, he laid claim to them. A shudder raced through him. He gentled the kiss, his mouth moving teasingly, sensually, persuasively over hers. Soft. Softer than the finest spun wool, they held the sweetness of nectar just as he expected. Its honeyed smoothness banished the aridness which had consumed his heart for so long. Hands slid down to cup her shapely rear, pressing her pelvis against his aching length.

Her whimper tore his intentions to keep the kiss light to shreds.

His tongue probed the seam of her lips, encouraging them to part. Groaning when they obeyed, he explored the sweet flavor of her mouth, touching her tongue, teasing it, drawing it into an intimate dance with his own.

The first hesitant response swelled his pulsing manhood. He ached to hold her closer. Ached to feel the softness of her breasts pressed against him. His bronze cuirass was an exasperating barrier. He wanted nothing more than to rip it off there and then.

Her moan vibrated through his fingertips; desire clenched his abdomen. One hand buried itself in her thick mane of hair. He tugged gently until her head fell back allowing his tongue to surge deeper into the silky depths of her mouth. He craved to draw deeply from the well of desire she aroused in him; to feel human again; to be nourished by an emotion more potent than the food of the gods.

Overpowered by a force greater than himself, he surrendered to the liquid fire flooding mind and body alike.

He had no right to kiss her!

No right to cause her heart to hammer to a staccato beat. To ignite a heady desire so that her body melted against him, to be reshaped into something new. To make the folds of her womanhood swell, forcing her to clench against the discomfort.

She must resist.

Her fisted hands uncurled. Calliope pressed them against his chest, commanding them to push him away. They refused to obey, curving around his broad shoulders instead, palms warmed by the armor she wanted to remove so she could feel his strength. His tongue touched her lips with an invitation she could not refuse. Absorbed by the sensual tremors rocking her body, they parted at his command, hands clutching him to support her quivering legs.

What was she supposed to do?

She had never kissed a man. Never wanted to. Until now.

His warm lips moved over hers, teasing, seeking a response. A sharp stab of feeling sent shock waves deep into her belly. She sighed; the small sound parted her lips, encouraging him to enter, to taste her essence.

His tongue made a swift foray. Lost in a battle between dismay and desire, Calliope failed to notice she was tentatively kissing him back. Grateful for the arm around her waist, she wrapped trembling hands around his neck to support her weak knees. Heat flowed from their joined lips to sweep through her like the river Phlegethon swept a fiery trail through the realm of Hades.

Only this was not death. His kiss brought renewed life to her like the first balmy spring wind heralded the end of the cold of winter.

How could she feel so safe in his arms? What had happened to her resolve to secure her freedom? To run faster than a deer away from the anguish awaiting her at the shrine.

Lulled by the gentleness of the kiss her fear waned. Calliope raised herself on her toes to follow his lead, wrapping her tongue delicately around his.

The hand at her waist clenched, then pressed her hard against the cradle of his lean hips. White heat burst in her head. She rubbed against the rigid rod thrusting against her belly, frantic to unveil a secret she had no name for. In the hidden nub between her legs, a wild frenzy grew more insistent, until it wiped every reason for remaining a virgin from her mind.

Calliope explored the tense, corded muscles of his neck, exulting that she had affected him like that. Thrust after thrust, her tongue delved into the depths of his mouth, savoring his clean male taste, reveling in the way their tongues danced around each other, a wild dance like that of the Maenads.

He broke the kiss, dragging a cry of protest from her. Cocooned in sensual silence, she ran her fingers delicately over the flush of dark color across his cheekbones. Her heart leapt—she had done that to him.

Then she lost the ability to think when he leaned down to kiss her neck, nipping the tender skin and ripping mewls of encouragement from her. Tilting her head to give him better access, she flattened her fingers against his scalp, closing her eyes on a drawn-out sigh.

Suddenly, cool air brushed against the spot where his mouth recently feasted.

Calliope dragged heavy eyelids open.

To find herself staring into brilliant eyes darkened to almost black, the pupils barely discernible. Something shifted in the air. Changed the energy between them. Fascinated by the emotions flitting across his features, she brought one hand to his mouth. Would his lips feel silky like they had when he ravished hers?

Calliope traced one curious fingertip over them.

A young girl reached down, plucked an iris, lifted the bright flower to the youth's lips.

The image faded, swallowed by the grey mist of her nightmares. Where had that vision lain dormant?

It was his fault. He had cast some spell over her.

She wrenched out of his hold and threw him a suspicious glance. He made no move to follow but she could see his chest heaved. He had barely drawn breath during their duel. Did kissing her require that much effort?

Warmth flushed her cheeks. With a groan she covered them, unable to look him in the eye. What must he think of her? She had kissed him, rubbed her aroused body against his, wanted him like she had never wanted anyone. She, a priestess sworn to remain virginal, had allowed desire to rule her.

Furious with herself she went on the attack.

"How dare you!" She spat on the ground at his feet.

Her shout startled the horses. They tossed their heads; their hooves churned the ground. He grabbed the bridle of the nearest stallion. They settled as if his touch possessed a magic hold over them.

As it had over herself she conceded bitterly.

"I dare, priestess. Do not call me Spartan in those tones again unless you want to be silenced more effectively."

She gaped at him. Was he threatening to kill her over a word?

"If you mean to kill me, who will wear the coronet and tell you what you want to know?" She paused to draw breath, planting hands on hips. "Is that why you kissed me? To frighten me into changing my mind. To believe I *want* to divine for you."

"I would never kill you," he stormed. "There are more effective ways of silencing a woman than killing her."

Air whooshed out of her lungs as understanding came. Her lips clamped against the admission his threat would not be a violation. Her traitorous body would no doubt welcome him.

"You cannot have me, Sp…." His glare brought her assertion to a spluttering stop.

Damn him, what else was she supposed to call him? "Only a priestess who is a virgin can wear the coronet. Despoil me and we can turn back immediately. I will not be of any use to you."

His face was devoid of expression. She burned to know what thoughts churned behind those enigmatic eyes.

"I would not despoil you. We both know you would come willingly." He went to her, wrapped a lock of hair around his finger. Gazing at it for a moment he let it drop and moved away. "We need to reach the shrine."

Calliope shut her eyes. His closeness did odd things to her insides. She had slipped once on the icy slope of a hill and slid, rapidly, to the bottom. She remembered the feeling of leaving her stomach behind. That same feeling overtook her whenever he came near her.

Her thoughts strayed to the coronet. She waited for the familiar fear to swamp her.

Nothing.

She ran a hand through her hair. Was this man a god in disguise that he could dissolve her fear?

"Since I must endure your company for some days yet, will you tell me your name?"

An uncomfortable silence followed. She hoped he would tell her so she did not have to refer to him as 'Spartan'.

"My name is Diokles," he answered in a slow, deliberate tone.

Her muscles tensed. She longed to run but there was nowhere to run to. The grey mist which inhabited her mind shifted, reformed. Why? Why did his name stir it in such a way? Was she somehow connected to this man?

Impossible. She was a priestess in the temple of Apollo in Apollysis.

"Diokles." She rolled the name over her tongue hoping to steady her racing heart. "Ah, yes, the glory of Zeus. Now I understand why your men called you the beloved of Zeus."

"Has my name disturbed you?"

"No!" she yelped, squirming under his intent scrutiny.

He lifted an eyebrow. "No? Your manner speaks otherwise."

"Are you a mind reader, Diokles?" An odd sensation trickled through her as his name came easily to her lips. A small voice insisted it was *him*.

But who?

She silenced the voice before it confounded her even more. Lifting her chin high she squared her shoulders.

"Your name, priestess?" he countered her question. "This time I want the truth."

"Calliope. High priestess of Apollo," she added, speculating on the hand which reached for her before he pulled it back, his face pale.

Silence hung between them heavy with more questions. Clasping her hands, she rubbed her sweaty palms together, blinking when he strode off to retrieve his helmet. She bit her lip, accepting all discussion was at an end. Once he donned his helmet, he became the inscrutable warrior hiding all thoughts behind it.

"We leave. Now."

She rolled her eyes. He had leapt into the chariot and waited, not doubting she would come to him. Arrogant, over-confident man! It would serve him right if she sprinted into the countryside. Calliope sighed resignedly. What other option did she have but to step in after him. She submitted her hands to be bound with an inelegant snort of contempt.

The brush of his skin against hers sent ripples racing up and down her spine. He tied one hand, checked the knot, and turned to pick up the reins. Resignation changed to disbelief. Was he testing her?

The warning look in his eyes gave her the answer. His largesse alone left her other hand free for her comfort. Any abuse of that freedom and she knew both hands would be tied before she could blink.

The horses broke into a trot then settled into a reaching canter. Calliope prayed he did not drive them too far this day.

The walk back to Apollysis would be that much longer.

CHAPTER TEN

The river was so cold. Flailing her arms, she gasped for air. Stay afloat, stay alive, she urged herself. Large as a coracle a bronze cup appeared. She must flee before it dragged her into its depths. A tight band gripped her chest. Every sluggish kick sapped her failing strength. She called to him for help, but he faded into the mist closing in around her. Despair clawed at her throat. Grey water swirled over her head.

Calliope snapped awake.

She could not see.

Hands thrashed wildly against the unknown threat smothering her. Short shallow breaths were making her light-headed. Surfacing from the clutches of the dream, her mind registered the brush of soft fabric against her fingertips.

It was her shawl.

The one she had wrapped around herself to keep warm.

Pushing it off her face she stared into the night sky. A full moon glowed and stars glittered with silvery light. The cool air chilled her exposed skin, but the lingering remembrance of the dream chilled her soul more. Her limbs felt as insubstantial as the lights above. Immersing herself in their unearthly beauty helped her pounding heart calm to a more even beat.

Gradually her eyes adjusted to the darkness. Calliope raised herself onto her elbows and looked around the small camp. The fire had burned down to glowing embers. No wonder she shivered. Next to her, the deep rise and fall of Diokles's chest betrayed the profoundness of his sleep.

Now was her chance to escape.

But how?

He had tied her ankles together the same as on the first night. The horses were tethered. Anyway, if she tried to steal one, they would betray her with loud whinnies. Moreover, she could not ride.

Diokles turned to his side with a grunt.

She froze, held her breath, and waited.

There was only the barely discernible up-and-down movement of his torso. The fight might have not wearied him, but his body must be recovering.

Earlier, the other Spartans had met them here. The meal had been a raucous affair. Enough to make her blush at the conversation. It deepened her desire to escape.

A glint caught her eye. She came to full wakefulness. The deadly looking xiphos he used when cutting meat lay next to him, exposed when he rolled over.

Did she dare?

Hermes, help me. The silent prayer summoned a guilty wince. Apollo would understand she consoled herself. After all, he had forgiven Hermes for stealing his cattle.

Eyes staring, she reached for it, her heart in her mouth. Every hoot of an owl made her jump. Her fingers closed around the grip. With infinite care she picked it up and started to saw through the ropes that bound her. The sharp, dual-edged weapon made short work of cutting through the cord.

Grabbing sandals and xiphos, Calliope stood, heart thumping, and tip-toed toward the sheltering trees. Every tiny noise raised the hair on her arms. Every so often she darted anxious glances at the sleeping man.

Finally!

Silently she slid between the thick trunks then hid behind one to slip on her sandals. Clutching the stolen weapon, she walked as quickly as she dared in what she determined the right direction. A wide swathe to her right evoked a muffled cry of glee. Yes. It was the road that had brought them here. The one which would lead her back to Apollysis.

No thought of safety or how she would accomplish the walk entered her head. Calliope wound stealthily through thick stands of trees, only leaving their shelter to check she still had sight of the road.

It did not take long for her knees to start shaking and to doubt the wisdom of her actions. She shook her head at the stranger inhabiting her body, wondering where her serene, sensible self had fled to. The one who stoically bore everything life threw at her.

A lump lodged in her throat. She worked her tongue, trying to moisten the dry well that was her mouth. Her mind began to play tricks so that she jumped at every sound, believing she saw something hide itself behind every shrub and low bush in her path. She wanted to run but running would alert the world to her presence.

Her hearing amplified to fever pitch. The crackle of breaking twigs beneath her feet sounded like thunder. Rustling sounds strung her nerves tight like the strings of a lyre. Diokles had warned her that first night to stay close to the fire.

She looked over her shoulder with a gasp as the loudest sound yet, echoed from somewhere to her right.

Maybe she should have stayed by the fire but she could not bear to go back.

Steeling herself, Calliope ploughed on, euphoria gradually replacing fear as she travelled further without incident. Her hands were covered in scratches from parting low-hanging branches. She brushed the stinging discomfort aside. She would make it home. Somehow find someone to take her there.

Time to check her bearings. Less cautious and more than a little over-confident, she leapt out from behind her cover of trees, smiling when the road came into sight.

A dense stand of shrubs opposite parted violently.

Tusks gleamed in the moonlight. A wild boar appeared in the gap.

Her smile trembled and died.

Instinct drew the hand holding the xiphos forward as the boar gave a ferocious grunt and charged. Calliope spun out of the way, thrusting at the tough hide, but the animal was too quick for her.

Her heart lurched in her chest and began to pound sickeningly in the back of her throat.

Frantic, she spared one quick look for a place to retreat to. One look was all she could spare, having to keep wary eyes on the boar which had begun to circle her like an enemy planning its next attack. Forced to turn on the spot to keep it in sight she shook her head to clear the dizziness.

The beast charged. More by luck than skill she managed to strike it and carve a gash in the thick hide.

An agonized squeal pierced her eardrums. In the blink of an eye, the boar lowered its tusks and attacked. All she could do was pivot out of the way.

Too late. One sharp tusk tore across her thigh.

Calliope shrieked.

The cut burned hotter than the sun. Gritting her teeth, she pressed a hand against it, but the boar was charging again.

She slashed at the animal, managing to keep it at bay. With her life about to end, she realized despairingly she really wanted to live without understanding the reason why. How long she would last against the boar would be the will of the gods. Her breath sobbed, her head pounded, and the pounding grew louder until the pain blinded her.

And grew even louder.

To resolve into the pounding of hooves, the trumpeting challenge of a stallion, then a dark blur rushing past so fast she felt the air move around her.

Through eyes half-closed by pain, she saw the boar lunge at the new menace, saw a familiar figure lift his own weapon and strike downwards with one mighty swoop. Without a sound the boar dropped dead. Its skull neatly cleaved in two.

Pressing a hand to her stomach Calliope stumbled to the side of the road and dry retched.

She had been close to death. So close. Now she must face an opponent no less dangerous than the boar.

A hand descended on her arm and spun her around. Calliope gulped. With no helmet every stark line of Diokles's face stood out in the bright moonlight like an accusation.

"I warned you to stay near the fire," he snarled, whipping the xiphos out of her hand. "Next time, obey me."

She stiffened. *Obey him*?

"I do not *obey* anyone who kidnaps me." Her sharp voice belied the excruciating pain of her gashed thigh. It was all his fault once again that she suffered. "I wish I had stabbed you before I left."

"And then what? The boar would have killed you." He stared at her intently. "Your thieving skills are praiseworthy."

Her brows rose. "There is nothing to commend in being a thief."

"Maybe not, but it shows resourcefulness," he countered, moving to her side to take an arm.

The hiss of indrawn breath told her he had seen the injury. Her mouth fell open when he squatted by her side and pushed her tunic up to examine the wound.

"There is nothing to see," she stammered, pushing his hands away.

"You are hurt. I will take you back and bind it." His tone warned her not to dissent.

"You will do no such thing. I can care for myself." Fire erupted in her cheeks. If she let him touch her bare skin there was no telling what might happen. The memory of the way he'd kissed her still held the power to arouse, no matter how much she tried to reason it away as merely being annoyed.

His growl was the last thing she heard before the world spun around her. With a whoosh of breath, she found herself atop the prancing horse, squirming as she realized he had picked her up and placed her there. Calliope grabbed a handful of coarse black mane and fought for composure. Expecting Diokles to lead the stallion, her heart slammed against her ribs when he vaulted up behind her.

She looked over her shoulder to meet his unfathomable gaze.

"Surely you can walk," she pleaded. "Your horse cannot carry both of us."

"Do not concern yourself with my horse. Your wound needs cleaning."

"But—"

"Stop talking." The clipped warning in his voice silenced her.

One arm snaked around her waist to clamp her against him. Calliope felt him kick the stallion into a canter. The rocking of his hips as he moved with the horse ignited a fire in the folds of her womanhood.

Grateful for the darkness hiding her hot cheeks, she clenched her jaw and tried to ignore the press of his chest against her shoulders, the hardness of his manhood rubbing against her lower back. She bit down on her lip to stop a betraying moan.

The fluttery feeling in her chest was simply worry she reasoned. It had nothing to do with the man sitting behind her whose body warmed her back like a furnace. He may have saved her but he was still the enemy. The man who had taken her from everything she knew; the man she must get away from; the man she must lean her body into, let her bare legs rub against his hair-roughened ones....

Calliope straightened up with a jolt.

"Sit still," he shouted, pulling her back against him.

"I am," she yelled back, annoyed with the rebuke. Her thighs gripped the horse's side harder. She simply could not risk a fall that might injure her more than she already was.

It was that kiss. Calliope's skin tingled at the memory. He had kissed her yesterday and now every cell she possessed was aware of him. Too much if her ragged breathing was any indication. How could one kiss affect her like this? A kiss from someone who should hold no attraction for her.

The abrupt change of gait pulled her out of her introspection. Her eyes bulged. They were already back at the fire she had decamped from earlier. Thinking she had travelled a good distance it was hard to admit it would take far more time than she hoped to walk to Apollysis.

She tried to slide off the horse before he touched her. Stopped by the arm around her waist, Calliope found herself pulled unceremoniously to the ground after he dismounted first.

Nerves stretched tight, she watched him walk to the fire pit, pile kindling onto the embers, and blow on them until the wood caught alight.

"Come closer to the fire. I need to look at your wound."

"More orders, Diokles?"

Diokles rubbed a hand over his forehead and managed to keep hold of his temper. "You are very provoking for a priestess. Come here before I make you."

She came, dragging her feet. Respect for her spirited determination to prove how thoroughly she loathed obeying his commands, disconcerted him. Only his Callisto had held his respect to this degree. Questions filled his mind, questions he burned to ask Calliope, but his priority was to tend her injured thigh.

The tunic was torn where the boar's tusk had ripped it. Placing his fingers between the frayed edges, he ripped it open to the hem, drawing a shocked gasp from her.

"You cannot do that! I have never exposed myself like this to any man."

He grabbed her wrists to stop her hands pulling the torn edges together.

"What you have done or not done does not concern me," he bit out, driven beyond his limits. "Your wound does. In Sparta, boys and girls exercise naked together. You have nothing to show which I have not already seen."

He smiled despite the frustration he felt. He would lay any wager her cheeks were redder than the flames flaring beside them. Flames that reflected in her lustrous eyes. What thoughts lurked behind them? Her lips were clamped shut. Not like yesterday when they had moved so sweetly beneath his. When he had kissed her and discovered a sweetness missing from his life.

With an angry grunt he reminded himself there was a more urgent matter to think about.

The wound was shallow, although blood continued to seep out. He rocked back on his heels. Easy enough to wash and bind the gash, but what if infection set in before he fulfilled his orders? He didn't want Calliope to die because he neglected to do everything within his power for her.

He ground his teeth. Failure was not an option.

Intending to carry her, he stood and made to pick her up. "Come, the wound needs washing."

"I can walk," she muttered, stepping away from him.

Meeting her mutinous look with a stern one of his own, he took her hand, leading her to the narrow ribbon of crystal-clear water below their camp. Crouching beside her he slashed the tunic with the xiphos until it exposed her thighs.

Diokles swallowed.

Moonlight silvered her skin with a pulsing iridescence, the shapely length of her legs sculpted to taunt and arouse a man. His hands shook as he tore the material he had cut away into strips. One piece he washed in the rivulet until he was satisfied it was as clean as possible.

First, he dabbed away the dirt and blood clinging to her skin. Knowing from experience the chilly water would sting the open wound, he washed it as gently as he could, her hiss of pain twisting his gut. A muscle twitched in his jaw all the while he cleansed the cut until he was satisfied. Binding her thigh with the cleanest strip of cloth was all he felt confident of doing with the limited knowledge he possessed.

Without preamble he stood and swung her into his arms and carried her back to the fire. Telling himself it was better she placed less pressure on her injured leg, he almost believed his own excuse.

Her silence was unusual. He had fully expected a hissing, spitting cat, but she avoided looking at him even when he set her on her feet. She sat immediately and stared into the flames.

"Tell me something." The jerk of her body left him wondering where her mind had retreated to. "You could have run a xiphos through me tonight and yesterday. Why didn't you?"

Her face was a study in confusion. Diokles reclined next to her, watching every nuance of emotion crossing her expressive features.

"I…I do not know." She drew a shuddering sigh and pulled her shawl over her bare legs. "Yesterday, I wanted to kill you when you fell to your knees. But an unseen force held my hand back. Your name was well chosen beloved of Zeus. I cannot defy the father of the gods if he wants you alive. It was why I did not stab you when I fled tonight."

Could he trust her explanation?

Chagrin at her inability to kill him came clearly through the melodious voice. He smiled inwardly. No doubt she would have made sure to finish him off permanently.

"Who taught you to fight?" He held his breath. If she were truthful it would answer the many questions plaguing him. She looked frightened, her hands twisting the ends of shawl.

"No-one." She dropped the shawl to rub her arms. "A priestess is not taught to fight. I stumbled across the discarded xiphoi and took one. I was angry you had killed people from my city. I wanted to punish you. Something took over me and helped me wield a weapon I had no idea I could use." Her voice trailed off.

Diokles waged a battle with his conscience. She was tired and probably in shock but the advantage he held was too good.

"You fought well. A lesser opponent would not have stood against you. Many of your moves I recognized. It is how our women in Sparta are trained to fight."

"I am not Spartan," her voice shook. "Just because I fought skilfully does not make me so. Do all of you think so highly of yourselves that you believe no-one else in the world can fight like you."

"You are provoking me again," he frowned, rubbing a spot on his chest. It was the same twinge which had heralded his collapse yesterday. He pushed it to the back of his mind to be dealt with later. "There is no false confidence in any Spartan. We men know our strength and our women know their worth."

Something akin to sadness flickered in her eyes. "If that is true then your women are indeed blessed."

Diokles gave her a searching look. She stared into the night though he had the impression her vision turned inwards to some place deep in her soul. She possessed a beauty to rival the sunrise which bathed his estate near the Eurotas River. The thick mane of hair fell around her shoulders in an untidy mass, her tunic torn and dusty. Even in her dishevelled state she was Aphrodite and Pandora merged into one. Her indomitable spirit, which refused to be cowed even though a hostage, presented the greatest threat to his peace of mind.

Yet that spirit had been shattered with a few words.

"Is your family still in Apollysis?" He wondered at the frightened, narrow-eyed look she gave him.

"I have no blood kin. I was adopted before I entered the temple."

"You were born in Apollysis?"

She tucked her legs underneath her and looked away. "I do not want to talk about it. If we must talk, then talk about something else, otherwise I want to sleep."

His stomach clenched. She was holding something back. Her strange words back in the temple when he asked if she was a native of the city burst clearly into his consciousness. The urge to press on was strong but even as he opened his mouth, unmistakeable shivers began to shake her body. He reached a hand to her forehead, grimacing when she flinched and leaned back.

"You have nothing to fear. Let me feel your forehead." The risk of infection setting in was very real. Only she could wear the coronet so he must do everything to keep her alive.

"I am cold, that is all."

He stared at her for a moment, then rolled to his feet and went to tether the stallion he had ridden. Returning, he tied her feet together and the ends of the rope around his waist. If she ran off again, she could become ill and collapse.

He raised an eyebrow when he caught her watching him with her mouth turned down. "Lie next to the fire. I will lie behind you."

"Do not lie too close."

He laughed. "As you wish. You will be warm at least."

Diokles lay down, pulled his cloak up for warmth, and tucked both weapons securely beneath him. The urge to move in closer and wrap her in his arms was overwhelming.

Mind churning, he drew in a breath and exhaled steadily. As galling as it was to deviate from his plans, he could think of only one way to resolve the situation.

"Sleep. If you are not better by morning you will see a healer first. After you recover, we continue to the shrine." Once she was on his home soil he would dig for information. Perhaps uncover what he needed to know without forcing her to wear the coronet.

A very un-priestess-like snort of derision lanced through the night. "Just where do you think to find a healer?"

"In Sparta."

CHAPTER ELEVEN

Lykos ground his teeth and fought a losing battle for patience.

Unable to sit still he paced the edges of the camp. A few stragglers still lingered around the fire breaking their fast. He stopped pacing and glared. It was past time they finished. He needed to do what he must. Alone.

He could wait no longer.

Whirling around, almost felled by the tunic flapping around his legs, he harried, snapped at, and tasked every single person with something to do. His heart raced. Revelation of Calliope's whereabouts would soon be his.

He spread out his traveling cloak around himself to shut out prying eyes. From beneath its folds he retrieved a small oak branch and bent over the smoldering fire like an old crone. Fingers trembling, he placed it on the embers, the scent of burning oak reminiscent of a warm summer night.

A quick, sweeping look showed everyone well out of earshot. He leaned in closer and began to whisper incantations known only to himself.

Images formed in the smoke. A fist of lust punched through his vitals. Calliope's tunic had been cut short; her shapely legs revealed to him for the first time. She was riding in a chariot—with the man who had stolen her. His fingers flexed, itching to reach through the smoke and rip the Spartan from limb to limb.

Emotions boiling, he peered fixedly as the images shifted, showing him where she was being driven. In the distance he could just make out four closely grouped villages, the mighty mountain rising like Zeus's aegis behind them.

Impossible!

But whenever he divined, he was always right. Which meant the hoplites sent to rescue her were dead at the hands of the Spartans. They would have returned by now if they were still alive.

Lykos rode the tide of rage building inside him. It seethed and churned like Charybdis's whirlpool. Unable to contain it he let out a furious howl.

A sound from behind brought him to his feet. Turning, he found himself face-to-face with Aeschylus whose forehead was creased with concern.

"What have you seen, Lykos? Is Calliope safe?"

"The men I sent to save her have failed," he roared, foaming at the mouth such was the strength of his rage. "She is almost at Sparta."

The older man's face blanched deathly white.

Lykos hid a gloating smile as Aeschylus wrung his hands. Inwardly he reveled in watching the other man re-learn how soul-destroying loss could be.

Burnt in his own memory was the day he first saw Calliope. He had taken one look at her nymph-like body, her beautiful glowing eyes and desired her for his own. Perhaps he would hunt her down in a chariot, sweep her away like Hades had done with Persephone.

And like Hades, he would take his consort, willing or not. Take her and her adoptive father's wealth. Unlike Demeter, Aeschylus would be left with nothing.

"You worry too much. I know her memories will not return." The secret pact he had made with the god of the Underworld assured it.

"You are certain?" Aeschylus demanded tensely. "How do you know that being removed from the temple, from Apollysis, will not bring them back?"

Lykos rolled his eyes. "Because of the water she drank. Nothing in this world can overturn its power."

"You say that as though the water possessed some secret. You never told me where it came from or what spells you cast on it."

"Let us not quarrel," Lykos soothed, needing to wipe the cloud of suspicion from Aeschylus's eyes. "The water was a gift from the gods."

A half-truth.

He had prayed to Hades, promised to worship him as the just and fair patron of Apollysis, even though the invisible god did not encourage earthly shrines for himself. Lykos's prayer had been answered with a gift of water from the Lethe. The river all souls drank from to forget their earthly lives after Charon ferried them across the Styx.

Undecided at the time how best to use it, he'd sealed the vessel containing the water, and hidden it in his private quarters.

Not long after Aeschylus arrived with a young girl. A girl, he claimed, who must be prevented from returning to her home for her own safety. The path to the wealth and power he craved became clear to him. So, he had come up with a plan and in return, Aeschylus had supported his bid to become high priest.

"To this day I question whether we did right in how we hid the girl," Aeschylus admitted in a hollow voice. "As long as I live I will never forget her terrified scream. She was little more than a girl and now is dead to the world."

"You are weak," Lykos hissed at him. "Do you remember how you persuaded me to help you stop her returning home? Told me her life was in danger if she returned. She is alive because of what I did and you have been able to play father to a new daughter."

In the blink of an eye Lykos found himself pushed up against a tree. The force of the impact drove the breath from his lungs. Apprehension, an emotion he had not experienced since his boyhood, shivered through him as he conceded he had underestimated Aeschylus's strength.

His head jerked back at the look in Aeschylus's eyes—cold and merciless—just like the eyes of the hunters who had pursued his parents.

"Never say that again," Aeschylus bit out with icy precision, releasing his grip on Lykos's tunic. "That girl was my daughter and now she has been condemned to a life of emptiness by both of us.

There are days when, Apollo forgive me, I believe she would have been better off dead."

Lykos took a deep breath and watched the man storm away. Chewing on his bottom lip until he drew blood, he speculated on Aeschylus's words.

Remorse was the province of the weak. The poor. He had dragged himself out of that pitiable state when he had escaped death by sheer chance. Never would he know hunger or fear or poverty again. He had made this promise to himself after his parents were hunted and killed during a purge of helots in Sparta.

He had sworn revenge.

Aeschylus represented the ruling class of Sparta; those who declared war on the helots. Lykos would take *his* daughter for his queen. The one the Spartiate had adopted and grown to love. It would be his first victory over those he hated—for their wealth; for their arrogance; for their cruelty. He, Lykos, king of Apollysis, for it was how he already thought of himself, prepared a vengeance Sparta would never forget.

When his army invaded the fertile region of Lakonia and laid waste to it.

The last curls of smoke were rising from the fire pit when Lykos beckoned a hoplite to him.

"Return to the garrison. Assemble all the men you can find and ensure they are armed and provisioned. I will meet you at the shrine in a few days. I have some other matters to deal with first."

"Yes, high priest." The hoplite mounted and wheeled his horse around, digging in his heels to urge the animal into a gallop.

Lykos made a mental note to reward the man for his loyalty. Just like he would reward all citizens who helped his cause. He thrust his chest out. The day drew closer when everyone would scurry to do his bidding without payment.

Looking around, he smiled at Lysandra, who eyed him with a look meant to see into the depths of his cold heart. He eyed her back with a promise of what she could expect when they were alone. The sinuous movement of her body teased a smirk from him. Let her think she had his confidence. He would never disclose his plans to her. She was only there to service his needs.

"Lysandra and Aeschylus, you will leave for the shrine and wait there until I join you." He swept an imperious hand at the remaining troops. "Four men will accompany me; the rest will go with you."

"Why the sudden change in plans, Lykos?" Aeschylus's voice carried distrust. "Dividing the men like this exposes us to more risk of an attack."

"Do not concern yourself," Lykos dismissed his objections. "I am going to retrieve Calliope out of Sparta so she does not reach the shrine."

The sharp intake of breath by those gathered around him simply hardened his resolve. If Calliope wore the coronet his plans would be revealed, his deception exposed, and his parent's death left unavenged.

"Lykos, I have allowed you to lead us since we escaped," Aeschylus pointed a warning finger at him. "But this is lunacy on your part. How do you expect to reach the city, never mind pass through it, without anyone seeing you? You will be cut down before you even see your attacker."

"I have my methods." Methods which included calling upon the god to make him 'invisible' to human eyes. He knew the darkest locations around the great marketplace; knew where to hide. He had used them all when he had escaped from the accursed city. "I will steal in during the night and snatch Calliope. By the time anyone realizes she is missing we will have joined you and hidden ourselves."

"You are delusional," Aeschylus stated in a hard voice. "You, an outsider, cannot just take a woman from Sparta. I am coming with you. I know where Diokles's home is. I will lead you there."

"You will go to the shrine as ordered," Lykos's voice rose. "Are you willing to risk being seen? A Spartiate who fled his home. Who put the life of a girl above the law of Lycurgus?"

"You are unwise to throw that in my face," Aeschylus glowered. "Recall who aided you to the privileged rank you now hold. I only take *orders* from Apollysis's ruling council."

Lykos paused. The deadly calm tone of his former collaborator disconcerted him. He had not expected him to argue with his plan.

He glared at Aeschylus, mind working furiously. He would not kill him until he had Calliope in his possession. Apollysis was occupied—he could not send him back. Lykos tapped a forefinger against his mouth for a moment. He could see no other way than the decision he reached.

"Bind him."

Aeschylus roared, struggling against the men forcing his hands behind his back. "You will pay for this one day. The gods will smite you, and your ambitions, whatever they are, will crumble to dust."

"Your words bore me," Lykos sniffed contemptuously. "My ambitions will be fulfilled no matter what you wish."

His secret army continued to grow. He had called down a curse upon an enemy he considered no more than an expendable hoplite. He would take care of Aeschylus. Nothing would stop him becoming king.

Lykos turned his attention to the cohort of men under his command. Their closed expressions sent a flicker of uneasiness through his mind. He looked hard into their eyes, sensing for treachery, but found none.

It must be his imagination.

Dismissing the momentary concern with a mental sniff, he selected those he wanted to accompany him. The rest would go with Lysandra and Aeschylus. Now he needed to hurry. If he could reach Calliope before she left for the shrine all the better. Either way, the outcome would be the same.

Aeschylus could think of no greater indignity than being led by another rider like a child. He prayed to Zeus to strike down Lykos, then to Apollo to protect Calliope.

"My lord?"

The low salutation intruded on thoughts of what he would do to Lykos once they were back in each other's company.

The eyes of the man leading him bored into his own. Aeschylus stiffened. This was a different man to the one who had spoken to him two nights ago. The look in his eyes pleaded for Aeschylus to speak but he needed to be careful; death awaited if he spoke to the wrong person.

Squaring his shoulders he embraced the risk. Calliope's safety meant more to him than his own worthless skin.

"Apollo's chariot lights the heavens," he whispered, waiting with bated breath. The reply could secure his freedom.

"And the huntress wields her bow by her brother's light," the guard replied, leaning closer. "Every man here is loyal to our city and to yourself. The high priest is unaware there is a rebellion fomenting against him."

"The gods will reward you for this." Aeschylus let go a sigh of relief and gave the man a conspiratorial nod. "But what of the priestess. I must escape without implicating any of you."

"Your escape is planned for tonight. I will untie you once everyone is asleep. Three men will be sent in pursuit but they are in fact your guard. The priestess need never know the truth. The rest of us must go with her."

Casting a glance to where Lysandra rode at the front of the column, a grim satisfaction filled Aeschylus. Surrounded by riders, she could not possibly hear them speaking above the noise of snorting horses and hooves striking against rocks. He had seen and heard enough to know she was Lykos's creature—from the way she paraded herself in front of the priest, to her bitter complaints to Lykos after Calliope had become high priestess. He had learnt to distrust her.

"What is talked among the men regarding Lykos?"

It was more than curiosity that niggled at him. Lykos had shown an arrogant and power-hungry streak since his elevation to high priest. Observing him strutting about the city as though he owned every soul within its walls intensified Aeschylus's concern.

"A small number support him; the rest do not trust him. He has become ambitious and the creation of this private army is concerning. Some whisper he plans to make himself ruler of our city although we are unable to prove it."

Shock rendered Aeschylus speechless for a moment. His gnawing suspicion about the priest's behavior appeared to be confirmed. Lykos had been quick to take charge, showing a tyrannical streak that made life uncomfortable for all. "Ruler? He cannot overthrow the governing council. The people would forbid it since the council members are chosen for the benefit of every citizen."

The hoplite looked off into the distance. "It is bad enough the Spartans have overrun Apollysis without our people turning against one another."

"Yes," Aeschylus agreed, worrying his lower lip as both fell silent. Only Lykos and a handful of the council knew he hailed from Sparta. Because of an oracle, he had left his home, his people, and his wealth to protect his remaining daughter in a place no-one would think to look for her.

That protection had come with a high price for she, too, had been lost to him. Calliope was all he had now and even her life might be under threat.

He must reach her before she wore the coronet.

CHAPTER TWELVE

The sights and sounds of the agora overwhelmed her senses.

Calliope stared wide-eyed around the vast marketplace spread out before her. There were the shouts of street sellers, the rumble of chariot wheels, animals protesting their restraints. Her ears rang with the cries of welcome directed at Diokles who held the high-stepping stallions to a walk. They tossed their heads, fighting the bit, and she stared in fascination at the play of muscles in his arms as he controlled both animals with enviable ease.

Used to the contemplative peace of the temple the temptation was great to stick her fingers into her ears.

Heart pounding in time with the clip-clop of hooves, she clutched the rail in a death grip and tried to control an overwhelming need to run. But where? How could she, a lone woman, escape this alien place?

Her mind reeled seeing the size of the crowd. Had the entire polis turned out to witness her humiliation? Embarrassed by the ruined tunic, she tugged the hem down in vain. Her hand brushed the strip of cloth covering the wound—a tangible reminder of why she was here.

Calliope gaped at the sight of so many women almost in equal numbers to the men. And none she could see wore a head-covering. Apollysis was not as strict as some of the other city states, but even so, few women ventured from their homes.

She sniffed in disdain. Everyone she knew said the Spartans were strange.

Her moment of superiority was short-lived.

Calliope began to shift restively, an uncomfortable tension building between her shoulder blades. Head swivelling to seek out the cause, she caught sight of the intent stares directed at her—some curious, others hostile. A few men leered, a painful reminder of how the Spartan troops in the temple square had ogled her.

That day felt like a lifetime ago.

Turning her head away she hung on to her composure and took a step closer to Diokles, hoping his presence would subdue most of the rabble. A light breeze blew a few strands of hair across her face. It brought relief to her heated cheeks and an awareness her head was bare. Spartan women might walk around without covering their heads but she was not one of them.

Calliope grabbed the trailing end of her shawl and draped it over her hair.

"Must you subject me to this humiliation?" she snapped in a loud voice. "Why didn't you warn me we were to come through the agora? They must think I am a slave or courtesan."

"You are neither," Diokles turned his head slightly so she could hear him. "And you do not need to cover your head."

"Just because your customs are odd does not mean the rest of the Hellenes are." She humphed and clutched the shawl closer.

He called out to a group of men before answering. "We Spartans are different in the absolute best of ways. In time you will come to understand this. I am taking you to my physician."

"There was no other way to reach the physician other than through the marketplace?". A remark tossed from a group of hoplites standing nearby brought a grin to Diokles's face and laughter among the crowd. She stared suspiciously, knowing she would not find whatever was said, amusing. "What did he say?"

"He congratulates me on winning such a prize as you."

She tried to convince herself the warmth flushing her skin was due to the heat of the day.

"I am not your prize," she heaved the words out from behind clenched teeth, restraining the impulse to jab a finger into his arm to drive the assertion home. She would likely crack every joint on rock-hard muscle. "Invading a peaceful city is not a great victory. Except for you Spartans."

The chariot lurched over an uneven paving stone throwing her against Diokles. Losing her footing, she stumbled, and had to grab his arm to steady herself. Wildfire scorched through every cell.

Snatching her hand back as though it had been burnt, Calliope grabbed the rail, fingers still tingling from touching his skin, and threw a fulminating look at the laughing faces in the crowd.

She turned the glare onto his back. He wasn't even looking at her, yet she was aware of him like no other man. He ripped incomprehensible emotions from her she did not want to feel. Why though?

Sweeping a glance over his tall powerful body gave her most of the answer.

She swallowed to ease her dry throat and went on the attack. "Did you plan to drive me through here so I could be mocked?"

He reined the horses to a stop and turned the full force of his gaze onto her. She found herself unable to look away, held captive by the gleaming depths of his dark eyes, eyes that commanded her complete attention. The memory of *that* kiss returned. Her lips tingled and parted on a outrush of breath.

Mustering every drop of willpower, Calliope pulled her gaze away and glanced downwards to hide the desire he would certainly see in her face. To her horror, her nipples had tightened, thrusting boldly against the light fabric of her tunic. One shaking hand pulled the shawl over her chest praying he had not noticed her body's response.

"I told you why we came this way." He paused, giving her a considered look. "For your safety it is better we did. Now everyone will believe you are mine."

"I am not yours!" It might be undignified for a priestess to stamp her feet like a recalcitrant child, but oh, how she yearned to. "Snow will fall in Tartarus before I belong to you!"

The smile curving his mouth set off a swarm of butterflies low in her belly. She wanted to take back the rash words. Too late. She had come to understand enough about this man to know her defiance simply meant a challenge to be overcome.

He brushed a slow finger down her cheek. "You will be."

Blood rushed to her head.

"Your arrogance is unbounded. You will never own me, Diokles, not ever." She thumped the rail, eyes watering from the pain that flashed up her forearm. "You cannot force me to stay with you. Once I have fulfilled your purpose—"

Calliope sucked in a frightened breath. They were back to the whole reason he had taken her hostage. To wear the coronet she feared would kill her or send her mad.

He shot her a keen look. "Will you tell me now why the coronet frightens you?"

It was unnerving how he could read her thoughts. She could see why he had risen as high as he had. "I don't want to discuss it," she mumbled.

"You will when we reach my home."

"Another order, *commander*?" she muttered under her breath, trying not to think about what would happen once they got there.

Would he expect her to share his bed? Something inside her melted, its liquid weight pooling in the heart of her womanhood. She squeezed her thighs to relieve the unfamiliar ache with little success. By Apollo, she would never give in to an inconvenient desire which would disappear once she was safely back home.

So when he moved past her she pressed back against the rail to avoid touching him. Eyebrows raised, she watched him step down and hold out a hand with a look that demanded her immediate compliance. Absorbed in her musings, she'd failed to notice they were stopped in front of a modest-sized building housing a small statue of Asclepius, the god of healing, set into a niche by the door.

"I told you yesterday I do not need to see a physician." Were all men so obstinate? "There is no infection, only a little soreness, and it stopped bleeding two days ago."

His face hardened. "Let the physician be the judge of that."

Opening her mouth to object, she shut it with a snap when Diokles wrapped one arm around her waist, urged her out of the chariot and escorted her through the open doorway.

Clutching her peony root balm, the physician's strict instructions ringing in her ears, Calliope looked about her with interest as they resumed their way down quiet, narrow streets. The buildings on either side of them were strange yet strangely familiar. They seemed to whisper to her, whispers of coming home. She shook her head in sad denial. Her home was far away.

Tears pricked the back of her eyes. Would she ever go back? She had forged a new life in Apollysis. She knew who she was there. Had overcome the mental anguish of being unable to remember anything about her life before she became a priestess. Was she doomed to never experience true belonging?

That army was your past, is your present, will be your future.

Why had those words come back to haunt her?

Sweat slicked her palms.

No!

It could not be.

She was Calliope, priestess of Apollysis, not some long-lost Spartan woman. The muscles around her eyes tensed and she blinked rapidly to clear her vision. Clinging to the rail, she breathed deeply over and over, fighting to tame her erratic pulse into its normal rhythm.

Her mind clear, the sound of female voices raised in song widened her eyes. It grew louder as they neared a doorway on their left. Her scalp prickled.

"Who is singing," she asked in a shaky voice.

"The chorus," Diokles informed her. "We are not barbarians despite what you think. Both boys and girls are taught music, poetry, and dance."

Her mouth dropped open. "Boys? Dancing?"

Diokles laughed. "If you marched and fought in a phalanx, you would understand the importance of footwork."

About to reply she still thought it singularly odd boys were taught dancing, the doorway opened as they came abreast of it. A group of young girls, dressed in tunics shorter than hers, spilled out onto the street.

Wide-eyed, Calliope followed their progress as they hurried toward the agora, the air ringing with their laughter. In the grip of a melancholy she could not explain, she failed to see the older woman following in their wake.

"Welcome, Diokles!" the woman cried. "Have you all arrived home so quickly."

"No, Melete. The priestess needed a physician."

Accepting the woman's deferential nod, Calliope inclined her head in return. She may be a stranger among them but she understood propriety and couldn't refrain from asking, "Surely those girls are not going by themselves to the agora without an escort?"

Melete blinked and stared hard at her. Calliope stared too, taken aback by the puzzlement wreathing the woman's face. She cast a furtive glance at Diokles. He wore an expression akin to working through a complex strategy as he studied Melete, who, with a final curious glance at her, left in pursuit of her charges.

Gripped by sudden uncertainty, Calliope injected more sharpness into her voice than she intended. "Who is that woman? Should she be encouraging those girls to go out in public dressed as they are."

Before she could blink, she found herself imprisoned between the chariot guard and Diokles's tall body. Her heart galloped in her chest and her limbs liquefied into the consistency of warm honey.

"'*That woman*' as you call her is a long-time teacher of the chorus," he murmured, watching her thoughtfully. "All Spartan children are trained and educated. It is why we are strong. Perhaps that is why you were able to fight me. Another woman from anywhere but Sparta would be unable to do so. Unless you are an Amazon." His eyes swept lazily over her slender, toned body. "And you are definitely not an Amazon."

Enthralled by the smoldering hunger in his eyes, it took Calliope a few moments to feel the subtle flexion of his manhood. Her lashes drooped. She swayed, pressing against him, watching his head bend closer, the brightness of the bronze helmet dazzling her eyes.

"Diokles." The plea whispered over his lips.

A loud hiss of indrawn breath catapulted her out of the sensual web embracing them.

Releasing an exasperated groan, Calliope clutched his cloak, dragging him closer until they stood toe-to-toe.

"How many more times must I argue with you that I am not Spartan?"

Her chest pressed against his cuirass. Too late she realized her mistake. Her irritation with his obtuseness only succeeded in melding their bodies closer. Releasing his cloak, she tried to twist away, almost toppling over the guard rail when she leaned back too far.

His arm shot out to stop her, the greave he wore warm against her waist. Its branding heat felt like a cool spring compared to the conflagration erupting between her legs.

"There will be no need of arguments," he stated in a low, husky voice. "Once you wear the coronet more than one question will be answered."

The thought of the coronet did not worry her so much as the sudden desire to drag Diokles's helmet off and plant her lips to his. His warm breath brushed over the skin of her face. She closed her eyes. If she kept them closed, she would not see the desire in his. Not see the trim beard lending him a forbidding, yet intensely masculine look. Not see the strong column of his throat which a rash impulse insisted she plant her lips against.

She drew in a deep breath, filling her senses with the earthy scent of his skin.

Every shred of will deserted her. She lifted her head, lips parting in forbidden anticipation.

"Not here," he groaned. "But in time my….."

She looked down to hide the desire he would see in her eyes and pushed him away. He did not move. Stealing a look between her lashes, her brows snapped together in concern. Diokles's lips were turning blue, one hand clutching his chest. She stretched out a hand, wanting to somehow help. For a long moment his eyes were lit by a feverish glow before color gradually returned to his lips.

"Are you—"

He cut her off with a dismissive wave of one hand. "There is nothing wrong."

But there was. Whatever ailed him, the attacks were growing in number. "I can help you, Diokles."

He turned away to gather the reins and slap the horses into a fast trot. Holding on with her free hand, Calliope shook her head and mused that an oath of purity presented no great burden.

Men were an impossible enigma.

CHAPTER THIRTEEN

The fertile plains of the Eurotas valley stretched before her. Unable to decide where to look first, Calliope tried to look in every direction at the same time. There were fields of barley interspersed with fields of wheat, their bright golden colors contrasting against the green of olive and fig trees. Grazing sheep dotted the countryside, resembling white balls of fluffy cotton, in contrast to the lush green grass not yet burnt by the summer sun.

She leaned forward curious to see where they were going.

A large house loomed to their right. Despite the sense of wealth and entitlement, an aura of melancholy clung to the building. It looked so forlorn, abandoned to weeds and the ravages of weather. An odd feeling overtook her. Like she wanted to run and embrace the house and heal it.

Why had the former occupants left what must have been a beautiful home?

Their pace slowed. Calliope glanced at Diokles, her forehead creased in a small frown. He was looking at the house, mouth compressed in a tight line, the knuckles of his hands white from the death grip on the reins. Even the horses appeared subdued. Sensing their master's mood, the normally spirited stallions did not protest being held to a walk.

"Who lived in that house," she asked tentatively. He started at the sound of her voice but said nothing. The silence stretched out until she began to squirm uncomfortably. Seeking to break the black mood which had descended over him, she said softly, "I see how it commands your attention. It must have great meaning for you."

He turned to face her and Calliope shrank into herself. His eyes blazed with a hard fury she had never seen. Not even when she had fought him. Now she witnessed the warrior he truly was—indomitable, ruthless, powerful.

"Meaning?" He gave a humorless laugh. "You are right, priestess, it has meaning, none of it good. The traitor who lived here fled. Better for Aeschylus to not return if he wants to live."

The hairs on the back of her neck rose. "Aeschylus?"

He must have read something in her voice judging by the piercing look he shot her.

"What does the name mean to you?"

"Nothing," she shrugged. Some instinct made her reluctant to mention her father bore the same name. It could not possibly be the same man. Her mind scrabbled to find a plausible lie. "There was a devout follower of Apollo by that name who worshipped often in the temple."

He looped the reins around the rail and turned the full force of his dark-eyed gaze onto her. Calliope squirmed under the intense stare meant to strip the layers away to see through to her mind.

"What did this man look like? Was he Spartan? Did he have a girl with him?"

Calliope blinked. The questions, thrown like weapons, left her shaken. "Why are you so interested in him? He is a citizen of Apollysis, not Sparta. He is the same as any other man in Achaea."

Not quite the truth although she would never admit it to him. Her adoptive father was taller; his skin closer to the color of Diokles's own, rather than the lighter olive-skinned shades of the other men who lived in Apollysis. "He isn't the only man in all of Hellas to bear that name."

"You did not answer whether there was a girl with him."

She chewed her lip, wondering why he was so insistent. What secrets did this house conceal that prompted Diokles to interrogate her? "Aeschylus has no children. That is why he adopted me."

She froze. What possessed her to tell him she was adopted? He did not need to know anything about her life, whether she remembered parts of it or not.

He cursed and pulled his helmet off. Calliope gasped. He had gone white around the mouth. His eyes, blazing in anger moments ago, were now devoid of feeling.

They looked bleak; dead.

"Are you certain?" Even his voice rang hollow.

"Yes," she replied, shaken by the change in him. "I once overheard him say he had lost his daughter."

Pain lanced his gut, his heart, his mind. Diokles stared at the priestess, fighting against the implication of her words. Did this mean Callisto was dead? Had she been taken hostage. Or had Aeschylus concealed her elsewhere.

A muscle worked in his jaw. He had no doubt now that the man who had adopted Calliope was the same man the priestess of Athena revealed had fled from Sparta. The traitor, Aeschylus. "When you say lost, did he say she was dead?"

Her expression grew wary. "No. Did….did you love this girl?"

Hearing the tremor in her voice, his eyebrows shot up. "We were to marry," he bit out. "Ever since I have searched for her whenever I could, prayed to the gods. Nothing."

But a small measure of hope lived in the form of Calliope. When she wore the coronet, she would not only divine the threat to Sparta, but also what had happened to Callisto.

All the way from the city he had berated himself for almost succumbing to the desire to kiss her. He could reason away the kiss after their fight. He had a mission to complete and had willingly used any means to bring her this far.

Ignoring the clenching of his gut, he argued that even if Callisto was dead, he could not allow himself to develop feelings toward Calliope. She was a priestess, even worse, an outsider. When he married, he would take a Spartan woman as his wife.

Yet looking at her, her mane of red-brown hair shimmering in the sunlight, her beautiful features pensive as she surveyed Aeschylus's old home with a look akin to deciphering a riddle, his body once more reminded him it needed something from her. He ground his teeth and willed his unruly erection to stand down. Never would he dishonor his promise to Callisto.

Diokles shifted, ready to leave, when she looked at him. Her amber gaze carried as much force as the punch he had taken to his mid-section during a pankration match in the agoge. Winded, barely able to draw breath, sheer will alone had helped him finally win against his opponent.

This woman would not be so easy to overcome.

He'd made a pact long ago to never again let emotion rule him. He had paid a heavy price the one time he had allowed it to do so.

"Was your family against your marrying?"

Her voice wove like a silken thread past his defences, ripping open old wounds, just like a whip had ripped open his back ten years ago. "Ask me nothing about my family. They are dead to me. Dead and buried and unlamented."

He grabbed her arm when she swayed, her face pinched and pale.

"At least you had a family you can remember," she rebuked him in a high, thin voice. "I cannot remem—"

"Believe me, priestess, the memories of my family are not pleasant." Then her words, the way she cut off what she meant to say, penetrated the bitter reminders of the past. "Are you saying you remember nothing of your family?"

He did not miss the quick frightened intake of breath.

"No, that is not what I meant! I know who my family is. Don't try to twist my words."

Diokles folded his arms and studied her. Framed against the peaceful green trees in the distance she exuded anything but peace. Her free hand moved agitatedly, rubbing her stomach, pushing her hair off her shoulders, clasping the hand holding the balm for her wound. She avoided his gaze as though concerned her eyes might betray some secret.

Relentless, he pressed further. "How did you lose your memory?" And almost smiled when she stamped a foot.

"I have not lost my memory," she shouted, losing her ingrained dignity.

Bone-deep certainty told him she lied. "I warned you before I see through lies. What else are you hiding."

She cast him another one of those looks meant to reduce him to a pile of ashes. "Nothing. I want to leave."

Diokles gathered the reins. Slapping the horses on their rumps, he kept them to a trot, allowing his mind to work through the small clues Calliope had fed him. There were too many questions and not enough answers, and the answer he yearned secretly for the most, remained a mystery to him.

As soon as he was certain her wound would not succumb to infection they would continue their mission.

By the time they halted in front of an imposing house built on two levels, Calliope's eyelids drooped, and she sagged against the rail. Looking up at the sky she judged it to be around the middle of the day. Mindful of her dust-covered skin she wanted to ask how soon she could wash herself and find fresh clothes.

Shading her eyes against the glare, she looked over the grounds. His estate stretched almost to the mountain range which formed a natural border to the west, crowned by a forbidding, imperious peak.

A cold shiver shook her soul. She could well imagine the Spartans somehow imbibing those very qualities at birth.

"Calliope?"

Startled out of her abstraction, she saw Diokles was already on the ground, his rugged maleness doing strange things to her pulse. "What is that mountain called?"

"You have not heard of Taygetos?" he asked incredulously. "It is named for the nymph Taygete, mother of Lakedaimon, the region where Sparta lies."

Calliope pressed her fingers to her temples, trying to relieve an inexplicable pressure behind them at the mention of the mountain's name.

"Are you unwell?" Concern laced his voice.

"My head is aching," she replied testily, certain his anxiety stemmed from the desire to have her wear the coronet for his benefit. "No doubt due to the constant traveling and sleeping on the ground."

"You have grown soft living in a temple," he mocked lightly. "You will regain your strength soon."

"From the moment you dragged me away you have delighted in offending me," Calliope fumed. "You implied I am weak, called me a harpy and a fool. Is there anything you have forgotten?"

Refusing to take his proffered hand she stepped down just as the household servants came spilling out of the courtyard. Calliope stiffened her shaky legs and drew herself up to her full height, once more the regal priestess. The polite masks covering the servants faces did nothing to hide the speculative looks thrown her way.

So it was ironic those same faces were overspread with delight on their master's return. They bowed to Diokles who in turn greeted them. Intrigued by the tableau before her, she felt she saw the man, not the commander. It was as if he allowed himself to be human here on his estates and not the driven warrior she knew.

His gaze swung to her. Discomfited to be caught staring she pretended an interest in a flowering bush growing against one corner of the house.

"Draw a bath for the priestess and bring her clean garments."

She shook her head in amazement at the way the servants almost fell over themselves to do his bidding. "Your servants are well trained," Calliope slanted him a look, surprised by his referral to her rank. "They would be worthy to serve in any temple."

"Erisa will attend you while you are here." He beckoned a woman waiting near the entrance to the courtyard. "You are free to roam the house and the estate but for your own safety do not try to escape. You will not see a kryptoi until one captures you. What they do with you—"

He lifted one shoulder in a way that sent cold chills from the top of her head to her toes. "Kryptoi?"

"The hidden ones who patrol the countryside. Young men sent out on a final test."

Hiding her uneasiness behind a world-weary sigh, Calliope lifted her chin to meet his challenging stare. "Your warning is unnecessary. All I want to do is eat then rest." And build up her strength for whatever fate awaited her.

Arching a brow, he left her to disappear into the house.

"Come, priestess."

Calliope studied the woman who was to be her servant, surprised and a little dismayed by the hostile tone. Resentment, barely veiled, shone in Erisa's flashing brown eyes. At a loss to understand her attitude, Calliope kept her voice calm. "If you do not wish to attend me you may find someone else."

"It is the master who gives orders here, not a hostage. Come this way."

Calliope bridled at the servant's rudeness. "If your *master* has ordered a bath drawn for me then I am not a hostage."

Erisa's mouth curved in a mutinous line before she turned away. Calliope followed her, disturbed by the short, significant exchange. She wanted to rebuke the servant's lack of respect toward a priestess but decided it would not be wise to aggravate her further. Her own position was tenuous at best. She, Calliope, had arrived into a world she knew nothing about. Perhaps Erisa was surly by nature.

Lost in her thoughts she quickened her pace to catch up to Erisa who was entering a doorway to their left. Calliope went in after her, stopping short on the threshold to stare around the spacious bathing room. Her tiredness melted away.

Built against one wall, the deep alabaster bath was already filled to the brim, steam spiralling off the surface. Hurrying closer, she dipped her fingers into the water, the warmth perfect to last for a lengthy bathe. After days of splashing in cold streams this was the closest thing to bliss she could think of.

"You may go," she directed the hovering servants, "and close the door when you leave."

She could not shed her torn, dusty clothing quickly enough. Dropping the tunic to the floor, vowing it would never touch her skin again, she decided to instruct the servants to burn it.

Holding the rim of the tub, Calliope climbed in, thankful the wound on her thigh only stung a little in the warm water. A smile of pure enjoyment wreathed her features. Savoring every pore of her skin opening, she immersed herself up to her neck, reclined against the back of the tub and prepared to relish the peaceful solitude.

Pinching her nose she ducked beneath the water, fancying she felt every speck of dust leave her scalp. Hair cleansed, she resurfaced with a broad smile. Not even her privileged life in the temple afforded such a luxury. Whoever the woman was that Diokles sought she would want for nothing.

A sharp pang in her chest wiped the smile off her face.

Calliope stared sightlessly at the wall opposite. Absurd to let the thought of an unknown woman arouse pain. She was not here to take her place. She leaned back again, thinking over the conversations with Diokles when a thought struck her. Perhaps he wanted her to discern the woman's fate.

The same pang shot through her again.

Am I jealous?

Oh, no, she was not going to fall in love with Diokles, regardless of how divinely masculine and gorgeous he was. She was a priestess and he a warrior bred by an alien culture. She clenched a fist and swore by all the gods she would not succumb to him.

Setting her mouth in a determined line she finished her bath quicker than she planned.

Not bothering to call the servants she stepped out and dried herself, carefully applying the balm to the almost healed gash. A delicious smell wafted from a jar placed on the small table in the center of the room. She breathed deeply, filling her senses with the beautiful scent of violets.

Dipping her hands into the jar she rubbed the oil into her skin, loving the way it banished the dryness, luxuriating in the fragrance. Violets were her favorite bloom, their shape, color and scent a constant marvel. Calliope let her mind ease into blissful oblivion, into—

A violet-crowned girl held back by strong hands, screaming, reaching to a youth being dragged into a cold grey mist.

The room whirled around her. Calliope groped for the chair beside the table and collapsed onto it. The pain in her heart throbbed with the pain of the strange girl. Resting her elbows on the table she pressed her forehead into her palms.

Then she recalled her earlier vision after Diokles had kissed her. It was the same two, older than in the first vision, but definitely them. She wracked her mind, needing to know who they were, why they were intruding into her thoughts.

There was a way to find out. She reached deep into her psyche the way she had been taught.

"What is the matter?"

The cold drawling voice cut her concentration. Furious at Erisa's intrusion, Calliope surged to her feet. "There is nothing the matter. Robe me quickly." The quicker she dressed, the quicker she could find a quiet place to ponder what the visions meant.

Brusque hands draped a fresh tunic in a beautiful shade of blue over her head. Feeling a jab on her arm she levelled an accusing glare at the servant.

"You must stay still if you do not want me to scratch you," Erisa warned.

Calliope sucked in a breath at the blatant lie. "I did not move," she said, her voice dripping quiet menace. "Be more mindful and do not scratch me again." She held Erisa's gaze until the woman flushed and finished robing her.

Sinking back onto the chair she pondered over the vision while another servant anointed her hair with rosemary oil.

Was she that girl?

A light film of perspiration clung to her skin which had nothing to do with the humidity in the room. If that were true, then who was she really? Who was the youth in the vision? Did she have a real family alive somewhere?

Tears stung her eyes as she thought back over the life she could remember. She had never known the love of a mother. Only the kindly Aeschylus had stood in the place of a father to the lost, frightened girl she had been.

"There is food waiting, priestess," the servant who oiled her hair told her. "Our master has been called away. He will not be back until late. I will show you where you are to sleep and where the dining room is. Please follow me."

Calliope stood somewhat reluctantly. Diokles had brought her here and now abandoned her to fend for herself. Floundering, out of her depth, she followed the servant outside into a large central courtyard enclosed by white-washed walls. She looked about her, interested despite her discomfort, noting the solidness of the building, the lack of any adornments.

Arriving at yet another room on the ground level, the servant bowed her through. Calliope thanked her, walking over to a table laden with fresh figs, cheese and warm bread. One sniff of the aroma wafting from the food brought her appetite back full force.

She seated herself on one of the stools and chose a plump fig. Its ripe sweetness exploded on her tongue. She sampled everything, licking her lips after every mouthful.

Sated, she propped her elbows on the table and surveyed the room through half-closed eyes, tempted to retire early to get some much-needed sleep. Maybe tomorrow an opportunity would present itself to explore the house and grounds.

She might even solve the riddle of the visions and why the sight of the mountain had disturbed her so much.

CHAPTER FOURTEEN

Calliope paced the length of the small comfortable room she had slept in. The tunic she wore, longer than the tunics of the servants but short enough to make her blush, swirled around her thighs. A film of moisture covered her face. The fine wool of the garment stuck to her skin. Warm morning air promised a hot day later.

The heat and her clothing were the least cause of her discomfort.

Her old nightmare had returned during the night. More vivid and disturbing than ever, her heart pounded from the recollection of how she had woken, gasping for air, hands thrashing against the sheet.

Stopping her incessant pacing she stared at the distant fields visible from her window. Obscuring the vista outside, the bronze cup of her dreams filled her vision. Water poured into it—water she drank in one long draught.

Then…nothingness.

Shudders wracked her body. She could not shake the feeling the nightmare had been her reality once. Ridiculous of course, still, the nagging suspicion would not leave her.

Because this time, the features of one man in the circle of men ringing her, sharpened into focus.

She knew him.

Certainty filled her, although the torturous scene faded before she could fully come to recognize him. Her dream world had changed, taking her back to a time before she drained the cup. A time when she herself seemed almost alien to the woman she was today.

The youth and girl of her visions had come into the dream, too. She'd seen him calling the girl back, raging when she disappeared into a swirling grey mist.

Calliope thrust her fingers into her hair.

She must be losing her mind.

Ever since Diokles had taken her away, fear and doubt had become her constant companions. The coronet hung over her as surely as if she was wearing it. Examining her wound earlier, she found it healing well, helped, no doubt, by the balm the physician gave her.

She bit her lip, tempted to stop applying it. The sooner it healed the sooner Diokles would insist they leave for the shrine.

Looking out the window into the bright light brought awareness of her gritty eyes. They burned because she did not sleep well. She could not sleep well because she was too restless.

She laid the blame for all her woes squarely at Diokles's feet.

A rumbled protest from her stomach reminded her she had been up since dawn. Calliope wiped her moist palms down her tunic. The thought of having to break her fast with him sent her tension levels soaring. No doubt he would ask her more questions about Aeschylus—questions she was not prepared to answer. One wrong word might make him think the man he carried a grudge against, and her father, were the same person.

Taking a moment to settle her humming nerves she walked out onto the landing.

The courtyard was a hive of activity. Servants flitted in and out of doorways, carrying oinochoes, filled with the flavorful wine she had sampled last night. Even diluted with water it had still made her light-headed. She had never drunk wine and was surprised to find she enjoyed the taste. Was this another quirk of the Spartans that they allowed their women to drink wine?

The aroma of freshly baked bread teased her nose. Diokles was nowhere in sight. Had he returned from his mysterious errand yesterday? She had eaten dinner alone, walked around the house, and eventually gone to her room to fall asleep without hearing or seeing him again.

Interested despite herself, Calliope walked along the landing, passing rooms opened for airing. Each earned a quick, disinterested glance inside, before she moved on. At the end of the landing one door remained closed.

Scalp prickling, every step she took closer felt like wading through thick mud. She stopped outside the door.

Instinct warned her it remained shut to imprison a great mystery. She choked back a nervous laugh at her fanciful imaginings. Nevertheless, the door drew her; beckoned; aroused a need to understand. Quelling her growing unease, she pressed an ear to it to make certain no-one was moving about in the room.

Her hand shook as she opened it and stepped inside.

No sunlight penetrated through the latched shutter. Trailing her fingertips along the walls, Calliope drew deep into herself, listening for clues buried in their silent witness. The sparse furnishings were covered in a thick coat of dust, testimony the room remained undisturbed for many years. An invisible cord pulled her further in, her feet raising dust clouds with every step.

Did she dare open the shutters?

Her fingers itched to let light and healing into the room. Not stopping to question the insistent need fueling her, Calliope unlatched it, pushing until a small gap allowed her to peer through to the vista beyond.

Commanding her attention, the mountain, Taygetos, loomed in the distance. Her chest tightened; her head ached. She struggled to breathe.

I must leave.

Blind to everything she whirled and made for the door. Her foot caught on the pallet in the center of the room. She pitched forward on a yelp of surprise, twisted her body, and managed to miss landing on the floor by a handspan. Even with her fall broken by the bed she was winded. Taking a moment, she went to push herself up—

The room was bathed in light. A woman lay on the bed wracked with the pains of childbirth. A newborn's cry. A gut-wrenching wail of heartbreak and loss.

Calliope wailed in sympathy with the formless voice. Doubled over, she tried to ward off the anguish permeating the room. It swept through her, drawing power from her own distress.

"Do you have a reason to be here?"

The voice—deep and subtly accusing—propelled Calliope to her feet. Chin trembling, she blinked rapidly, dazzled by the light illuminating the doorway where Diokles stood like an avenging deity.

"Do you mean to frighten me to death?" her voice shook. Gradually her eyes grew accustomed to the light, allowing her to see the muscle working in his jaw, the cold, intimidatory glint in his eyes. Counting three heartbeats to steady her still-racing pulse, she continued. "I'm sorry if I intruded. I wondered why this room remained closed when all the others were open. I….I am sorry."

He walked in. She halted her stammering apology, wincing in the knowledge she had violated his privacy.

Silence hung like a heavy shield between them. He stared at the bed, the emotions crossing his strong, rugged features giving Calliope pause. Useless to wish for courage to reach up and wipe the torment from his eyes, smooth the white line of tension thinning his lips. Instead, she clasped her hands together to stop them trembling.

She waited for him to speak but his attention remained on the bed so long she felt impelled to say something.

"Who did this room belong to?" She kept her voice soft and even to mask the suspicion she might know the answer.

His eyes bored into hers. "What did you see?"

Calliope blinked, her earlier sympathy for his feelings forgotten. If he chose not to answer her, she could choose to lie. "I saw nothing. Merely lost my footing and hurt myself when I fell."

The hard look on his face spoke volumes. "If you had hurt yourself that badly you would still feel pain." He paused. "I was there when you succumbed to a vision after I kissed you. Your face wears the same expression now. Tell me what you saw."

The accusation hit with the ferocity of a thunderbolt, the reminder of their kiss unleashed wildfire inside her, which only made the throbbing in her head unbearable. Calliope pressed her fingers against her temples in a vain attempt to ease the discomfort.

Then the tension of the last few days boiled over.

"I saw nothing, Diokles. Do you hear me? Nothing! I am tired. You brought me here to heal so I can—"

Her mouth clamped shut. Always the coronet loomed between them. She must remember he only cared about the threat to Sparta—she was merely the means to reveal it.

A fleeting expression crossed his face. Regret? Concern? Tensing, she waited for another verbal barrage.

Her stomach rumbled loudly in the quiet bedchamber.

With a twitch of his lips, he stepped aside. "Join me for breakfast. The food is ready."

There was no mistaking the order in his voice. Calliope straightened up and walked past him glad to leave the eerie room behind. Not looking back, she heard the door close behind her.

What had she seen in his mother's room?

Confident he would find out, Diokles pushed aside the bitter speculation the vision contained another missing link to his family's miserable past.

Watching Calliope nibbling the tasty food in front of her without enthusiasm strengthened his certainty she had seen some vision. A vision that tore at her soul given the gut-wrenching cry he'd heard.

"Can you ride?" His eyebrows shot up when she almost jumped out of her seat.

A baleful look preceded her reply. "Is riding yet another luxury women are permitted in Sparta?" she huffed. "I have never ridden."

"I saw how you admired my stallions." He worked hard to hold back a smile. Even glaring at him her beauty remained undiminished. "I have a horse that would suit you."

She leaned forward, resting her forearms on the table. "I do not understand why you are offering to teach me to ride. Are you not afraid of my escaping?"

The suspicion in her voice confirmed to him she was not one to be easily fooled. "You are an intelligent, spirited woman. Doing nothing will drive you mad. As for escape, I warned you of the kryptoi. Mounted or on foot makes no difference to them."

She drew back from the table. "You know nothing about me. Are your constant threats reserved for me or is it something you do all the time?"

This time he could not hold back the laugh. "A warning is not a threat. I am trying to protect you."

Wariness crept into her eyes. "Yes, so I can divine some danger to Sparta."

He sobered instantly. Damn those amber jewels and damn his manhood for responding to their clear depths. An air of secrecy hung around Calliope cloaking the woman within. She presented an enigma he burned to uncover.

Diokles ground his teeth. He wanted to not admire her feistiness and courage or succumb to her dangerous allure. She might be a mystery, but he must solve two pressing mysteries first, one involving a woman whose memory he still held in his heart.

"Yes, priestess, that is of utmost importance." Surprise lit those astonishing eyes. He used the title deliberately to remind her and himself why she was here. "We will reach the shrine quicker on horseback."

Her face closed against him. "I am not hungry anymore."

Diokles reached over to grab her wrist before she could get up. He could not afford to have her collapsing from lack of food in the days ahead.

Touching her was like being struck by lightning.

Warmth sizzled from her skin. His fingertips tingled. The hitch in her breath told him she felt it too.

Time stood still.

He stared into her eyes, then dropped his gaze to the swell of her breasts, heaving enticingly with every breath she took. His own heart pounded in his chest. A soft whimper brought his gaze back to hers. Trapped in liquid amber, he was unaware of drawing her hand closer; unaware of the moment he turned her palm up, raised it to his mouth, prepared to press the soft skin to his lips.

A sudden commotion outside and running footsteps broke the spell. He thrust her hand away, angry at himself, at her, at the world.

"What has happened," he demanded of the servant who hurried through the doorway.

The man bowed. "Master, your friend Acastus has arrived."

Diokles shot to his feet. Acastus, here?

He glanced at Calliope. She sat as one transfixed, staring at the hand she held in front of her face. An apology hovered on his lips, dying unsaid. By Zeus, why should he apologize for something he sensed would bring solace to both.

"I will leave you to eat," he announced, fighting down every protective instinct when he spied moisture in the eyes she turned up to him. He left quickly before he gave in to the need to take her in his arms and comfort her.

The dust coating Acastus's face and cloak spoke of a hard journey. Diokles handed him a skyphos containing a dilution of water mixed with his best wine. Half-irked, half-amused, he watched his friend finish drinking in one long draught.

As soon as Acastus returned the two-handled cup to a servant, Diokles confronted him. "You left your command," he stated in an accusing tone which also carried a question.

Acastus's head reared back in affront. "Do you believe I would leave if Apollysis was not secured? Or carry news of importance for you."

Diokles clapped his second-in-command on the back. "It was wrong of me to assume that, but this campaign has not progressed to plan. I should've already uncovered the threat and be returning the priestess to Apollysis." *Failure is not an option.* "What is the news?"

Acastus took a deep breath. "Questions have been asked about this threat. I asked privately if anyone from Sparta had come to live in the city. Always we find people eager to save their skins. I was taken to the house of a man who has lived in Apollysis only a few years."

Diokles stilled. "The traitor, Aeschylus?"

"Possibly," Acastus frowned. "The informant told me he is a wealthy man who arrived with a young girl, who soon after, was never seen again. He believes she may have died because this man adopted the priestess you took hostage."

If his heart had been ripped from his body he would feel less pain. The muscles of his face felt like they were carved from stone;

his stomach hollowed out while he fought to control the rage clouding his mind. He must think; plot his next move; act on it.

"The priestess told me much the same." How could he think when his world had been stood on end. "Could the informant describe the girl who arrived?"

"She was blond, just coming to maturity," Acastus replied with reluctance. "He remembers well because everyone in Apollysis is dark-haired."

"Then she is dead," Diokles stormed, smashing a fist against the stone wall. Physical pain was dwarfed by the desolation clutching his gut, his heart. "Callisto is dead. Years wasted searching. Aeschylus possesses the wealth to buy himself security. It is him."

"You do not know for certain she is dead," Acastus cautioned. "What if Aeschylus hid her after he arrived? I also learned a small group escaped. A priestess, a priest, some men. The rest were recaptured."

Diokles stared off into the distance. He wanted to send orders to follow the group and deal with them accordingly. The directive from the council was unchanged—uncover the threat in Apollysis. This remained his priority. Personal vengeance must be pushed aside. For now. "Any word what the threat to Sparta is?"

"Veiled hints," Acastus replied. "A former hoplite heard rumors a secret army is being assembled. He cannot, or will not, say who by or where they are concealed." He ran a hand over his brow. "Strangely, the people loathe the high priest. Some mutter he assembles this force."

"A priest!" Diokles took a deep breath. Every possibility needed to be considered. "Come inside and eat before you leave."

When Acastus made no move to follow him, Diokles sent him a sharp look, surprised when his friend averted his gaze.

"I heard you brought the priestess here," Acastus spoke as though making up his mind whether to say anything. "Melete stopped me in the city. She heard the priestess speak and swears she recognized her voice." He waited a heartbeat then said, "You once suspected this priestess might be Callisto—what is it, Diokles?"

Renowned for her memory, hope stirred Melete might be right. Immediately the crushing hand of death squeezed his heart. Through fading vision he saw Acastus's face pale. His head swam;

followed by the now familiar heat flooding his body, allowing him to breathe, clearing the hope from his mind.

"This pain has plagued me ever since I took the priestess away." Acastus was the only person he would have trusted with the knowledge. "Whenever I start to think she is somehow Callisto, I glimpse the gates of the Underworld opening to me."

"Perhaps it is the god's way of telling you it is not her."

Diokles sent him a pitying look. "You do not sound even remotely convinced, my friend."

"A curse?"

"Perhaps. Or I am being punished for some neglect." Brow knotted in concentration, Diokles ran the problem through his mind like he did battle tactics. "Tomorrow I meet with the council. Afterwards I will seek counsel from Athena Chalkioikos. You are to tell no-one."

"You know me better than to think I would betray you."

Diokles gave him a half-smile of apology. "No-one must suspect I am unfit to lead." Instincts honed through years of battle warned of a sinister undercurrent. "There is more at stake than we see. I will request an enomotia to secure the shrine. Come inside."

Leading the way, Diokles rubbed his chest where a residue of pain remained. He reminded himself Calliope did not recognize him or anything about Sparta. His mouth flattened. Until he fulfilled his vow to find what happened to Callisto, there would be no thought of replacing her with someone else.

Especially by someone who was not Spartan.

Her legs shook like a newborn foal's. Calliope collapsed against the wall, palms pressed against warm stone to stay upright, and released the breath backed up in her lungs. Her pulse kicked and jumped to a crazy rhythm as she imagined Diokles finding her listening.

A fervent need to hear news about her home had prompted her to follow him. Pressed against the wall, alert for any servant who might see her, she had stolen alongside the house, coming to an abrupt stop when she heard their voices.

Now she wished she had stayed inside.

A sour taste invaded her mouth. From Acastus's words, she concluded only a handful of those she helped escape, were able to evade the Spartan cordon. She hoped Aeschylus was one of the men spied in the group who evaded capture.

Her stomach flipped over. Was Aeschylus really the Spartan who had fled from his homeland? She wiped a hand across her eyes. Why had he not told her? Calliope racked her mind, trying to recall a girl with him, and came up with nothing. Her inability to recall things worried her more than ever.

She needed to move through the fog shrouding her mind. Return to her past. Remember who her family were. Calliope stiffened. Melete claimed to recognize her voice. How could she; they had never met. The woman mistook her for someone else.

And why had she felt pain in the region of her heart on hearing Diokles speak of the unknown Callisto? She gathered it was the name of the daughter Aeschylus claimed he had lost.

Jealousy? Impossible.

How could she be jealous of a dead woman. Diokles was not her lover or even a potential lover. She was a virginal priestess immune to human desire.

Yet whenever she locked gazes with Diokles she grew warm in parts of her body where she never expected to feel that way. Imagined like never before what it would be like to tame such a man.

She closed her eyes, throat contracting over a swallow. Yes, he had been tempted to kiss her. Now she speculated if the kiss was simply a means to bend her to his will. Because only she could wear the coronet to divulge the answers he needed.

Perhaps the time had come to cast aside her fear, harness the courage she possessed, and wear the coronet. She, too, would find answers. Answers to what she saw during the rapture which continued to torture her soul. Answers about her childhood.

She needed them as much as Diokles did.

Calliope turned back to the house, determining to take up his offer to teach her to ride. The quicker she reached the shrine, the sooner she could find the truth.

CHAPTER FIFTEEN

A gentle breeze lifted Calliope's hair off her neck. Cooler than yesterday, snowy white clouds floated across the sky, at times obscuring the sun. Neither the day, nor the news she had recently received, caused the trembling of her limbs. Resisting the urge to scratch her head she marveled at her composure.

Earlier, the physician had examined her wound and declared it almost healed and safe from becoming infected. Knowing his diagnosis meant the day she would once again wear the coronet loomed closer, she had waited for the familiar terror to seize her. When it did not, she worked hard to hide her surprise from Diokles, who remained with the healer, telling her to wait for him near the agora.

Flanked by two male servants and a grudging Erisa, Calliope strolled past stalls carrying a myriad of wares. She speculated whether the servants accompanied her for her protection or to ensure she did not attempt to escape.

The snatches of conversation that reached her ears concerned politics and war. Pursing her lips, Calliope mused whether the military power which was Sparta, ever concerned itself with philosophy.

At least they paid proper homage to the gods. The priestess in her approved the statues, stopping to bow to Apollo, and his twin, Artemis. Peering up into the face of Apollo, she felt a tug of worry, praying that Lysandra and the other priestesses she had helped escape, were alive and well.

The reason Diokles had carried her off pushed all other thoughts out of her mind.

Expectation hummed along her nerves. No fear seized her throat, or clenched her stomach, or covered her body in a cold sweat. Was she finally ready to confront whatever she had seen when she first wore the coronet?

What if the secret belief she harbored over the years manifested itself? That the coronet possessed the power to restore her memory. What revelations waited to unveil themselves?

The agora was not the place to ponder on such a momentous possibility. Calliope turned her eager gaze back to the wares on display.

There were merchants selling exquisite handmade fabrics. She stopped to admire some brightly patterned wool, the like she had never seen before. It slid through her fingers, silky, soft, the tactile cloth drawing an appreciative sigh. Even if she possessed the means to buy it, the fabric was too fine for a cloak and too warm to wear as a tunic in Apollysis.

Nodding to the merchant she moved on. Further along, elegant vases and figurines were on display; the former decorated with battle scenes befitting the people they were being sold to.

On the opposite side of the assembly hall wine and food merchants shouted the freshness of their produce. Calliope smirked. How convenient to have the wine sellers so close to the main buildings. The council and members of the assembly could refresh themselves immediately after finishing the important business of government.

Once she had looked over all the stalls, she drifted leisurely to one of the quieter avenues which led to the central square.

Seeking shelter under a tree with a canopy large enough for their party, Calliope prepared to dispatch one of the men to fetch water, when Erisa surprised her by offering to go instead. The servant declared a water pitcher was not heavy. She had a small purchase to make which she could do on the way. Unable to dissuade her, Calliope watched her leave, trying to dispel the idea there was more to Erisa's insistence than at first appeared.

She leaned back slowly against the trunk. She could pass her time observing the people walking past while she waited for Erisa to bring water, and Diokles to return from wherever he had gone.

Fetching water provided the perfect cover. For all she cared Calliope could die of thirst.

Ducking and weaving in the shadows, Erisa stole back to the agora. A tidal wave of resentment seethed through her, swirling high in her stomach, driven by an all-consuming passion to be rid of Calliope.

She drew the shawl closer around her head and draped it over the lower part of her face. No-one must recognize her who might carry word back to Diokles. She slipped from column to column, leaving behind nothing more than a whisper of movement, panting at the risk she took.

The Apollysian man who had accosted her during her last visit to the market square was her quarry. Her mouth curved in a humorless smile. After many assurances, she managed to convince him he could trust her not to betray him, even suggesting in a low voice they work together to achieve their goals. Her only desire was to protect his identity and help him restore the high priestess to her rightful home.

He did not need to know she longed to scratch Calliope's eyes out every time she witnessed the way Diokles looked at the priestess. Given the chance she would push the woman off Taygetos without a qualm. Ever since her arrival, Erisa's plan to finally lure Diokles into her bed, had been scattered to the four winds.

Now she simply wanted the wretched woman out of her life.

At last she saw him, furtively waiting near the north-western entrance to the city. Knowing he pretended to be a worshipper of Athena, on a pilgrimage to her temple, she held all the advantages in this pact of deceit.

Concealing herself behind a column Erisa beckoned to him. He hurried over immediately.

"What news?"

"They will leave for the shrine soon," Erisa muttered, eyes darting back and forth. "His friend, Acastus, arrived yesterday and left not long after for Apollysis. I overheard Diokles order him to wait there until the priestess is returned. She is allowed some freedoms although abducting her off the estate will be difficult."

"Then you better devise a plan to lure her away," he growled, the threat in his voice meant to intimidate. "The high priest is already impatient at the delay in finding her."

She drew back to look down her nose. The flash of momentary fear in his eyes curled her top lip in a sneer. "Be very careful. I am certain you do not need reminding you face a greater danger than your threats pose to me."

One word from her in the wrong ears meant certain death for him and he knew it.

"The high priest will reward you handsomely for the assistance you give us," he assured her in an ingratiating voice.

Erisa inclined her head in condescending agreement. In her mind she called the man all kinds of fool. Such a paltry reward meant little. A spy's payment paled into insignificance against her ultimate prize.

Her Spartiate father had left his unwanted half-caste daughter in the care of her helot mother and never seen her again. Because of her parentage she was considered a free woman. When she married Diokles, she would enjoy a life of ease, wealth, and possess the position in society she deserved.

The first time she saw Diokles remained vivid in her memory. Returning home, carrying wood to her mother, she had spied him among a group of youths and her body had instantly burned with passionate longing. Even then he had stood taller than the others, his demeanor almost godlike to her admiring eyes.

Discovering who he was, she secured a position in his father's household. On his death the estate naturally passed to Diokles. His living in the agoge at the time meant she needed to cultivate patience; wisely use the opportunities which came her way. Close to fulfilment, her plan to seduce him suffered at the hands of fate when he was assigned command of the force to take Apollysis.

"My gratitude to the high priest," she smirked. "Word will be sent as soon as there is anything of importance to tell you. I must return now. To be seen together would spell disaster for our plans."

Erisa parted from him with no acknowledgement, no sign of farewell, and hurried away to fetch water. While the ewers were being filled she mused over possible excuses she could offer for her delay.

Her mouth twisted. It did not matter whether Calliope believed her excuse or not. Soon the woman would be gone. Then she, Erisa, would have Diokles in her bed and in her life where he should have been already.

CHAPTER SIXTEEN

Arms folded across his chest, Diokles leaned against a column in the cella, waiting for the priestess to come out of her trance.

Perched on the highest knoll which served as the acropolis of Sparta, the temple of Athena Chalkioikos provided sanctuary for whoever sought it. The spacious courtyard hosted important public events in honor of the patron goddess. Bronze plates, depicting scenes of gods and legends, covered the interior walls, shining with a burnished gleam.

His eyes moved to the statue of the goddess of wisdom. The sight never failed to stir him.

A spear held in her right hand, a shield in her left, this likeness of Athena represented everything Diokles held himself to be. Everything Sparta was.

Strong. Immovable. Invincible.

Today, though, he sought the goddess's wise counsel.

Ensuring Calliope was attended properly, he stayed on with the physician. After explaining his near-death moments, the healer had asked a myriad of questions, poked and prodded him at length, pronouncing him physically fit.

Leaving Diokles none the wiser.

Recalling how he had shouted at the man he had known all his life he heaved a sigh of regret. The healer had cowered, then rallied to suggest he seek answers from the gods.

A whisper of movement brought his attention back to the priestess. Seeing her rise and turn to him he strode briskly to meet her.

Puzzlement wreathed the woman's features. Rarely did he feel doubt, but it enveloped him now.

"Diokles, the goddess has answered me." She fell silent for a moment then clasped her hands. "I do not understand why the reason for your malaise was not divulged to me, however, Athena has advised to give up your search for the girl you remember."

If the goddess herself descended from Olympus, snatched the spear from the hand of the statue and thrust it into his heart, the pain in his chest would be no less.

"I swore an oath to save her," he stormed, uncaring of the priestess's reproving look. "I do not go back on my word."

She drew herself up on an outraged gasp. He was forcibly reminded of another priestess glowing with anger when her god was impugned. He would have laughed if the threat of failure did not beat at him like a whip.

"You dare question the wisdom of our patron goddess?" she berated him. "Why did you seek counsel if you do not believe? I have told you what the goddess has spoken: give up the search; the girl you knew no longer is."

He fumed. Spartans spoke plainly, not in riddles. "Is she alive or dead?" he asked from between clenched teeth.

His primary purpose, of course, was to discover the yet-to-be-revealed threat to his city. But if the man who had brought news of it spoke the truth, then Calliope would be doubly helpful to him. He cast his gaze round the temple, coming to stop on Athena. Her message obscured his usual clear-headedness.

Maybe her fellow Olympian, Apollo, would cast light on whether Callisto lived, or d—

Diokles stopped the thought before it could form, refusing to give it credence. All he understood was he needed to take Calliope to the hidden shrine. He would countenance no delay.

"The gods understand your anger, Diokles," the priestess laid a sympathetic hand on his arm. "Love and grief are not just the domain of mortals. The message may simply imply you need to open your heart to see your path forward clearly. To search with a closed heart is to not see what is before you."

To not see what was before him.

Diokles mouthed the words, deliberated on them, let them settle into his mind. He thought of Calliope. He fought a daily battle to stop himself falling under her spell; to deny victory to his desire for her. Yes, she was a priestess; she was not Spartan; but what if the gods were giving her to him in place of Callisto? So many possibilities struggled for prominence his head pounded under their combined assault.

A mortal could not fathom the workings of the immortal mind.

He passed a heavy hand over his eyes. "You have done well. I will follow the counsel given to me." Turning to leave he sent her a wry look. "If I can make sense of it."

The sun, now blazing higher in the heavens, hit Diokles like a firebrand. A mild breeze wafted through the courtyard and carried the scents of the market to him.

Prior to coming to the temple he had apprised the council of the taking of Apollysis and what information he'd already learned. While they voiced their disapproval of his return, he gave them sound reasons why, stressing the importance of ensuring the health of the high priestess. Relief had washed over him when they accepted his explanation, granting approval of his plan to leave in the next day or two with an enomotia.

Marching down the hill he kept in mind to offer a proper sacrifice to Athena once he arrived home. His thoughts turned to Calliope. Taking a deep breath to counter the tug in his groin he went in search of her.

Always searching.

The thought seared into him, mocked him, irritated like a burr. He quickened his pace, glancing neither right nor left to avoid being stopped by people making their way to the temple.

He had preparations to make for a journey which held the potential to alter the course of his life.

Calliope tapped her foot. The staccato beat sounded a note of disapproval. She craned her neck trying to spot Erisa among the throng of people passing where she waited.

Surely there must be water available closer than wherever the servant had chosen to go. She herself, could have gone to the river, filled the water skins, and returned by now. Calliope moistened her dry mouth, envying the two servants seated on the ground, quietly talking between themselves. It might be beneath her dignity to join them but she would welcome the opportunity to rest her legs. Standing in one spot proved tiresome.

Her heartbeat ratcheted up a notch. Diokles should be returning soon as well.

Diokles. Every moment in his company tested both her temper and a desire she ought not feel. All five senses would have to be taken from her to stop her noticing his masculine appeal. Her strength and stamina, honed by days on the road, meant she welcomed the early morning walk to the city. On one rocky stretch her foot had turned over a loose stone and she'd been thrown against his arm. The brief contact shot sunbursts of energy into every vital part of her. Those rock-hard muscles had left her in no doubt he was every inch a man and a warrior.

She pressed a hand to her stomach. By all the gods there was that insidious throb between her thighs again!

Calliope studied the people going about their daily business, thankful they provided a distraction from her wayward thoughts. The men wore their beards neatly clipped and hair braided down their backs. Their proud bearing and muscular physiques spared them from appearing odd.

More surprising was the number of unaccompanied women. In the marketplace of Apollysis women were rarely seen. If she ventured out of the temple she veiled herself and went in the company of a servant. Here, some women were veiled, others bare headed. If Erisa did not loathe her she could ask the servant why this was so.

Calliope sighed. Whatever the reason she applauded the Spartans for the freedom granted to their women.

From one breath to the next, the air around her swirled, full of uncertainty and an indefinable something else that raised the hairs on her arms. She was about to suggest to her companions they move on, when the woman she had seen on her arrival materialized in front of her.

Calliope started, one hand flying to her chest.

The older woman bowed and spread her hands contritely. "I am sorry if I startled you, my lady. My name is Melete." She peered intently. "Do you recognize me?"

The sudden interest in the eyes of the two male servants prompted Calliope to draw her aside.

"I do not know you," she whispered in a shaky voice. She drew back from Melete who continued to study every detail of her appearance. "How can you think such a thing? I am a stranger in Sparta."

"Forgive me," Melete stared even more closely. "You remind me a little of Callisto, the daughter of Aeschylus, who left many seasons past? It was my privilege to teach her." Melete's eyes took on a faraway look, her lips curving into a fond smile. "Her voice was sweet like the Muses and she could handle a sword as well as a man."

Calliope's blood ran cold.

She had used a sword once to fight a warrior.

The urge to flee, anywhere, overwhelmed her, sent her heart racing. Struggling to breathe past the panic gripping her chest, she reasoned it was foolish to even contemplate any connection to Aeschylus's mysterious daughter. In a moment of sheer desperation, fighting for her freedom, Apollo had guided her hand.

Calliope struggled to find words to deny what she'd heard. Looking anywhere but at Melete, she finally caught sight of Erisa carrying a pitcher of water. Instinct warned her to not let the two women meet. "The gods have confused you," she insisted. "I am not this girl you taught. Please leave me, Melete."

Crestfallen, the woman walked away. Gripped by a strong desire to run after her to apologize, Calliope swallowed the pang of guilt. She never spoke to servants, or supplicants, so rudely, but her mind reeled from what she had heard.

The noises of the city faded as she turned her focus inward. Deep in her heart she discovered an eagerness to reach Apollo's shrine to rival Diokles's own.

Would the whereabouts of Aeschylus's real daughter be revealed while she divined the threat to Sparta? What would it reveal about Aeschylus?

If this Callisto lived, would she, Calliope, lose Diokles?

A sharp intake of breath shocked her awareness back to the present. Later, she promised herself, desperately pushing the dilemma to the back of her mind. Later, she would find an opportunity to escape into solitude; contemplate feelings which had grown without her noticing.

Calliope succeeded in calming her inner turmoil just as Erisa arrived. Motioning the two men to come drink, she turned on the servant. "Much as I am grateful for the water, were you constrained to fill the pitcher in the river."

"I have some small skill in healing," Erisa snapped. "I stopped to help someone injured by a fall."

Calliope's brows rose as she took the cup of water Erisa handed her. Could she believe her? Erisa's furtive expression rang warning bells as though a koudounia played in her head.

"Our master approaches."

Calliope looked over her shoulder irritated that her cheeks flamed as soon as she saw him.

Diokles strode toward them, tall, proud, his steps swiftly closing the distance. People parted for him to walk through, some hailing him, others respectfully nodding their heads. He stopped beside her sending her breath juddering in her lungs.

Then her brow wrinkled in concern as she spied a combination of determination, anger and despair raging in his eyes. She longed to ask if the physician had discovered some worrisome ailment.

He looked down at her as though seeing her for the first time. Her heart tripped. Seeking to give comfort Calliope reached out a questioning hand. In her side vision she caught the astonished stares of the male servants, the envious disapproval glaring from Erisa's eyes.

She dropped her hand to her side.

"We leave," Diokles ordered them.

About to object to his high-handed command, Calliope found herself hurrying after him when he immediately strode off, confident all would follow him. She stared at his back certain she could feel the very air around him radiating irritation. Her own irritation grew the further they walked from the city. There was no opportunity to talk to him given the pace he set.

He had better be prepared to speak with her when they reached his house. For her own sake, the sooner she wore the coronet, the sooner she would understand what her past held, and what future the gods had marked out for her.

CHAPTER SEVENTEEN

"Why does the coronet frighten you?"

Anticipation hummed along his nerves. Diokles hoped Calliope now trusted him enough to explain her reluctance to wear such a gift. From Apollo no less. Lifting the kylix to his lips, he drank a long draught of blended water and wine, the potency increasing the tension gripping every muscle instead of relaxing him.

She'd been peeling a fig when he spoke. Now she stared at it as though surprised to find it in her hand. Eventually she raised her eyes to his. The power of her amber gaze, clouded by a mixture of doubt and determination, drove a pang of remorse through his gut. His hand clenched around the handle of the kylix to stop himself dragging her off the stool, and into his lap, to reassure her she had nothing to fear.

They had arrived back in time for a late lunch. The visit to the temple whetted his appetite to find out more about her, so while the men normally dined separately, this time he invited Calliope to eat with him.

"I could not trust you at first but much has happened which has greatly lessened my dread. Things I have heard and seen, your concern for my welfare." Calliope shifted in her seat. "I wore the coronet just one time. I was told I collapsed, writhing in agony, the moment the sapphire touched my forehead. Lykos, the high priest, said he saved my life by giving me water containing secret herbs to drink. Try as I might, I cannot recall anything I saw. To protect me from possible death I was never allowed to go back. No-one else can wear it because only a virginal high priestess is allowed to do so."

Diokles let out the breath he'd been holding. She gazed beyond him her lovely face tinged with regret; perhaps regretful of things she could not recall. "Does this Lykos possess knowledge of magic? He may use it to confuse you about what you saw."

Distaste flooded her expressive features at the mention of the high priest. Rubbing a hand over his beard he brooded over her reaction.

"Perhaps he has," she conceded shakily, placing the fig on her plate. "He is cunning enough to rival a wolf."

Diokles's mouth hardened. He sensed an undercurrent rippling beneath her words he did not like. His blood boiled imagining the unknown priest trying to lure Calliope into his bed. Even though he himself held no right to her, she summoned every possessive and protective feeling within him to the fore.

He braced himself. "You know why I brought you here. Tomorrow I complete preparations for our departure. While better to travel at night, for your comfort we leave early the following morning. Are you prepared to do what you must?"

Fire flashed in her eyes. He drew back, drinking in the sight of her flushed, resolute face, heady and intoxicating as pure wine. The urgent tug in his groin insisted he stand and take her in his arms. Reminding himself he must not jeopardize his mission he pushed the impulse aside.

"Yes, I am, even if it means risking death." Her voice rang strong and certain. "You want answers, Diokles. So do I. I hated you when you first threatened me to wear it. Now, now I am eager to get there like yourself. I want to know what I saw the one time I wore it. I want to know how I lost my family. I want to know why I cannot remember parts of my life."

A smile curved his mouth as her fisted hand pounded the table to emphasize her resolve.

"Your courage impresses me," he commended her. He spoke no less than the truth—her refusal to succumb to fear, and his demands, had impressed him since their first meeting. His keen mind ran over the practical details of getting to the shrine in the shortest possible time. "I will instruct someone to show you how to ride later." He leaned back with a considering look. "Something tells me you will have no trouble riding a horse. A chariot will hold us up too much."

"Ah, you possess a gift to see through the eyes of the gods," she quirked an eyebrow at him. "I never rode in Apollysis so your confidence is misplaced. I don't want to fall off and break my neck."

His eyes locked on her mouth, curved in the first real smile she had given him. He swore Eros himself shaped those full, soft lips. How would they feel under his own? Yielding to his kiss with no barriers of duty or enmity between them?

Diokles blinked to break the spell. He saw her eyelashes flutter, as if she too, snapped out of the same enchantment. "I know *you* see visions. Speak of what you saw that first morning in the room above."

She waited a heartbeat before saying, "I saw a woman, twisted in pain, on the bed. She was wailing, grieving, because something had been taken from her."

Through half-closed eyes he searched her features. She was not lying but he sensed she held an important part back. "It was my mother's room. My mother's room where on her deathbed she told me secrets which drove a knife deep into my heart."

"I am sorry I intruded." Around her bent head the mane of red-brown hair draped over her shoulders.

Diokles wrestled a sudden need to bury his fingers into its lush thickness. Sleek and shining, its silky length goaded him, tested his control.

"It does not matter anymore." He almost believed it. "Do you remember anything about your family?"

She shook her head. "No," she mumbled through a heavy sigh. "I always wondered whether the coronet showed me what happened to them. I even hoped it would restore my memory." She drew her shoulders back. "If there is a threat to Sparta brewing in Apollysis, I want to know who is behind it. I do not want to see my home destroyed, lives lost, to satisfy one person's ambition."

Pride in her words swelled his chest. “Your bravery is worthy of any warrior.”

He broke off as Erisa arrived bearing warm bread and a platter of cheese. Placing the food in front of him, she surprised him with a warmer than usual smile, then leaned forward to refill the kylix, one breast pressed hard against his shoulder. Surprised by her boldness, he tensed, stopping short of pushing her away when Calliope averted her gaze, a flush of color staining her cheekbones.

“You may go,” he ordered sharply, moving the kylix and himself out of Erisa’s reach.

The dark look she sent Calliope as she left, pleated his forehead into a frown, until a flash of clarity left him shaking his head. Now he recalled small incidents since Erisa entered the household while he was still in the agoge. Taken together the reason for her animosity became clear. On his return he would leave her in no doubt she had no chance of luring him into her bed.

Diokles reached for bread at the same time Calliope did. Their fingers brushed against each other. Those large, beautiful eyes widened, whether in shock or surprise he couldn’t tell, but the way she jerked her hand back betrayed she was affected by his touch. Smiling inwardly, he tried to ignore the heat the light contact had ignited in him.

“I am curious why a priestess of your obvious beauty chose to remain chaste.” Diokles reasoned talking would distract them both. He hoped. “You are not the Pythia nor do many of the gods require it. Has no man ever tempted you away from your chosen path?”

A stab of jealousy knifed through him as he asked the question.

“It is my duty and honor to serve the gods,” she replied. “I owe my sanity to them. Losing my memory…I cannot explain the pain in my soul, the despair. Every waking moment I screamed silently. I wanted to curl up and die. Becoming a priestess brought purpose and meaning to my life. I help to heal others, even if I cannot heal myself, by being a conduit to Apollo when my people need him.”

“So you helped those in the temple escape,” he accused without heat, offering her the platter of cheese.

“Of course I helped them. I wanted to save whoever I could.”

Pleased she accepted the proffered cheese, he pressed on. "You, however, chose to remain behind. Is the high priest as courageous? I hear he is greatly disliked."

Disgust wrinkled her nose. "He is a loathsome, self-important despot."

Blood rushed to his head. "He tried to bed you." It was not a question.

"You are very perceptive for a warrior," Calliope returned with some surprise. "Yes. He knew I swore an oath to remain virginal." She grimaced. "Lykos did not care, but he was too afraid of Aeschylus to—"

Darkness fell on his heart at the mention of the traitor's name. He leaned forward to rest his forearms on the table. Calliope looked like a hunted rabbit, eyes darting left and right, seeking an escape route. "Are you certain he adopted you? I know he is not a native Apollysian. Has he ever said where he came from?"

She gave a world-weary sigh. "We have already spoken about this. My father is not Spartan."

"Yet you call him father." He winced as the strongest cramp he had felt so far almost crushed his chest.

"Of course. He has loved and protected me. Something any father does for their child."

Spartans never retreated although pushing Calliope about her father would destroy the fledgeling trust building between them. He had the information Acastus provided, reminding himself this battle was not against an enemy armed with spears and xiphoi, but a battle to uncover the identity of the man in Apollysis.

And always behind him, like an avenging fury, lurked the threat of death whenever he suspected this woman was not who she appeared to be.

The subject of the high priest was another matter. "Is Lykos capable of creating a secret army?"

"I cannot answer with certainty," she replied hesitantly. "Lately, many have questioned his behavior. He struts through the city, even the temple, acting like he reigns over everyone."

His gaze sharpened. "Strange conduct for a priest. Did he somehow remain hidden amongst the people after we left?"

"I discovered he fled leaving all of us priestesses behind." She compressed her lips. "There is no reason not to tell you now, and without myself or Lykos, no-one will find the opening. There are tunnels leading out of the city. That is how I managed to get everyone to safety."

Diokles tore off a piece of bread and dipped it into the wine. The combined flavor exploded on his tongue as he considered what Calliope had told him.

She was right. Useless to send someone racing to Apollysis to tell Acastus of these tunnels. No escapees were likely to return through them while Spartans held the city. "Have you ever heard him speak about an army?"

"No. I cannot think him capable of raising one." Her brow wrinkled as she helped herself to cheese. "Where would he house these men if they exist? No-one has noticed anything untoward."

He believed her. Whoever was behind the build-up of hoplites the spy told the council of, they would take care to keep them out of sight.

"This is what I hope you can reveal. Eat. The food is all produced here on my lands."

He took his own advice, eating enough to see him through to the larger meal in the evening. In the comfortable silence that settled over them, he enjoyed seeing Calliope eat with gusto, savoring every mouthful. Her small sighs of approval, the way she licked her lips in appreciation of the ripe figs, sent his stress levels soaring higher than during any battle.

How could watching someone eat arouse him?

Finally sated, she sat back, a contented smile illuminating her face. "If it were not wrong, I would compare this meal to the feast of the gods," she said. "I am curious though. Do men and women normally dine together in Sparta?"

He shook his head. "I asked you to join me in the hope you might reveal something to make travel to the shrine unnecessary." Not disclosing his other reasons was the smart, strategic move.

Diokles stood when she did. Unthinking of the consequences, he took her hands, pressing his lips to the smooth skin.

"Do not worry," his voice rumbled from somewhere deep inside him. "A healer will come with us. Both he and I will accompany you into the shrine. You will not die."

Her eyes locked on his mouth as he spoke. Through the pounding of blood in his head, he heard the hitch in her breathing, felt the trembling in her fingers. Arousal crashed through him with the unstoppable might of a phalanx.

Were the gods truly giving him Calliope as Athena's priestess had intimated.

Releasing her hands, he cupped her face, moving closer until their bodies were almost touching. Reining in a need which demanded relief, his thumbs slid over high, silky cheek bones, her soft gasps the only sounds in the slumberous afternoon silence.

With infinite care he explored her lips, running his fingertips over their fullness, the whisper of breath across his palms more erotic than a naked nymph. With every touch he sought to understand her; understand why she almost caused him to forget an oath he'd sworn to honor.

She smelt of violets and spring. Warm, potent, alluring. Trailing one hand down her neck, he pressed a brief kiss against the warm skin, relishing the tiny whimpers which fueled the desire fighting to be freed from the restraint he imposed on it. He needed to see her; see the intensity of feeling he pulled from her, reflected in her face. Long lashes half-covered her eyes, lips parted over shuddering breaths, breaths his heart beat a ragged tattoo in time with.

Throwing caution to the winds, he traced a line down the side of a breast, fingers coming to a rest lightly beneath its fullness.

"Diokles?"

The look of wonderment in her eyes, coupled with the way she breathed out his name, snapped him back to reality. Regardless of whether they both wanted each other cold logic reasoned it could not happen. Not yet. At least not until their mutual demand for answers was satisfied.

Cradling her against his chest, he buried a hand in the lush mane of hair, allowing himself the pleasure of massaging her scalp. "Remember you wanted to run me through with a sword."

"I may still want to."

Diokles laughed. "You would have to surprise me in my sleep. Even then there is no guarantee of success."

Calliope curved her lips trying to hide the fact her heart hammered in her chest. "Are we eating together tonight?"

He released her. "I always eat with my syssition in the evenings—my mess group," he explained in answer to her quizzical look.

She covered her disappointment with light mockery. "Another Spartan tradition?"

Nodding, he said, "Ask any of the servants to prepare whatever food you choose. I may not see you tomorrow. Prepare to start early the day after."

As he left her Calliope refrained from pointing out the hope that Erisa would not be preparing her meal. Given the way the woman had draped herself over Diokles earlier, she now understood Erisa loathed her because she wanted Diokles for herself.

Calliope touched her face where her skin still tingled from his caresses. Staring at the wall she relived the flare of excitement the lightest touch of his fingers had evoked. She had almost collapsed against him, perturbed by the strength of her desire, reluctant to admit she wanted more.

She needed time to think. To sort out her emotions. If she lived up to his prediction of her riding abilities later this afternoon, she would ride alone over the estate the next day.

Hearing footfalls behind her Calliope swung round in the hope it was Diokles returning. Her half-formed smile died on seeing Erisa starting to clear the table. The expression on the servant's face was akin to her having smelt something unpleasant. Lysandra had looked at her the same way on that fateful day she helped her escape.

Was she destined to be plagued by jealous women who had no foundation for their envy?

"If there is anything you want, priestess, you may ask me to bring it."

"I will not trouble you," Calliope answered coolly. "I can ask someone else to prepare me a meal."

"The master instructed me to attend you. I do so only because he has willed it."

She lifted her chin to lock gazes with Erisa who continued to glare defiantly. "You are determined to provoke me. Whatever you may think I am here because your master needs a priestess. I am not here to marry him or steal him from any lovers he may have." She bit off each word with icy precision needing to dispel the disquiet caused by the gleam of triumph in Erisa's eyes.

"You may *yet* be rescued," Erisa claimed with an arch look. "Perhaps someone has followed you who will take back word to those who seek you."

Calliope shook off the tingles of dread creeping along her nerves. "You are mistaken. No-one knows where I am."

Erisa tossed her head and walked out carrying the empty platters. Calliope followed her more slowly. Why did Erisa sound so certain someone was looking for her? Ridiculous to even consider the possibility. Erisa wanted her gone and would say anything to achieve her goal.

Passing the bathing room Calliope glanced inside and considered asking the servants to fill the tub. She leaned against the door frame, arms crossed, thinking through the practicalities. She had no idea how many days they would travel. Better to wait until tomorrow evening to wash. There would be little chance of a warm bath once they left.

Calliope rolled her eyes then continued up the stairs to her room. Here she was, planning her next bathe, when in two days she would undertake perhaps the most important journey of her life.

CHAPTER EIGHTEEN

Early morning light peeped through the shutters. Birds sang in the distance; nearby a cock crowed. Calliope rubbed her gritty eyes, opened them slowly, and rolled over onto her back. A weary yawn stretched her mouth.

She threw an arm over her forehead, chest rising and falling on a long breath, as she relived the night. Tossing and turning, sleep had eluded her, then been punctuated by dreams of escaping a sword which chased her into the mists.

The temptation to curl up and resume sleeping beckoned strongly.

Another sigh escaped as she lay there trying to convince herself to rise. She always started her day breathing deeply and listening for divine wisdom in her heart. Tired as she was it would be futile to meditate now. Her mind refused to even consider doing anything as remotely difficult as focusing.

Close to her window the whinny of a horse brought her to full alertness. Her brow pleated as she struggled to comprehend yesterday's events after Diokles left her.

She rode a horse.

And not just walked. The perioikic—a free non-citizen—renowned for his horsemanship skills, had stood open-mouthed when after helping her mount, she'd quickly accustomed herself to the horse chosen by Diokles. She must have been taught to ride, and ride well, the perioikic claimed. The skill, he stressed, once taught was never forgotten.

How was it possible?

Calliope squeezed her eyes shut while she struggled to recall ever riding a horse. One by one the muscles in her face tensed from the effort until a headache threatened.

Taking her time, she got up, grimacing when her leg muscles protested, thankful she'd kept up her physical strength. The more she rode, the more the muscles would strengthen, and the stiffness plaguing them now, disappear. How she knew this, how she possessed the ability to ride, simply represented more dilemmas to unravel.

She dressed in a fresh tunic, ran a comb through her hair, and pushed open the shutters, inhaling the morning air. No clouds dotted the sky. The air was still, golden light starting to bathe the fields. Leaving her room Calliope hurried down the stairs, grinning in anticipation of what no doubt would be a delicious breakfast, and an early start to her ride.

As she crossed the courtyard a sound drew her attention to the entrance. She stilled, staring at Diokles, who was preparing to mount his horse. Heart beating a ragged tattoo, she drank in the sight of his body in the short tunic—the bulge of muscle defining his limbs, the wide shoulders strong enough to carry any burden.

He must have sensed her engrossment because he turned to lock gazes with her. Stomach dancing as though a troupe of Maenads celebrated inside it, she felt an invisible cord binding her to him, growing stronger like a hardy vine.

Her mouth dried. Her tongue swept out to moisten equally dry lips.

Calliope summoned a tentative half-smile which broke their absorption in each other. He left the horse, purposeful strides carrying him into the courtyard

"I did not expect to see you this morning," he said, dark eyes sweeping over her.

"I woke early," she managed, smoothing her hands down her tunic. "I plan to ride over your estate if I may."

He took her hand raising goose bumps over every inch of her skin.

"Of course." He hesitated as though reluctant to leave. "Ride toward the mountains. You will find a stream where you can rest if you need to. The horses are trained not to leave their rider."

"You were right about me not having any trouble riding." She looked down at their joined hands, then raised her eyes, unnerved by his intense scrutiny. All of a sudden, taking refuge in the dining room seemed an excellent idea. "I will see you tomorrow."

Pressing a hand over her breastbone, Calliope hurried away, scolding her still ragged heartbeat into a more sedate pace.

Diokles stood unmoving as he watched her leave.

His eyes drifted upward, seeking the closed door to his mother's room. Had she told him all her secrets on her deathbed or had some gone to the grave with her?

He refused to think about his father.

Rubbing a hand over his rigid jaw he felt the weight of expectation settle on his shoulders. Everything recoiled in him whenever he thought of his duty, the duty of every Spartiate—raise strong sons and daughters for Sparta.

His hands clenched into indomitable fists as the past rose like a phoenix to flood his mind with memories.

The first time he saw Callisto at the *Gymnopaidia*, the festival where young men and women often paraded naked, eyeing off potential spouses, he promised himself one day she would be his. To discover she felt the same strengthened his conviction to marry her once she reached her twentieth year.

Yet, tearing him neatly in two, were the memories of Calliope's caresses; his response to them; how it felt having her pressed to his body. The torment, pain and longing of the years fell away beneath her soothing touch.

Would it be so wrong to persuade Calliope to leave her former life behind? To marry him if his search failed. How would she look swollen with his child?

He grew hard in an instant. With a muttered imprecation, he strode out of the courtyard before a servant witnessed the bulge in his tunic, cursing his throbbing member from one end of the Peloponnese to the other. If he showed up at the agoge still erect the ribald ribbing at his expense would never end.

Mounting, he nudged the stallion into a canter, clenching his jaw against the discomfort of riding in his aroused state. He fervently hoped the pain dampened his ardor by the time he reached the city.

Calliope came out of her musings to an awareness she had lost track of time.

Astara, the mare she had ridden yesterday, proved to be well-trained and as disciplined as Diokles himself. Giggling at the thought she looked up to the heavens. The sun sat high over the horizon—it must be almost the middle of the day. The mare ambled along, perfectly behaved, giving her time to think over the morning so far.

Not far from the main house she had discovered cheese and winemakers working in white-washed structures keeping them, and their produce, cool. Calliope had asked to see their work not just out of idle curiosity. She wanted to see whether witnessing everyday life on the estate would spark some recollection of her past.

She had listened while they explained how the white cheese she ate yesterday, required storage in brine once it curdled, and been shown the leather bags specially kept for that purpose. Calliope's mouth watered remembering the way the rich creamy flavor had lingered in her mouth long after she'd finished eating.

One of the winemakers had brought her a cup of wine, proudly informing her it was made from the estate's own grapes. Diluted, it still retained its strength, so she limited herself to a few appreciative sips. Riding a horse after drinking potent wine was not a combination she wanted to risk experiencing.

The gentle whisper of a warm breeze over her skin turned her attention to her surroundings. A light sheen of sweat glistened on Astara's coat, reminding Calliope how long she had been out. Guiding the mare in the direction Diokles had instructed, her eyes were drawn to the summit of Taygetos. The odd misgiving she had felt on her arrival stirred in her spirit again. The vision she saw in Diokles's mother's room flashed through her mind. Strange that she should remember it now.

Averting her eyes she raised her face to the sun, opening herself to its energy and healing strength, feeling her hips rock in time with the mare's gait. The warmth dispeled the unease and allowed her to fully relax for the first time since leaving Apollysis.

An image of Diokles materialized behind her closed eyelids. Caught unawares, Calliope squirmed, kindling a firestorm in her secret parts. Worrying her lower lip between her teeth she tried to understand what drew her to him despite him abducting her from her home.

Did her body recognize some subliminal connection between them?

Yes, he was handsome in a tough, rugged way which, to her surprise, appealed to her more than she wanted to admit. She had met better-looking men who stirred no desire within her. He was hard in the way this land bred its men and very much in control. In contrast, she witnessed the delight of his servants on his return; seen the hoplites under his command respectfully defer to him.

Calliope shifted the reins between her hands.

It was the way he touched her. As though he discovered a different woman beneath the cloak of serene priestess she always wore. In his arms she knew security; believed nothing could harm her ever again. He had shown tenderness—something she never expected. Even the way he had touched her breast was reverent rather than crude fondling.

Heat flamed through her. The soft folds of her womanhood grew heavy as the heart-stopping images played out in her mind.

Why, oh, why, could she not remember what she saw under the sacred enchantment?

Diokles had intimated Lykos might have used magic to confuse her. Could he have tampered with her memory? Never hearing of such a thing before she shook her head against the likelihood it was true.

Her mind gnawed over the dilemma like a dog gnawed a bone. Melete had confused her with Aeschylus's lost daughter. Did she resemble the girl in some way? Was this the reason Diokles was drawn to her? Because he discerned some quality in her reminding him of a woman he once loved?

Perhaps still loved.

Her muscles tightened. Would *she* ever be loved and wanted for herself?

Sadness engulfed her at the thought. Peering into the distance she fancied she could see the empty house—owned by a stranger bearing the same name as her father—which sat brooding over neglected fields. The house which had affected Diokles profoundly.

The Sphinx could not pose a more difficult riddle than those she faced.

Movement in her side vision caught her attention and she reined the mare to a stop. Her eyes swept the distant groves, coming to rest on a man holding the reins of a horse, half-concealed in the shrubs. A woman emerged from behind a stand of fig trees to the man's left.

Calliope stiffened.

It was Erisa.

While too distant to clearly see the woman's features, she recognized the clothing, the arrogant tilt of the head, as Erisa removed the cloak covering her. Squinting, Calliope studied their body language. They stood close to each other, not touching, though she could discern their lips move as they spoke.

A film of sweat covered her body. For some irrational reason she wanted to gallop down and confront them, demand to know why they met in secret, what plot they were hatching. Her fingers tightened on the reins as another possibility struck her.

A lover's tryst? If so, accusing Erisa of subterfuge would only make the situation between them more untenable.

A plaintive whinny made her cringe. Bending low over the mare's neck, praying she remained unnoticed, she breathed a sigh of relief on seeing them engrossed only with each other.

Calliope loosened the pressure on the bit and patted the bay neck. "I'm sorry, Astara," she whispered, keeping an eye on Erisa and the unknown man. They did not stay long. She watched them part ways, waiting until they disappeared to sit up again. Urging the mare into a trot, she continued on, confident neither of them noticed they were being watched.

Soon she spied a glistening silver ribbon in the distance. Grass gradually gave way to narrow pebbly banks on both sides, filled with clear sparkling water rippling between them. Calliope almost believed the water sang to her, inviting her to sink into its reflective depths.

Eager to cool herself, to forget all her worries even for a short time, she located a shallow ford and crossed to the other side.

An olive grove grew to her right, tall trees crowned by spreading boughs of dense, green leaves, providing shelter from any weather.

The serenity of the place spoke to her soul convincing her nothing sinister could happen here. She would water the mare and wash herself before returning.

Sliding to the ground, she untied the knot in the reins, patted the large white star on the mare's forehead and left her free to graze. Straining to hear any sound of another horse, or man, nearby, Calliope only heard the occasional call of a bird. Satisfied, she removed her sandals, tucked her tunic into the belt around her waist and waded knee-deep into the stream.

She washed her face, then scooped a handful of water to drink, entranced by the light sparkling over it. Laughing softly at her imagination she drank her fill. Another quick look reassured her she was alone, except for the mare, who having finished drinking, started to crop the lush grass.

The deepest part of the stream reached to her waist. Crouching, she dipped her head back, her long hair fanning out over the water. Elation filled her heart. Apollo had finally answered the prayers she offered devoutly over so many years. In the deepest part of her soul, she knew she would wear the coronet; find her memories; recall what she saw that one time.

Revelation would be hers tomorrow.

Perhaps even her salvation, although she could not say from what.

Calliope rose and waded out, her bare feet gingerly picking their way over the smooth stones. Squeezing water from her tunic she searched for a comfortable place to dry herself.

One tree looked promising. Large, leaf-laden branches swept the ground. Carrying her sandals she headed toward it, delighted with the seclusion it afforded. Dropping onto the grass she wriggled into a comfortable position. The dappled light beneath the canopy cast a somnolent glow over her.

She rested her head on the smooth trunk and closed her eyes with a sigh of pleasure.

Warm air flowed over her damp skin like a lover's caress, the soporific stillness soothing her spirit. Opening one eye, she checked on Astara, warmed to see the mare crop her way closer to where she sat.

Drowsiness weighted down her eyelids. Calliope fought to keep them open, vowing not to fall asleep. She needed to practice her riding and return in time to prepare for the journey to the secret shrine.

She would not succumb to sleep…..

Head lolling to one side a smile lit her face as she fell into a fitful doze.

CHAPTER NINETEEN

Calliope jerked upright and pressed hands to her burning cheeks.

She blamed the heat suffusing her body on the half-dream whose after-effects still had her heart knocking erratically against her ribs. The dream where her naked body pressed against Diokles, had seemed so real, she almost expected to see him sitting next to her.

Gulping in much-needed air, she glanced around the grove, relieved to see Astara close by. The mare stood in a patch of sunlight, eyes half-closed, dozing, her whole manner contented.

A loud splash broke the silence of the afternoon.

Calliope froze and jerked her head in the direction of the stream.

Had Erisa and the man the servant met earlier found her resting place?

It was her own fault if they had. She had lingered too long, fallen asleep, and left herself vulnerable. Keeping low to the ground, Calliope silently rolled onto hands and knees, then crept in the direction where more muted splashes echoed through the air. Her pulse thundered in her head as she searched for patches of ground devoid of dry leaves to crawl over, hoping she could somehow observe whatever, or whoever, it was without being seen.

There!

A gap in the thick foliage provided the perfect spot. She edged her way to it wincing when one knee accidentally crushed a few leaves. The crackle echoed loud in her ears. Another loud splash at the exact same moment masked the noise she made.

The breath she unconsciously held gusted out on a long, relieved sigh.

Reaching her goal she pressed closer to the ground and warily peered around the rim of leaves.

The hand holding the branch tightened, unheeding of rough bark stabbing into her flesh. Nothing made an impression on her stunned mind except the sight which stood before her eyes.

Diokles stood knee-deep in the water.

Naked.

Her hungry gaze tracked the droplets of water winding a seductive path down the bronze skin of his back. Faded white lines marred the otherwise smooth perfection. Her heart grew heavy at the thought of him being whipped, but her growing arousal drew her eyes back to the water rolling over his taut buttocks.

Surely he was a god descended from Olympus in all his glory to enthral mere mortals such as her.

While her eyes devoured every sculpted tendon and sinew, her belly tumbled over itself as though it were a master gymnast competing in Olympia. Calliope tried to swallow but her tongue was dry as the leaves underfoot. She fought a mad whim to relieve its aridness by licking every drop of water clinging to his skin.

Her mouth opened on a silent moan.

Heedless, she leaned in closer, her weight bending the branch which promptly gave way, leaving her spread-eagled on the ground, her surprised cry ringing loudly in the tranquil afternoon air.

Panting heavily she pushed up off the ground and threw a panicked look at Diokles.

Please let him ignore me.

Calliope scrambled backwards only to snag her foot in a dense cluster of twigs. Sobbing in frustration she plucked frenziedly at them, but all she managed to do was scratch herself, and leave her foot still tangled.

She cast another panicked glance his way.

Their eyes locked.

His intense stare pinned her to the spot. In contrast to his utter stillness, her limbs shook like the branches of a tree shaking in a high wind. Heat bloomed in her belly, unfurling a river of fire whose warm tendrils stoked every nerve-ending to fever-pitch. The soft folds between her legs swelled, moistened, started to throb to an unfamiliar sensual rhythm.

A strangled sound issued from her throat.

He left the water, approaching with a measured, commanding step.

Her heartbeat raced to a gallop, then propped into a shuddering cadence. Calliope staggered to her feet. A strange buzzing filled her head at the sight of faultless masculinity drawing steadily closer. She locked her shaking knees, crossed her arms and thrust her chin up, striving for a measure of control.

He was magnificent. Every muscle honed to almost god-like perfection by the harsh military training every worthy male Spartan was subject to.

Remember the naked men you saw at festivals.

But not a man such as him a wicked voice taunted back.

In her priestess duties she'd barely noticed them, seeing only bodies in need of ceremonial cleansing.

The throb between her legs grew in strength, catching her in its irresistible grip, reminding her she was a woman with a woman's needs. Despite her best efforts not to look her avid gaze locked on his manhood. Not limp like those she had seen during the festival of Apollo but springing erect and proud from a nest of black hair.

A bead of sweat rolled into her eye. Blinking to clear her vision, Calliope turned her face away, desperate to look anywhere else. It was wrong of her to succumb to the spell of his masculine beauty. Concentrating on a nearby tree she counted the birds roosting on its branches to distract herself.

Unable to count past two she conceded defeat.

An unseen power commanded she turn her head to face him, watching and waiting as he came ever closer; close enough for her to feel the heat emanating from his body; see the pounding of his heart beneath the rippling muscles of his chest.

"I—" Calliope croaked, swallowed, and managed to force the words past her dry throat. "I need to go and prepare for tomorrow," she whispered, grimacing at the huskiness of her voice.

Instead of turning to leave she swayed toward him.

Caught in the glittering depths of his eyes every coherent thought fled when he cupped her hot cheek.

His free hand massaged her shoulder. "There is time," he insisted thickly. "My preparations are complete."

"Then I must go."

She had to go before both yielded to the passion building between them. The rigid control he imposed over himself was palpable. Every taut muscle proclaimed his desire. From his broad shoulders to the tumid erection from which she quickly averted her gaze.

Her eyes followed his line of sight to where the hard points of her nipples pushed against the soft material of her tunic. Even as she drew her long hair forward to cover them, she knew it was too late. Both had seen the evidence of her arousal.

He pressed her closer. "Let me hold you, Calliope."

A tiny part of her still capable of reason protested his nearness would go beyond holding. "This is dangerous," she whispered.

"Tomorrow will change the course of our lives," he said. "We both need strength to face whatever fate holds for us."

He was right. She would never again be held by a man in this way.

Surrendering to the comforting haven of his arms, Calliope leaned into him, feeling his heartbeat merge with hers. Lost in the moment she was unaware her hands were journeying on a sensual exploration of his warm back.

The subtle massage of his fingers, at her waist, on her back, sank her into a world she had yet to discover. Her hands moved of their own volition, sinking lower with each sweep, relishing the feel of his skin. Never had her breath shuddered as it did now. Lifting her head she stared at his mouth, fascinated by the tic spasming near his beautifully carved male lips.

She pressed a wondering, questioning kiss to his chest. His entire body stiffened further if that were humanly possible.

And then his hands, those hard, capable, masculine hands, ran up her back to her shoulders, pushing the tunic down, baring the softness of her breasts to a man's gaze for the first time.

By the grace of Apollo I should be pushing him away.

Logic told her she must, but logic fell to a stronger opponent. Transcendent desire commanded her hand to shape the high, proud cheekbones; commanded her fingertips to explore the planes of his face, trace a path of wonderment over his mouth, until they curled around his neck, pressing his head downward so their lips could meet.

The sun warmed her closed eyelids in the same way his lips warmed hers, playful caresses driving everything of importance out of her head. Who she was, the oath she had made, the answers she needed, all melted into nothingness. Head falling back against the support of his arm, she parted her lips, consumed with longing for his kiss. Her tongue curled around his, glorying how his body convulsed beneath her touch.

Caught up in a wondrous new world she dipped her tongue into his mouth. She yearned to taste him; to conquer him. The corded muscles of his neck were hers to explore, the sweat slicking his skin hers to taste, just as she savored the knowledge she affected him so completely.

The release of her lips drew a moan of protest from her throat. Heedless of her actions, Calliope rubbed her aching nipples over his chest, the sensation of skin sliding over skin, searing her mind. He stood still as a statue, but the feel of his erection pressed to her belly, reminded her he was very much flesh and blood.

What was she doing?

Half-heartedly she pushed at his chest. Unable to escape the iron band of his arms, she studied the drops of water clinging tenaciously to the smattering of dark hair narrowing temptingly down his body.

Resting her cheek over his heart, she whispered, "Diokles?"

Whatever she was asking for his answer came swift and sure.

She met his seeking kiss with her own demands. Legs trembling, Calliope clung to him, fingers digging into the rock-hard biceps for support. She luxuriated in the light woody scent clinging to his skin. It reminded her of cistus, its aroma all the more potent when blended with his own unique male essence.

Never had she felt so alive.

Wanted.

Recklessness, unfamiliar and thrilling, stirred. She had no energy to question where it sprang from. To question why she tilted her head to allow him to nibble and suck the sensitized skin of her neck, his hot breath liquefying her bones.

Trapped in a bubble of sensory delights, Calliope swayed in time with the rocking motion of his hips. She craved some glorious remedy to ease the fiery need erupting between her legs. Her fingers threaded through his sleek damp hair to massage his scalp.

She heard him groan, felt cooler air brush her neck when he abandoned it to suckle a breast.

"No, we cannot…Ooh!"

Her inchoate denial was driven into oblivion by his tongue circling the hard point of her nipple. Breathless, she clutched his head, wondering how it was possible for a mortal to bear this much pleasure and remain alive.

"Look at me."

Calliope peered through her lashes, held in thrall by his flushed face, the depthless black pools of his eyes. His clever fingers traced a sensuous path down her neck to brush over one burgeoning breast. Enchanted she could make this powerful man tremble, her eyelids drooped as he turned her around, her back to him, sighing with each kiss he bestowed on her temples.

The throb in her feminine folds grew more insistent.

His hands taking the weight of her breasts as though worshipping them buckled her knees. Right then, she could not fathom anything more beautiful than seeing the contrast of his fingers to her much paler flesh, the callused skin of his hands tender against her softness.

Lifting her hands to cover his, certainty filled her with the knowledge she had waited for this moment without knowing it. Here was the reason why she had never offered herself to another man.

"Calliope."

Her name burst through the cocoon of passion he had enveloped them in.

"Yes," she sighed, tilting her head to gaze languidly at him.

"Only one woman has ever done this to me," he told her hoarsely. "Until now."

His words were cold water dousing her ardor.

"You still think I might be the woman you lost." She tore out of his embrace to face him. "I cannot hide I want you, Diokles, but not like this. Only if you can look at me and see Calliope of Apollysis, instead of someone you obviously still hold in your heart."

The words came from the depths of her soul leaving her amazed by their simplicity and truth.

His hands moved to frame her face. "You misunderstand me, Calliope. I see only you."

The struggle with his conscience melted away like the winter snow brushed by a warm spring wind.

The goddess's message to give up his search had brought pain and hope. Pain for a lost future; for being forced to renege on his oath. Hope, in being free to admit this woman could shine light onto the darkness in his soul.

Bowing to the urgent need driving him, Diokles swept her into his arms, swift strides carrying him to the center of the grove. Using his strength, he dropped to his knees, lowering his precious load onto the soft grass. Laying himself beside her, his hungry gaze feasted on the woman making his head spin. Her face glowed, the expression of sweet longing making her amber eyes shine brighter than jewels.

Trust and surrender he read in her face, the message reaching deep into his scarred heart like a healing salve.

He must be patient. Must rein in the raging need convulsing his body.

What was it about her that crushed his control to dust? Astounded to see the tremor in his hand, he stroked her flushed face, the skin soft as silk, traced the slender neck with his fingertips, before sweeping down over her breasts. Her hips thrust upwards, their plea for attention almost undoing his control.

Gritting his teeth, he pressed a light kiss at the base of her throat, let it linger, his lips riding the contractions of her throat muscles, which betrayed how much she welcomed his touch.

Sweat beaded his forehead. He trailed kisses over her chest, glorying in every whimper of need he drew from her. A droplet of sweat fell off his forehead to anoint the valley between her breasts.

He bent to lick it like a man dying of thirst under the hot sun. Her hoarse cry of need echoed in his head.

His heart swelled. He had marked her as his woman.

Inhaling the scent of violets belonging to her alone, he pressed a hand over her mons, coveting it as though it was the greatest treasure he possessed. Her hips bucked like an unbroken horse, sending his loins convulsing in sweet agony.

In the grip of a driving hunger demanding immediate release, he pushed her tunic up to expose her long, lean legs. Caressing them with the same adoration he had shown her breasts, he swept long, slow strokes upwards, coming ever closer to the center of her desire.

A niggling caution clamored to be heard.

Diokles ignored it.

Ignored the order insisting he stop, think, before an irretrievable point was crossed. Absurd to even consider stopping. Not when he stared, enraptured, into the beauty of her aroused face, the lips plumped and parted by the passion he himself brought to life.

His arousal commanded him. Commanded his hand pay homage to her inner thigh. Luxuriate in its smoothness. Her legs parted like flowing water, allowing him to glimpse the soft, pale curls covering her womanhood.

His burning gaze riveted onto the moist heart of her. Carnal flames seared his body, every muscle taut to the point of pain. The rush of blood hardened his aching length even more. He reimposed control, returning to kiss her eyelids, the tip of her upturned nose, the corners of her lips.

His hand, though, refused to comply with orders, sliding over her flat stomach, over her womanly hips covered by a thin tunic, offering little barrier to his feeling the heated skin beneath. Lower still, until his fingers threaded through damp curls to lightly press the pulsing nub they hid.

Her mindless wail of his name proved his undoing.

Clutching at his remaining lucidity, Diokles fought the urge to blindly thrust into her welcoming warmth. He slicked one finger over her again and again, wanting her to reach the pinnacle of ecstasy before he filled her luscious body.

Her incoherent demands obliterated whatever control remained.

Easing his weight over her, he leaned on his forearms and held on to the last shred of discipline to take her with finesse.

His teeth clenched with the effort. She was a virgin and.....

Biting off a groan of disgust Diokles rolled onto his back.

Chest heaving painfully he stared at the clouds disturbing the blue of the sky. For one moment of gratification he almost ruined his best chance—perhaps his only chance—of discovering the truth. Even worse, failed to complete the mission entrusted to him.

Failure.

The word struck like the whip which had once struck his back.

Cold, hard reality crashed through him. Useless to wish it could douse the burning, unsatisfied need ripping him like the piercing thrusts of swords.

Fury at his loss of control surged through him. Keeping his eyes fixed on the sky, he took a deep breath, speaking words torn from his heart.

"I will not make you break your vow."

He jumped to his feet and walked stiffly to the stream welcoming the pain every step cost him.

Finding the deepest part he sank below the water.

If only she could fall back into the comatose state she had been dragged out of.

Aching from unfulfiled release, Calliope propped herself on her forearms. Every muscle tightened like the strings of a lyre at the sight which met her appalled gaze.

Honesty insisted she confront the shame of her disheveled appearance. Her legs were spread wide, the tunic a crumpled mess around her waist. The rosy peaks of her breasts still glistened where Diokles had anointed them.

She closed her eyes against the reality of what had almost happened.

What she had allowed to happen.

Nothing excused her wanton behavior.

Mindful he could return any moment Calliope sat up. Shaking hands pulled the tunic over her shoulders and pushed its length down to cover her legs. Drawing them up to her chest, she wrapped her arms around her knees and rested her forehead on them.

Too soon for comfort a whisper of movement intruded on her humiliation. She sneaked a quick glance just in time to see Diokles pulling a tunic over his head.

She was not ready to discuss her rash behavior. If she sat without moving he might leave her alone. What could she say to him that would not smack of hypocrisy? Recalling how she welcomed his touch, even urged him on, she hung her head, blessing the long hair which shielded her flushed face.

The crackle of leaves underfoot announced his return. Calliope curled further into herself when he sat down beside her. Counting the beats of her racing heart she waited for him to speak.

The silence dragged on stretching her nerves to breaking point.

She could not bear it.

"You must think I am some kind of wanton," she mumbled into her knees. "I cannot explain my loss of control. Why I would so easily break my own vow." Mouth falling open, appalled at the realization, she lifted her head to face him. "It may have been broken already," she sobbed.

Anger flamed in his eyes. Disconcerted by it after what they shared Calliope drew back.

"Was this a ruse, priestess? Pretending to enjoy my lovemaking while hiding your real motive. Did you want *me* or want me to take your innocence so you could jeopardise my mission?"

"Priestess!" She thumped her fists on the ground finding relief in losing her temper. "You call me that after what happened. Do not dare to accuse me of duplicity, Diokles. I would not contrive to risk my purity, my home, my chance to recall the past, for something as fleeting as the wind!" Forgetting her embarrassment, desiring nothing but to thump him for his obtuseness, she jumped to her feet. "You embrace me as though worshipping a goddess and accuse me of trickery in one breath!"

What she saw next in his expression ignited her rage. "Do not laugh at me!"

"I do not mock you." His smile grew wider. "Your spirit and fire are admirable but I have to consider all possibilities and you may have unconsciously planned to trick me. Remember my troops are still in Apollysis."

"You remind me of the threat to my home after we made love," she hissed.

In one fluid motion he rose to his feet. Wide-eyed, she watched him take her hands, and draw her close.

"You are not so naïve," he stated quietly. "I did not take you fully. I have just as much to lose by my actions as you do, Calliope. How would you feel if you were unable to learn the truth of who you really are. Never be able to discern what threatens both your home and mine."

Shaken by his words, tears stung the back of her eyes as she acknowledged the truth of what he said. She would not succumb to tears. If she allowed herself to cry she needed good reason to do so.

"Every day I live with the despair of not knowing my past," she choked. "Yet how can I know uncovering it will bring me joy? Am I better off not knowing?" She paused. In wearing the coronet she could save many lives. "I want to divine the threat to Sparta. Whatever it is, I now see it presents a threat to Apollysis, too."

This time she did not struggle when he drew her into a gentle embrace. She sought to absorb some of his strength and courage.

"You need to know else you are living a half-life." He released her and stepped away. "After we both have our answers you will be taken home if you wish it."

"Of course I will go with you," she sighed, looking into his finely drawn face. "But first I must offer sacrifice to Apollo in atonement. Do you trust me to go to his temple?"

His brows met in a formidable line. "Amyklai is a day's journey."

Calliope spared him an affronted glare. "I do not care. Please Diokles, this is important to me. And to your mission."

He raked a hand through his hair. "You drive me to the edge. Go, since you think it so necessary. Erisa will accompany you."

Calliope shivered.

"Is there no other servant who can come with me?" She debated whether to mention her suspicions that Erisa loathed her out of misguided jealousy. She owed the woman no favors. However, there was no reason to bring Diokles's wrath upon her. She herself would be gone soon.

"She is your servant while you are here. Two men from the household will provide escort."

"And they will all make sure I do not escape." She groaned at the thoughtless remark. She did not mean to snipe but her nerves remained on edge.

The warning look he sent her did nothing to ease her tension.

"You would be unwise to try."

"You still mistrust me?" That hurt. "I am not foolish enough to try."

He ran a hand through her hair the gesture weakening her knees.

"Go to Amyklai," he rumbled. "It gives me an extra day to complete long-neglected tasks before we leave."

She watched him stride to his horse, his proud bearing possessing the power to send eruptions of need through her. Hugging herself she waited until he mounted and rode off.

Once he was out of sight she walked over to where Astara still grazed. Leading her to a fallen stump, Calliope stepped onto it and sprang onto the mare's back, letting the horse retrace their path, her own mind too preoccupied to choose a way home. However much she rebuked herself on her lack of judgement, heat continued to flood her body at the remembrance of Diokles's lovemaking. Bordering on tenderness she speculated whether he was falling in love with her.

What would she do if it proved true?

Intimacy with a man was not for her. She pledged not to fall into such a trap again.

Pushing aside the thought which whispered she was halfway to falling in love herself, Calliope brooded on how close she had been to forever losing the opportunity to divine answers capable of profoundly affecting her life, and the lives of others.

Nothing, and no-one, would stop her now.

CHAPTER TWENTY

Foreboding beat at her like the wings of a Stymphalian bird.

Calliope shivered and attempted to convince herself the pressure bearing down on her head was due to the weather. She glanced at the clouds overhead. Rolling in sometime during the night, they had trapped yesterday's warm air beneath their thick cover, ensuring an oppressive morning. Catching the scent of rain her gaze swept the overcast sky hoping the day stayed dry until after their return.

Another shiver prompted her to draw the shawl tighter around herself.

Behind her Erisa carried cypress branches to light the sacrificial fire. Calliope swore she could hear resentment in every trudging step of the woman's feet. She pursed her lips remembering the scene in her room after telling the servant she was required to accompany her.

Her hand tightened around the ends of the shawl.

Erisa had turned surly and uncooperative. Only when she suggested the servant speak to Diokles, did she grudgingly accept. That same afternoon Erisa remembered an errand she had in the agora. This morning some time had passed before she appeared.

Suspicions niggled at the edges of Calliope's mind. Unable to pinpoint the reason for her uneasiness over Erisa's behavior, she could only assume it was due to witnessing the woman reappear both times with a smirk marring her face. A smirk designed to mock her, Calliope, as though Erisa possessed knowledge of some secret.

She firmed her lips and attempted to convince herself her suspicions were unfounded. She would not allow them to distract her today. Her uneasiness stemmed simply from being in unfamiliar territory, accompanied by two silent men from Diokles's household and a surly servant.

Useless to wish he was with her. Another sleepless night revealed he had not returned from his evening meal. He was probably still overseeing provisioning for their departure.

She quickened her stride.

"How much further to the temple?" She tossed the question over her shoulder to Erisa.

"Are you tired, priestess? Perhaps you are not used to walking far in your privileged life."

Calliope came to an abrupt stop. Unable to credit what she heard, she turned to face the woman, giving herself time to swallow the rash words that threatened to escape.

"You are insolent." Her voice dripped ice. "Have a care, Erisa. I grow weary of your constant provocations. No servant has ever had reason to speak to me the way you do. If your rudeness continues I will turn a blind eye to your punishment."

Grim satisfaction filled her when the woman tensed, her face flushing an angry red.

"Of course, because you think you have our master's favor, you assume you can mete out punishment."

"I do not have his favor," Calliope cut her off with a wave of her hand, trying to ignore the sensual images flitting inconveniently through her mind. Praying the heat in her cheeks did not reflect on her face, her embarrassment reminded her all too clearly of the reason for this pilgrimage. "I do not order punishments on a whim, Erisa, but you are leaving me no choice. I will not tolerate disrespect simply because you are jealous of what you believe his intentions are toward me."

Erisa's mouth pinched so tightly the lips turned white. Menacing intent resonated in the woman's aura. Calliope held her breath, muscles tightening, ready to repel an attack she sensed was imminent. Erisa could be capable of anything.

In the next heartbeat Erisa dropped her gaze, her shoulders slumping. Rather than insist on an answer she turned to the two men whose presence provided relief from Erisa's animosity.

"How much further?"

"It is just over the next rise, priestess," one answered.

Were her ears deceiving her or were his words slurred? Inclining her head in thanks, she lengthened her stride, upping the pace. From the corner of her eye, she noticed the man who had spoken, stumble, his companion clumsily helping to right him.

She shot both a worried look.

They could not possibly be drunk this early in the day. Could they? She slowed, waiting until they caught up, dismayed to see their faces pale as snow, a shimmer of moisture covering their foreheads. She could not believe that Diokles would send two sick men to protect her.

They motioned for her to keep walking. A moment's hesitation and she set off again, frowning at Erisa's impassive features, which showed no concern for the condition of her fellow servants.

In a short while they reached Amyklai, the fifth village which made up the polis of Sparta. Calliope began to breathe more freely as the tension felt her.

The temple of Apollo rose before them. Energy vibrated through her heart, gladness warmed her soul, and a thrill sizzled through her quivering body. The long walk, taking a good part of the morning, had been worth it.

About to relieve Erisa of her load Calliope sucked in a worried breath. Both men swayed, then their legs buckled beneath them as they sank to the ground. She hurried over to see if she could help. "What is ailing you?"

Neither summoned the energy to reply. Calliope looked around frantically, seeking help, but the temple stood quiet and empty.

Gripped by a sense of urgency she snatched the cypress branches from Erisa's arms. "Run to the village and ask for a healer."

Watching to ensure Erisa did her bidding, she then turned her attention to the two men again, disconcerted to see one lying down and curled into himself as though in great pain. "Be strong," she encouraged, wishing she could give them more aid than just words. "Help will come soon."

Hastening to a small altar on the far side of the temple, she placed the branches on the smooth stone and withdrew two small rocks from the pouch around her waist, striking them until a thin curl of smoke spiralled up.

Blowing on the fire to encourage it to light quickly, Calliope entered the temple itself, depositing an ivory seal as an offering. Diokles had presented it to her before he left to join his peers, explaining the seals were normally offered to Artemis Orthia. Too flustered to meet his gaze, she thanked him with downcast eyes, murmuring it was fitting she could offer a token sacred to Apollo's twin in recompense.

Bowing low to the likeness of the god she returned outside to kneel before the altar. Immersed in the scent of burning cypress, she turned her mind inwards, the spot between her brows throbbing whenever it connected with the divine, arms lifted in prayer, beseeching forgiveness.

Calliope came out of her trance to find the fire reduced to embers. She winced at the stiffness of her knees as she rose. Maybe she was growing soft as Diokles once claimed.

She must check on the men. Praying Erisa had returned, she hurried to the front of the temple where she had left them.

Her heart lurched in her chest.

There was no-one in sight.

The skin on the back of her neck crawled. Panic fluttered in her abdomen as though a trapped bird beat its wings inside. Fighting an overpowering need to flee the place, Calliope tried to logically reason away the men's absence. Perhaps they had been taken to the village.

Silence weighed down on her like a smothering cloak. No birds sang, no wind sighed through the trees. Only a subliminal threat hummed, unseen, spreading dark tentacles through her senses.

Her shallow breathing turned her dizzy. Feeling she was about to succumb to panic, Calliope dragged air into her tight chest. She needed to get to the village. She needed to stay calm; not break into a reckless run.

In a thin, high voice she called, "Erisa."

"Do not waste your breath, she will not hear you."

Her high-pitched yelp almost deafened her.

It could not be him!

No. She was overwrought and imagining things. Holding her head high, fists clenched to stop her hands shaking, she sought the last person she wanted, or expected, to see. "Show yourself!"

He slinked into sight from behind a large column. The blood drained from her face leaving ice-cold dread in its wake.

"Lykos! You...How...?"

"I am relieved to find you unharmed, high priestess Calliope. We have been searching for you ever since the fall of Apollysis." He rubbed his hands together. "It is time to return you home."

Calliope took an involuntary step away. Danger hovered in the air and permeated through her skin like a noisome irritant. She studied the pale eyes she had never trusted, the weak chin, the leer adorning his narrow, lupine features. She remembered catching sight of the exact same leer directed to her in the past when he thought she wasn't looking.

Even as her vision tunneled, her body wound tight like a coiled snake ready to defend itself.

"How did you find me, Lykos?" Good. Her voice sounded steady and strong. "I know you escaped through the temple tunnel before the Spartans invaded." Impossible for him, or anyone, to have tracked them given the speed of Diokles's horses. "The three hoplites who followed me were defeated by the Spartan commander."

She recoiled when he spat on the ground.

The expression on his face turned ugly. "Yes, we all know the brutality of the Spartans. You do not need to question how we found you. Just know I am here to save you." He took a step forward.

"Stop, Lykos," she held a hand up, pleased her voice rang with authority. "I am not in danger whatever you may think."

"You cannot go to the shrine without me," he shouted. "You forget what happened the one time you wore the coronet? If I had not been there you would have died!"

Calliope gaped at him. "How do you know I am going to the shrine?" There had to be a reason he risked everything to follow her. "What are you afraid of? That the coronet will restore my memory? You and Aeschylus always insisted I could die if I wore it again. Well, I do not believe you." Arms akimbo, she planted her feet and glared at him. "I will go to the shrine. I will wear the coronet. I will find out the truth. Neither of you can stop me!"

Fury mottled his face red. It fueled her own anger and made her more determined to seek the truth. His behavior proved everything she always suspected him of being—a petulant child who shouted and stamped his feet if he did not get his way. There would be no greater way to deny his selfish demands than to wear the coronet.

"You too should learn to value your life, Calliope. It is not for you to determine what you do with it but for the gods."

"And for you I suppose" she threw back, easing her way past him. "Think your absurd thoughts if they make you feel better. I do not need your permission to wear the coronet."

A shadow passed over Lykos's face. A palpable shift in the air plucked her rapidly fraying nerves like the talons of an eagle. He was muttering something under his breath, his eyes flicking between her and the road. Rattled by his erratic behavior, Calliope frantically scanned the ground, hoping to find a strong piece of wood to use as a weapon.

He stalked closer. She sucked in a breath knowing she must run faster than the wind.

Lykos stood between her and the village. Calliope turned and bolted along the road back to the main polis. Every instinct screamed to place the furthest possible distance between her and the priest. Sobbing for breath she risked a glance over her shoulder. He followed without hurry, a smirk just discernible on his face.

Her throat tightened.

Blind to everything except her need to escape, she missed seeing three horsemen emerge from the cover of trees, spreading out until they surrounded her. She slid to a stop, trembling, gasping, scanning their faces for any sign they would help her.

She recognized one. He was Apollysian. That meant the others were, too.

"Stand aside and let me pass," she panted, hand pressed against the sharp pain digging into her side.

"We take our orders only from the high priest," the man directly in front of her said coldly.

But the fleeting look of regret crossing his features sent hope surging through her. "Stand aside for your high priestess. Your duty is to me as much as it is to the high priest."

Without warning both her arms were seized from behind. Cruel fingers dug hard into her flesh, promising to leave bruises. Cursing herself for not keeping an eye on Lykos, she stood upright despite the pain, and the knowledge her hands were being tied together. None of these men would see her fear.

"Where is my servant? The two men who accompanied us?" Could she talk these hoplites around to release her? Thoughts careened violently in her mind until one stood out like a beacon of light.

Diokles.

The connection between them was a gift from the gods given for this very moment. She tried to reach out to him through the bond between their hearts and minds. However impossible it seemed, he must come, or her memories would be lost forever and the danger to Sparta never uncovered.

"Your servant rendered us a great service," Lykos gloated. "She will not lift a finger to help you. The others were dealt with in the same manner your Spartan finished the hoplites first tasked to save you."

A sob escaped her. "So, they are dead. I pity you when Diokles learns of their fate."

"I am not afraid of this, *Diokles.*" He said the name as though spitting something revolting out of his mouth. "As for the unfortunate men, a little Mandrake wine taken at breakfast, switched by a servant wanting revenge…."

Her blood ran cold.

As the words trailed into silence, the cunning of the plan almost brought her to despair. Even knowing the treacherous servant faced severe punishment once she was discovered, Calliope found no pity in her heart. The harm Erisa had done was incalculable.

She glared at each of the men, memorizing their faces.

"You will not escape punishment," she warned them in a voice full of cold menace. "Either by my hand or by the Spartans." The corners of her lips lifted into an angry smile when they squirmed uncomfortably in their saddles. Turning to glare at the hateful presence behind her, she offered him another chance to reconsider whatever he was planning. “Let me go, Lykos, unless you want the wrath of Apollo to fall on you.”

He laughed in her face. “I follow only one god which is myself. I only pretend to believe in or worship any other.”

Her jaw fell. “Do you hear yourself?” she cried. “May the gods smite you for such pride.”

He touched a finger to her cheek. She recoiled in disgust and clamped her lips shut to avoid retching.

“If I am to be cursed then I will first do what I always wanted to.” He addressed the hoplites. “Take up positions along the road. Make sure I am not disturbed.”

Calliope’s mouth worked soundlessly. These men of her own city prepared to leave her to the mercy of Lykos? As they disappeared between the trees she found her voice. “Come back,” she yelled after them, “Come back!”

Rage spilled over when they ignored her pleas. To desert her in this moment of need gave her yet another reason to see them punished. She threw Lykos a dark glower hoping it impaled his black heart. Any other time she would revel in the unease flickering across his face.

His pale, beady eyes dropped to her chest. She pushed away the fear curdling her stomach. Channelling defiance, she imagined seeing it grow and expand like a massive shield to protect her.

“Let me go, Lykos,” Calliope bit out through clenched teeth. “Touch me and you will not need to wait for the gods to smite you.” Deliverance would come. She did not know how she knew. Until then she must find the words to stall him.

“Ah, but soon I shall have the satisfaction of taking a long-desired prize.” His voice rose. “You spurned my passion, priestess. Ever since you came to Apollysis I wanted you. Then to thwart me you took a stupid oath of purity. I could not touch you in the temple, you were always in the company of others. Now you are at my mercy!”

Bile burned her throat. “I did not take the oath because of you,” she hissed. “I had another reason. I always despised you. You are arrogant, greedy, and selfish. I know you bedded other priestesses. I heard them talk. You did not care whether they enjoyed it or not, whether they worshipped you and were forced to endure the sight of you with another. So long as the great priest, Lykos, satisfied his lust."

A ringing silence followed her denunciation. She had heard the Spartans were sent to battle with the admonishment to return, carrying their shields in victory, or die in glory, and be carried back on them. Calliope straightened to her full height.

She would take those words for herself.

Her defiance was her shield.

Surrender was weakness.

She would not surrender.

Her chin rose higher as he sauntered closer, close enough for his body odor to wrinkle her nose in loathing at the combination of lust and sweat. Her bound hands might be a handicap, but she could still make the fool sorry if he tried to overpower her.

"You shall be mine, Calliope. My prisoner, my queen, my concubine, whichever you prefer. Never again will you need to fear the coronet." He grabbed her arm and pulled her roughly away from the road.

She stumbled and almost fell.

"What do you mean, queen? You are mad!"

He simply continued to pull her after him without answering. Shuffling to keep up with his strides she fought to stay upright. He would pounce on her like a wolf pounced on a lamb if she fell.

Once again, she silently called to Diokles, willing him to somehow find and save her. Why did this part of Lakonia have to be so fertile? Densely packed stands of trees grew on both sides of the road. How could she leave a sign?

Then an idea burst into her mind as though sent by Apollo himself.

She had chosen to wear a long tunic which might prove to be her savior. Crouching slightly, she took a careful step, trod on the hem, and heard the satisfying rip as a portion of the fine fabric tore away. Heart in her mouth she glanced surreptitiously at Lykos who kept walking. Triumph hummed through her.

"I warn you one last time, priest, let me go if you know what is good for you." Her racing heart pumped blood much too quickly around her body. Calliope shook her head to relieve the pressure on her scalp. She must remain clear-headed to spot any chance of escape.

A low savage laugh rattled the calm she strove for.

"You accused me of doing as I please. That is what I am doing now, my beauty, what I please."

He stopped inside a grove of trees. Calliope whimpered as thoughts of another grove on a halcyon day filled her mind. Shutting her eyes tight she recalled how Diokles had treasured her, recalled his gentleness, his reverence, the way he controlled his own desires. She clutched at the memory like a dying person clutched at life.

By closing her mind she could disassociate herself from what Lykos was doing. The possessive way he touched her neck, his hot breath wafting over her skin, nauseating her. If he dared to kiss her neck she would tear him to shreds with her teeth.

Then he touched her breast.

Her wrath burned hotter than the fires of Tartarus. In her mind she was back in the temple in Apollysis biting another brute who prepared to attack her. A strangled scream escaped her throat, frenzied, wild, wiping out every modicum of civilized decorum. Calliope recoiled from the vile hand tormenting her.

Pivoting, she sunk her teeth into the flaccid skin of his wrist.

Through the buzzing in her head she heard Lykos's agonized roar as he tried to shake her off. His free hand rained blows to her head. She refused to let go. The harder he hit her, the harder she bit him, drawing blood when she almost bit through to the bone.

The blows ceased but her respite did not last long.

His fingers twined into her hair and yanked without mercy. Pain exploded in her scalp. Calliope let go of his wrist, spitting blood out of her mouth in disgust. His face was a study in rage and animal desire.

Twisting herself out of his reach, she swivelled on one foot, using her body weight to propel herself forward as she lashed out with the other, managing one swift kick to his vitals. Her bound hands did not allow her to gain enough power to hurt him properly. Instead, to her horror, she fell, hitting the ground hard, calling down curses on him from every god she could think of.

Calliope scrambled away as Lykos followed her down. She was too slow. Despair crashed through her when he pinned her to the ground with the weight of his body. Her heart stuttered, then raced with a speed she feared would kill her.

"You will pay for this," he lifted his bruised and bloodied wrist in front of her face. "Today marks the first payment. I will be the first to possess you. You will never know what the coronet would have revealed. You will not need to."

His maniacal laugh rose from the depths of Hades.

"Damn you, Lykos! Damn you to Tartarus for all eternity." She thought of Diokles again. Now, when she was about to be violated, she realized she loved him. Had grown to love the man he was. "There is no life for you once Diokles finds out—NO!"

Before her appalled gaze he turned into a madman. His eyes gleamed in a demonic, possessed way, reminding her of the Furies, his mouth stretched in a parody of smiling anticipation.

He squeezed her breast roughly. Dry retching, she spat out bile, vowing revenge with every sobbing breath she drew into her lungs. His clammy hand pushed her tunic up, sliding along her thigh in a sick travesty of a caress. Calliope squirmed beneath his loathsome weight trying to slam her knee into his groin.

"Do not attempt to hurt me again," he panted, licking his lips as he rested his hand on her hip. "Surrender to me like your peers and you shall see how kind I can be."

She ached to wipe the lascivious smile from his thin lips.

Permanently.

Her bound hands dug into the small of her back, the stabbing pain making her eyes water, realization dawning that her hands were losing feeling.

Calliope bared her teeth. "Force me and I swear by Apollo I will take my own life. I will throw myself off the roof of the temple damning your name so all citizens of Apollysis can hear why I chose death. I swear it!"

For one blessed moment she thought her words had pierced the lust clouding any rational thought left in him. He stiffened, paused, looking at her with an expression akin to fear. She held her breath, hating the odious weight of him lying on her.

There was only one man she yearned to feel on her.

He would come to save her. She didn't know how she knew, but she knew.

An anguished sob escaped as the cloud lifted and insane greed returned to Lykos's face.

"Your choice my beautiful priestess. Even to possess you once is enough."

The fabric of his tunic rubbed against her hip. Her struggles became more frantic. She could feel hysteria bubbling high in her chest.

Calliope dug deep for control only to lose her grip on it when his stiff rod settled between her legs.

"*NO*!"

Her scream merged with a new voice which echoed like thunder through the air.

"*LYKOS*! Release her!"

CHAPTER TWENTY-ONE

He had heard her call.

Had come to save her.

It must be him who lifted the weight of the monster off her body. Calliope stared at the sky and sucked blessedly fresh air into her lungs. Something warm and wet slid past her ears. Blinking her eyes simply released more moisture.

Tears?

She never cried.

The more she tried to stem them, the harder they fell, until they flowed like a thermal river down the side of her face. It was as if coming so close to being violated by the man she loathed beyond all others, opened the flood gates to every feeling dammed behind the veneer of serene priestess.

She would stay strong; concentrate on the task of restoring her memory; rejoice her prayers for salvation had been answered. She would survive this ordeal the same way she survived the loss of her memory.

Grunts of fury, mixed with guttural cries of pain, echoed in her ears as the stasis gripping her faded. The sound of flesh connecting with flesh, one sickening thud after another, pounded through her awareness. Calliope wearily tilted her head in time to witness Lykos sink to his knees, coughing and heaving, then curling up on the ground like a wounded animal.

Let him feel pain her mind gloated. He deserves it.

The man hurrying to her was not who she expected to see. Who she most wanted to see, though he, too, claimed a part of her heart. Strong, caring hands clasped her shoulders, carefully lifting them, until she was able to shift herself into a sitting position, every muscle trembling and aching.

She gaped at him through a curtain of tangled hair. "Aesch—"

A cough rasped from her parched throat while a thousand sharp thorns jabbed into her wrists where the rope still cut her flesh.

"Please untie me," she croaked.

Helped to her feet, Calliope wanted nothing more than to sink against her father's comforting bulk. Calling on reserves of strength she stood unmoving while he cut the knot with one swift stroke of his knife. Rubbing her hands and forearms to restore circulation she managed a weak smile of reassurance. Not that it convinced Aeschylus who frowned darkly at her bruised wrists.

"Water."

At his terse command a man came forward carrying a water skin. Calliope rinsed her hands, then took several small sips, swishing the water around her mouth, removing the taste of Lykos's blood. Every mouthful she spat out she imagined spitting out all residue of him.

Running her tongue around her teeth to ensure no taint of blood remained, she lifted the skin to her dry lips, drinking deeply, blessing the cool water soothing her raspy throat.

Refreshed, she handed it back to the man, who bowed and left her with Aeschylus. "Did you find the piece of material I tore off? Is that how you found me?" she asked in a firmer voice.

"No. We have been following Lykos for several days," Aeschylus placed a protective arm around her. "A judicious coin in the right place set us on the road here. We rode under the cover of the forest where one of the men heard you cry out."

Calliope released a breath and rested her head against his shoulder. "Thank you."

Receiving no response, she looked up at his face and drew in a sharp breath. Rage warred with loathing for supremacy in the stare he directed at Lykos. That look alone was deadly enough to cleave the priest in two.

"You possess no honor, Lykos. Did all my assistance mean nothing," he roared. "How could you even think to do this to my ch—?"

Too numb to notice the abrupt way Aeschylus cut off his words, Calliope began to shake, clutching Aeschylus's arm when she swayed unsteadily.

"Would you rather she knows the truth," Lykos raged. "She is prepared to go to the hidden shrine. With *him*! Are you ready to die?"

"Better to die than to see Calliope degraded. I will not forget this, Lykos, nor forgive you." Aeschylus raised his free hand and bent his head to her. "We leave for Apollysis before we are discovered here. You will accompany us priest so I can keep watch on you."

Calliope's confusion grew when two armed riders came into view, pulling one of the hoplites who had abandoned her, behind their horses.

She stared at her father. "How is it these men obey you? What is going on? Where are the others who were with Lykos?" The questions tumbled out, her interest heightened, needing to understand a situation she had no idea existed.

"Unlike the priest and his cohort these men are loyal to Apollysis and its people." A grim smile curved Aeschylus's mouth. "The *others* sought to stop us....and failed. The prisoner is the only one left. Come, I brought a horse for you."

Sadness filled her heart knowing Aeschylus would be unhappy with her decision. But he needed to know. Calliope opened her mouth to speak then shut it like a trap.

Had she heard him correctly?

"What do you mean you brought a horse for me?" His face blanched. A frown pulled her eyebrows together. "I never rode in Apollysis. Why do you think I can ride?"

"I meant you can ride behind me," he replied in a rush. "My horse can carry us both."

"I cannot go back." She clasped one of his hands affectionately between both of hers. "I will return after I have been to the shrine. I promise we will talk then." To her consternation his features tightened, distress clearly visible in the pinched look around his eyes. "I do not want to cause you pain but I must do this. Ever since

I left Apollysis I see visions which I do not understand. I must find my memories in order to find myself."

Better not to mention Diokles's mission.

"No good will come of going to the shrine," Aeschylus protested. "I will ensure your safety once we return home."

Calliope glowered at the priest standing a few feet away, pressing on his nose. Her heart rejoiced over the spots of blood decorating his face. He deserved every one of them for what he intended to do to her. "I go nowhere where the priest goes," she insisted coldly.

"Please come away. It is too dangerous for you to—"

The rest of his words were drowned in the thunder of hooves racing toward them.

"My lord, Aeschylus," a third rider shouted in a panicked voice. "Spartans are coming."

Diokles!

Strength flooded her nerveless body. She whirled to face Lykos, fingers curling into her palms so hard the nails almost pierced her skin.

"Whose death is near?" The acid in her voice would have dissolved marble pillars. She met his look of pure hatred with a mocking smile, watching in satisfaction while Lykos was roughly pulled onto a spare horse, tied and taken away.

Turning to Aeschylus she grabbed his arms. "Leave quickly," she implored. "None of you will be left alive once they know what has happened." His ashen face made her heart weep.

"Not unless you come with me," he whispered in a voice laced with pain.

How could she ignore his plea?

Racked by indecision, an indecision stemming out of love and respect for her father, images flooded her mind to remind her of the early days in Apollysis. The fear, the sense of loss, most of all the aloneness. "I cannot. Go! Diokles thinks you are someone he has sworn vengeance against—are you ill?"

The man who had been her rock, shook like a leaf, even his lips trembled, his eyes filling with anguish. On the verge of calling one of the hoplites to help him she stopped when he emphatically shook his head.

"He is mistaken," he said thickly. "I am as far from being that man as I could be."

Calliope searched his face through slitted eyelids trying to make sense of his words. A film of tears covered his brown eyes. Compassion moved her to hug him tightly before urging him in the direction of the waiting men. A last pleading look, then he left her, running to mount his horse, and was soon swallowed from sight by the thick forest.

"May Apollo guide you safely home," she whispered. Calliope listened until the pounding hooves were no more than a distant echo.

She must find Diokles.

Pushing her distress into a distant corner of her mind, she consoled herself that there would be time later to wash away the memory of Lykos's filthy hands touching her. Time to heal.

She forced her reluctant legs to move, gaining strength with each step, then more urgent as she fought the instinct to run. Alone, exposed, her mind conjured images of enemies lurking in the bushes ready to jump out and attack her.

She shuffled into a sluggish jog.

Each shallow breath cost her as though she carried the weight of the heavens instead of Atlas. If she ever saw Lykos again she would kill him. The brute deserved the wound to his wrist. There was no going back to showing him grudging respect. No apologizing for the injuries she caused him.

All the creative ways she had imagined in the past of ridding herself of Lykos raced through her mind. Each one breathed life into her smoldering anger. Imbued her with fresh energy to keep going.

She thought of the men who had died because of her and vowed to ensure their bodies were found so they could be given proper burial.

A sudden bright flash shook her out of her vengeful fantasies. In the distance she spied a burnished light bobbing and weaving through the trees. Adrenaline sent a surge of power into her legs. Breaking into a run, Calliope rounded a bend in the road, heart leaping as she saw the riders.

"*Diokles!*"

Joy lent her wings. Abandoning all pretence of control, heedless of her own safety, she collided with his stallion. The huge animal half-reared, trumpeting its surprise and displeasure. Undeterred by the milling hooves, she grabbed Diokles's arm, leaving him no time to rein to a stop, and dragged him to the ground as though her life depended on that one act.

Throwing herself into his arms, she uttered glad, mindless cries. Cradled against his chest, melting into the living heat of his body, the feeling of safety and comfort overpowered her. Through closed eyes she breathed in the subtle scent clinging to his skin.

"Where is the priest?" he demanded.

The strength of the demand vibrated through her. "You know!' She drew back to search his face. "Has Erisa returned? Did she tell you?"

Calliope fell silent. She thought she had seen the extent of his anger. How naïve to think she understood him? Bloodless lips stood out in a face mottled red, a hard fury blazing out of his eyes which were fixated on the direction she had appeared from.

He would make a dangerous enemy.

"Do not go after him," she urged. "We must get to Apollo's shrine first. He does not want me to wear the coronet."

Something in her voice brought his piercing gaze to her face. Calliope kept her features impassive while he minutely examined them though nothing could hide the evidence of her ordeal. Her tunic was dirty, threads hung from the delicate material, bruises stood out livid against the pale skin.

While he barked out orders she tried to swing her long hair over her arms but he pushed it back.

"Return to the city. Tell the men we march tonight." He pointed to four of the silent hoplites. "Follow the priest and those he fled with. If you find them inside our borders….you know what to do."

Calliope tugged at his arm uncaring if she needed to beg on her knees.

"There is one you must spare. A man called Aeschylus. He adopted me after I lost my memory, gave me a home, family and saved me from losing mind. Just now he saved me again. Please, Diokles, tell your men to spare his life."

"He was here," he thundered.

Calliope jumped back frightened by the black frown crossing his face. By the gods what did she say that was so wrong?

Certain she heard his teeth grinding she whispered hesitantly, "Diokles?"

"Spare this man. I will deal with him."

CHAPTER TWENTY-TWO

He would deal with him?

"Why would you *deal* with Aeschylus? He is a kind man who does not deserve death."

His bitter laugh assaulted her ears.

"Kind? Where was his *kindness*," he flung the word like an epithet, "when he dragged his daughter from Sparta, screaming, never to be seen in ten long years."

Calliope tensed, pulse thudding to a heavy, dull rhythm.

"What are you implying?" She drew back, wary of the raging fire evident in his eyes. "That my adoptive father is the man you swore revenge on."

"Yes." He fisted one hand. "You did not reveal before that this is the same man who adopted you. Are you protecting him?"

"No! It cannot be. How many times do I have to tell you he is not Spartan." Calliope thrust shaking fingers through her hair and started to pace. "He never spoke of Sparta to me or knows anything about it. Listen to yourself. This is why I withheld my relation to him because I feared you would assume he was the same man."

She stopped in her tracks puzzled by his expression. It looked like he waged war within himself over what he wanted to say.

"I told you we learnt of the threat from a spy," he spoke in measured tones. "The priestess of Athena came down from the acropolis to advise the threat was real." His chest expanded on a deep breath before he continued. "She looked at me and told of a Spartan who escaped to Apollysis." He gave her a piercing look. "I believe it is the same man."

"Even a priestess cannot always divine the thoughts and will of the gods," Calliope insisted. "He would not hold something so important from me. No, Diokles, both of you are wrong."

"Perhaps you are wrong," he countered. "Time will prove who of us is."

She gave a startled cry when he lifted her into his arms. Calliope speculated on the bleakness in his eyes. She yearned to erase it, holding back, unsure whether he would welcome her comfort. He held her like she was the most precious thing on earth, but she needed reassurance his heart would not forever be held by a lost love.

He sat on a flat rock jutting out of the ground and settled her in his lap. "What happened?"

"You are giving orders again," she complained half-heartedly to distract him. Worrying the inside of her lip, she pressed her face between his shoulder and neck afraid of his reaction once she revealed her ordeal. "We need to go," she mumbled against his skin, drawing in his scent, finding solace in his embrace.

"Calliope," he growled with a hint of impatience. "Men and supplies are not readied in an instant. Speak."

With a heavy sigh she started to recount everything she recalled of her journey to Amyklai. Encouraged he let her speak without interrupting, her voice grew stronger, telling of how she sent Erisa for help after reaching the temple. She confessed her suspicions about Erisa hating her because she claimed Diokles's attention. The servant's smugness and insolence on the journey as though she harbored a secret.

Raising her head she gazed into his eyes. "I called for you in my heart and prayed you heard. Is that how you knew to come here?"

He held her closer. "The krypteia discovered Erisa and her henchman. Information was swiftly extracted and brought to me."

Calliope winced, not wanting to imagine what happened to the prisoners. Instead, she recounted the sudden, inconceivable arrival of Lykos, the disappearance of Erisa and the two men accompanying them and trembled all over again.

"They are dead," she choked past the lump growing in her throat. "Lykos implied as much. Their bodies must be brought back for burial. They died protecting me."

The still fragile emotions she held in check reached the limit of their endurance. Throwing her arms around him, she clung like a limpet clung to a rock, welcoming the quiet, healing tears washing away the horror of what had happened.

Diokles stroked her hair—long, comforting strokes he often used to settle a fractious young horse. The ghost of a smile curved his lips, imagining her annoyance if she knew he compared her to a horse. The way she clung to him showed her trust that he would keep her safe.

Some emotion he did not want to examine too closely moved in his chest.

A glance at her face showed she no longer wept, although her cheeks still bore tear tracks, the odd droplet clinging to her skin, testing his control when he just wanted to kiss them away. Her eyes glowed through a film of moisture. She looked more beautiful than ever.

If he showed her comfort now she would never find the strength to recount her suffering. As much as he loathed himself for making her relive the torment, he instinctively knew she was strong enough to bear it.

Keeping his touch soft lest he frighten her, he reached for her hand, lifting it to his lips to touch light kisses on the broken skin where the rope had cut. "What did they do to you?"

"Lykos brought men with him," she sniffed. "He was always a coward. He tied my hands behind me."

A tight band squeezed his head. Did he really need to hear this given the anger churning in his gut? His lips twisted. He had insisted she tell him; he was now honor-bound to listen. "Then?"

He clamped an iron hold on his emotions, already suspecting what he would hear. As his unease grew, so too a fierce desire rose in him to protect her.

She began to speak hesitantly, then all at once the words poured out like a torrent of gushing water.

"He sent his men away to keep guard. He…he touched me. I thought if I did not move he would lose interest. But….then….he touched my…my breast. I panicked. I bit his wrist. I bit him hard, Diokles, as hard as I could. I tried to hurt him with my knee but lost my balance. I fell. He followed me down….he wanted to force himself on me….he would have taken me worse than an animal. He lay on top me, keeping me pinned down, he almost—you're hurting me!"

Calliope whimpered and squirmed in his lap, but the whimpers were powerless to douse the rage which burned through his heart and mind. Feeling a tug he looked down, shocked to find his fingers crushing the hand he still held.

Shame flooded him. She had been through enough already without him adding to her pain. Easing his grip, he rocked her while his mind raged.

Diokles struggled to control an avenging fury worthy of Alecto herself. His free hand curled around the hilt of his sword, squeezing hard, welcoming the pain. He wished it was Lykos's head between his hands; he needed to crush something to release the red mist clouding his vision.

The fate of the priest was sealed.

He flattened his lips, understanding what Calliope's fate would have been if help had arrived too late. "You are not fit to go anywhere. Rest today. We can leave tomorrow."

"No! We must leave today. You cannot allow them to reach the shrine first."

"No, Calliope." He held firmly onto her wriggling body. "You have endured enough. I decide when we leave."

The outrage on her face flooded him with relief although he was careful to keep his emotions in check. A warrior could not allow emotions to rule him. Judgment became clouded; wrong decisions were taken.

"You saved me from something worse than death itself," she argued. "But you do not know what is best for me or how strong I feel. Only I know what I am capable of."

Her defiant anger bore testimony that the ordeal had not broken her spirit. Unable to stop a smile he observed lightly, "You speak as though you are a woman of Sparta."

She continued to fight his hold. He released her reluctantly, watching as she jumped to her feet to glare at him. He had to stop himself leaping after her and kissing her into compliance.

"All the more reason for me to wear the coronet," she shouted, balling her hands into fists so the bruises on her wrists stood out. "It is not just about your mission, Diokles. I need to understand who I truly am and where I came from."

Concern for her well-being waged a battle with the knowledge she spoke the truth. Yes, Athena had spoken through her priestess. Told him to give up his search. Yet his heart still retained a small kernel of hope barricaded within it. The barricade he'd erected ten years ago to soften the blow of his loss.

If he must go back on his oath he needed to entertain no doubt his betrothed was indeed lost to him. No matter how much he had grown to lo—

Diokles pushed the word out of his head. All focus must be on the mission entrusted to him. Whatever madness brewed in his emotions could be analyzed later. "We leave as soon as we are provisioned," he announced as he rose to his feet. "Even if it means you sleep on the hard ground tonight."

She gave a weak smile at the reminder of how she had complained during their time on the road. "Kiss me," she whispered.

He went to her, keeping the kisses soft, planting one at each corner of her mouth, over her closed eyelids, no demand or heat in them. Returning to her mouth, he kissed her tenderly, wanting to dissolve the trauma she suffered, until her attempt to snuggle closer brought him up short.

He broke the kiss and stepped back.

Every breath he took brought a hint of Calliope's essence with it. Despite the nightmare she had been subjected to, the scent of violets still clung to her skin. Memories stirred. Of his mother; of the girl he had loved. He tightened his hold on the quivering woman who had brought his heart back to life.

"Diokles?"

He knew what she wanted to ask. It was a question he did not possess an answer to. Whistling to his stallion he turned to help her mount. A brow lifted when she stood her ground.

"Look at me, Diokles."

He wondered briefly where she had learnt the art of torturing a man. "There is no time to argue if you insist on leaving today."

She stared then looked away. He waited, discomfort clawing his chest in the drawn-out silence.

"We reach the shrine," she said, holding her head high. "I wear the coronet. Reveal the threat you spoke of and find my memories. What happens to us if Apollo reveals this Callisto is still alive?"

Her words pounded through him. Diokles stared unseeingly over the Eurotas river rushing between its banks. The sight did nothing to calm him or grant him wisdom.

This woman had insinuated herself into his life. He must shoulder the blame for his weakness.

There were no easy answers to give her. "I don't know," he replied heavily.

He cursed under his breath when her face crumpled. He was incapable of making her any promises. The words she wanted to hear, he could not utter, even though he was forced to resist the urging of his heart to say them.

"Then we are back to where we started," she choked. "Hostage and captor. Can we leave now. I can't bear to stay here another moment with this uncertainty hanging over us."

Cursing himself and the Fates, Diokles lifted her onto the stallion's back. He had intended to sit behind her and cradle her in his arms. Now he could not bring himself to do so. Instead, he picked up the reins and jogged beside his horse.

Relieved when she remained silent, he kept his gaze on the road, glancing occasionally to check she continued to sit securely on the big-boned animal.

There was nothing to speak about until the truth came to light.

At least nothing which would not cause more pain to them both.

CHAPTER TWENTY-THREE

The four winds scattered pieces of her heart across Lakonia.

Calliope kept her eyes resolutely fixed between the ears of her horse. From the moment they returned to Diokles's house yesterday she sensed an invisible wall between them. A wall she did not know how to breach. To spare herself pain she avoided speaking to him unless she needed to. In a small way it lessened the grief of believing he would never love her.

Despite all they had faced together since their first meeting, he still retained the memory of another woman, regardless of his feelings for her.

A wistful sigh escaped into the late morning air. He'd admirably aided her efforts to maintain that distance. They had bumped into one another while breaking camp where they'd rested during the night. Her lips twisted, recalling the swift turn of his body out of her way as though she carried some disease. Reduced to the avoidance of any physical contact hurt.

A gust of wind caught his red cloak, blowing it across her arm, the fine wool softly brushing her skin. She clenched her teeth and resisted the urge to grab the cloak and rub her face against it.

Wrapped in her own cloak of misery Calliope paid no heed to the tall cypress trees lining their route. Did not hear the singing of birds that flitted between the frond-like leaves. Did it matter whether she died or lost her mind? Once she revealed what he wanted to know he would have no further use for her.

She dashed a solitary tear away. She would not cry over him.

A desultory glance over her shoulder showed the line of men on horseback. Each carried a shield that looked solid enough to crush rock. Marveling at their strength, she remembered the morning Lysandra roused her out of the nightmare, remarking on Calliope's powerful grip.

Was she stronger than the others because some twist of fate might prove she was Spartan?

Her lips firmed in a tight line. She must know even if she feared the truth.

What would Diokles do if his betrothed was dead? Alive in another land? Would he leave her, Calliope, to continue his search, scarring them both in the process? Her mind churned over the same questions until her head pounded.

"Halt."

Bands of tension constricted her forehead and chest. "Why are we stopping?"

Diokles turned his brilliant dark eyes on her. Caught in their thrall, she stared back, acutely aware of the attraction humming between them. She noticed his hands tighten on the reins, his horse tossing its head in protest.

She understood his anxiety. Uncovering the lurking menace to his home comprised only half the reason tension simmered between them.

Learning the fate of another woman hung over them like a dark cloud.

"The men and horses need watering." His tone was detached as though the reason should be obvious. "The shrine is a short ride from here."

Each staccato sentence pierced her like a shower of arrows. Calliope waited until he dismounted and removed his helmet. She wanted to touch his face, wipe away the wariness in his eyes. One hand half-rose—she pulled it back, unable to cope if he rejected her. If she touched him, she would collapse in his arms, and they had no time to lose.

"I want to reach there quickly," she insisted, sliding smoothly to the ground. "I feel like my life is more precariously balanced than ever."

"It is not just your life," he said quietly. "The lives of my fellow citizens depend on you."

Sending him a narrow-eyed glare, she bit out. "Thank you for reminding me Sparta always comes first in your consideration." She held herself stiffly, disappointment swamping her, a disappointment she had no reason to feel. "Tell me, commander, what happens if Apollo reveals *I* am the danger? That your Callisto is dead?"

A muscle worked in his cheek before he looked away. It would have hurt less if he'd physically struck her.

"I have spent these hours asking the same questions and receiving no answer." He took her hand to press a searching kiss on her knuckles, sending a thrill of pleasure through her. "I honor the woman you are, Calliope—beautiful, strong, courageous. Should your words prove true—"

He released her hand.

The glimmer of regret she spied in his eyes did little to ease the pain skewering her stomach, her chest, her scalp. Her eyes devoured his tall body as he strode to where the small Spartan force gathered on the bank. Running after him to demand, even plead, he make his intentions clear would do no good. She understood him well enough to know him immovable once his mind was made up.

She really wanted to shake him to his senses. Calliope flexed her stiff fingers at his stubborn refusal to admit his feelings. She witnessed them expressed in a myriad of ways—the worshipful way he had pleasured her, the way he held her after her ordeal, the kisses they shared.

She had fallen in love with the man he was—ruthless, compassionate, dictatorial, honorable. The contradictions meant nothing. She had gifted him her heart.

The dry grittiness of her mouth clamored for relief. She walked off and found a small cluster of bushes a short distance away which guaranteed a measure of privacy. Stepping between them, she sank to her knees, exhaling in bliss as she rinsed dust and sweat off her skin. Sunlight sparkled on the stream. She scooped the glittering water into her cupped hands, imagining she drank liquid light.

Once she quenched her thirst Calliope sat back on her heels. Staring into the rushing water she shook her head in wonderment. Her life had altered so dramatically in such a short time. She had changed so much, she barely recognized parts of the new person inhabiting her body. She had discovered strength, skills and a sensuality she never dreamed she possessed.

What else would she learn about herself?

And it all came back to Diokles.

Yes, he had dragged her from her home, made her bear privations, but he somehow summoned forth the person she was now.

She had endured—she'd grown stronger. She had fought with him—she did not lack courage to confront obstacles thrown her way. She'd almost made love with him. Calliope quivered as heat spiralled from her face to her toes, finding odd comfort in discovering she was more than just an emotionless, enigmatic priestess.

"We are ready to leave."

Startled out of her reverie, she twisted round to see Diokles walking toward her, his sandalled feet making no sound on the soft ground. How long had she sat on the bank immersed in her thoughts?

"Good. The sooner we get there the sooner I can return to Apollysis."

Gratified her words snapped his head back, she still hesitated to take the hand he held out, afraid she would pull him toward her to kiss away any lingering doubt from his heart.

Taking a deep breath, she braced herself for the touch of skin on skin, curling her fingers around his battle-toughened hand.

Pulled to her feet, her free hand clutched his arm to steady herself. For one blissful, magical moment, she stared into his eyes, seeing the exact moment his heart took over. His gaze dropped to her mouth. Her pulse quickened, prompting her to take an infinitesimal step closer.

She heard his sharp inhalation. Saw his dark head bend toward her.

Her lips parted.

In the blink of an eye a shadow crossed his face. He stepped back, face wiped clean of any expression, once more the inscrutable commander.

Calliope hung her head to hide the stark need devouring her. The hand resting on her back scorched through the thin fabric of her tunic, searing her soul, even as it seared her skin. That same hand had once stroked her body with unimaginable tenderness.

It proved sweet torture when he helped her onto her horse. The feel of those large, capable hands spanning her waist, wrung her senses to fever-pitch, each individual nerve-ending sitting on a knife edge.

His sudden spring onto his mount sent her mare wheeling in a circle. The hoplite closest to her caught the bridle to hold the animal steady. Thanking him, she noticed the others either avoided her gaze, or inclined their heads in a gesture of respect. In Apollysis she had been ogled and borne the brunt of hostility. Calliope barely summoned any feeling of triumph at the change.

As they moved off, she prayed the truth would conjure the same favorable change toward her by the one man who mattered.

The sun burned high in the heavens when Diokles reined his stallion to a halt in a grassy hollow which sat behind a small hill covered by laurel trees. His fellow hoplites dismounted around him; helot servants moving to tie ropes around tree trunks to secure the horses.

A danger sense honed through many battles raced down his back. An eerie silence hung over them making his skin crawl. Glancing up, he read no omens in the sky, although the air remained motionless, as though the gods themselves held their collective breath.

A fine film of sweat broke out on his brow. No military training could prepare him for what might happen this day.

Dismounting, he drove the spike of his spear into the ground and rested his shield against it. He turned to help Calliope dismount, a simple act which challenged his vaunted self-control. The touch of her soft hand goaded him to drag her into his arms and protect her from the world. His heart and head waged an ominous battle which promised to breach the wall holding back every hurt imprisoned behind it.

How could he consider giving his heart victory when his head reminded him why he'd persevered to reach this place? Despite the priestess's counsel, everything he stood for, everything he was, demanded he honor his oath.

Yet his heart played traitor, demanded he honor his feelings for this woman, whose valiant spirit drove her to freely accept whatever fate had in store for her.

A pinched look haunted her eyes. He yearned to return the spark of joy to them and spoke without thinking.

"If you fear for your life, Calliope, I will take you back to Apollysis."

Her face grew so pale it looked like all blood had drained from it. He took a step closer, ready to stop her collapsing at his feet.

"Have the gods robbed you of your reason?" she whispered incredulously. "You threatened to raze Apollysis unless I wore the coronet. Now that I have conquered my fear, now that I need the truth as much as you do, you want me to choose to leave."

Her words split him neatly in two. His orders remained unchanged. To determine his future he needed certainty his oath no longer bound him.

Could he unearth a way to fulfill both decrees without causing Calliope more pain?

"Your well-being is paramount. The gods will grant me the knowledge I need." His voice rang with the unswerving belief Zeus would answer him. "I would rather you left now, safely escorted home, than suffer any kind of harm."

The sudden flare of suspicion in her eyes surprised him.

"Is your concern about me, Diokles, or concern for yourself over what I might learn?" she hissed. "I believe *you* are now frightened of the truth. You did not answer what would happen depending on whether your Callisto is alive or dead. Will your vaunted honor be impugned because you kissed me, Calliope, priestess of Apollysis, as though I am the most precious woman on earth? Because you almost made love to me, *me*," she jabbed her finger to her chest. "And now, rather than face the truth, you want to retreat from it. I heard Spartans never retreated."

The scornful darts she hurled hit their mark. He stiffened and took her arm, dragging her out of earshot and the covert glances cast their way.

"True, we never do, we are not cowards." Her accusations galled him, striking too close to his integrity. "Your beauty can tempt any of the gods but I never go back on my word." He offered his hand, but she stepped away, driving thorns of bitterness deep into his vitals at the distance she deliberately placed between them.

He could not reassure her she and Apollysis were safe. His mission remained uppermost in his mind, although, buried in a dark corner, lurked the personal cost he might face—to leave this beguiling woman who had gotten under his skin.

"So, no more discussion is necessary, Diokles." Her chin lifted. "We are here. I will do what you asked of me."

He breathed deeply to quell the anticipation coursing in his body. Always single-minded in battle it grated to admit his control was being severely tested. "Since you are resolved I will go in with you."

He walked back to retrieve his weapons, signaling his peers to follow. His probing gaze never wavered off the narrow path ahead of them. It wound like a coiled serpent around the hill and led to a concealed entrance discovered by his scouts weeks ago.

Matching his pace to Calliope's, every step they took drew his nerves tighter until they hummed like the strings of Apollo's lyre.

"DO NOT ENTER!"

Diokles spun, crouched and raised his shield to protect Calliope. Her swift gasp, her shocked cry of '*Lykos*', drove him to push her behind his body. A quick glance showed his peers already moving to form a phalanx and fight for Calliope's right to enter the shrine. Growling deep in his throat he welcomed the surge of blood he always experienced prior to a battle.

He cast a swift assessing look over the enemy massed below. They might outnumber his men, but Spartans never asked how many they had to fight, only where the enemy were. Strange so many hoplites followed the priest—

With the speed of one of Zeus's thunderbolts understanding flashed into his mind.

Here stood the threat the spy had spoken of. Which meant the priest was behind the building of this secret army like Acastus had hinted. The fool had over-played his hand and betrayed himself.

He searched out the two men he most wanted to meet. Spying Lykos standing, bound in righteous fury, to the rear of the Apollysian troops, bloodlust swept through him like a mighty river.

The priest would be the first to feel his sword.

Muscles coiling, Diokles shifted his gaze to the man guarding Lykos. He would be next.

"Go quickly," he prompted, pushing Calliope toward the entrance. When she grabbed his arm he pulled her further up the hillside, the shield providing cover against a surprise attack.

"Diokles, leave now, let me negotiate with the Apollysians so you may all get out alive."

Her words carried a punch that he swore winded him. "You are not serious!? Would you go back to the man who almost violated you? To the half-life you yourself said you were living? No, Calliope, whatever it reveals to you, wear the coronet."

He stared into her eyes, urging her to go. The words *I love you* floated into his consciousness, breaking free from deep inside his soul.

Stunned, reluctant to utter words that could never be retracted, he started to repeat the exhortation to go, when a voice he had not heard in ten years bellowed over him.

"Diokles, you have walked into a trap. Let her go and prepare to die."

"No, Aeschylus, *you* must prepare to face Charon," Diokles roared, hand crushing the spear he held in a death-grip. "Atropos has cut the cord of your life."

Pain blossomed in his arm where Calliope's fingernails dug deep.

"What has Aeschylus done to make you call death upon him?" she implored. "You do not even know him."

He glared at the man he hated. "I know him. I told you he robbed me of the greatest treasure of my life."

"He is a good man…" she trailed off as his words sunk in. "Are you…are you saying he is Spartan?"

His contemptuous laugh grated out. "You hear, Aeschylus? Calliope says you are a good man." Despite the distance stretching between them, he read fear and shame on the older man's face and speculated on the latter.

Diokles turned to the woman beside him. Watching her stare, white-faced, at him then at Aeschylus, burdened him with guilt, but he owed her the truth. "The priestess was right. He is the man she revealed fled his homeland. He is also the father of Callisto. He has lied to you." Calliope slumped and held his arm even tighter. Her distress lifted his anger to a new level.

In a voice which thundered with the ferocity of a fierce summer storm Diokles taunted the man he vowed revenge on. "You have failed, Aeschylus. Now you will pay the price I swore to exact from your traitorous hide. Light will shine on the truth today."

"No!" the older man raged. "She must not wear the coronet for her own safety."

"Safety?" Diokles snarled. "To return to the *safety* of living in the temple beside the animal who tried to violate her."

"Do not enter the shrine, priestess!"

"What are you afraid she will find, *priest*," he spat the title out. Satisfaction swept through him on hearing the very real panic in both men's voices. "Do you fear she will uncover the nest of vipers planning to provoke a war they cannot win?"

"The high priestess wore the coronet once and almost died," Lykos yelled. "Only I can save her."

Diokles froze. Never in his life did indecision cloud his mind until now. Damn them all, he would not sacrifice Calliope to uncover information, no matter how vital.

"You are not to wear the coronet," he ordered her, each word costing him. "Hide yourself until we defeat these men, then I will take you home."

"No," she stamped her foot, moving further up the path. "My decision, Diokles. I am prepared to risk everything."

"Calliope, if he speaks the truth…."

"Lykos, tell the truth!" Her derisive laugh cut him off. "I am only surprised I did not suspect his motives earlier." Hands firmly planted on hips she thrust her chin forward. "I am going to wear the coronet. Neither you, nor Lykos, nor Aeschylus are going to stop me."

No matter how long he lived he would never forget how she looked in this moment. Color returned to tinge her cheeks, her amber eyes glowed like fire, the glint of determination evident in their depths.

She had never looked more beautiful.

And no time remained to argue further.

Accepting her decision, he stepped back even though his heart feared the consequences awaiting her. "May Apollo guide and protect you."

Her tremulous smile warmed his spirit, then she turned and ran to the entrance, disappearing into the depths of the cave.

Diokles turned an implacable gaze on Lykos. "If she has gone to her death yours will swiftly follow," he roared. So close now. He swept his tongue over his lips, tasting the battle ready to begin. "If you lie, you must go through me to stop her."

"NO! Attack now."

As the priest shouted the order, Diokles gathered himself and took a flying leap to his place in the phalanx, the men seamlessly reforming around him. He brought his shield up, overlapping the man next to him, spear balanced in his right hand, the tip pointed in deadly intent toward the enemy.

"March."

As one, the phalanx advanced. A feral smile curled Diokles's lips as he watched the Apollysians hesitant approach. Few were brave enough to actively seek to engage Spartans in pitched battle.

Then the phalanxes crashed into each other.

Vision tunneling to any attacker engaging him, Diokles heard the drum of his pulse; felt the blood pump in his veins, giving him strength to carve his way through all opposition.

The screams of the mortally wounded were background noise in his awareness. He glared into the eyes of the man in front of him, thrusting with lethal force past the shield the other held.

Making the most of the advantage of higher ground, Diokles felt the give of the enemy hoplites, faltering under the inhuman strength of his peers pushing them back.

Step by dogged step, he closed the gap between himself and the two men standing a safe distance from the fight, who were now shouting at each other.

The brute who called himself a high priest and thought himself a conqueror.

The traitor who had blighted ten years of his life.

Both would pay.

Soon.

CHAPTER TWENTY-FOUR

Apollo! Help me!

Calliope gazed into the stone eyes which looked down on her, unmoving, yet in her heart of hearts, she held an unshakeable belief—that this day, the god she served would hear and grant her prayers.

The sacred coronet rested between his feet. Its radiance drew her gaze to the shimmering sapphire stone, its deep blue lustre casting a luminescent glow over the walls of the cavern. Legend held Apollo himself set the gem within the circlet of gold, endowing it the power of divining truth, of seeing into the future.

A shaft of sunlight burst through the small fissure in the rocky ceiling. She blinked incessantly to diffuse the dazzling light almost blinding her eyes.

Nervous energy ran up and down her spine.

Would she remain sane, even alive, after she wore it?

She did not want to die. She needed to live. To learn the secret of her past. To leave behind the bleakness blighting her life.

Most of all she yearned to know whether she and Diokles stood a chance of a life together.

Diokles, the man she loved, now fighting for his life, for Sparta and her right to seek the truth.

A niggle of disquiet wormed its way into her mind. Calliope clenched her hands—she would not give in to it. Together, she and

Diokles had crossed so many hurdles to come here, that to fail now was unthinkable.

Pushing the malevolent doubts away her eyes fell upon the ceremonial bow, the quiver of arrows beside it, propped against one side of the altar. Her fingers itched to pick them up and join the battle raging outside. She wanted to see justice done but must trust to the gods and Diokles to mete it out.

Her battle was here. Wasting time thinking over consequences was not going to give her the knowledge she craved.

In a dream-like state she glided to the altar.

A deep silence reigned. Calliope heard every whistle of breath she inhaled, every beat of her heart drumming in her ears. She hesitated, feeling cool air flowing out from the depths of the cave to whisper over her skin, lifting the fine hairs on her bare arms. The stillness cloaked her, weighing down her limbs, smothering her senses.

Closing her eyes she reached deep into the calm center of her spirit. In that quiet space she acknowledged the cause of her hesitation—the fear of discovering the unknown Callisto still lived and she would lose Diokles to her.

Calliope half-opened her eyes and drew her shoulders back vowing to fight for his love.

Looking into the face of her god she believed with unwavering faith Apollo would help her to victory.

All her awareness centered on her hands, moving forward slowly, solemnly, while her pulse raced faster than Balios and Xanthos, the immortal horses of Achilles. Concentrating on the spot between her eyebrows, where deep inside her mind saw through divine eyes, she immersed herself into a trance, trembling fingers reaching for the circlet of gold.

"Do not touch it, Calliope."

Her racing heart slammed into her rib cage, propping to a momentary standstill, then skittering into an unsteady rhythm. Calliope spun so quickly she over-balanced, grasping the altar to break her fall, eyes widening in disbelief.

"*Lysandra!* How did you get here!?"

"Yes, it is me," the other woman smirked, coming closer, every swaggering step proclaiming menacing intent. "Lykos does not want you to wear the coronet. I assured him I would do whatever I need to stop you."

"Stop me?" Calliope yelped. The back of her neck prickled uneasily as Lysandra's smirk grew wider. After all the years of knowing Lysandra, a curtain finally lifted, showing her a different woman to the one she thought she knew. A woman holding unshared secrets behind the strange glint in her eyes. The same glint she remembered seeing the day the Spartans invaded.

"Why, what does Lykos stand to gain?" Calliope regarded her warily. "I am prepared to face danger, have been preparing for weeks."

"Lykos does not want you to. That is reason enough." Lysandra laughed, a high-pitched grating screech. "I should have been high priestess in the temple not you! Always you were chosen ahead of me. Lykos will be grateful I stopped you."

Calliope reeled, completely at a loss to understand the vitriol directed toward her. Surely she heard wrong. Like a poison brew dread bubbled in her mind. She wracked her memory for some clue to explain Lysandra's jealousy, something she had said or done to antagonize her.

She found nothing.

"Why are you saying this now? In all these years you never hinted you were dissatisfied." A lump of sadness rose to lodge in her throat. "We shared a room, food, even our secrets of the temple and the rites. What did I ever say or do to make you hate me this much?"

"You entered the temple and ruined all my plans," Lysandra shrieked. "I wanted Lykos to favor me. I desired him, craved to be his lover. Then you arrived and he saw no one except you. I saw how his eyes followed you even if you did not. He would lay with me, or other priestesses, to assuage his passion because you took an oath of purity. Lykos could not touch you without consequences. Did you enjoy driving him mad with lust, Calliope? He only made you high priestess because of his pact with Aeschylus." She paused with a sly look. "And I never shared *every* secret."

Calliope reached out to clutch the cold stone of the altar, intensifying the coldness gripping her heart, a coldness born of the spite she clearly heard in Lysandra's voice. Unable to credit even a fraction of the accusations, shock held her silent, the band of tension circling her chest making her fight for every breath.

Suddenly, boiling anger rose to melt the tension. How dare the woman blame her for something she was innocent of.

"Let us not play games." Grim satisfaction filled her on seeing the cunning smile on Lysandra's face falter. Her voice grew hard. "What secret do you claim to know?" Calliope demanded. "Tell me, or I promise, I will make you tell me in a way you will not enjoy."

The last thing she expected was Lysandra to unsheathe a hidden dagger at her waist. Calliope crouched into a fighting pose when her rival began to stalk her. Impossible to believe Lysandra strove to kill her but one penetrating look showed her how wrong she was. An ugly expression marred Lysandra's face as she sought an opportunity to attack.

Grief, anger, determination all swirled inside her. Calliope tracked Lysandra's every move, her entire focus now on the hand clutching the dagger. Lysandra was a fool to think she could best her.

"Whatever this secret is, I refuse to bargain with you." Her soft measured tones dripped a threat greater than any weapon. She kept pace with Lysandra ready to pounce at the slightest hint of an attack. "I defied Lykos. I held a sword and dueled a Spartan commander. Drop your weapon. Do not force me to hurt you."

"Have you never wondered why Aeschylus adopted you?" Lysandra mocked her. "Why he always treated you as though you were the child of his own flesh?"

Calliope shuddered at the unholy glee in the woman's eyes.

"No, because I know he is a good man." Immediately the words left her mouth, she remembered Diokles's threat to harm Aeschylus. A cold wave of foreboding smashed into her. She rode it and then shook it off. "Your paltry tactics fail to distract me. Move out of my way."

"You do not need to wear the coronet, Calliope," Lysandra gloated. "Aeschylus is your real father only you do not remember."

It cannot be!

"You lie," Calliope managed to whisper. She gritted her teeth to hold back a howl of misery fighting to be set free. She must not succumb to despair. "You lie," she accused in a stronger voice. "I would not trust you to tell the truth anymore."

Heartbreak burned through her very cells, consuming her and everything she held to be true. A myriad of questions battered her mind which throbbed from the onslaught.

Did Lysandra lie or speak the truth?

All the suspicions Diokles had voiced came rushing back to her. Could his assertion be true that she had somehow been robbed of her memories? Did the real reason Lykos and Aeschylus keep her away from the shrine lie in what she had seen, rather than the coronet almost causing her death?

If Aeschylus was indeed her real father why had he not told her?

Caught in a maelstrom of uncertainty, Calliope's thoughts reeled drunkenly from one possibility to another, until she wanted to scream for the storm to stop. A supreme effort of will calmed her mind and ceased the endless wave of questions.

Except one.

It rose out of the foam of the receding wave, filling her perceptions, stunning her with its meaning. One hand clutched the tunic above her heart.

She fixed Lysandra with a baleful stare which prompted the woman to move out of her reach. "You are wise to fear." Calliope heard the chill in her voice. "Leave now. Leave with your life while you can."

"I warn you, Calliope, I am not afraid to use my dagger. The coronet should be mine to wear not yours."

A guttural laugh escaped Calliope's throat. "And I thought you wise. Only the high priestess is permitted to wear the coronet. Are you so ready to risk everything, perhaps even your own life, without knowing the consequences?"

A faint, nebulous voice whispered a suggestion in her head. Her startled gaze flew to the statue behind her. Had she truly heard the voice of Apollo or just the desperation of her own mind?

Yet, the idea could work.

Feigning compliance, Calliope dropped her head. "If you are so determined to wear it, I will stand aside." Moving to the right of the altar, she took care to brace herself against the wall, satisfied the bow stood within easy reach.

Disgust knotted her stomach on seeing the mixture of greed, triumph and pride light up Lysandra's expression. For one brief, tantalizing moment, she toyed with the idea of letting the shallow woman wear the coronet and face the consequences.

The voice of wisdom reasoned the risk would be too great. The coronet's power might be destroyed if worn by anyone other than herself.

Calliope waited, unmoving, every muscle coiled, ready to pounce at the opportune time. Her lip curled watching Lysandra trip in her indecent haste to reach the altar. Calliope took in the tableau—the priestess standing side-on to her, the dagger in her right hand, the fatal mistake of switching it to her left….

Swift as a striking snake Calliope lunged for the bow, seized it, and swung the wooden limb hard across the back of Lysandra's free hand now grasping for the coronet.

The woman's agonized yell of thwarted rage echoed in the confines of the cave.

"Damn you," she shrieked, rushing forward, dagger raised over her head.

Calliope leapt out of striking range and landed flat-footed on the rocky floor. Digging her toes in she swiftly assessed the situation. Lysandra was armed but she remained blind to everything except her own fury. As she pounced, determined to deal a death blow, Calliope feinted, then jabbed the pointed end of the bow into a vulnerable leg. Screeching, Lysandra lost her balance, falling onto the hard floor of the cave.

Flinging the bow aside, Calliope threw herself onto Lysandra, grabbed the wrist of her weapon hand and squeezed hard.

Disregarding the yells almost bursting her eardrums she held on with a strength born of desperation. The betrayal by her so-called friend drove all pity from her heart. The harder Lysandra held onto her knife, the harder Calliope squeezed her wrist, surprised not to hear bones popping.

"Drop the dagger," Calliope growled, her tone of voice surprising even herself. "Drop it. I will show you no mercy. I will bite through your wrist like I bit Lykos when he tried to ravish me. I have too much to lose and everything to gain."

"Spoken like a Spartan woman," Lysandra hissed then spat in her face.

Calliope wrapped her free hand around Lysandra's throat, ignoring the terror widening the woman's eyes.

"Stop!" Lysandra struggled harder. "No!"

The panicked plea failed to sway her. "*That* is one of the answers I need," Calliope yelled angrily. "Am I Spartan or Apollysian or someone else entirely. *Drop the dagger*!"

The hand wrapped around Lysandra's neck started to bleed from deep scratches where the desperate woman clawed it. She shed the blood gladly—in time, the scratches would heal, just like the scars of her mind would heal.

Her impatience mounting, Calliope squeezed tighter. Lysandra's throat muscles worked beneath her palm as she struggled to draw breath. Calliope watched the face below her own turn ashen, stunned and saddened that Lysandra hated her with such passion, she would choose death instead of relinquishing the weapon.

She felt the struggles growing weaker. The hand attempting to remove hers fell away; the other hand, Calliope saw, finally dropped the knife. She picked it up and tossed it into the furthest reaches of the cave.

On a gusty sigh of relief, she pushed herself up, taking care to keep a tight hold on Lysandra. Even though she would obviously stab her without a qualm, Calliope abhorred the thought of killing her rival unless her own life was truly in jeopardy.

Hardening her heart to the sputtering coughs emerging from Lysandra's no-doubt bruised throat, she rolled her over, face to the ground. Digging her knees into the small of the woman's back, Calliope swiftly untied the belt at her waist, using it to bind Lysandra's wrists together. Pulling the knot tight, she spied a plinth on the opposite side of the cavern, solid enough to secure someone to. She jumped to her feet, dragging the dazed Lysandra in her wake and tied the trailing length of the belt around it.

Now.

Now she would learn everything.

On trembling legs Calliope stumbled back to the altar. With proper deference she lifted the coronet using both hands as she had been taught. The thrum in her fingertips matched the power throbbing in the blue depths of the sapphire.

A power she would soon harness.

A breath, a heartbeat, she waited; prayed to Apollo for guidance and protection.

She lowered the coronet around her forehead, the cool gem settling over her hot brow. Kneeling, Calliope placed her hands on the feet of the statue and closed her eyes.

Swirls of light burst behind her eyelids. She could not see the sapphire glowing with heavenly light, only feel the pulsating warmth against her skin. She cried out, clinging to the feet of her god—a safe anchor in the kaleidoscope of colors threatening to drown her inner vision.

Fire licked through her hands, flowed up her arms, moving gradually through her body, until it swelled into a mighty inferno to sweep rebirth into her heart and mind and soul.

Calliope flung her head back as her spirit left her body on an upsurge of rapture. She flew, light as air, hands reaching out to touch Apollo's chariot, the chariot of the sun. Lost in timeless transcendence she pressed them to one fiery wheel.

Unearthly energies seared away the cold fingers of forgetfulness. Her body jerked and shuddered. In her mind's eye she saw the grey mist, her grim companion of many years, spiral from her head and dissolve into the sky like smoke disappearing on the wind.

Trapped memories hidden by the mist flew out of their imprisonment.

In front of the abandoned house she saw on her arrival in Sparta, a violet-crowned girl struggled against the man holding her, screaming to the youth to save her from being dragged away. She recognized the youth now; saw the torment and anger in his face, the combined efforts of three men needed to hold him back. The girl's terror swept through her heart to become her own. She embraced the terror, gave it succor, then released it to evaporate into the bright heavens above.

She saw the same girl lifting an iris to the youth's lips. He took the flower, kissed it, then kissed her palm. She remembered the softness, the firmness, of his lips. The sweet certainty she was loved.

From an earlier time, a familiar man emerged, smiling at her with love and pride reflected in his eyes. She ran to him, her love just as strong. A fair-haired older woman dragging a younger version of the girl off the horse she rode at the boy's home. This woman struck a discordant note, but its jarring reverberation was soon eclipsed by the jubilation filling her.

More memories of her life rushed back. They jostled for prominence, until one needing the most healing, claimed victory over the others. It helped her understand the nightmare which haunted her nights all these years.

She gasped, recognizing the faces of the men who had circled her. Relived the moment icy fingers froze her mind when she drank from the accursed bronze cup.

Saw the coronet ripped off her head by Lykos when he realized her memory returned, saw herself bound and held while the same chill water was forced down her throat, robbing her of every sense of self a second time.

Hot tears spilled out over her face, warming the cold skin even as the sun's warmth rekindled light and life in her spirit, melting the horror of what she witnessed into oblivion, never to return.

Gradually the fiery warmth mellowed. Now she understood her ability to do things she never dreamed possible. Understood the reason she experienced desolation on the one occasion she wore it.

Understood why she secretly believed her memory could be restored.

Her joy knew no bounds. She longed to dance and shout her exultation to the world. Glorious hope for the future overcame the sadness of her loss.

In the midst of her rapture Apollo turned his radiant face toward her. She lifted her head, listening, certain something of great importance would be divulged to her.

Inside her head the god's words echoed.

A keening wail shattered her spirit all over again. The utter, futile, despair that fed it broke her connection with the divine.

Callisto collapsed on the ground, hennaed hair trailing over her face, fists beating uselessly upon the hard stone.

CHAPTER TWENTY-FIVE

So close.

Close enough to catch the scent of their fear.

Diokles disregarded the sweat rolling into his eyes. To wipe it away, to blink, was to invite the slash of an enemy weapon into an exposed limb or neck. He bellowed over the clash of weapons, urging his peers on, feeling air rattling in his lungs. They moved in unison, thrusting spears with deadly accuracy between their heavy bronze-covered shields, smashing through the opposing phalanx.

Almost there.

Cold merciless intent drove him painstakingly closer to the two men who would not escape punishment once he reached them.

Muttering a prayer to Ares he leaned all his strength into the shield and pushed. Felt the ranks of men behind him press forward, as though endowed with superhuman power, driving him into the Apollysian lines.

He broke through, enemies falling at his feet like saplings in a mighty wind.

"Engage at will," he roared.

Two attackers rushed to challenge him. Lunging his spear at one, he bashed the other with his shield, swiftly dispatching both.

The path to his chosen targets cleared.

In the blink of an eye the scene changed.

He saw an enemy hoplite disengage from the main battle. Saw Aeschylus about to run the priest through with a xiphos. Saw the hoplite fell Aeschylus with a blow to the back of the head and release Lykos.

Diokles let out a loud curse. No-one but he would deal out justice to the traitor.

A whisper of motion warned him seconds before he instinctively crouched and pivoted in time to throw off another attacker as if the man was no more than a fly.

He turned to see Lykos gape at him, horror freezing the priest's expression as Diokles strode toward him, blood-stained spear held at the ready. He met the priest's maddened glare with a pitiless one of his own; welcomed the surge of blood to his head when the coward fled. He loped after him, poised to strike a fatal blow to anyone foolish enough to stand in his way.

One thought reigned uppermost in his mind—*kill Lykos*.

Diokles kept his pace steady. The longer he ran, the easier he breathed, stamina cultivated through years of distance running. His sandaled feet, immune to discomfort, relished the challenge of the stony ground beneath them. Unlike the priest ahead, who slipped and stumbled, seeking the easiest path.

Diokles snorted in disgust at this display of weakness.

A grassy field loomed ahead to the right. He gauged Lykos would get there first and attempt to sprint toward the cover of trees beyond. Proving him right, Lykos raced over the level ground the moment he reached it, cloak streaming out behind him, betraying his desperation to escape.

Time to end the chase. Time to stand and fight. No mercy softened his heart as he increased his own speed, moved sideways to angle his attack, then threw the heavy weapon in Lykos's direction.

The spear struck true. A cold, triumphant smile curved Diokles's mouth, seeing the flapping cloak pierced, just as he intended, the bronze point imbedding itself in the ground, accompanied by Lykos's cry of surprised terror as he fell.

Digging into his reserves of energy, he sprinted the last few paces to the fallen man, who tugged wildly at his cloak. Fury consumed Diokles when Lykos, giving up on the cloak, attempted to pull the spear out of the ground.

How dare the priest think to use his own weapon against him.

Lykos still tugged frantically when Diokles reached him. Like a cat toying with a mouse, he unstrapped his shield without haste, drew a fist back and dealt the priest a powerful blow to the jaw, uncaring how Lykos's head snapped back; uncaring how the crack of the man's shattered teeth sounded in his ears. He pulled the spear free and tossed it out of reach.

Grabbing a handful of tunic he dragged the accursed man to his feet.

"You are not worthy to wield a Spartan weapon," Diokles growled and pulled Lykos closer until the hateful features loomed a hand-span from his own. "You have failed. She has already learnt the truth."

The sneer growing on the priest's loathsome face fired his blood to boiling point.

"The truth," Lykos laughed gratingly, spitting blood to the ground. "The truth will not help her or you. You think you have won. You are wrong. Victory is mine."

Chest heaving, Diokles glared at him, aware of an evil undercurrent. A swirling unease bubbled to the surface. The priest would be skilled in the art of deception. He would need the wisdom of Athena to cut a swathe through every lying utterance.

"Your head is addled by lust," Diokles hissed, unsheathing his xiphos. "Whatever soul remains in you must beg the ferryman to take you without payment."

He drew his hand back to deliver the killing blow.

"The high priestess is Aeschylus's daughter who you seek."

"You lie, priest."

"No! I tell you it is her!"

Blind-sided, Diokles failed to see the blazing expectation in Lykos's eyes. A roaring, rushing wind filled his head which threatened to burst through the heavy bronze helmet.

Glorious hope expanded his heart….

Then without warning he sank to his knees, felled by the vice encircling his chest, squeezing life and hope out of him. Black spots danced in front of his eyes. Fighting certain death, he dragged air into his lungs, feeling the oxygen clear his brain.

The words of Athena's priestess in Sparta echoed in his mind—give up the search. The priest must be lying to save his miserable life.

The belief grew, snuffing out the short-lived flame of hope.

The vice around his heart eased.

His vision cleared to find the point of his own spear against his throat.

"How satisfying to take my revenge this way," Lykos jeered. "A Spartiate at my mercy. You will die kneeling at my feet. I begin to exact my revenge from this moment. A life for a life!"

As the priest's voice rose to a scream, Diokles found himself growing calmer, his mind rapidly considering the options available to him. A mad light gleamed in Lykos's eyes. In this state of mind he was dangerously unpredictable, however, consumed in his own rage, the priest was incapable of clear-headed thinking.

"You kill me and then what?" Diokles taunted him. "Do you think Calliope will fall into your arms if I am dead?" He needed to keep Lykos talking, extract information from him, discover why the lunatic hated him.

Lykos's eyes bulged in their sockets. "She will be mine regardless of what she wants," he raged. "Your death marks the first of many. Your *peers*," his lip curled over the word, "will be hunted down the same way my helot parents were hunted and killed. I will not rest until my army, the army I assembled and command, has left your precious polis a wasteland."

"Now I know you are mad." Diokles expected to feel shocked, instead, a hard-bitten resoluteness poured into his spirit. Here, in this field, he conquered failure and completed the mission entrusted to him, discovering who, and what, the threat comprised. He would conquer this madman, too, then return to deal with Aeschylus in the same way.

Energy coiled inside him, building, ready to spring, left arm tensing, ready to grab the spear. Diokles clamped down on a crazed impulse to laugh in the priest's face. Blind to everything but his thirst for revenge, Lykos had overlooked the xiphos still clutched in his right hand.

An evil cackle broke the silence. Then Lykos spoke in a low, triumphant voice. "Go home on your shield, Spartan."

Preternatural reflexes bent Diokles backwards as Lykos moved to drive the bronze tip deep into his throat. He felt the graze on his skin, heard a roar of fury leave his mouth. His left hand clamped around the cornel wood shaft and shoved it aside.

Muscles flexed and burned with the effort, his innate strength overcoming the priest, even though Lykos held the advantage of being upright on his feet, able to lean his full weight into the effort to kill him.

Teeth bared, mind fixated on defeating Lykos, Diokles pushed the spear further from his neck, deaf to the priest's disbelieving yells, raising himself up by degrees. When Lykos started to lash out at his kneecaps, trying to cripple him, he roared again, finding a fierce potency in the sound, giving him the impetus to stab the xiphos deep into the priest's leg.

Feeling Lykos's grip slacken on the shaft, Diokles sprung to his feet, ripping his spear from the priest's hands as Lykos, cursing and howling, tried to staunch the flow of blood.

Throwing the spear aside a second time, Diokles grabbed Lykos by the throat and hauled the priest to his feet. He stared hard into the pleading beady eyes and whispered in a dangerous voice, "Prepare to enter the Underworld."

"Have mercy," Lykos cried, clutching Diokles's wrist with both hands. "Have—"

"Mercy!" His rough laugh cut the air. "The same mercy you showed Calliope when you almost violated her. Pray to Hades to show you mercy. I have none."

Burying his xiphos into the hateful presence, Diokles drove it in to the hilt.

He held onto Lykos through his death throes. In the moments before life receded from Lykos's eyes, Diokles read malicious triumph in them.

"Remember this," Lykos rasped. "You will never possess her. My death guarantees…."

Cold dread wormed its way into Diokles's heart as he released the limp body. Lykos remained a liar to the end. He convinced himself the priest's threat meant nothing except the last ramblings of an evil mind.

Pulling his xiphos free, Diokles bent to wipe it clean on the grass. He wanted no remnants of Lykos to taint his weapon in any way. Sparing no backward glance at the dead man, he sheathed it, retrieved spear and shield, and ran to re-join the battle.

Imperative he return quickly.

Return to punish a traitor to Sparta in the way he deserved to be punished.

Return to convince a certain strong-willed priestess that her future lay with him.

CHAPTER TWENTY-SIX

Slivers of light flickered in his vision.

Aeschylus squeezed his eyes shut against the glare. He blinked and groaned, the sound convincing him he was still alive.

He pushed himself onto his elbows, wincing as pain shot through the throbbing bruise on the side of his head. Gingerly pressing his fingers to the spot, relief swamped him on finding no blood. Heaving his protesting body upright he cursed Lykos and the hoplite who'd freed the priest.

Urgency beat at him. He needed to find his daughter before more harm came to her.

Still groggy from the blow seconds passed before the sounds of battle registered in his dazed mind. Aeschylus took in the scene, mouth dropping open, appalled by the number of bodies on the ground. Bodies of men loyal to him and the city that had sheltered him. He would not allow any more to die because of Lykos's demented ambitions in a fight they could not win.

Summoning strength honed from his own days in the agoge, he bellowed, "Apollysians, drop your weapons and surrender!"

Every man obeyed instantly. Switching to his native Lakonian Doric, he shouted to his former peers. "Spartans, the prisoners claim sanctuary in the name of Apollo." The effort to speak loudly left him dizzy.

Relief sagged his shoulders when they stopped fighting, albeit their blood-stained weapons held ready to attack. They did not glance his way, but he sensed their surprise at hearing him speak their dialect, so different from most of Hellas.

He knew he could still die but at least further bloodshed halted for the moment.

The feet of a warrior appeared before his eyes, over-shadowing where he sat, blocking his view.

He knew who stood there.

Aeschylus raised his head wincing as pain shot through it. Staring at the transverse crest on top of the bronze helmet, he glanced down to meet unfathomable eyes and the pitiless face of impending death.

"I know you intend to kill me, Diokles. It is no more than I deserve." Aeschylus coughed, realization striking him that the Spartans only stopped fighting because of their commander's return. "I call on Zeus to whom you were dedicated to stay your hand until I speak to Callisto and yourself."

"You are right, death awaits you, nothing will prevent it," Diokles confirmed roughly. "You robbed me of the woman I intended to marry. I swore an oath to find her, searched over ten years whenever I could, only to discover I was too late. Callisto is dead."

The hard menace in his voice carried enough threat to terrify an entire army.

Aeschylus paled. "No, you are wrong! Callisto is here, alive. Please, you must believe me." The merciless unyielding light in the younger man's eyes chilled him to the bone.

"You lie, just as your priest, now dead, lied. The gods do not lie. You will join your dead daughter soon."

Aeschylus threw a despairing look toward the hill. Where was Callisto? Somehow he must convince Diokles she was indeed alive. Enough misery had been suffered. He possessed the power to prevent its continuance. "Diokles, I ask nothing of you except to let me live long enough to explain."

"Silence! You dare mock me. Did you listen when you dragged your daughter away? No. Yet you expect me to listen to you now."

Tears stung the back of his eyes. Aeschylus acknowledged them, refusing to fall prey to their weakness. He was Spartan. A Spartan did not fear death. He stared it defiantly in the face.

No, the tears sprung from a well of grief deep enough for him to drown in. Grief, because he would not have the chance to beg forgiveness from his daughter. Grief, because she and the man she had always loved would be separated forever. Grief, because neither would learn the secret he carried in his heart.

He did not cower as Diokles drew his weapon. He would die, brave and resolute, proud of his heritage, proud of being a Spartan.

Through narrowing vision he saw the xiphos coming toward him.

Waited for the blow that would send his soul to eternal damnation.

Waited for a blow that never came.

A clang against the xiphos jerked Aeschylus out of his spiral of grief. An arrow bounced and skittered away. He saw Diokles wheel to face this new threat. Another arrow bored into the ground between them quivering with intimidating intent.

Aeschylus spun his head in the direction the arrow had arrived from.

This time a lone tear escaped.

His daughter walked slowly down the hill.

Dread, like the beating wings of the Furies, battered Diokles.

Something was wrong.

The footfalls of the woman approaching him dragged heavily as though a great burden beat her every step deeper into the earth.

Soon she was close enough for him to see her face. Whiter than the snow which crowned the sacred heights of Olympus where the gods dwelt. No light showed in her staring eyes.

A lump of tension fomented in his stomach. "Calliope?"

She flinched at her name. The bleak look she gave him constricted his throat, strangling further words. Despite the bow in her hand, the quiver of arrows slung behind her back, she looked utterly defeated.

"I have seen and learned the truth, Diokles. Lykos has assembled a secret army not far from Apollysis. His plan was to conquer Lakonia as some form of revenge." She glanced at Aeschylus who shook his head imploringly. "You are released from your oath. The woman you sought is dead."

This must be what the men who died between the clashing rocks of the Bosphorus experienced. Every bone throbbing in pain; the breath stolen from their lungs in an instant. He swung away, teeth bared, restraining his temper with difficulty. He wanted to curse everyone—the gods, Aeschylus, his father, himself.

All the wasted years. Hoping. Searching.

For what?

Rage impeled him to where his men were holding the prisoners. Shouting orders gave him some solace but failed to calm the maelstrom of emotions whirling inside his heart. His quest to fulfil his oath snatched out of his hands by cruel fate. The reality grated over already frayed nerves.

He needed to think. Plan his next move.

Every so often he glanced back. Seeing her and Aeschylus arguing creased his face into a frown as he covertly studied them. Distress riddled her features. He wanted to snatch her away. Keep her safe from everything in the world which could hurt her.

Aeschylus reached out as though begging her to do something. Diokles's gaze sharpened when she doubled over, her long hair falling over her face, fingers thrusting through it.

His scalp tightened in sympathy with her agony.

Diokles drew a shuddering breath. The words he had hesitated to say rose like a phoenix buried beneath its own ashes. There on the field of battle he understood himself. He had come to love her. Instinct whispered she would be the woman to bear his children. Strong sons and daughters for Sparta.

True, she was not Spartan, but he would find a way to have her accepted as his wife.

Calliope and Aeschylus still argued. Whatever caused the discord between them he needed to know the reason. The desire to understand grew more intense when both clamped their mouths shut as he re-joined them.

"There is a problem." It was a statement demanding answers.

"No." She kept her eyes averted. "I told Aeschylus of the priestess Lykos sent to stop me. She is bound within the cavern. Someone must retrieve her."

Diokles drew his head back. The words were flat as though she remarked on the weather.

He reached out to her. "Come with me."

"No!" She twisted her hands. "I mean, I must return to my city."

"We will return together. There is much I need to say to you. Without witnesses." He cast a meaningful glance to where Aeschylus was rising unsteadily to his feet.

She dropped the bow to plant both hands on her hips. "Again you order me. I have done what you asked of me. I wore the coronet, divined the tru—," she stumbled over the word then rallied to finish. "Divined the truth, told you what you wanted to know. I ask you to keep your part of the bargain to remove your warriors from my home."

He should be angry. He really should. Somehow her demands only served to arouse his admiration. She had woven a spell over his senses which until today he resisted acknowledging.

"We need to speak." He took her hand, intending to lead her somewhere private. Confusion stirred when she refused to move.

"There is nothing to talk about." Her voice rose. "Nothing, Diokles, can't you understand."

He shook her lightly to keep the hysteria he heard in her voice at bay. An unforgiving jerk of his head signaled Aeschylus to leave. The older man hesitated, then hurried away from the savage look Diokles impaled him with.

"Tell me what is wrong." He brushed her hair back, tucking the silky length behind one ear. "What did you learn that stole the light from your eyes?"

"I told you already what was revealed to me. No matter how much you insist, there is nothing more to be said."

Only hard-earned control helped him hold onto his patience. She kept something back. He heard it in her constrained voice, thick with tears. "What are you not telling me? Whatever has upset you let me help you bear it."

"No-one can help me," she whispered. "Especially you. Go! Go, take your army. Return to Sparta a hero. You will soon forget me."

"Forget you? Impossible to do when I love you?"

Her face went from white to grey faster than storm clouds brewing over the mountains of Atlas.

"No, you do not." She sucked in a sobbing breath. "Do not torture me with false promises. I will return to my duties as high priestess. You will return to Sparta and marry a Spartan woman to carry on your family line. It cannot be me."

Her words stabbed deep to kindle a fiery anger. He controled it. To let it loose meant failure when his future rested on convincing her to return. Marrying someone he did not love, even a little, would just perpetuate the disaster of his parent's union.

It killed him to see the dullness of her eyes; eyes which glowed like jewels when he had kissed her. He searched for the words to make her understand, to rekindle the fire of life inside her.

"There is something between us," he insisted, taking hold of her shoulders, resting his strong hands lightly on them. Memories rose of those shoulders laid bare to his hungry eyes. He swallowed, determined to ignore the signals from his body. "I saw you looking at me when you thought I was unaware. I resisted you because of my oath and yours. Released by the gods I am free to ask you to come back to Sparta with me."

"You say you love me but how can I be sure. Deep in my soul I know I will forever question whether it is indeed me you love or the memory of a woman you perhaps see in me."

"You did not worry who I thought you were that day by the river." He ignored the sudden flush to her cheeks, wanting to draw out the fighting spirit she possessed. "You welcomed my touch, my caresses, you gave—"

"Stop, stop, stop," she cried, clapping her hands over her ears. "We had an agreement, Diokles. I kept my side of the bargain. You are honor-bound to keep yours."

He ground his teeth at his inability to break through her stubborn resistance. "I will honor what I promised you. If you happen to remember what we shared, I will wait in Apollysis, but only until we crush Lykos's army."

"Do not wait."

He strained to hear the words. An emotion he could not define crushed his soul. "Since you cannot bear the sight of me two of my men will stay to escort you back when you are ready. I return now with the prisoners, including Aeschylus."

She clutched his arm. "No. Leave Aeschylus to me. I must speak to him," she implored. "Please. I swear by Apollo and Zeus he will return with me to Apollysis. We have nowhere else to go."

Diokles stared at the soft hand clutching his bicep. A muscle worked in his jaw. It strained him to fight off the impulse to sweep her into his arms and carry her off to where she belonged.

With him.

Her plea went against his better judgment, yet he was unable to deny her. "Speak to the traitor if it is so important to you. Two horses will be left for your return."

He shrugged out of her hold and left to re-join his peers.

Callisto pressed her lips together until they turned numb.

She could not beg him to come back. To take her in his arms and give the comfort she sought.

Could not ask him to declare his love again.

She knew he loved her.

She could never tell him how she knew.

Following his every move she committed to memory his proud bearing, his strong, sculpted warrior's body. These memories she would keep in her heart to ease the burden of the lonely days stretching out ahead of her.

This would be the last time she saw him.

There was no choice.

She had to send him away.

His life was worth more than her happiness.

Through burning eyes she saw her father released, saw him try to say something to Diokles, who turned his back on the older man and walked away. Her father's shoulders slumped in defeat.

She knew his pain. Her own body sagged under the weight of the same crushing anguish.

Diokles did not look in her direction again. Callisto saw servants leading horses to their riders, the prisoners, on foot, corraled between them. True to his word two horses were tied to a tree. Then the entire mass of humans and beasts began to depart.

She sank to her knees, wrapping her arms around her middle, rocking backwards and forwards. If he had tied her between his black stallions and sent them galloping in opposite directions, the pain of being physically torn apart would have been easier to bear.

A veil of tears obscured her vision. She dashed them aside with the back of her hand vicariously needing to witness Diokles leave. She spied Lysandra among the prisoners before the entire cohort rapidly dwindled to specks in the distance.

Her father was hurrying to her. She could just make out the confused distress wreathing his face.

Callisto reached out a trembling hand in the direction the Spartans had left.

"Diokles, I love you."

CHAPTER TWENTY-SEVEN

He has gone.

The single thought ran over and over in Callisto's tortured mind, beating at her like Hephaestus beat at an anvil with his hammer, taunting her, making her head pound.

She wanted to roll over and die.

Warm hands rested on her shoulders. Fear closed her throat. Readying herself to throw them off she recalled her last words to Diokles begging him to free Aeschylus.

She clutched those hands. Hands, which in her childhood always carried a solution to any problem she faced.

"My child, why did you lie and send Diokles away? Weeping will not bring him back."

Her father's strained voice echoed the pain in her heart.

"I am not weeping," she averred, though she craved to. It might provide some salve to her soul to cry out her misery, but she would not do so. Not now she possessed the truth—she was indeed a Spartan woman. A Spartan woman did not weep or admit defeat.

A Spartan woman battled her way to victory no matter what obstacles stood in her way.

Lifting her head she stared at Aeschylus through a curtain of tangled hair. Callisto wanted to wipe away the deep lines etched on his face and the torment dulling his eyes. He appeared to have aged ten years since she last saw him.

It would take much more than a simple caress to unburden the emotion which oppressed him.

Another part of her longed to lash out. To scream questions to her father. To demand why he saw fit to practice a soul-destroying deception over so many years. Callisto composed herself but was unable to prevent the utterance of one crucial word.

"Why?"

The simple question carried the full force of her pain.

The grimace contorting her father's features twisted her insides. What could he say that she wanted to hear? Then a daughter's affection, long suppressed, insisted her father remained the same man who always showered her with the love her mother never had.

She took pity on him and gave him time to collect himself. "Why did you tell me I was adopted? During the rapture I saw myself drinking out of a bronze cup. You and Lykos were there. The liquid looked like water but so much colder than the coldest streams on the earth. After I drank, I lost my memory of you, our home, everything."

He seemed to shrink into himself. Callisto's heart skipped a beat at the sight of his face—pinched, pale and full of pain. So many wasted years. So much of her life snatched away.

Fury ebbed and flowed within her like the tidal forces of the sea, eventually settling to lap at the edges of her consciousness. Raging at her father would not return the lost years or heal her heart.

"I cannot undo what has been done." Aeschylus's voice broke. "I can only hope you will understand and try to forgive me."

Callisto's eyebrows rose along with her curiosity. His shoulders bowed down like an old, old man, so different to the image she held of a tall proud man, a spring in his step, and twinkling eyes. Eyes, which even as a child, she remembered thinking masked a hidden sadness.

She pressed light fingers on his arm when he hesitated.

"It is too late for regrets," she kept her voice soft, but resolute. "I need to understand so I can begin to heal the wounds of the past."

And with sudden clarity she recognized he had not completely abandoned her. He'd watched over her, ensuring Lykos never over-stepped the boundary she placed around herself.

Callisto allowed him to help her up. A large rock loomed out of the ground to their left, worn smooth and flat over time, large enough to seat them both. She traced a weary path to it where she collapsed. Her entire being felt listless, her energy drained by the last few hours. How she wished sleep would embrace her for days then wake her up to a different reality where all her trials were merely a bad dream—the revelation from Apollo; Lykos's attack on her; Diokles's abrupt departure.

How she managed to stay lucid bore testimony to her heritage.

Making room for Aeschylus, she bit her lip when he dropped heavily to sit by her side, a bone-weary sigh escaping him. Regret? Shame? She wanted to hurry his explanation, to learn everything immediately.

Digging deep for patience she summoned a small smile of encouragement and squeezed his hand.

"I loved a woman before your mother became my wife," he began without preamble. "We agreed to marry, but her father intervened, having already planned to wed her to the son of an ephor, whose family were distantly related to one of the kings. I returned from a campaign to find her already married to…."

Callisto sat unmoving, enthralled by this unveiling of family history. It all made sense to her now. The constant arguments between her parents. Her mother's coldness toward herself because she was a mirror-image of her father.

"Who did this woman marry?" Her voice rang sharper than intended because a frisson of impending doom tingled through her.

She fidgeted, the silence stretching out, watched his mouth open and close, as though he longed to keep the words buried, never to be heard by anyone.

"Diokles's father."

Callisto gave profound thanks to the gods she was sitting down.

Every dark emotion whirled, threatening to overpower her. A painful gasp penetrated her dazed mind. She looked down to find herself squeezing her father's hand so tightly his fingertips were turning white. Easing her grip she stared at a distant rocky outcrop.

Her early years came marching out of distant memories. She again heard the bitter barbs her parents hurled at each other. Her heart moved in her chest remembering the visits to Diokles's mother. Ianthe had been a beautiful, haunting, dark-haired woman, who had taken Callisto under her wing. She pressed a fist to her mouth to stop a cry of wretchedness. Ianthe had loved violets. She had learned to love the scented blooms alongside her.

"Where is my mother?"

"She refused to leave with us," Aeschylus answered flatly. "Akantha knew I did not love her. The marriage was arranged by her father, also an ephor at the time, possibly in collusion with Diokles's grandfather. Following your birth you were given over to servants to be cared for. She stayed on in our home after we fled."

Callisto's anger shifted to her mother.

"She is no longer there. The house is abandoned. Diokles drove past there on the way to his home but refused to say who the estate belonged to." She looked back at Aeschylus. "Did she never try to find out what happened to me?"

"No," he gave her an apologetic glance. "I was so proud when you became high priestess, certain I had secured your safety. I sent a letter to Akantha via a trusted servant. He came back without ever seeing her." He rubbed a hand over his face. "Perhaps she had already left."

Callisto ground her teeth at the mention of her former rank.

"What pact did you make with Lykos? Lysandra told me that was the sole reason I became the high priestess. Did you never suspect the spineless fool wanted me in his bed?"

Aeschylus hung his head. "Not immediately." He gave a jerky sigh. "As time passed, his passion became obvious in the way he ogled you, tried to touch you at every opportunity. I noticed and thereafter spent more time in the temple to keep watch. I warned him that if he brushed aside the vow you made the gods would punish him."

Callisto scowled as more understanding dawned. "I took that vow to thwart Lykos, but I now believe a greater reason existed. Some place deep within me, the memory of Diokles lived, untouched by whatever I drank, even if I was unaware of it."

Heart thudding, skin tightening on her face, she came to the moment which could no longer be put off.

"How did I lose my memory?"

Guilt, shame and fear chased each other across her father's face. For a moment she was afraid of what the answer might reveal. A flush of heat suffused her body and left her limbs feeling weightless. Aeschylus looked away, whispering so quietly she needed to bend her head closer to hear him.

"I sought counsel at Athena's temple. The priestess advised to take you to safety in Achaea and make you forget your life in Sparta." He twisted his hands. "When we arrived in Apollysis I asked for assistance at Apollo's temple. Lykos assured me the—potion he called it—would ensure you forgot where you came from but not harm you in any other way. Just as the battle started here he goaded me with the truth. The 'potion' was water from the Lethe."

Callisto leapt to her feet as though the rock beneath her burst into flames.

"*The Lethe!*" She traced crazed circles over the ground. Wrapping her arms around herself she held on tightly, fearing she might still be spirited away to meet Hades. "*What were you thinking of*? Water from the river of forgetfulness! I could have lost all sense of myself forever! How could you have allowed the priests to do that to me? It is meant for the souls of the dead so they never recall their earthly life. I could have—"

"I did not know at the time," Aeschylus managed to gulp past the tears pouring down his face. "You were always a brave child, beautiful, strong and reckless. I knew Diokles, trained him in the agoge, understood why he loved you, even though you were not yet fifteen and he five years older. His father was an influential but violent man who discovered why Ianthe did not care for him in the way he believed she should. I feared for you if his son turned out to be violent like him. Discovering you and Diokles pledged to marry his father came to see me. He threatened to see you dead rather than agree to let you marry his son."

"Was my banishment some sort of revenge?" she accused mindlessly, reeling at the revelation of how close she had been to death. "Did you take me away from everything I knew as punishment on Diokles for the sins of his father? Or because if you could not have happiness then neither could I?"

Her father's mouth dropped open, his face turning whiter than the snow which crowned Taygetos in winter.

"No," he choked out. "I only ever thought of your safety."

Remorse and her own guilt crashed into her.

Shamefaced, Callisto hung her head, wishing uselessly she could recall the senseless words born out of shock. Her father had never failed to show his love and care during their time in Apollysis. And he had not trusted Lykos, evidenced when he pursued him to save her from the priest's demented plans.

"I am so sorry." Her voice trembled. Unsurprising given the rioting emotions swamping her: a desire to hurt her father; to embrace him; to leave him; to give thanks to Apollo for her salvation. She drew in three breaths and strove for calm. "I need to know the pact you made."

"Lykos requested my support to build a stronger force to protect Apollysis. He was very careful to hide he planned to style himself king in order to invade Sparta. I never suspected anything." He rubbed a hand over his neck. "I agreed on condition he make you high priestess, giving you rank, status and protection. I prayed hard your spirit would find satisfaction in your new life."

He turned a pain-wracked face to her. "Oh, my Callisto, can you ever forgive me?"

Callisto gazed into the brilliant blue of the sky unmarred by clouds. One cloud still darkened her horizon, though. Lykos. Her hands itched to wrap around his neck. She lay all blame at his feet. His miserable hide should be—

"I do not remember seeing Lykos among the prisoners," she cried. "He must be found."

"He is dead. Diokles killed him."

"I am cursed by the gods," Callisto wailed, turning wild-eyed to meet the stunned look on her father's face. "I found myself and lost Diokles. You asked why I lied to him. Lykos has damned him so that if he recognizes me he will die."

Shock and a stunned amazement gripped her on seeing her father react to her words. In Apollysis he exuded civilized control. Before her eyes sat a man tearing at his hair and cursing the priest he once aided.

"I should have killed him myself long ago," he raged. "He must have called down the curse after Diokles took you away. There was no other reason for Lykos to do it. How do you know this?"

"Apollo spoke to me during the rapture. He told me of the curse. I could not bear to see Diokles dead at my feet."

Her heart, along with every hope, had died in the cave.

"It is all my fault," Aeschylus sobbed. "I ought to have suspected Lykos's ambitions. The people of Apollysis loathed his arrogance. Some whispered mutinously. The men fighting here today wanted to return to liberate the city. He forced them to accompany him as he grew ever more maddened in his search for you. After Lykos pronounced me a prisoner, their assistance enabled me to escape and save you at Amyklai. My spies told me he was buying loyalty from any man who agreed to follow his dictates. Seeing Lykos's instability during the journey here, many secretly pledged allegiance to me."

"How did he obtain the Lethe water?" Callisto pressed. "That should be impossible."

Aeschylus groaned. "He never said. Lykos would not have qualms about striking some terrible agreement and not revealing the secret to anyone."

Sorrow poured into her heart. Sorrow at losing Diokles, sorrow for what both she and her father had endured in their different ways. Hot tears welled to burn her eyes. They spilled out over her cheeks in a warm flood. This time she welcomed them, needed to taste every drop of salty moisture, cry the pain out of her heart, cleanse and make peace with herself.

Callisto stared at her father, the man who loved his daughter so deeply he protected and betrayed her in equal measure. Her watery gaze shifted in the direction the Spartans had left. She'd sent Diokles away with anger in his heart. Anger she herself conjured in him.

Did he know about his mother and her father? There was so much she needed to ask him, too; so many things she needed to tell him.

She had loved him before their fathers destroyed their lives. Unaware of his real identity she'd learned to love him all over again.

Only to discover she could never have him. Lykos's death made certain of that. The curse could not be broken without him.

Torn, she watched Aeschylus rocking back and forth, face covered, tears leaking past his fingers. She had always loved her father better than her mother. He was the one she confided in, asked for advice, who comforted her when she needed comforting.

Now it was her turn to comfort him.

Callisto went to him and wrapped her arms around his shaking body. Wordlessly she pressed her cheek against his bent head, listening to their muffled sobs merge together.

In the quiet solitude near the sacred cave she found some lightness restored to her soul. The serenity of the place poured balm on the open wound of hurt and betrayal. After so many weeks of uncertainty, Callisto felt clarity and peace pour into her, clearing her mind of turmoil, enabling her to think.

She had no sense of how long they sat there. Startled to see the sun low on the horizon, she tapped Aeschylus's shoulder. "We need to leave." He lifted red-rimmed eyes. Hers must not look much better she thought with a sad smile. "There is a dwelling not far from here where we can shelter overnight. Then we ride to Apollysis to ensure the city is freed. You must not tell Diokles who I am. Lie. Give him any excuse, any reason, but do not let me have the grief of seeing him die…father?"

He was looking at her with a strange light in his eyes.

"Apollo gave you knowledge of the curse," Aeschylus said in a steadier voice. "What if his father reveals how to break it?" He sat up. "We detour to Olympia first to pray for Zeus's mercy. I cannot bear to see you suffer more than you already have."

Callisto nursed a cautious hope. She yearned to believe it possible, but the gods often toyed with human lives. On the other hand, they showed favor if it pleased them. She thought back over her life as a priestess—the privations she willingly accepted and the selfless dedication to her duty.

Surely she had earned the right to ask the king of the gods to grant her this one boon.

"If we hurry we can reach both Olympia and Apollysis within a few days," Callisto agreed, calculating that with a good pace they could manage it. "Diokles will not wait long."

"Can you ever forgive me?" Aeschylus asked in a broken voice. "I failed my city, my honor, and most of all, you, my daughter.

Regardless of the reason, I ran. A Spartan does not run away in fear."

Her mouth stretched into a wan smile. "I can barely reconcile myself to anything. It is all too overwhelming. When I do, I can promise to forgive you with all my heart."

The grateful hope wreathing her father's face summoned fresh tears.

She threw her shoulders back. No time for tears. A journey of hope awaited. Callisto hurried over to where their mounts stood half asleep under the shade of a tree. Untying both she beckoned her father over.

Mounting, she turned in the direction of Olympia, sat deep, and nudged her horse into a gallop.

She had no time to lose.

CHAPTER TWENTY-EIGHT

Callisto marvelled at the sight of the temple—magnificent, imposing, mighty—as befitted the god to whom it was dedicated.

She brought her hands together, staring wide-eyed at metopes and triglyphs depicting the twelve labors of the hero, Herakles. To one side, the sacred grove where altars stood under the hot sun, beckoned. But she must be patient and follow her father up the three unequal steps leading into the temple itself.

Stepping into the cella, a profound peace settled on her spirit, even as she gazed in breathless awe at the massive ivory and gold statue of Zeus towering over them. It shone with a brightness to dazzle mortal eyes.

A whisper of sound behind them turned her attention away from contemplating the father of the gods. The high priestess of Olympia glided over the shell rock floor. Callisto resisted the urge to kneel in her presence. She had never met anyone brimming with so much dignified serenity.

After exchanging greetings Callisto explained the reason they sought the counsel of Zeus. She waited in nervous anticipation while the priestess tilted her head as though listening to a message from Olympus itself.

"Go to an altar on the western side of the temple," she instructed them. "Apollo graces the pediment on that side. Your offering will be doubly blessed. I will commune here with Zeus then come to inform you of his judgment."

"Thank you," Callisto clasped hands with the priestess. Beckoning her father—who had stood respectfully to one side while they spoke—he accompanied her to retrieve the already gathered gifts of laurel leaves and wild fruit. Nerves humming, she proceeded to the side of the temple where they'd been directed.

Callisto lit the fire. Immediately her mind flooded with images of doing similar in Amyklai. A fine tremor shook her hands as she recalled the reason for needing that particular reparation. She only had to imagine Diokles in all his glory for her heart to start racing and her blood to turn into liquid fire.

Could love overcome the curse threatening to keep her and Diokles apart?

Aeschylus's hand settled on her shoulder as she knelt before the altar. She covered it with her own and turned her sight inward.

Time had no meaning in the space where she immersed herself. Callisto prayed until she felt the squeeze of her father's fingers. She started and gazed at him quizzically wondering why he'd disturbed her so soon.

"The priestess approaches," he explained.

Her stomach free-fell to her toes and back. Over her booming heartbeat she prepared to hear words carrying the power to lift her to ethereal joy or consign her to a life of wretchedness.

"Priestess Callisto," the high priestess inclined her head. "The Olympian has spoken. While the curse-maker lived Zeus would not defy the oath made to his brother, Hades, except to sway Diokles's mind from recognizing you."

Callisto felt sweat break out on her forehead and run down the sides of her face as though she'd just finished sprinting in the stadion.

"Zeus has decreed the curse is able to be broken."

On a cry of elation Callisto dropped to her knees and raised her arms in prayerful thanks. The same elation swept away the remaining vestiges of darkness from her heart. "Then I may reveal to Diokles who I am?"

"You may after you have been purified at Delphi."

"Delphi!" Callisto cried. "But—"

The high priestess gave her a stern look. "Do you question Zeus's will?"

Callisto sank back onto her heels. "No, of course not," she sighed, pulse racing in the knowledge of how much more time this added to their journey. What if Diokles left Apollysis thinking she had betrayed her promise to return with Aeschylus?

Would he consider it a betrayal and try to find them with vengeance still filling his heart. She feared for her father's sake.

"Go to Delphi," the high priestess exhorted. "Apollo's priests will purify you of the curse and release you from your priestess vows."

"I am grateful for your counsel," Callisto thanked her in a strained voice. She rose to her feet and turned to her father. "There is no time to lose. We must return before Diokles leaves. I want all of us to go home to Sparta together."

The Olympian priestess instantly dashed her hopes.

"Aeschylus, you too are required to atone," the priestess pronounced the verdict. "The gods understand your choices were made out of love and a desire to protect your daughter. You are to remain in Apollysis when Callisto and Diokles return to Sparta."

"No!" Callisto cried. She had just found her father, however flawed he was. Now to be denied the chance to rebuild their bond was akin to having a sword run through her. "Is there no other way?"

"This is my deserved punishment," Aeschylus interposed before the priestess could reply. "I chose the way I thought fit to protect you my daughter but you paid too high a price. I accept Zeus's judgment unreservedly."

"I do not want to leave you—" Callisto bit her lip to stop herself railing against fate.

Her father pressed her hand, silently asking her to hear him out. "I have lived my life and made my choices. It is time you and Diokles begin your life together and do the same."

"Zeus is merciful," the priestess spoke again. "There is hope for you, Aeschylus. If your secret is found and returned to Sparta, you too, may return."

With that pronouncement, she glided away, leaving Callisto gaping at her back. Wrenching her eyes away to look at her father, she stared in concern at his bloodless face, his eyes staring at something only he could see. "What does she mean?"

"Do not ask me now. No, Callisto," he insisted when she started to interrupt. "This is something you and Diokles need to hear together."

For a moment she considered whether to force him to reveal this great secret but almost immediately discarded the impulse. Every moment they spent here arguing meant wasted time. "I will wait," she agreed, earning a relieved smile from him.

Callisto led the way to their horses at a run.

A journey to Delphi awaited.

Her nerves were stretched to breaking point and the torrential rain outside seemed to mock her desperation.

"Sit down, Callisto, there is nothing you can do except wait," Aeschylus raised his voice to be heard over the thunder.

"I cannot rest," she stormed, striding back and forth between the walls of the small cave. More a recess in the rock face, it was deep enough to shelter their horses, Aeschylus and herself. "Ever since we departed Delphi delays of all sorts have beset us. Now this!"

She waved a frantic hand at the storm raging beyond the entrance.

"You told me Diokles gave you an ultimatum of when to return." Aeschylus leaned back against the rocky wall. "Depend upon it, he will wait for you."

Callisto stopped her pacing and met her father's confident gaze. "I wish I could believe it. You said you trained him in the agoge. You know how determined he is once his mind is made up…"

She trailed off, too tired and anxious to contemplate the consequences. They had pushed themselves and the horses once they returned to the Peloponnese. Although distance and time had been reduced by handsomely paying to sail across the gulf instead of returning via Corinth, it still meant days of hard riding. Every muscle cramped at the thought of doing more of the same.

Even if Diokles still waited for her would he be ready to listen?

She had sent him away without explanation. Made him think she cared nothing for him. She worried her tongue over her teeth. Could she now make him understand the reasons why she refused to come with him when he had almost begged her to?

Somehow she would persuade him.

"Sit beside me," Aeschylus held out a hand. "Apollysis is only a day or two away. We will eat something soon, but first, tell me has the purification brought you peace?"

"Yes, in so many ways." Callisto relaxed her tense shoulders and went to sit next to him. "I feel another large part of me has been resurrected. Last night I dreamed of the one time you took me to the shores of the Ionian Sea. I remember chasing the waves." She smiled wistfully at her father. "Life was much simpler then."

He cupped her head to rest it on his shoulder like he had done so many times when she was a young child. Callisto gulped over the ball of tears in her throat.

In one way the long journey had provided a blessing. She had rediscovered the man she remembered from her early years in Sparta. His keen intelligence, his passion for his family, his quick wit and empathy. They had shared their hopes, fears, and regrets. She basked in the quiet love and acceptance flowing between them once again.

"Are you sorry you needed to sell your two rings to pay for our passage, food and an extra horse?"

"Not at all," he replied. "Personal adornment is not something Spartans indulge in. I wore the minimum of jewellery in Apollysis to blend in with the people."

Callisto lifted her head, running fingers through her hair to push it off her face. "I am glad there are no regrets. You too have suffered all these years."

"Your hair is growing," Aeschylus observed, peering at her head. "Your natural blond has started to reappear all over your scalp."

"Diokles may not recognize me now," she half-heartedly joked. "If he does not want the real me anymore, I will stay with you now Lykos is dead."

Aeschylus gaped at her as if she had gone mad. "If you think Diokles does not want you, you are in sore need of returning to Delphi for more healing."

CHAPTER TWENTY-NINE

Diokles stared over the agora of Apollysis. Fate had robbed him of one woman. He was now doubly cursed by fate. Calliope did not want him. He would leave and renew his search for the traitor who masqueraded as her father.

The tide of dark thoughts racing through his mind threatened the self-control he prized. In defence, he kept himself occupied overseeing the preparations for their departure—ensuring everyone under his command left Apollysis and the flame-keeper performed the appropriate sacrifice to Artemis so the army could eat on the way home. The tense muscles around his eyes betrayed no flicker of feeling while he answered questions and issued orders.

The pressure in his jaw sent arrows of pain through his face to feed the dark resignation within his soul. A resignation he never expected to experience in his lifetime. On his return to Sparta he would have to choose a wife. He would be damned before he allowed anyone to accuse him of not fulfilling his duty as a Spartiate or laugh that he was unable to find a woman who would marry him.

Flushing out the last remnants of Lykos's supporters had taken longer than planned. The extra time allowed him a sort of reprieve from thinking too much about finding a wife and siring children. He'd held on to a slim hope Calliope would return before he left.

Any Spartan worth the name wanted a spirited wife. A wife whose amber eyes a man could drown in, soft skin to brush against him, beauty to dazzle his eyes. A wife whose indomitable spirit commanded his deepest respect and admiration.

Regrettable that Calliope's betrayal overrode all those qualities. Leave and forget her the angry part of him urged; find another woman at least worthy of respect regardless of whether she stirred his desire or not.

He shrugged. Right now he had more important things to command his attention.

Hearing his name called Diokles looked up to see a hoplite running toward him.

"Word has been received the advance party intercepted a man and a woman riding in from the south," the hoplite relayed quickly. "The man has been taken prisoner. The woman is attempting to fight them."

He did not need to hear anymore. Leaving the hoplite staring, Diokles sprinted to the nearest horse, vaulted onto its back, and galloped out of the city gates.

"Let him go!" Callisto glared at the men restraining her father. A hoplite, who she surmised was in charge by the way the others deferred to him, laughed at her.

"Your demands are futile." He studied her keenly. "You are the high priestess who left with our commander some weeks ago."

"Yes, I am, and I insist you take me to him." Uncaring they all dwarfed her in height and breadth, Callisto rolled her eyes and wondered how long it would take to get the message through their thick skulls. Spartan men were a breed apart.

The leader frowned. "Both you and the man—"

"My father," she shot back.

"—and your father," he continued without missing a beat, "are prisoners. We….what madness is this?"

Callisto had stomped back to her mount to pull a xiphos from the sheathe hidden behind a fold in the saddle blanket. The astonished expressions on the faces of her countrymen would have amused her any other time, but she was tired, she was cranky, and she had no patience left to debate their position.

"No, Callisto, do not fight," Aeschylus shouted despairingly. "You will get yourself killed."

Ignoring her father's plea she raised the xiphos to point it at her opponent's neck. "Release my father and take us to Diokles. Fight me if you dare."

The powerfully built man stepped back a pace. "You are *Spartan*!?"

Callisto choked back intemperate laughter. Her memory must really be returning with a vengeance. A recollection stirred of witnessing a friend's father, a huge bear of a Spartan warrior, almost cowering under his wife's anger. And, she had unwittingly spoken in their native dialect. "I will answer your question with this," she flicked the xiphos and braced her feet.

She waited. And waited. The leader drew his own weapon, reluctantly it seemed to her eyes, his moment of indecision allowing her to spring a surprise attack, furiously slashing her xiphos across his body, pouring all her strength into the blow. He bent backwards, rolling out from under her assault. Callisto heard the mocking cries from the onlookers and saw the angry frown change his entire attitude. He would never live down allowing a woman to best him.

Disengaging, she jumped out of reach and went on the defensive when he followed, ready to make a real fight of it.

"Stop!"

The familiar voice thundered over the group. Engrossed in the fight Callisto had not registered the swift drum of hooves brought to an abrupt halt. Suddenly every man stood to attention. She heard Aeschylus cry out; felt her heart jump joyfully in her chest.

A smile tugged her mouth as Diokles dismounted and strode toward her. The smile grew wider with every step that brought him closer. Even when he snatched the xiphos out of her hand, eyes blazing, lips compressed, she had to restrain herself from hugging him.

"Release the man and leave us," he ordered, waiting with barely concealed impatience, while the advance party hastily obeyed and continued on their way.

Callisto allowed herself the pleasure of feasting her eyes on the tall, proud, strong warrior who held her heart. His silence did not fool her. Across his beloved features swept an intriguing mix of anger and hope. A nerve ticked near the corner of his mouth. That mouth had kissed her senseless. Her lips tingled, anticipating his kisses for eternity.

"Do you never learn, Calli—"

Knowing the name he was about to call her she pressed a hand to his mouth to stop his exasperated outburst. The look in his dark-as-night eyes changed abruptly from blazing anger to blazing desire.

Callisto moved closer so that their bodies were almost touching, thanking the gods Diokles wore only his tunic. Holding his gaze, unable to stop smiling, she whispered, "Do you remember the iris I gave you?"

The breath whooshed out of her lungs when he swept her into his arms. Laughing, she hooked hers around his neck, pressing joyous kisses over his chest, his beard until he stopped her with the simple expedient of covering her mouth with his own.

The kisses were light, tentative, taking her on a journey of rediscovery. They brought back memories of the kiss they shared after agreeing to marry. Memories of the day she secretly tracked him when he had been sent out on a ritual survival test. She had plucked an iris and stolen a kiss while he berated her for placing both of them in danger of severe punishment. Memories of the strength contained in his arms even as a young man. The muscles of the man he had matured into were strong enough to never allow her to be taken away again.

Forgetting her father, forgetting everything, she snuggled closer, relishing his hardness, his power, his ability to read her desire for his caresses. He deepened the kiss to the point she struggled to breathe. Her hands buried themselves in his braided hair, tugging until he lifted his head, delighted by the flush of color across his high, bronzed cheekbones which betrayed how aroused he was. The love burning in his eyes warmed her soul.

"You knew who you were at the shrine," he accused. "Why did you lie?"

Callisto explained how she learned of the curse which could have killed him. Expecting the storm breaking over her, she pressed her fingertips to his lips to stem the flow of heated words. "I would not risk your life, ever, for anyone, even myself. My father insisted we ride to Olympia to pray to Zeus to break it. We took so long to return because I was counseled to go to Delphi to be purified and released from my priestess vows." She paused, waiting for him to accept he owed their reunion to Aeschylus. "May he join us?"

Menace rippled through the air. Seeing the swift, dark look he directed toward her father, who stood well away from them, she cupped Diokles's cheek. He promptly turned to her. Satisfied she commanded his attention Callisto opened her mouth to speak but he interjected.

"I swore punishment against those who wronged me," he fumed. "Do not expect me to so easily forget what compeled me all these years."

Callisto stepped back and planted her arms akimbo. She knew why Diokles's lips twitched despite his anger. She had adopted the same stance on countless occasions when she'd disagreed with him in the past.

"Do you think I found it easy to forgive?" she hissed in a tone of voice which reared his head back. "At least I gave him the chance to explain. I was hurt, Diokles, furious, but I chose to listen, however hard it was for me to make that choice. You need to listen, too. There is a secret he carries he says affects us both. Allow him to speak then decide whether it is enough to end your vow of revenge."

She shivered when his eyes raked over her. Beneath his fury she sensed the deep hunger he held at bay. Hunger neither could indulge just yet. Callisto held his gaze showing him with her eyes she wanted him just as much.

"Do not push me into a corner," he warned. "Your father ruined our lives, yet you stand there and defend him."

Sending him a lethal glare she jabbed a finger into his chest. "You are a stubborn fool," she shouted, not batting an eyelid when his eyes widened in silent outrage. "Yes, he ruined our lives, but you need to know why. If you still mean to kill him after you learn his reasons, I will take back the xiphos and duel you for his life, the same way I once dueled you for my freedom."

His jaw sagged. "I would not lift a sword against you, Callisto," he raged. "I will stand back and you may run me through."

"Now who is pushing whom into a corner?" She waited, feigning patience, not daring to breathe, watching the muscles flex in his forearms as he clenched and unclenched his fists in the fight for control.

Unable to bear the suspense Callisto rested her hands on his chest.

"Please, Diokles," she cajoled softly. "For me. If you kill him that one act remains a cloud over our love." When he started, she knew she'd struck a chord. He stared into her eyes, annoyed, captivated, then brought her hands to his lips, pressing a lingering kiss to each palm. Every pleasure point she possessed lit up in fiery need.

"You drive a hard bargain my love." Releasing her hands he motioned Aeschylus over.

Callisto smiled tremulously as her father came to join them, apprehension in his steps. An uneasy silence fell; a silence none of them knew how to break. Studying the expressions of both men she shook her head. Her father appeared anxious, her beloved ready to combust at the slightest wrong move. Her priestess training had included how to play the role of peacemaker. All the experience she garnered she would use to keep peace between the two men.

"Whatever needs to be said can be said back in the city," she ordered, casting a meaningful look at Diokles.

"We can talk here," he shot back

"No, in the city," she insisted, looking around her. "Since our horses have been taken we will have to walk." She tossed her head in Diokles's direction. "You can use the time to cool your temper."

Not waiting to see whether the two men followed, Callisto set a brisk pace toward the city. While more expedient to speak here where no-one would overhear them, she knew exactly how Diokles would react when he heard how she lost her memory. Inside the city walls, surrounded by the trappings of civilized life, by his peers to whom his conduct meant everything, she counted on his honor to restrain himself.

Grimacing, she admitted she too, had no idea of how either of them would react upon hearing the secret Aeschylus had yet to reveal.

CHAPTER THIRTY

As Callisto walked through the city gates, she was struck by the hive of activity which greeted her. Apollysians warily emerging from their houses; Spartans preparing to leave. The latter sight prompted her to thank fate that no other delays had hindered her return.

And Diokles had kept his word.

Walking proudly by the side of the man she would spend the rest of her life with Callisto's happiness soared as they neared the acropolis. The agora, the principal buildings, and yes, even the temple, remained untouched since her departure.

A smile lifted the corners of her mouth. She had walked through the fire of her destiny, found the courage to wear the coronet, saved herself and the city that had been her home these past years.

"What are you thinking?"

Callisto beamed and touched Diokles's arm. "That you are honorable. Apollysis is undamaged for which you have my undying gratitude." She saw he was in his commander mode, his features impassive, but as far as she was concerned, the warmth in the gaze he turned on her made up for it.

"I loathed threatening you at the time," he admitted. "It went against every personal code I live by."

"There is something I have been wondering about," she said, tilting her head to give him a considered look. "Would you really have burned the city to the ground if I refused to wear the coronet?"

"If it was the only course remaining to complete my mission, yes." He raised an eyebrow when she gasped.

Indignation shook her then morphed into a resigned sigh. "Of course. I should have remembered. No surrender. No going back unless a mission is completed."

Diokles squeezed her hand. "The ways of our people will return to you in time."

A handful of citizens found the courage to acknowledge her as she passed. Callisto returned their greetings. The number of people moving around raised her concerns over finding a place private enough for them to talk. There was nowhere in the temple she could think of. Slowing her pace to address Aeschylus, she asked, "Is there a place in our home where we can speak?"

He shook his head. "The servants are loyal, but this is too personal to risk being overheard. There is a room at one end of the portico in the agora," he told them. "It has the advantage of one door and one small window. Many private meetings are held there. Come with me."

As they followed Aeschylus across the agora, Callisto frowned on seeing Diokles summon two hoplites who fell into step with them.

"They will remain outside to ensure no-one overhears us," he answered her unspoken question.

Too nervous to speak she nodded her thanks.

They caught up with Aeschylus as he opened a door and beckoned them through. Stepping inside, she glanced back to see the two men standing on guard a few paces away, then Diokles closed the door, shutting out the world.

It was gloomy inside. The only light came through the small window. A few stools ringed a low table in the center of the room. She moved to sit next to Diokles while her father took a seat on the opposite side.

No-one spoke. Diokles sat like a motionless statue. Aeschylus twisted his hands.

Callisto closed her eyes, called on every shred of diplomacy she possessed, then reached out to still her father's incessant handwringing. "Remember what the priestess in Olympia said. Reveal this secret so you can come home."

She sat back, feeling Diokles's palpable tension wash over her. Concerned he might flare up at any moment she placed a hand on his arm.

Aeschylus gulped a whistling breath. "My children, this will not be easy to hear. It is a burden I have carried a very long time."

The quaver in his voice touched her deeply. "Go on," she encouraged.

Nothing could have prepared her for what her father said next.

"Callisto, I told you Diokles's father threatened your life." His expression asking for understanding, he looked straight at Diokles. "Your father wanted another son, but a battle injury meant he had to find a genitor. Knowing Ianthe and I had wanted to marry he absolutely refused to consider me.

"Your mother fell pregnant with my child without his knowledge. When our daughter was born, she was immediately taken to be exposed on Taygetos. Ianthe managed to get word to me. I dispatched a trusted servant to save your half-sister. He was seen fleeing with her and recognized to be from my household.

"The person who saw them is dead but for a long time he held the threat of revealing this to your father, Diokles. When I finally refused to aid him further, he told your father, who confronted me, threatening to kill Callisto to prevent you marrying each other."

Shock and denial held her rigid in her seat. Callisto sneaked a look at Diokles, sucking in a frightened breath at his mask-like features. Beneath her fingers the muscles of his arm tensed to a marble hardness.

The significance of her father's words penetrated her mind. She did not care about the unknown betrayer. Futility shook her until she wanted to scream. "Does that mean I cannot marry Diokles?" she choked.

"Of course you can," Aeschylus exclaimed. "The child is half-sister to both of you, but you and Diokles are not related by blood. How could you be?"

A hard band of tension she had been unaware of loosened from around her chest. As the reality of having a half-sister sank in, her breathing smoothed into an easy rhythm. After all the years of inner turmoil the shattered fragments of her existence were melding into a cohesive whole. "Does anyone know where she is now?"

"No. My servant sent word to say they'd safely escaped, but nothing has been heard since." Aeschylus ran a hand over his face. "I have no idea where he and his wife fled to. To keep them all safe I never sought to find them."

A fire leapt into life inside her. Determined to discover her half-sister's whereabouts she began to plan a return to Amyklai and ask Apollo's help. The visit to a place where she had come so close to having her life shattered would also heal any lingering trauma of what she'd suffered at Lykos's hands.

Decision made she turned to Diokles. Callisto's mouth dried. His eyes bored into the wall opposite them as though it had done him a personal wrong.

Desperate to reach wherever he had retreated to behind his armor of control, she whispered, "Diokles?"

When he did not answer she leapt to her feet and gripped his broad shoulders. She wanted to protect her father from the storm brewing inside the man she loved, but she sensed he needed protecting from himself, too.

Only the feel of Callisto's hands kept him anchored to his seat. Pain he could not recall ever experiencing cut deep grooves into his heart. Diokles stared at Aeschylus's bent head, the man he hated, the man he swore vengeance on, and saw a man tortured in spirit the same as himself.

One question rose above all the others. "What happened to make Callisto lose her memory?"

He had to respect Aeschylus for not looking away when he confessed. The longer Diokles listened, the stronger the seething mass of rage grew, taking over every cell of his body. Like molten lava it searched for a weakness from where it could erupt. He needed to contain it, smother it, if he hoped to retain any semblance of rationality.

Too late.

Diokles sprang to his feet with the speed of an arrow loosed from a crossbow.

"You could have killed her," he roared, blind to Callisto's wince of shock. He paced the room raging within himself for not being there to protect her. "And then what? You would have lost both your daughters. You are a fool, Aeschylus, yet blessed by the gods. I swore to kill you only to find my revenge thwarted by what you tell me. My father is fortunate he fell in battle else he would be paying the price you were meant to pay."

He brushed past Callisto's outstretched hand to stand alone at the window. Squeezing his eyes shut he dug deep for calm he could barely feel, biting back the words of denial, of betrayal, of the pain he wanted no one to hear. Instinct told him Aeschylus spoke the truth.

Behind his closed eyelids he was back in his mother's room, her anguished features swimming into focus. On her deathbed she confessed to him her long-held love for Aeschylus. That it was he who had taken Callisto away.

Why did she not tell him about his half-sister?

He fisted a hand. He would never know the reason. His eyes snapped open as a vivid image flashed across his mind.

"You knew." He stared at Callisto, demanding the truth. "You saw something in my mother's room the morning I found you there." She came and wrapped her arms around his waist. He crushed her to him, needing her warmth and love to anchor him against a perfect storm of emotions threatening to tear him apart.

"I could not bear to tell you I heard a woman in the pains of childbirth," she half-sobbed into his chest. "That I heard a newborn's cry; the same woman wailing. I sensed so much grief it almost overwhelmed me."

A choking sound brought his attention to Aeschylus whose shaking hands covered his face. He hugged Callisto even tighter, trying to banish the desolation hollowing out his being.

How many wasted years swearing vengeance on the wrong man; unaware of his half-sister; the loss of Callisto. Dismantling the room with his bare hands might sweat out the bitterness choking him, but it would only give fleeting relief, only leave bruised hands to match his bruised emotions.

He needed time—time to come to terms with the past.

Passing a hand over his eyes he looked down at Callisto. She was the sun his world revolved around, the calm center where he found solace. Resting his chin on the crown of her head he bit back a splutter of laughter. Calm their relationship would not be. She was too strong and fiery, too much her own person.

Now she was restored to him. The festering wounds scarring his spirit could begin to heal in her soothing embrace.

Hearing the door open and shut he knew Aeschylus left to give them privacy.

For a while he simply stood in the same place gently rocking the woman in his arms. By the time he released her a measure of calm had settled over him.

"I wanted to believe it was you that first day in the temple." He ran his fingers through the silky strands of hair. Passing a hand over her head, he spied a golden glint covering her scalp. He smiled. His Callisto was truly returning in every way. "I had not seen you in ten years, your hair another color, a different name and you did not recognize me. Every time you defied me I was reminded of how you did the same when we were younger."

His mouth quirked when she threw her head back and laughed.

Sobering, she explained the reason. "My hair was hennaed from the time I became high priestess. They told me the color must be red to signify the fire of the sun. It was so easy to hide my identity after I lost my memory. I never remembered being blond." She tilted her head engagingly. "Have I changed so much since I was fifteen?"

"You have grown into your beauty. I remembered a girl and could not see the woman she had become." He ran a possessive look over her face. "Your eyes were a darker brown as a girl, now they are like amber jewels."

He stared deeply into them, saw the exact moment desire intensified their color to a smoky gold. He grew hard, his arousal coming with a speed only she had ever been able to summon. Fighting the insistent urge to take Callisto into his arms, kiss her senseless and make her his, he reminded himself now was neither the time nor the place.

"When I first saw you I thought you were a mountain of a man," she confessed. "Somewhere along the road to Sparta I found myself resisting a growing attraction to you. It surprised and shocked me because I never desired a man during my years as a priestess. When the time came to go to the shrine, I, in my Calliope persona, feared the course you would take if…well, if *I* were alive or dead."

"I told you I wanted you when you claimed 'Callisto' had died." He held her gaze. "I developed feelings for 'Calliope', although neither of us could have known I fell in love with you all over again." He tensed and shifted uncomfortably. "I cannot answer what I would have done if you had told me the opposite."

"Nothing will be gained by knowing the answer," she absolved him of any guilt, then winked saucily. "Anyway, I was already planning how to win you if the Fates proved to be unkind to me."

Alerted by the seductive tone of her voice, Diokles studied her features in minute detail. There was a familiar glint in her eyes and a pert smile played around her lush lips. He would wager his black stallions she plotted to spring some surprise on him like the time she tracked him to the woods, stealing a kiss and more. His burgeoning manhood tightened painfully at the memory.

Stepping back from temptation, he took her hand, reveling in the feel of her slender fingers enclosed in his, and led her to the door. "You always were the rebellious one," he scolded with a grin. "Any belongings you wish to take, retrieve them now and meet me at your father's house. I need to speak with him and help arrange his journey to Sparta….why the frown, Callisto?"

"You did not comprehend what I said earlier," she spoke in a strained voice. "We cannot take my father."

Diokles stiffened. "Why not?"

As Callisto explained the atonement required of her father, he fought back the impulse to race back to the shrine, find Lykos's body, and kill him again. Cursing the priest to eternal damnation, Diokles understood if not for Zeus's mercy, Lykos's evil plan would have separated Callisto and himself forever.

He felt the long-held vow of vengeance break inside him, washed away by gratitude toward the man he once swore to kill. "Your father loves you. I am not surprised he subjected himself to Zeus's will for your sake."

"I understand that," she said sadly. "I wanted us all to leave together, to see my father restored to his rights as a Spartiate, but unless our half-sister is found, he may never be able to return."

The haunted look in her eyes touched a nerve. Her hurt was his hurt. To protect the woman he loved from more grief he would find a way to release her father from an injustice he did not deserve. Opening the door, he led her outside, his keen mind already running through possibilities. "Come to your father's house as soon as you are ready."

"I will not be long," she assured him.

Diokles motioned the two hoplites to resume their duties. Watching Callisto walk, straight-backed, head high, toward the temple, he thought his visit to Aeschylus could be considered his atonement to her father.

CHAPTER THIRTY-ONE

Standing at the base of the temple steps, Callisto took several deep breaths to steady her tingling nerves. The last time she'd walked down them she had done so as a prisoner. Now she ascended them a free woman in every sense of the word.

A mission within the temple awaited her.

Pausing in the pronaos she took a moment to wonder at the strange voice whispering she did not belong here. It disconcerted her, especially as her heart ached a little on seeing the familiar sights, reminding her of the years she'd served here.

The corners of her mouth lifted on an enveloping wave of warmth. She would always remember this temple, the people of Apollysis, with affection for offering two strangers a home.

Sudden movement brought her out of her introspection. With a glad cry she opened her arms, meeting the onrush of her fellow priestesses, delight etched over their faces, embracing her, their eager questions filling her ears.

In the clamor of greetings, of accounts of their own escape, Callisto related the details of what had occurred from the time she left till now; expressing relief to find them all safe and well. In turn, they told how some had stolen back into the city, while others were forcibly returned when their hiding places were discovered.

The torrent of conversation had barely died down when a discordant note undulated through her body. Callisto looked around to seek out the presence she sensed watching her.

Lysandra stood apart from their happy group, face an expressionless mask, taking in the scene.

Callisto felt anger rise like a hot bubble in a steaming spring. Her eyes bored into her onetime friend who studiously avoided her gaze. Bruises still colored Lysandra's neck though no remorse knocked at the door of her conscience. Yes, she had inflicted those bruises, however, she had allowed the other woman to live. Lysandra's willingness to kill her proved she would not have been as generous.

Callisto reminded herself the gods had granted her victory on all fronts. Time to put the plan she'd recently spent agonizing over into action. Her father and Diokles would disagree vehemently if they knew, but she possessed more sense than to tell them. Her decision might cause consternation amongst the priestesses, among the people of Apollysis, though she hoped all would eventually accept and understand her reasons.

She approached Lysandra, shaking her head in mock admonishment when the priestess flinched. "The bruises will heal. I give no apology—you would have done the same to me, if not worse."

Lysandra opened her mouth to speak but Callisto cut her off with an abrupt wave of her hand. No amount of insincere excuses could make amends for Lysandra attempting to stop her wearing the coronet.

She placed herself next to Lysandra then faced the open-mouthed priestesses. "Sad though I am to leave many of you, I return to Sparta, my real home, today."

Cries of dismay filled the air. They warmed her soul and brought a fond smile to her lips. She risked a sideways glance at Lysandra who wore a pinched look around her eyes. "Which means I must appoint a new high priestess to succeed me."

She steeled herself. Her decision did not sit well in her mind. Two priestesses among their number deserved the ascension more than Lysandra, but, locking gazes with her adversary, she prayed the latter would learn a valuable lesson. "As you are next in seniority will you accept the post of high priestess?" She stifled cynical amusement at the utter stupefaction spreading over Lysandra's face.

"I—"

'Good, then it is settled," Callisto interrupted. "Lykos is dead. Since no other priests returned the ceremony of elevation may be passed over." Lysandra still looked as though a bolt of lightning had struck her. Callisto inclined her head and walked away in the secure knowledge she would never see her again.

The good wishes and blessings continued a long time. Everyone was reluctant to let her go. Callisto hugged those she had formed close friendships with and hand-clasped the rest. Now that the time for departure grew closer, tears pricked the back of her eyes, aware she was leaving a large portion of her existence behind, not just good friends.

Even more time passed before she was able to extricate herself, crying and laughing in equal measure, declaring she must go soon. A final hug, a final wave, she started to make her way out to the square, but prompted by an unseen force, she directed her footsteps to her old room one last time.

Opening the door she gazed around in wonderment. The clothes and furnishings remained the same as when she left it weeks ago. The sleeping pallet unmade, the cloak she had been preparing to wear on the day Diokles arrived, lay discarded where she had tossed it. Callisto picked it up and ran the fine material through her fingers.

Never could she have imagined how much her life would change when she first saw the Spartan troops massing on the hills above the city.

She had come full circle.

Folding the cloak, she laid it on the bed and turned to leave. A glint caught her eye. By the bed lay her priestess knife, precisely where she always left it each night. The bright blade beckoned. She picked it up, considered taking it as a memento of all she had accomplished here, then dismissed the momentary impulse. The person she had been in Apollysis had proved to be an illusion.

She went to return the knife to its former place when an idea struck. Her eyes widened—the gesture would be so fitting. Taking the knife she walked out without a backward glance.

Callisto hurried back to the cella. Kneeling before the altar she offered a prayer of gratitude. Then, taking her knife, she laid it reverently at Apollo's feet.

Stepping back she bowed low to the god she once served.

Her mission was complete.

It was time to go home.

Diokles hurled himself off his horse, sweat pouring down his face and down the horse's dark flanks. Beckoning a helot servant, he handed him the reins of the prancing stallion.

"Walk him until he settles," he ordered, then called out after the departing man. "Do not let him drink too quickly."

"I thought you planned to visit Aeschylus."

Diokles pivoted to see Acastus approaching him. Wiping the sweat off his brow with a forearm, he managed a self-conscious smile. "I needed to clear my head and accept that some things I held as truth, were wrong." Reflecting on his mad ride Diokles rubbed his jaw. "It was not easy."

Acastus clapped his back in a way guaranteed to topple anyone other than a fellow Spartan. "You rode out of the city as though the Furies pursued you."

"It did me good." Trust in his long-time friend enabled Diokles to share the news he had learned in the last few hours. His curiosity rose with the same speed Acastus's grin faded when he mentioned the existence of his half-sister. "Something troubles you," Diokles stated, watching Acastus keenly.

An uneasy silence followed until Acastus, a far-away look in his eyes, finally spoke. "I will restore your half-sister to you. Once home, my preparations to leave will be swift."

"Sparta cannot afford to lose a warrior like you," Diokles frowned. "No, someone else can go."

"Do not try and stop me." Acastus pointed to Diokles's arm. "It is the least I can do to atone for that scar."

An inner prompting insisted there was more to Acastus's resolve than atoning for the scar he himself barely noticed. He had learned over the course of his life, sometimes the hard way, to trust his hunches implicitly.

Diokles studied his friend's face long enough to spy a flash of emotion, quickly suppressed, cross his features. Out of respect he would not press Acastus to disclose the reason why he wanted the mission so badly.

"Permission has to be sought from the polemarch," Diokles cautioned, still sensing an undercurrent. "If granted, you have my gratitude, in addition to any provisions you may need."

"At least we are in agreement." Acastus clasped Diokles's forearm. "We are ready to depart whenever you finish your business with Aeschylus."

Diokles continued to watch Acastus until the latter was out of sight then ran a hand over the back of his neck, trying to make sense of the exchange. Preposterous to think his friend continued to harbor guilt over inflicting the wound which scarred his left forearm. Honing fighting skills formed part of their training. Weakened by the whipping he'd received his reflexes had not been quick enough to avoid the blow.

His arm flexed remembering the reason for the punishment. The man he was about to visit was a reminder of that day. Old, habitual anger rose. He doused it before it took hold. There remained no reason to keep its flame burning his emotions.

Refreshing himself in a nearby fountain, Diokles made his way to the cluster of private homes, asking a passer-by for directions to Aeschylus's house. Standing outside the white-washed stone building he took time to breathe out the tension in his body. He thought of Callisto, of his love for her, of the still incomprehensible truth which made the man inside not the monster he had held him to be.

Diokles pushed open the door and stepped into the welcome coolness of the vestibule.

A scream, followed by the sound of pottery shattering, dropped him into a defensive crouch, reaching for his xiphos. A servant stood over the broken remains of an expensive urn, an expression of almost comical fear on her face.

He straightened up slowly to not frighten her any further. "You are in no danger. Where is your master?"

The woman opened her mouth but only managed a terrified croak. Diokles exhaled an exasperated sigh then spied a man running toward them from the courtyard visible through the open doorway.

"What happen—"

"Your face shows the same fear as your servant's, Aeschylus," Diokles mocked him without malice. "I am not here to attack you. We need to talk, and not in front of your household."

"Hagne, bring refreshments to the dining room. Do not concern yourself over the broken urn." Aeschylus gathered his scattered wits together. "Come with me, Diokles."

Diokles followed him to the upper floor into a spacious room. Recognizing many of its furnishings he came to an abrupt stop. "You carried all this from Sparta? I remember the speed with which you left."

"Yes," Aeschylus half-smiled at the amazement on the younger man's face. "Fleeing Sparta, our home, the life we were raised to, broke my heart. Your father's threat made it imperative we flee. Whatever we could not take was later despatched to us by trusted friends."

Diokles drew his brows together. The mention of his father stung deep. He wondered whether that wound would ever heal. However, it presented an opening to broach a painful subject.

"I am here to discuss my mother, not my father." His head snapped back in astonishment at the broken look on Aeschylus's face.

"I cannot ask your forgiveness for the love I bore your mother. I can only ask you to forgive the unintentional hurt I caused you."

Folding his arms across his chest, Diokles held Aeschylus's gaze, his esteem for Callisto's father rising further when the older man returned his look. This man had taught him to throw a spear with a true aim. Diokles remembered him as a hard, but fair, taskmaster, constantly challenging him and his fellow squad members to go beyond themselves. He had looked up to him more than his own father. Nor could he fault Aeschylus's love for his daughter, his commitment to Sparta, and his generosity.

"The birth of my half-sister was kept from me, easy to do since I was already in the agoge." He found freedom in speaking of a time in his life he had not shared even with his closest friend. "My mother never spoke to me about it, not even on her deathbed, when she confessed you took Callisto away."

"Do not blame your mother," Aeschylus appealed on a broken sigh. "She died trying to protect you, Callisto and myself. From the messages she smuggled to me I know her spirit broke after our daughter was taken from her. Ianthe was not permitted to hold or suckle the baby. There is no doubt grief sent your mother to an early grave rather than anything else."

Diokles blinked away the moisture blurring his vision. Warriors did not give in to weakness. They met and solved challenges. "Why you thought Callisto should lose her memory is beyond me." He raked a hand through his hair. "Yet I understand you loved her enough to protect her. Compelled by Athena's counsel I released one oath. It is harder to do so a second time." He squared his shoulders. "I release my oath of vengeance for Callisto's sake and because of what you told me."

"I already told Callisto the reason," Aeschylus rubbed his eyes. "I, too, took counsel at the temple and received advice to take her away and make her forget everything." He fisted a hand. "She paid too high a price."

Diokles gripped the hand the older man held out to him, unsurprised by the strength it still contained. "She did, although both of us are blessed to have her back unharmed."

"If I am able to come back to Sparta, may I visit my daughter once she is settled in your house?"

"Certainly, you are free to visit her." Silent laughter shook him. "I could not deny you entry even if I wanted to. My life would be in more danger than in any battle. Callisto fought me once, threatened to a second time, so I would rather not give her any reason to try a third time."

"With a xiphos!?"

"Naturally," Diokles laughed out loud. "Your daughter always was, and still is, a true woman of Sparta." He saw a father's pride brighten Aeschylus's eyes. It mirrored the love and pride he felt for the woman who would one day bear his children.

"Of course, I am a woman of Sparta. How could anyone doubt that?"

Both men's heads whipped round to find Callisto hovering in the doorway. Diokles felt his heart move as she glided toward them. He reached out to take her hand, his hard, calloused fingers closing possessively over her much smaller ones.

"I have completed what I intended to do and have come to say goodbye."

Diokles heard the catch in her voice. He squeezed her hand, imbuing some of his courage to her, then released it to accept the skyphos of wine brought in by the servant, drinking it in one long draught.

Giving Callisto a smile of reassurance, shaking hands once more with Aeschylus, he left them alone to make their farewells.

One final check of the army and he would begin the journey home with his betrothed.

CHAPTER THIRTY-TWO

"I thought I might find you here."

Callisto's mouth curved in a secretive smile. Taking her time, she turned in the direction of the deep, strong voice which would always possess the power to make every pleasure point sing in ecstasy.

The delicate folds between her legs swelled as she envisioned her plans.

Holding his gaze she went to him, steps measured, hips swaying. The hunger gleaming in his night-dark eyes loosed arrows of heat into every nerve ending.

Smothering a whimper, she took his hands, lifting them to her lips to press lingering kisses over each knuckle. His fingers clenched around hers. The simple gesture sent her belly into free-fall as though she had jumped off a cliff into the sea.

"If you agree, I want your mother's room to be mine. Past time to let light into it to remove the darkness of what happened here."

"Any room is yours to choose," Diokles released her hands to embrace her, planting a lingering kiss on her brow. "This is your home now to do with whatever you wish. The servants are yours to command."

Callisto laid her cheek on his chest, rejoicing in his racing heartbeat. He belonged to her. This proud, brave warrior belonged to her alone. She snuggled closer, relishing the way his fingers massaged the back of her neck. "Your people have welcomed me so warmly though I'm glad Erisa was sent away. I think she hated me."

"She betrayed you," his voice hardened. "And betrayed my trust. I discovered a man was asking about you in the agora the day we arrived. Erisa heard and made herself known to him. Jealousy drove her to tell him of your plans. That, my beautiful one, is how they managed to ambush you at Amyklai."

"No need to speak of that time anymore," she said, pressing her fingers over his mouth. Tenderly prising them away he nibbled each tip, singling out her middle finger to suckle. Callisto rubbed herself sinuously over his body, uncaring she could not hold back a moan that spoke clearly of her hunger.

"Will that make you forget?" Diokles whispered in her ear.

Air jammed halfway up her chest. His voice was throaty, full of promise; enough to make her light-headed from the blood pounding through her veins. "Yes," she choked the affirmation past a throat tight with anticipation of what was to come.

Temptation stood before her and the bed behind. Was she really going to deny both of them? Callisto wavered; torn between pushing Diokles onto the bed or making them both wait until they were driven mad by the delay.

Keep to your plan.

Her inner voice was right. Not giving herself time to reconsider, she moved out of his embrace. "The servants are already attending to their tasks. They might overhear us." His brow lowered, the puzzled expression forcing her to quell an urge to laugh.

He had no idea of what awaited him.

She gifted him a melting look beneath her lashes that promised pleasurable reward for his patience.

A furtive glance showed his tunic tenting away from his body. Callisto closed her eyes and smirked. Their first time should be special. So, where better she asked herself, than in that shaded grove where they once treasured each other.

"Remember the day we almost made love?" she breathed, sensing the rigid control he held over himself. How long would it take for her to shatter it? "Meet me by the stream in the same place in two hours?"

He drew back, dark eyes glinting. "Why there?"

Feigning modesty, she looked at her feet to hide the excitement she knew must be written clearly on her face. "I will explain once we are there. Promise me you will come."

"There is nothing to promise," he growled. "I will be there."

Where was she?

Diokles surveyed the surrounding area, senses alert to any ambush. Even here, on his own land, he did not drop his guard, or disregard the training that meant the difference between life and death.

"Callisto?"

A loud splash broke the silence. Cursing his inattention, he reached for his absent xiphos. He had left weapons behind, certain the only battle he would wage would be an extremely pleasurable one.

Then he caught sight of her, submersed in the clear water, smiling the alluring smile of a woman intent on seducing a man.

The wreath of violets circling her head made a potent contrast to the short blond hair. His hungry eyes probed the surface of the water, drinking in the sight of her slim, naked body. His manhood sprang to immediate attention.

Blond hair?

Diokles blinked. And blinked a second time and stared to make certain the gods had not addled his brain. "Who stood in for me at the wedding?"

A seductive laugh was his answer, the sound raising his pulse to dangerous levels. Watching her swim lazily into the shallows he bit back a groan when she stopped short of the bank.

"Are you coming out, Callisto, or do I need to come in and get you?" he challenged, his voice coming from a deep untapped reservoir of desire.

Her pouting lips and heated eyes promised paradise was within reach. "I am yours to command." Mouth curled in an impish grin, she qualified, "at least this time."

Diokles stood stock-still while she rose out of the water, heart drumming a staccato tattoo as she walked languidly to him, more beautiful than any naiad, breasts gently bouncing with every step. Mouth dry, he dropped his gaze to the coral buds crowning them, pebbled into enticing mouthfuls by the cool water. Feasting on the sight of the perfect globes his hands itched to hold, the aridness of his life was swept away.

He waited with a hunter's stillness. She stood close, not touching, smiling an invitation that ripped at his control. A pulse pounded in her neck. His erection throbbed painfully in reply.

"No-one stood in for you, my love," she murmured, placing a hand over his heart. "As custom dictates, I must shave my hair for the wedding, so I asked a servant to cut the length back to my natural color. Calliope is no more. She was an illusion. Now, and for the rest of our lives, you will make love to me, Callisto."

Heart full to bursting point, Diokles ran a hand over the short spikes, lifting the crown of violets off her head. Their elusive scent teased his nostrils, reminding him of the freshness of spring, of new life. Just as one day Callisto would bring new life into the world when she bore their children. "Always," he promised on a deep groan, lifting her into his arms to first slake his hunger at her breast.

Drinking in the scent of her, clean and crisp from the water, he suckled one coral bud, its pert hardness tempting him to take it between his teeth. Her fingers dug into his scalp, the pressure holding him to her breast. Unnecessary for her to do so. Here was where he had longed and hungered and thirsted to be.

Lifting his head, Diokles drank in the sight of her. Eyes half-closed, lips parted—his woman in exquisite surrender. If the world ended right now he would not care. Seeing his Callisto with the glint of arousal in her eyes, her face flushed with ardor, encompassed all his world.

He would worship her as she deserved to be worshipped.

Lowering her, he tilted her head over his arm to press a kiss to her throat. Sliding his lips along skin warmed by the sun and his caresses, he ministered to her other breast. She collapsed against him, pliable and liquid like warm honey, forcing him to tighten his hold to keep her upright.

Lost to everything but the woman in his arms, Diokles traced the indentations of her spine, fingers sliding over the silk of her back, moving to cup her bottom. Massaging the firm cheeks, the mewling moans issuing from her throat inflamed the desire searing them both, his own hoarse breathing echoing loudly in his ears. Somehow through the haze of passion clouding his mind, he heard her call his name over and over, pleading for fulfilment.

He would give her that. Show her the heights of delight true lovers scaled together. They had pledged themselves in their youth. Now as man to woman they would pledge themselves in the deepest and most intimate way possible.

Diokles drew away, silencing her cry of protest with a searing kiss. Cradling her to his chest, he strode quickly toward the sheltered olive grove and the privacy it gave.

The feel of her body sliding over his throbbing manhood as he set her on her feet, spurred him to strip off his tunic with a speed which almost ripped the garment in two. Spreading it over the ground he dropped to his knees to press a lingering kiss on her belly, throat constricting when she knelt to join him.

Her amber eyes glowed, mesmerising him, her hand wrapping around his erection. Diokles struggled for breath, an impossible task when she squeezed him, her touch tender and teasing. She had done the same when she had broken all the conventions of their society to find him during his survival training. The only time in his life he had ever come close to feeling terrified, especially for her, knowing severe punishment awaited both if a member of the krypteia had found them together.

"I want you, Diokles, with every fibre of my being. I love you."

"You humble me, my Callisto. You are the sun my world revolves around." He brushed shaky fingers over her face, warmed by the sun and passion. "I will be as gentle as I can."

No matter how many times he had confronted enemy spears, Diokles could not remember his hands trembling like they did now. Carefully lowering her onto the tunic, he savored the sight of her reposing like a goddess, the flicker of sunlight through the foliage dappling her olive-toned skin, the languid lift of her arms reaching to shape his chest.

The touch of her hands on his bare skin, the press of her fingers, the undulation of her body, dragged a groan from deep in his soul. The juncture of her neck and shoulder, enticed, drew him to press his lips to the tender skin.

"Look at me." Her eyes were hooded, the amber irises shining through narrow slits. Holding her gaze for long moments, he read in their depths everything he yearned to see. Her desire stoked his own ever higher.

Diokles traced his fingers over the planes of her face, over her throat, exulting to feel it convulse under his touch. Lower his hand journeyed until it climbed the peak of one breast to rub over the taut nipple.

An incoherent cry burst from her lips.

His tenuous hold on control shattered.

No power on earth could stop his hand roving over her exquisite body. Threading his fingers through the soft curls covering her womanly secrets, Diokles prayed his pounding heart would not give out on him. Alert for any sign of hesitancy, he slid one finger between the moist folds, watching through hooded eyes as her long legs parted and her body arched like a bow when he stroked the hidden nub.

He rolled onto her, supporting his weight on his forearms. "I will take you to the heights of Olympus," he vowed in a voice thickened by the depth of his feelings.

"Diokles—"

He kissed her deeply, seeking the warm recesses of her mouth. Her tongue wrapped around his in ever-growing urgency, tasting his mouth as he did her own. Diokles broke the kiss to suck in much-needed air.

His arrested gaze roved over rosy lips plump and moist from his kisses, eyes glazed with the fiery arousal he had called forth, her silky skin tinged by the same heat consuming him. Diokles licked its warm sweetness, discovering what aroused her the most. Every taste, every breath, filled his senses with the scent which belonged to his Callisto alone. He paused to swirl his tongue in her navel. Her wailing demands almost sent him over the edge.

Pressing moist kisses down her belly, he finally reached his goal, inhaling the fragrant muskiness between her folds. The scent of his woman. Every protective, primal and possessive instinct flooded him. He parted the moist curls to stare hungrily at the swollen nub which pleaded for his touch. Bending closer, he laved his tongue over it again and again.

He gloried in Callisto's mindless cries, heart bursting from the knowledge he was pleasing her. Fire seared his body, stoked hotter and wilder, by the pain of suppressed release. He must hold on so she could experience the all-consuming pleasure first. Tasting his woman was all he wanted. The mingling of their juices, his saliva and her moistness, rendered the sweetest ambrosia, the very food of the gods, tasteless.

With every sweep of his tongue her thrusts grew faster and wilder. Holding her steady, he increased the pressure until her keening scream of release rose in a mounting crescendo to the sky above.

Her chest rose and fell with the effort required to breathe. She was still alive even if, for one radiant instant in time, she swore she had flown among the stars.

Panting breaths gradually settled into a regular rhythm. Callisto recalled the rapture she had experienced while wearing the coronet. She'd mourned later, convinced she would never recapture the feeling. Now with Diokles's warm body settled beside her, one muscled arm thrown possessively around her waist, she rejoiced in being able to experience the same rapture once more.

Overwhelmed by the contentment she felt, Callisto traced quivering fingers over his beloved features. "I sometimes wondered what it would be like between a man and a woman," she confessed. "You know I was planning to seduce you that time you were sent out on your survival test."

"You always were a tease," he smiled wickedly into her eyes. "Remember how you flaunted yourself in front me during the festival of youth. I decided then you would be mine."

"I came to the same decision," she purred deep in her throat. "No other girl was going to stand a chance."

Stretching like a contented cat she gloried at the possessive light shining in his eyes. Callisto sneaked a look at his manhood pressed between them. Even though she hungered for him the sight widened her eyes. He was so big. Running her tongue over her lips she wondered how they could possibly fit.

"Do not be afraid," he whispered into her ear. "We are made for each other."

She reared back in surprise. "Are you able to read thoughts?" His slumberous glance told her otherwise.

He cupped his hand over her moistness. “I do not need to read your mind to know your body will accept mine.”

“Oh!” Her eyes widened at the intense pull in all her feminine parts so soon after her first ecstatic release. Guided by instinct older than time, she threw a leg over his narrow hips.

The world spun as she found herself on her back, Diokles looming over her. He resembled a god descended to earth solely for her gratification.

Power. Looking at the face of the man she loved Callisto luxuriated in her womanly power. Enchantment. It emboldened her hands to take a journey of sensual discovery from his shoulders all the way to his taut buttocks. She dug her fingers into them delighting in the rock-like strength she found there. Sliding her hands upwards again she soothed the ridged skin where a lash had once struck deep.

“What happened,” she asked, wanting to wipe away the shadow that crossed his face.

“Not now,” he muttered thickly.

“Then make me yours, Diokles,” she sighed in a smoky voice, pressing his head down to hers.

Eyes drifting shut, lips parted, she opened to his kiss. No duel this time, only their tongues touching and tasting, weaving a sensual magic she never would have believed existed.

She wrapped her arms tight around his back, desperate to absorb, and be absorbed by him. Her legs parted of their own volition to wrap around his waist. His tumid manhood weighed heavily against her feminine heat. Callisto gasped and writhed beneath him in a frenzy of excitement.

“I want you,” she panted, running her hands wildly over every inch of his sculpted body that she could reach.

Nothing could have prepared her for the explosion of mindless delirium when he probed a finger, then two, into her warm, wet center. Boneless, her legs collapsed either side of him, spreading wider to accommodate his narrow hips. She bucked like an untamed horse, her inner passage clenching around his thrusting fingers.

“Do not stop,” she cried out in agonized disbelief when he withdrew his hand. Surely he would not have brought her this far to leave her wanting.

He kissed her forehead. "Trust me, my love."

His heart thundered against her breast. The sweetest drumbeat in the world. She caressed his sweat-slickened skin, her own moist skin sliding luxuriously beneath him, her enjoyment of the sensation voiced in throaty moans she made no effort to contain.

Fixing her gaze on his face, Callisto decided she could look at him forever. His eyes were closed, sweat beaded his forehead, his long hair fell to one side like a curtain that shut out the world. Longing to see him in the throes of passion, she raised her head to nip his neck, then daringly slipped a hand under her thigh to cup him.

Feeling his erection probe the heated passage that yearned for his possession, Callisto murmured, "Diokles, please."

He slipped into her welcoming heat, taking such infinite care, the quick hiss of pain as he broke through her virgin barrier, was quickly forgotten when he claimed her mouth in a soul-shattering kiss.

Rocking her hips to the rhythm he set, her inner passage gradually stretched and yielded, enabling him to thrust deeper. Senses attuned to his, she settled into the dance of lovers, where both innately understood every step and nuance of each other. The sensation of his body rubbing the peaks of her breasts sent her wild, the mounting excitement becoming unbearable, her new-found knowledge recognizing what the pressure building in her core meant.

Impatient to reach the gloriously dizzy pinnacle again, she thrust upwards with increasing frenzy.

"Now," she commanded him. "Diokles, now!"

Meeting the quick, hard thrusts with her own desperation—once, twice—the surge of ecstasy engulfed her a second time. Digging her nails into his back, Callisto wailed as her mind went blank. One part of it that revived registered Diokles's muscles tensing tighter and tighter as an inborn wisdom whispered he was close to his own climax. One final convulsive thrust, then long, guttural groans filled her hearing, even as the warmth of his seed filled her womb.

Callisto smoothed trembling hands over him; long, languid strokes, feeling the sun overhead warm their exposed skins. Lying beneath him, she marvelled at a tranquillity of spirit beyond anything she experienced. Their melded heartbeats slowed, returning their breathing to normal.

At least his did.

"I cannot breathe," she complained in a muffled voice.

In a flash he rolled onto his back. Sated, replete, Callisto draped herself over him, resting her cheek on his broad chest, loving the way the coarse hair smattered over it tickled her breasts.

"You should have said something sooner," he stroked her waist then choked out a laugh. "I suffocate my bride before the wedding."

"I am not your bride yet," she teased in a voice made sultry by his clever hands on her body.

"You will be soon," he placed a finger to her lips. "We will marry, you will live in my house, and regrow your hair. For a while at least."

"So arrogant," she teased while secretly admiring his assurance. "What would Lycurgus think of you?"

She hid a smile when he had the grace to shift uncomfortably.

"I follow our laws," he declared. "But after the time lost to us, would you deny me the pleasure of seeing your hair one more time like it was in our youth."

She stared through the curtain of foliage which protected them from prying eyes. Placing her hand over his heart, she felt its vigorous beat, full of love; for her. "Of course not. I teased you because you went into full commander mode."

A comfortable silence fell over them. Callisto mused it was a chance to luxuriate in the closeness of their bodies, the languid movement of fingers sliding over choice areas. Hers traced his jutting hipbones, pausing as the white seam of an old scar on his arm caught her eye. "Tell me what happened to your back?"

His chest rose and fell on a deep breath under her cheek.

"I was training as a kryptoi at the time. Word came to me you were being taken away." His free hand covered his eyes. "I broke every rule leaving my duty and going to stop you. You saw what happened when my father arrived. I was taken away and whipped by him for disobeying orders, for leaving my fellows." He stared deeply into her eyes. "I would risk all again for you."

Callisto bit back a sob. She would be brave and not weep for what he had endured because of her. Lovingly touching his cheek, she murmured, "Turn onto your stomach."

Grinning at his raised eyebrows, she prodded his side until he acquiesced. Pushing herself up to straddle him, the feel of her moist center settling into the curve of his lower back, awoke slumbering arousal.

Leaning over his back she trailed kisses along the ridged skin in a kind of healing ritual, smoothing away the darkness of the lost years, of the punishment they had endured in different ways. She wished she possessed the magic to vanish the ridges—all she could do was show her love.

Her heartbeat gained speed to match the rapidity of his increasingly laboured breathing. With a mischievous smile, she pressed a line of kisses past his waist, then swooped to bite one rock-hard buttock, laughing when his entire body convulsed, almost toppling her off him.

"Callisto," he growled warningly before flipping over to look at her.

Resting her hands on the ground, she leaned in to touch the tips of her breasts to his chest, thrilled by the color tinging his aristocratic cheekbones. "Is there a problem?" she asked in a throaty whisper.

He slanted her a knowing look. "There will be if you keep doing that."

"I have much to learn about love," she goaded in a low, seductive voice, now trailing fingers over his mouth and down his neck. His sharp inhalation stirred an answering tug. "Is it possible to do what we have done many times in the course of a day?"

She saw his mouth move but no sound came out. Elated to realize she had rendered him helpless beneath her, Callisto studied the much smaller male nipples. Was he as sensitive there as she was?

A little surprised by her daring, she licked a forefinger then rubbed it over one, delighted how he spasmed in reaction. Hiding a smile, she committed his response to memory, certain it would prove useful whenever they argued.

Consumed by a sudden need to test the limits of his sensual endurance, she explored his ribcage, the bronze skin stretched tight over it, his flat stomach. Wiggling her hips down his body, her eyes grew wide seeing his manhood swell. It was all so new to her, but her inquisitiveness drove her on. Holding her breath, she touched the drop crowning the tip, bolting upright when his erection lifted of its own accord.

"You are playing with fire," his hoarse voice warned her.

She licked her lips. "You sound as if you are in pain." Catching him staring at her mouth as though he meant to devour it, raised hopes for a repeat of their lovemaking.

"You will be too sore if we make love again," he told her with a sigh of regret. "Better to wait and enjoy it to the full tomorrow."

But the gleam in his eyes told her he could be persuaded to change his mind. Callisto trailed her nails over his skin to stop short of his burgeoning manhood. Leaning closer she teased in a sultry whisper, "Well then, teach me how to please you."

His throaty groan was music to her ears.

"You are giving me orders already," he complained in a strangled voice. "Whatever you want to learn I will teach you for the rest of our lives."

Letting him guide her hand Callisto surrendered to the exquisite joy in her heart, knowing a lifetime of loving waited to be shared with this magnificent man.

"Forever," she agreed, wrapping her hand around him.

THREE WEEKS LATER

"I am surprised Callisto chose to come here."

Diokles gusted out a resigned sigh. "She insisted," he said, as both men drew closer to Apollo's temple at Amyklai.

"And you of course agreed," Acastus grinned, stopping to study his boyhood friend. "Over the years I watched you grow hard, even violent, when you were crossed. Finally, Zeus has smiled on you."

Diokles's throat tightened. "You are right. Losing Callisto fed the darkness I inherited from my father. There are things I did in battle I want to forget."

"We all have done things in the heat of battle we would rather forget," Acastus pointed out. "What is Callisto praying for?"

"She is trying to divine whatever information she can to help your search. She hopes to at least provide a name and place where you can start."

"Whatever she sees is enough." Acastus stood tall in his conviction. "I will find your half-sister and bring her home to Sparta."

"I do not doubt your success," Diokles stated confidently. "Although, it might prove a long, dangerous mission. Subterfuge may be needed."

"Your memory fails you, my friend. Remember when we were boys in the agoge, I disguised myself so well, I fooled even you?" Acastus threw back his head and laughed. "Do not look so irritated about a boyhood prank."

Diokles rubbed his chin. "I have trouble reminding myself I am only a man who can make mistakes. Let us see whether Callisto has finished."

The lingering scent of burnt cypress wafted through the temple. Alerted by the sound of approaching footsteps, Callisto rose to make a final obeisance, hurrying out to greet the two men who approached. No, two warriors, she amended; both toned, well-built, fit, walking with an assurance earned over a lifetime of effort and sacrifice.

One of them held the power to ignite love in her heart. It was to him she ran, a smile wreathing her face. "Her name is Xanthia," she told Diokles, then faced Acastus. "I saw an island, its name remained a mystery, though golden sand and towering cliffs filled my vision. Horses ran along the shore and a woman ran among them. I could not see her face. I am sorry I cannot tell you more."

"It is more than enough," Acastus asserted. "I heard of such a legend from a servant in my father's household. He is old now, but his mind is still sharp. I will speak to him; see if he can enlighten me further."

"Thank you," Callisto took his hand between both of hers. "I pray for your safety and success."

Acastus took his leave. Waiting until he was out of earshot, Callisto turned to the silent man by her side. "Did I thank you for making your peace with my father?"

"At least three times every week since we arrived home." Diokles kissed the top of her head. "In a few weeks I have gone from loathing your father, to respecting him once again, and respecting his devotion to you, however misguided. I learned of a half-sister and forgave my mother's memory, thanks to you."

"I have done nothing," she slapped his bottom playfully. She too, had much to thank him for, not least her confidence which blossomed each passing day.

"Do that one more time and you will pay."

The flare of heat was instantaneous. "Are you promising, Diokles?" she teased in a sultry whisper. Sweeping her lashes down to hide the mischief she was certain danced in her eyes, she slapped him again.

And gave a yelp of laughter when he swung her into his arms, stalking off to where their horses were tethered.

"You are playing with fire again," he warned in a husky voice, releasing her to slide down his body.

"I want to play with fire," she breathed against his mouth. "Living fire. You, Diokles. Always. I want your child. I want to hold the child of our love in my arms. I want—"

He cut her words off in the best way possible. Callisto met the lips swooping down to claim hers. She kissed him fiercely, imbuing it with all the love in her heart. The kiss gentled, became tender, the hand supporting her head trembled. She gulped for air when he released her lips.

"I love you, Callisto. I loved the girl you were. I love the woman you are now. When I realized feelings grew toward the priestess I captured, I resisted. I swung between believing it might be you, and doubting, when the curse almost killed me. Still, you insinuated yourself into my heart in a way I did not expect." He framed her face with his hands. "I want to come home to you for the rest of our days. I want to hold our children when I return from battles, lie in your arms and be at peace?"

"I love you, Diokles. Even when I argued with you, cursed you after you took me away from what I thought was my home, I fell in love with the man I came to understand. I, too, fought my attraction to you, refusing to succumb like other hostages who fell in love with their captors." Callisto threw her arms around him. "Now, I long to give you strong sons."

And she would she promised in her heart. Strong sons brave and honorable like their father.

"A son or daughter what does it matter? We are Spartans; either is welcome." He gazed off into the distance. "Of course, our son will have a better father than I did, and our daughter will be as beautiful as her mother."

"We should hurry home." Her voice a low purr, she ran her hands up to loop them around his neck. "Standing here talking does not fulfil our hopes."

"Perhaps our child already grows within you." He placed a protective hand over her belly. "Although it is best to make sure." His fingers slid lower.

"Of course," she spluttered, half laughing, the air leaving her lungs when he nipped her neck. "Race me back," she murmured into his ear.

"I will let you win. This time," he teased, lifting her onto her horse.

Did she really want to race him? Callisto held out a hand, his quizzical look prompting a smile to curve her mouth.

"I want us to journey together, Diokles, now and always."

Love swelled inside her as she watched him take her hand and plant a kiss on the palm to seal their agreement. Callisto knew then that however long she lived, this moment would always remain etched in her heart.

Ingram Content Group UK Ltd.
Milton Keynes UK
UKHW011947220323
418981UK00004B/125

9 780987 640727